Also by Lucy Score

T0005670

THE CORPSE IN THE CLOSET

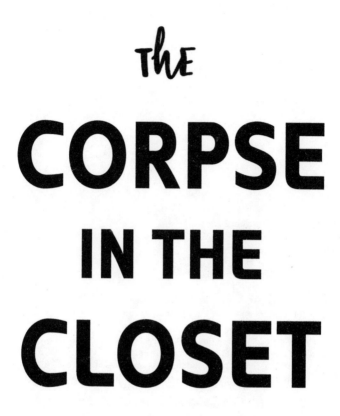

LUCY SCORE

Bloom books

Copyright © 2021, 2024 by Lucy Score
Cover and internal design © 2024 by Sourcebooks
Series design by Nicole Hower
Cover illustration by Hannah Burr/Lott Reps
Cover images © artvea/Getty Images

Sourcebooks and the colophon are registered trademarks of
Sourcebooks. Bloom Books is a trademark of Sourcebooks.

All rights reserved. No part of this book may be reproduced in any form or by
any electronic or mechanical means including information storage and retrieval
systems—except in the case of brief quotations embodied in critical articles or
reviews—without permission in writing from its publisher, Sourcebooks.

The characters and events portrayed in this book are fictitious or
are used fictitiously. Any similarity to real persons, living or dead,
is purely coincidental and not intended by the author.

All brand names and product names used in this book are trademarks,
registered trademarks, or trade names of their respective holders.
Sourcebooks is not associated with any product or vendor in this book.

Published by Bloom Books, an imprint of Sourcebooks
P.O. Box 4410, Naperville, Illinois 60567–4410
(630) 961-3900
sourcebooks.com

Originally published in 2021 by That's What She Said Publishing, Inc.

Cataloging-in-Publication data is on file with the Library of Congress.

Printed and bound in the United States of America.
LSC 10 9 8 7 6 5 4 3 2 1

To David. The biggest heart, the broadest chest, the kindest soul. We miss you.

1

This was not how she was going to die, Riley decided. Not sitting on a concrete floor in a musty TV studio surrounded by idiots.

The helmet-headed blond on her right was muttering under her breath about lawsuits. On her left, Riley's ex-husband, Griffin Gentry, rocked in place and whimpered about the dry-cleaning fees for his mohair suit.

Neither of them was smart enough to realize just how much trouble they were all in.

But Riley knew that, barring a miracle, none of them would be walking out of Channel 50 alive.

"How long are we going to have to stay like this?" the blond demanded. "This lighting is giving me a headache, and I need to make four dozen cupcakes for the marching band bake sale tomorrow."

"That's my chair," Griffin complained when the gunman sat down behind the anchor desk.

"Let the man with the gun sit in your chair," Riley advised.

"Just great," Griffin whined when the gunman lowered the seat. "It's going to take me forever to get it back to the right height."

"Oh, please," Valerie hissed from her position between cameras one and two. "You put it as high as it goes, and we all pretend you're a normal-size human."

"Let's focus on the real problem here," Riley said. "That guy has killed several people so far, and he has more on his list."

"No one wants to kill me! Everyone loves me," Griffin insisted.

"Have you continued to devolve, or was I really that stupid when I married you?" she wondered.

"Personally, I think it was a combination of both," the camera one operator at her feet chimed in.

"Hey, Don," she whispered. "Long time, no see."

"How's it going?" the hefty mustachioed man asked.

"So what's he going to do after he's done messing up my chair?" Griffin hissed, tugging at his collar. "You don't think he'll do something terrible like—"

"Kill you? Anything could happen at this point," Riley said.

"*Kill me?*" he croaked. "I was going to say *make me look silly on the air.*"

Her ex-husband had gone from indignantly inconvenienced to anxious. Beads of sweat appeared on his spackled forehead.

Griffin was a nervous sweater. And he was very, very nervous. He looked as if he'd been hosed down.

"Look. He's one guy with a gun. There's sixteen of us in here. If we attack him in order of least important person to most important person, most of us will survive," the blond said.

"Obviously, I'm the most important," Griffin said, latching on to her idea.

"You read things from a teleprompter and wear makeup," the woman scoffed. "I'm a *mother*. I'm raising the future of our country."

"Your kids are in college," Riley pointed out.

"And they still need their mother! I'm last. Griffin can be next to last," the woman conceded.

"Bella should be next to next to last," Griffin decided.

2

On cue, Bella Goodshine, perky weather girl and his new fiancée, popped up next to him and held out a hand to Riley. "Hi! I'm Bella!"

"I know who you are!" Riley yelled.

The gunman spun around in his chair to glare at her.

"Sorry," Riley said. "But she keeps introducing herself to me!"

"Didn't she steal your husband?" the blond asked.

"She sure did," Griffin said. He was still sweating.

"This must be really awkward for you," the blond observed.

"It's not great."

"Don't mind Bella," Griffin said, reaching for Riley's hand. She snatched it away. "She has female face blindness."

"Female face blindness?" Riley repeated.

Griffin nodded. "She only recognizes men. It's a medical condition."

Riley blinked slowly, then shook her head. "I'm not dying here with you people."

"So who should be first in line to attack this guy?" Griffin asked. "I never cared for Armand. I don't like his urinal cake placement."

"Fine. He'll go first," the blond decided. "Then maybe that guy over there by the bagels. I don't like his shirt."

"That's Rose. She didn't sign my birthday card this year. Maybe she should go first?"

"You people can't just decide who lives and who dies," Riley hissed. This was what was wrong with the world. People like Griffin, who had an overinflated sense of importance, wielding power over others.

Nick was going to kill her. That was if she survived her own murder.

2

Six Days Earlier
11:47 a.m. Wednesday, August 12

"Abso-fucking-lutely not," snarled Nick Santiago, dimpled private investigator and barely reformed bad boy as he fisted his hands in the cop's shirt and bared his teeth.

Life could go from blissful summer day to bonkers in a very short period of time, Riley realized as she clung to her boyfriend's back. Not ten minutes ago, she—Riley "Middle Name Unacknowledged" Thorn—had officially moved in with him. But before they could christen the new king-size bed, everything had, of course, gone straight to hell.

She blamed her batty mother's tarot prediction for copious amounts of strife and turmoil.

The universe waited all of twenty seconds before delivering said strife and turmoil in the form of a surprise visit from Riley's formidable grandmother. Elanora Basil, president of the North American Psychics Guild, had proceeded to cast a pall of judgmental disdain that could be felt throughout the entire run-down mansion and large portions of Harrisburg, Pennsylvania.

It had gone downhill from there.

Now Nick was assaulting a cop. Not just any cop. His ex-partner and frenemy Detective Kellen Weber.

"Calm the hell down," Riley demanded through gritted teeth as she tried to pry Nick off the detective.

"Do you require my assistance?" The deep baritone came from the large, impossibly muscular Black man in the doorway.

"Stay out of this, Empire State Building," Nick snarled.

"I got it, Gabe," she promised her part-time spiritual guide and full-time friend. "But thanks."

"I am always available for punching Nick in the face if necessary," Gabe promised. After the briefest of hesitations, he gracefully dodged the melee in the kitchen and helped himself to a frozen Snickers, which he devoured in two bites before squaring his massive shoulders and disappearing again.

Elanora had that effect on people.

"Don't make me arrest you, Santiago," Weber rasped from his prone position on the kitchen table.

Nick growled in response. The pony-size dog at their feet mistook the noise for a game and barked joyfully.

"Not now, Burt," Riley told the dog as she landed a series of slaps to Nick's hands.

Finally, he released the detective.

"The last time she got involved with an investigation, she got shot," Nick snarled. "The answer is no. She's not doing your job for you."

Detective Weber stood and straightened his tie. He was an attractive man, always dressed as if he was ready to take a disapproving in-law to the Olive Garden after church. "Assaulting an officer is against the law, dick," he reminded Nick.

"Pretty sure a jury would make an exception for you, assface."

She slid off Nick's back. "Can you two idiots keep it down? If my grandmother hears—"

"This is precisely why I am here."

The mint-green kitchen suddenly seemed very small and very cold as Elanora, terrifying matriarch and nationally known psychic medium, stepped into the room. Her sniff was full of derision.

She was petite with ramrod posture and looked as if she wore a coat hanger under her layers of flowing black. With her pinched frown and sterling hair swept back from her face with bird feathers, she reminded her granddaughter of an older, disappointed Stevie Nicks.

Briefly, Riley wondered if her grandmother had murdered the bird that donated the feathers. Nothing seemed out of the realm of possibility when it came to Elanora.

"Your behavior is positively unseemly. My granddaughter is most certainly not getting involved in another homicide," Elanora announced briskly, glancing at the case file Weber left on the table. "She is dangerously untrained, and I have absolutely no faith in her ability to control even the most basic of powers. Look at the two of you. One minute alone in a room with her, and you're behaving like children."

Riley rolled her eyes. "Thanks, Grandma." Elanora preferred *Grandmother*. Riley preferred to mess with her just a little bit.

Nick pointed in Elanora's direction as he leaned into Riley. "Listen to your scary grandma. You're not doing it."

He was lucky he was hot even when his dimples weren't on full display. He was also lucky that Riley was a patient woman. He was new at this boyfriend thing. So she could ignore the occasional gung-ho alpha blunders and tolerate the adorable macho overprotectiveness. Because deep down, she knew he was still tied up in knots over their recent adventure in taking down the city's mayor, his communications director, and a few bad cops.

Both she and Nick had walked away with a bullet hole apiece as souvenirs. While she'd moved on, he was still stewing about it, and like a good girlfriend, she was giving him the space to stew about it.

Elanora gave Nick an imperious glance followed by a stiff nod. "Perhaps you're not as useless and uneducated as you appear to be, Nicholas."

It was practically a gold star.

"Thanks?" he said.

"While I appreciate you all feeling as if you have the right to make decisions for me, you don't," Riley announced. "None of you do."

"That's right. This is Riley's decision," Weber said smugly.

"Kiss-ass," Nick snapped.

"You two, out." She nudged her grandmother and boyfriend toward the door.

Burt barked and cocked his gigantic head.

"You can stay. You trust my judgment," she told the dog.

Elanora's eyes narrowed. "I did not come here to be ignored while you continue to make a mockery of the guild."

"No, but you did arrive unannounced. You can't expect us to drop everything and entertain you."

"*Entertain* me?" Elanora scoffed. "My daughter and granddaughters are blessed with psychic gifts that should have foretold my arrival."

"Yeah, well, they didn't. So you can't expect me to drop everything right now. Go home with my parents. Drive them nuts. You like doing that. We'll catch up soon."

The disapproving lines on her grandmother's forehead deepened. "I am very disappointed—"

"In me. And everyone else. And life in general. I got it, and I'm not saying you're wrong. We'll deal with it later, Grandmother."

"We most certainly will."

Elanora swept from the room in a huff, and Riley turned to face Nick. "And you," she said.

"Me?" He pointed at himself and produced both dimples. Weapons of mass devastation.

"Yeah, you. You're the one who said you could handle dating a psychic." She didn't exactly choke on the word, but she did cough.

"Thorn, this has nothing to do with you talking to dead people and reading minds. I don't give a shit about your psychic training. You haven't been trained to defend yourself. You barely survived the last time you got tangled up in a case. Hell, you threw a gun at the bad guy. You can't expect me to pat you on the back and tell you to get back out there and bring home a win."

"You really do need to teach her to shoot," Weber cut in.

"I don't if she stays away from murderers."

"Oh, come on. You're being dramatic," she complained. "One measly bullet hole in a love handle didn't put me anywhere near death's doorstep."

"Don't tell me it was one 'measly bullet hole' when you almost let a madman drown you in the goddamn capitol fountain."

Oh, that.

"Nick." She crossed her arms over her chest. He was putting on a front, but underneath it, she could sense the fear that kept him up at night.

Not again. I can't lose her.

She slammed the metaphorical garage door shut in her head. As a psychic girlfriend, she tried very hard to give Nick and his inner monologue privacy.

"Riley." He mirrored her posture, hiding his inner turmoil under a cocky, sexy facade.

"Let me hear Detective Weber out," she said gently. "Looking over a case file isn't going to put me in mortal danger." At least she hoped it wouldn't. "You have to trust me."

His jaw clenched under his sexy stubble, making his dimples pop again. "For the record, I don't like it. And you," he said, turning on Weber. "If she ends up in trouble or gets hurt, I will personally choke you to death with your stupid tie collection."

"Nick." She sighed.

"I'm not leaving," he insisted, pulling out a chair from the table and attacking one of the banana muffins Gabe had baked that morning. The man was an angel in the kitchen. Burt trotted over and put his head in Nick's lap so he could inhale muffin crumbs.

The problem was, Riley didn't really *want* to consult on a case. Especially not another murder. Especially not when, as

8

her grandmother so meanly pointed out, her powers were not exactly under her control at all times. Which technically was her own fault for denying their existence for the past thirty-four years.

However, she'd also spent the last several years doing what she'd been told in both a dead-end job and her deader-end marriage. She was due for a rebellion.

"Look, I don't know if I want to get involved," she told Weber. Nick's smug grin had her adding, "But I'll hear you out."

They both took a seat at the table. She picked up a muffin and gestured for Weber to help himself.

"It's been a week, and we've got nothing," he explained, opening the file and laying out a series of photos of the body.

Muffin lodged in her throat.

The victim was a woman of indeterminate age due to obvious and extensive plastic surgery. She could have been in her forties or her sixties. She had a deep, orange-hued tan, swollen duck lips, unnaturally rounded cheeks, and a frozen forehead. Both her hair and her lashes were longer and thicker than those found in nature.

The body was face up on plush white carpet with what was most likely a look of surprise. However, given the enhancements, the overall effect was that of a life-size sex doll.

Thankfully, there was no blood or obvious cause of death.

Riley found it Alanis Morissette "Ironic" that the victim had fought aging tooth and nail only to meet an early end.

Her nose twitched, and somewhere in her head, she thought she heard the echo of a laugh. A practiced, insincere, nasally giggle.

She shivered and picked up a photo of the body taken from a distance. The woman was sprawled on the floor of a large walk-in closet. The kind featured on reality shows set in LA. There was a tufted velvet hassock in the corner. Floor-to-ceiling shelves housed shoes, most with skyscraper-high heels. Luxury-label purses, jeans, and tops hung in precisely spaced intervals and organized by color.

She whistled. "Someone with a closet like that lives in Harrisburg?"

Harrisburg, Pennsylvania, wasn't exactly Los Angeles. If there was a family tree of U.S. cities, Harrisburg would have been a bumpkin third cousin who kept getting divorced. But with several large health systems in the area as well as a nearby candy fortune, local pockets of money still existed.

"Her name is Bianca Hornberger. She was forty-four. A stay-at-home mother of two kids. The husband is a software engineer," Weber explained.

Nick wiped the last of the muffin crumbs onto the floor where Burt expertly hoovered them up. "You look at the husband?"

Weber shot his ex-partner a bland look. "No. It never occurred to me to look at the spouse. Let me go ask him for an alibi."

"Don't be a dick. I'm sorry for messing up your fancy shirt and tie."

Riley shook her head. Men's ability to be infuriated one second and then trading good-natured insults the next fascinated her.

"Yes, I looked at the spouse," Weber said. "His alibi is airtight. He was at work in meetings with dozens of witnesses all day. Didn't get home until eight and called 911 within minutes of walking in the door."

There was a tightness in her chest, almost as if she couldn't catch her breath. Her nose twitched again.

"Cause of death?" Nick asked.

"Suffocation," she said quietly.

Both men looked at her.

Nick got up and squeezed her shoulder before moving to the sink to fill a glass of water. He put it in front of her and sat back down, dragging her chair closer until his body crowded hers. He might have been new at this boyfriend thing, but the man was a natural.

Weber met her gaze. "That's right. Medical examiner found signs of asphyxiation."

Riley's head was slowly filling with puffy pink and blue clouds, but she couldn't see through them. "There's something else," she guessed, squinting at the table.

Weber's mouth tightened. "Yeah. This stays between us. This detail hasn't been made public. But the coroner found a fancy pair of underwear lodged in her throat."

"She choked on her own underwear?" Nick asked.

The clouds stayed too thick for her to see more than glimpses. She shook her head. "No. I think there was a bag over her head."

The look the detective gave her was triumphant. "There was a plastic bag with only her prints on it found next to the body. Coroner thinks the thong down the throat happened postmortem."

"That's just creepy," she said as the clouds dissipated.

"I need your help with this one," Weber said. "So far, the investigation has turned up no leads, and my gut says this wasn't random."

Riley blew out a breath. "I'll think about it and get back to you," she told him. "You do get that my grandmother isn't wrong, don't you? I'm not very good at this whole psychic thing."

"You were good enough to save your best friend and this son of a bitch here."

"Technically, I saved her," Nick cut in. His grip tightened comfortingly on her shoulder.

"If you want to get technical, *I* saved *both* your lives," Weber added. "You owe me. So I'm calling in the favor. I need your help with this one. Otherwise, a murderer is going to walk free."

Ugh. The last time she'd allowed herself to get involved in an investigation, she'd ended up at the bottom of the capitol complex fountain with a bullet hole.

The media circus that had made her life a living hell was only now beginning to calm down. The last thing she needed was more attention. She had two bins upstairs full of emails and letters from strangers begging for her to find lost items, contact dead relatives, and deliver predictions on future sporting events.

"I need to think about it," she said.

"I'll take whatever help you can give me," Weber said, ignoring Nick's scowl. "The longer this case goes without a lead, the colder the trail gets. I need to give this family some answers."

"Answer's no," Nick announced. "Not happening. Take your muffin and go."

3

The temporary offices of Santiago Investigations were crammed into the music room on the first floor of the crumbling Bogdanovich mansion on Front Street.

Sure. There was a kick-ass view of the Susquehanna River through the front windows. And yeah, Nick was saving a shitload on rent. Plus, it kept his commute to the two minutes he'd been accustomed to when he'd lived in the apartment above his previous office. Before the whole arson thing. It wasn't good manners to look a gift office in the mouth. But the place had its "quirks" too.

For one, the music room smelled like mothballs and old cardboard. It was stuffed to the ceiling with dusty flea market artifacts and heavy pieces of ugly furniture. It looked as if no one had stepped foot across the threshold in two decades. Given the fact that the Bogdanovich twins were in their eighties, there was a good chance they'd forgotten the room existed.

Lily Bogdanovich had spent the first few days of office setup opening old boxes and drawers, then exclaiming over random finds.

"I haven't seen this meat cleaver in years."

"So that's where my erotic fire poker set got to."

The bigger issue—besides dusty penis-shaped fire pokers—was the fact that the space wasn't wheelchair accessible yet, which meant his cousin Brian couldn't get inside. This led to its own set of problems. When Nick offered to foot the bill for a ramp, landlord Fred Bogdanovich and another tenant, Mr. Willicott, had volunteered to build it themselves.

Since Brian was more than happy working from home, and since toupeed Fred and the elderly Denzel Washington doppelgänger Willicott were only charging him for materials, Nick stupidly agreed.

They'd been hammering away for a week and a half, pausing only to yell incoherent questions and answers at each other.

As far as he could tell, neither man had ever successfully constructed anything more complicated than a sandwich. Each afternoon, they submitted their receipts to him for items including hammers, nails, wood, meatball subs, and matching stools on which they ate their meatball subs. Every day after they called it quits, Nick went outside to inspect their work and found the same thing: a disaster that resembled nothing close to a ramp.

But all of that paled in comparison to the biggest issue with his temporary digs.

He could no longer hide behind closed doors when he was pissed off at an employee or vice versa. Which meant he was getting the full force of his new office manager's displeasure. Riley was doing her best to ignore him since the completely legitimate concerns he'd raised that morning.

He didn't like being ignored. He'd prefer it if she just stood up and called him a stupid asshole. Santiagos understood yelling. But this simmering silence gave him entirely too much time to begin doubting his stance.

He scooted the ancient brocade armchair away from the marble-top parlor table he used as a desk and stared at her. She'd commandeered a scarred library table near the fireplace and had set up a tidy little workstation with a scanner, laptop, and printer. Her office supplies were organized in matching desktop accessories. Neat rows of paperwork were labeled with sticky notes.

Update.

Scan.

Shred.

File.

She frowned at the computer screen, glanced at the documents in her hand, then efficiently stuffed them into the shredder at her feet.

It was exactly what she'd done to his heart when he'd found her submerged in that fucking fountain. The fountain he hadn't been able to drive by since.

When he'd met Riley two months prior, he'd absolutely taken note of those big brown eyes, those full lips, and the temptation of curves. But it had been the whole package that had him falling face-first in lo—ike. *Like.* Her snarky wit. Her self-deprecating humor. The vulnerability that made him want to stand up and promise to keep her safe for the rest of her life. Though he'd very nearly let her down in that area. It still gave him nightmares.

She was calm in situations that called for hysteria. For instance, getting shot and nearly strangled and drowned by a deranged asshole. She hid junk food from her mother. Played reluctant tech support and chauffeur to her elderly neighbors. She had a habit of leaving her vehicle at crime scenes. And she stole a dog while accidentally breaking up a dogfighting ring.

The caveman bachelor in him hadn't stood a chance.

And the stubborn, independent, delusional, I-can-take-care-of-myself woman in her didn't either.

She needed him to look out for her. And he was going to take care of her whether she wanted him to or not.

"I can feel you staring at me," she said without looking up from her screen, where she was probably organizing his life into spreadsheets.

"I'm trying to decide how mad I am at you," Nick announced, kicking back and putting his feet up.

"No, you're not. You got over it an hour ago," she shot back blandly, clicking a pen and scribbling something on a sticky note.

Dating a psychic had its upsides. He didn't have to talk about his feelings because his girlfriend already knew what they were.

"What are you doing?" he asked.

"Scanning last week's paperwork into the server and shredding the ones that don't require physical copies."

It turned him on when she organized shit for him. One of the reasons his office had burnt to the ground so quickly was the fact that he'd been sitting on two years' worth of paperwork that he never got around to filing.

He stood and wound his way through ottomans and boxes labeled *Doll Heads* and *Goose Figurines* to get to her.

He leaned against the corner of her desk and stretched his legs out.

"I don't like you getting involved in another case," he said.

She looked at him. Finally. And his heart did that idiotic little tap dance it always did when those big brown eyes locked on to him.

"Really? Gee. Why didn't you say something when I was clinging to your back trying to pull you off your friend?"

The tone of her voice had his blood racing south well above the legal speed limit. The woman made sarcasm sexy.

"Weber's not my friend," he insisted stubbornly.

"He saved both our lives," she reminded him.

"He didn't save our lives. He aided in our continued survival," he hedged.

"Look, I'm not excited about the idea of getting involved either—"

"Good. Don't. Let's go have sex."

She rolled her eyes, but he didn't miss the way her gaze skimmed over his crotch.

"I'm not excited about it," she continued. "But that doesn't mean I shouldn't do something. A woman is dead."

"And you're alive. I'd like to keep it that way."

She sighed and pushed away from her computer, coming to stand between his outstretched legs. He liked when she came close enough for him to reach out and grab her, to reassure himself she was real and breathing and his.

Nick reeled her in so she was standing between his thighs.

The pulse at the base of her throat fluttered temptingly.

"Thorn, I almost lost you." His fingers slipped under the hem of her shirt and traced the round pink scar that still starred in his nightmares.

She bit her lip, then looped her arms around his neck. "Refresh my memory. Do all your investigations go that way?"

He ran his hand through her thick brown hair, brushing it back from her face.

"No."

"Then there's no reason to think that Weber's case will either," she said, raising her voice to be heard over the incessant hammering.

"You don't even want to do it. Why the hell are you even considering it?" he demanded.

Nick Santiago lived his life according to a succinct code of conduct.

Rule #1: Rules are meant to be broken.

Rule #2: Don't date members of the same generation in the same family (e.g., sisters or cousins) within three years of each other.

Rule #3: Don't do shit you don't want to do.

Riley, on the other hand, had been born a good girl. She wanted to make other people happy by doing what they asked. And while the whole good girl thing was a major turn-on for him, he didn't like how other people could use it to take advantage of her.

"I'm an *adult*," she told him. "Adults do things they don't want to do all the time."

"Yeah, like right now. We should be having sex on that dusty-ass couch over there. Instead, you're pretending you have a choice when you know there's no way in hell I'm letting you investigate a homicide."

"I think it's called a divan," she said.

He stood and walked her backward until her legs hit the hideous brocade upholstery and she sank down onto the cushion. He followed her, covering her body with his.

Her breath caught, and her fingers dug into his shoulders.

"We're at work," she whispered.

"I'm the boss, remember?" He trailed his mouth over her jawline, nipping at the skin of her neck.

She shivered against him. "I think you're taking the boss routine a little too seriously."

The hammering outside stopped abruptly. "Look at that, Willicott. I think we built it backward," Fred shouted.

"What?" Willicott yelled back.

"I *said*, 'I think we built it backward!'"

"How the hell should I know which way is starboard?"

"For the love of God," Riley muttered under him.

"Ignore them. They're adults," Nick said, shifting his hips against her to add weight to his argument.

Her legs parted, and he settled between her thighs. She was wearing a pair of running shorts that were cut high on the leg. He liked them on her—but not as much as he was going to like seeing them on the floor.

"I don't think we settled anything," she reminded him as his mouth hovered over hers.

He looked into those eyes under their heavy lids and thick lashes and felt himself physically ache for her. He'd never had this before. Never wanted a woman with this prolonged kind of intensity. It scared the hell out of him and added to the thrill of it.

If something scared Nick Santiago, he preferred to run right up to it and slap it in the face. Metaphorically speaking, of course.

"We'll settle things later when you're too dizzy from orgasms to argue."

She gave a breathy laugh, and everything was right in the world. He had his tongue in her mouth and his hand on his fly when the pocket doors flew open.

"Whoops! Well, since you're not naked yet." Mrs. Penny—their purple-haired, glasses-wearing roommate—sauntered into the room, shoving things out of her way with her cane. She was dressed in wrinkled cargo pants, Birkenstocks, and a WINK 104 visor. She had a bullhorn in her free hand.

Riley groaned and shoved at Nick's chest. "Get off."

"I was trying to," he shot back.

"What do you want, Mrs. Penny?" Riley asked, wriggling under him. It didn't help his state of arousal. "And why do you have a bullhorn?"

"I was protesting whales over on Woodbine Street. Don't worry about it. You got a new client, Santiago," she said, kicking a rolled-up rug out of the way. A puff of dust rose up from it.

"Who?" he asked, feeling depressed as Riley adjusted her tank top to cover up her great rack.

"Whales?" Riley repeated.

"Dunno. Younger gal," Mrs. Penny said, ignoring Riley.

"Younger" didn't help, seeing as how Mrs. Penny was eighty years old. That made a large chunk of the earth's population "younger."

"She's waiting across the hall. Didn't want to bring her in in case you two were already naked."

As Mrs. Penny bellowed this information, Nick guessed the client had just learned how unprofessional her new PI was.

He dropped his forehead to Riley's. "We need a new office with a lock on the door."

She gave him a friendly peck on the mouth and squeezed his ass through his jeans. "Behave. We'll revisit this later in addition to our fight."

On a low growl, he let her up and tried not to think about how much he couldn't wait until later. It was one thing to get caught mauling a sexy brown-eyed employee. It was another thing to meet a new client with an obvious hard-on. He'd never placed much importance on professionalism, but now that his offices were temporarily housed in a three-ring circus, he felt some pressure to deliver a reasonably professional experience.

"Fine. Come with me. You can start a case file if she doesn't get scared off by our roommates."

Riley perked up. He'd promised to show her the ins and outs of being an investigator but had been putting it off. It was a hell of a lot harder to get hurt or almost murdered by doing paperwork. So far, she hadn't complained, but Nick knew the clock was ticking.

They followed Mrs. Penny across the hall and found Lily Bogdanovich plying the woman with tea and cucumber sandwiches. Lily was newly obsessed with the show *The Crown* and now insisted on serving tea every day in 1950s-style dresses.

Tea usually bled into Mrs. Penny's happy hour. Most residents didn't make it to dinner, being too drunk and too full of tiny weird sandwiches.

The client was tall and attractive, with her dark hair worn in a short puff above a colorful headband. She was in a killer business suit and hot-pink stilettos. The purse she'd slung over her shoulder was the size of a Shetland pony. She paced back and forth in front of the bar as she snapped orders into her phone.

"Yeah. I gotta go. I'll be back in time for the meeting. Uh-huh. I don't care. Deal with it." She disconnected the call and slid her phone into the gigantic bag.

"Hi. I'm Nick Santiago," he said, offering his hand.

"Shelley Rupley," she said. Her grip was brisk and firm, as if she spent a lot of time shaking hands.

"Shelley, this is my office manager, Riley."

"Hi." Riley gave a little wave as she set up her laptop on the round parlor table near the organ.

"Nice to meet you," Shelley said, glancing at her smartwatch.

"I'll just leave these teeny-tiny cucumber sandwiches here in case anyone gets peckish," Lily trilled.

"Thanks, Lil," Nick said.

Lily gave a curtsy and a toothy grin before backing out of the room.

"What can I do for you, Shelley?" he asked as they settled themselves around the table.

"My ex-husband, Larry, is missing," Shelley said, interlacing her fingers on the table. The face of her watch lit up, and she glanced down at it. Riley started diligently taking notes, and Nick decided to spend time later fantasizing about a sexy secretary role-play game.

"When is the last time you saw him?" he asked.

"A week ago. I picked up the kids at his place. We have three. Kids, that is," Shelley said, glancing down as her watch lit up again.

"How long has he been missing?"

Shelley shrugged. "I don't know. I saw him last Wednesday. But he hasn't responded to any of the kids' texts since Saturday. Not even Ellen's. She's the good one," she said to Riley.

Riley made a note that Ellen was the good one.

"So he hasn't been heard from since…"

"I think he left a voicemail for Kyle—he's the troublemaker—Saturday morning," Shelley said as her watch lit up yet again. "I need you to find him," she said, leaning across the table, a dangerous gleam in her eyes.

Nick recognized it as one his own mother had displayed during his harrowing teen years.

"You see this?" She pointed at the watch. "These are appointment reminders, emails, messages from my kids. My oldest is packing for college. Another one needs a ride home from some student government summer camp thing this afternoon. And I've been ducking the soccer coaches' calls all day on the third one because he can't respect the authority of the whistle."

Riley's fingers flew over the keys.

"In the meantime," Shelley continued, "I've got a meeting with marketing in an hour, and then I have to fire someone by the end of the day. I don't have time for a missing ex-husband."

"That's a lot to handle," he observed.

"It is. I need you to find my ex-husband so I can go to the beach in ten days with my girlfriends. No kids. No men. No work. Just wine and pizza and books. I. Need. This." She stabbed the table with a sharp fingernail. "I've got my Kindle right here. I've been reading the same book for six months because every time my ass hits a chair, a kid needs something. Or work calls. Or someone is bleeding. Or there's another fire in the microwave. He owes me this. I haven't gone to court over all the child support he hasn't paid. The absolute least he can do is take his own damn kids for a long weekend."

Nick knew a woman on the edge when he saw one. "Have you talked to the cops?"

She rolled her eyes and let out a humorless laugh. "Of course I did. After Larry's work said he hadn't been in, I called the police. They made me wait forty-eight hours before they were even willing to go knock on his door."

"And?" he prompted.

"And nothing. He didn't answer. They said they'd look into it. They seem to think that just because he's disappeared before means this is more of the same."

"He's disappeared before?" Riley looked up from her screen.

"We had our first kid at twenty. That man was not ready to get married, much less raise four kids. Once we started having kids, every once in a while, he'd go out for drinks with the boys and not come home for two days. He was clinging to his youth. Drinking too much. Staying up all night playing video games."

"Four?" Nick repeated. "I thought you said three."

Shelley grimaced. "Damn it. Alice is the quiet one. I forget about her sometimes since she's the low-maintenance one. Anyway, this is much longer than any previous quest to recapture his youth or escape his life. So since the cops aren't worried, I'm going to pay you to worry. Worry and find him and bring him back so I can go to the damn beach and read my damn book!"

The woman looked down at her watch again, and Nick felt the frustration simmering beneath her surface.

"I'm happy to take the case, Shelley," he said. "Let me take this off your plate so you can focus on your job and your kids."

Her eyes filled with tears, kicking Nick into panic mode. He thrust a box of tissues in her direction. He hated when women cried in front of him. Nothing made him feel more useless.

"No one said being a parent was going to require every second of my day for the rest of my life. No one told me that once kids get just a little bit independent, then the real worrying starts. And no one sure as hell told me to marry a guy who could do dishes and drive kids to basketball practice instead of the cute one I met in seventh grade. Not all seventh graders grow up to be men."

Riley was nodding sympathetically, and Nick could only guess how big of a seventh grader her ex-husband, Griffin Gentry, had been.

"I *need* this weekend. My *sanity* needs this weekend," Shelley said.

He cleared his throat. "How about you give me some details about your ex-husband, and I'll get started right away? I've got a fee sheet that explains—"

"I don't care if it costs me every dime in the kids' college fund. Half of them probably won't go anyway. I'll pay you whatever you want. Just find my ex and have him back here by next weekend."

"Do you have a recent picture?" he asked.

She reached into her cavernous bag and pulled out her phone. "I'll text you a couple."

In the first, Larry Rupley stood in the center of four kids looking like he'd rather be anywhere else. He was a pudgy white guy who'd gone bald on top and soft in the middle. He looked bored and checked out in each of the photos Shelley forwarded.

"Where does Larry work?" Riley asked.

"He was a billing representative for United Alpha Dental Insurance."

"Was?" Nick noted the past tense.

"When I spoke to his supervisor on Monday, she said if he bothered showing up again at the office, he was fired," she explained. "Larry always had a problem with being told what to do. Especially if he didn't feel like doing it, and he *never* felt like doing it."

Nick was familiar with the type. Passive-aggressive little shits who would do the bare minimum and do it badly just to weasel out of any further responsibility.

"Is there a possibility he disappeared so he wouldn't have to take the kids for your beach trip?" he asked.

Her expression darkened. "If that's the reason why he worried me and my kids, then he's going to be in a world of hurt when I find him."

The faint song of a power saw erupted from outside. Riley's nose twitched, and her face drained of color.

"Excuse me," she said, jumping up from her chair and racing for the front door.

One second later, there was a shout and the saw cut off abruptly.

Nick waited a beat, and when no one started yelling for 911, he resumed the meeting.

"Shelley, I'm going to need as much information on your ex-husband as you can give me."

"I'll tell you whatever you want. Birth date, Social Security number, favorite food, shoe size."

"Sounds as if you know him well," he ventured.

"That's what you do in a relationship. Well, unless you're Larry. After twenty-plus years together, he still didn't know when my birthday was or remember that I'm allergic to almonds. I knew him well enough to know that we couldn't stay married. Some guys just never grow up. And eventually a woman needs a man who's willing to put down the game controller and pick up the damn dry cleaning without being asked six times."

Nick felt a little warm under the collar. He made a mental note to ask Riley if she needed anything dry-cleaned.

"Let's start with hobbies and friends."

"He doesn't have a lot of friends. The kids said he did just start jogging. Apparently getting a divorce reminds a man that he needs to put a little effort into his appearance." Shelley huffed out a breath. "He'll just fix himself up for the next woman, and once he gets comfortable, it'll all go to hell again."

He made another mental note to go to the gym.

Riley came back inside carrying a circular saw. Neither she nor the saw was covered in blood. Nick considered that a victory.

"Great. Last question. Is there someone who will let me in to look around his place?" he asked.

Shelley reached into her luggage-size purse and produced a key ring. "Help yourself."

"We'll take a look and see what we can find," he promised.

4

Riley let herself in the back door of the mansion with her haul of groceries and packages. She made a right into the kitchen, Burt on her heels with a new chew bone clutched delicately in his huge mouth.

She found Gabe staring mournfully at a carton of ice cream that looked doll-size in his hand.

"What's wrong? Ice cream headache?" she asked, hefting the bags onto the counter.

He glanced up at her with pathetic brown eyes that held the pain of a thousand broken hearts. "I am saying farewell to a good friend." With a whimper, he tossed the ice cream in the trash can.

Burt felt like the trash can put the ice cream in his territory and shoved his face in the can.

Riley wrestled the dog out of the trash. "No more farting," she warned him. "Why are you giving up ice cream?"

"Elanora wishes for me to resume my practice," Gabe said, still staring into the trash.

She shooed the dog out of the room and returned to her friend and sometimes spiritual advisor. "My grandmother does things her way. Her way doesn't have to be your way."

He shook his head slowly. "She is right. How can I guide you in your journey if I have strayed from my own?"

She laid a hand on his massive bicep. "Gabe, buddy. Ice cream isn't straying from your journey. It's a pit stop. Everyone loves a pit stop."

"Not Elanora. She is right. I must recommit myself to being pure in mind and body."

Riley narrowed her eyes. "What does that mean?"

"It means no more ice cream. And no other distractions."

Uh-oh. Her nose twitched and a vision of her sister, Wander, floated into her head. She suddenly had a very good idea of what "other distractions" had concerned her grandmother.

"Desires of the flesh stunt your spiritual growth."

Elanora Basil was a mean old lady.

"I'll talk to her," Riley promised. "She spends too much time in the guild and forgets that there's a whole world out there just waiting to be experienced."

"Elanora said experiences are for those with small minds."

"Yeah? Well, she also says that summer vacations are for stupid children worried about burning out their brains with year-round education. So I wouldn't take her too seriously. We'll figure out why she's in town and when we can look forward to her leaving."

"She is disappointed in the spiritual guidance I have offered you. That is why she is here. To take over your training."

Riley shuddered. Gabe had been nothing but a muscly, sweet guiding light since showing up unannounced at the mansion and presenting himself as her official teacher of psychic things. His gentle guidance had helped her tiptoe into the realm of a semi-functioning psychic.

She reached into one of the shopping totes and handed him a carton of moose tracks ice cream. "I got this for you to enjoy because you've been a good friend and a great teacher. Don't let one crabby medium ruin that."

His grateful smile was blinding. "I will always be your friend, Riley Thorn."

"Good. Now eat your ice cream."

"I will help you carry your bags upstairs, and then I will return to enjoy my special treat."

"That sounds fair."

He left her outside her door on the third floor and practically sprinted down the stairs to get back to his beloved ice cream.

Riley let herself in and stopped in her tracks.

"What in the—"

Nick Santiago was cooking. And it smelled *good*.

He looked up from the stove and flashed her a dimpled smirk. "Good timing," he said, pulling the pan off the tiny two-burner stove top.

"What is that?" she asked, floating toward the smell of garlic and sizzling onions.

"Chicken fajitas," he said and tilted the cast iron skillet so she could see. His forearm and bicep flexed indecently. She liked when they did that. "It's my specialty."

"You have a specialty?" she asked. "I mean, outside the bedroom."

He shot her one of his patented underwear-combusting looks. She dumped the bags on the floor and took the beer he offered her.

"What's the occasion?" she asked.

His broad shoulders rose and fell carelessly. "Just felt like making my girl dinner. Consider it a date night."

On their first "date night," Nick had accidentally seen her naked and then bribed his way into her apartment with pizza just so he could stake out her neighbor's place.

"You're acting weird," she decided.

His eyebrows shot up. "Me? Weird?"

"You moved us in together without consulting me. Refurnished everything. Yelled at me about a homicide investigation. Now, you're cooking me dinner. What's going on behind those dimples, Santiago?"

"Nothing's going on. Boyfriends cook dinner for their girlfriends all the time. They also yell at them about homicides."

Riley remained skeptical. "You don't have to go full-speed ahead, you know. You're new to this relationship thing. I'm not expecting you to whip out a diamond ring and a 401(k) beneficiary form."

"You have a problem with us living together?" he demanded.

She scanned the space. The new couch. The big flat-screen. The dining table that looked as if it could handle the weight of an entire Thanksgiving feast. "No. I'm just worried that you're jumping into this faster than you should."

Very deliberately, he took the beer from her, took a sip, and set it down next to the stove. Then he hooked his fingers into the waistband of her cutoffs and pulled her into him.

"I like fast," he whispered darkly in her ear.

Yes, yes, he did. And he'd been turning her into a speed freak too. Shoving her out of her comfort zone into free fall. Except every time she was certain she'd plummet to her death, he'd been there to catch her.

"I'm starting to like fast too," she said, deciding dinner and state of the union relationship talks could wait.

She sank her teeth into his earlobe. He hissed out a breath, and his fingers tightened their grip on her hips.

"What do you say we see how this table holds up to combined body weight?" she suggested.

He growled low in his chest and turned the stove burner off. "It's got a max load of five hundred. I checked," he said, picking her up and carrying her toward the table.

She wrapped her legs around his waist and held on tight.

He slid her ass onto the table and stood between her thighs, staring down into her eyes.

"I like you, Thorn."

She heard the catch in his voice and melted like cheese under a broiler. "I like you too, Nick."

He shook his head. "Uh-uh. I *like you* like you."

She felt dizzy and warm and really, really turned on.

"I *like you* like you too," she whispered.

"Promise?" His lips were a breath away from hers.

"Cross my heart," she said, dragging his mouth down to hers.

Nick Santiago could kiss. He could make a professional career out of it. Women would pay him to kiss them breathless and make them feel like the center of his universe. Not that she was going to bring up the idea right now. Not since it was *her* breath he was stealing and *she* was the center of the universe.

She didn't know how she'd gotten this lucky. Why he'd hurled his bachelor lifestyle out the window for a chance with her. But rather than overthink it, she'd just go with it.

She was so busy enjoying his mouth on hers that she didn't hear the door when it flew open. "Riley, got another bin for you!"

Fred Bogdanovich, in a Pink Floyd T-shirt, very short yoga shorts, and his summer toupee—it was blond—burst into her apartment with the energy of a much younger man.

When she tried to pull away, Nick clamped a hand to the back of her head and continued to kiss the hell out of her while waving his other at the wayward senior citizen.

"Oops. Didn't know you two were busy canoodling," Fred said, dropping the plastic tub next to the door.

"We need a new apartment," she told Nick's mouth. "One where we don't know our neighbors."

"Guess I'll just leave you to it." Fred paused and sniffed the air. "Hey! Fajitas. My favorite."

Nick's delicious assault on her mouth didn't let up as Fred bebopped into the kitchen and helped himself to a plate before leaving.

She liked him. More than liked him.

Nick Santiago had no idea, but she was in love with him. She'd get around to telling him. When she was sure the information wouldn't send him into anaphylactic shock.

His hands were at her waist now, skimming under the hem of her shirt. When his fingers found her skin, every hormone receptor in her body lit up like a Christmas tree.

"I'm so into you, Thorn," he said, continuing to ravish her mouth with his expert-level talent.

"Yeah. Me like you too."

His mouth curved against hers in smug satisfaction. "Me like you too?"

"Shut up and keep kissing all the grammar out of my head," she said, fisting her hands in his T-shirt.

It lasted for all of thirty seconds, until her nose twitched and a chill descended on the room. Nick didn't notice it. His libido was in overdrive, and in general, the man pumped off more heat than a five-alarm fire. But Riley knew what it meant.

There was an imperious knock at the door.

"Go the hell away," he snarled.

Before his hands could continue their pilgrimage to her breasts, the knock came again.

Riley tensed under his touch. "Yeah. We have to get that."

"Nicholas, get your hands off my granddaughter's breasts and open this door," Elanora called from the hallway.

With extreme reluctance, he took a step back. "Shit. Fuck. Dammit." He abandoned her on the table and flung the door open. "Can I help you, Elanora?"

She was still dressed in head-to-toe black, but she'd swapped the bird feathers in her hair for a somber black scarf.

"I doubt that very much," Elanora said. "I'm here to extend an invitation to you both."

"Oh goodie," Nick said. "You couldn't do that by text?"

Riley finally regained the use of her legs and slid off the table. People didn't talk to her grandmother that way. She stepped between them just in case Elanora had mastered any interesting magical combat powers.

"You two will join the rest of us for a family meal tomorrow. Bring Gabriel," her grandmother announced.

Burt wandered in through the open door, giving Elanora a wide berth. He sat down on the other side of the couch and peered over it with suspicion. His tongue peeked out of his gigantic mouth.

"You may also bring your very large dog."

"Gee, thanks, Grandma. But Nick and I have a lot of work—" Riley began.

"You will both be there. It's long past time that this family remembers its roots. There will be no more lollygagging."

"I never liked lollipops," Nick cut in.

Elanora shot him a withering look that would have had a lesser man quaking at the knees.

"Not a fan of the sense of humor, are you?" he asked, rubbing a hand over his stubbled jaw.

"A sense of humor is a waste of energy. This world is not a humorous place. People live. People die. People commit to their responsibilities and hone their gifts. There is no room for humor or fun." She spat out the word as if it was a different kind of f-word.

"Ever been skydiving?" he asked.

"I am far too busy dealing with the living and the dead to hurl myself from any mode of transportation."

"Water skiing? Or is your kind not allowed to get wet?"

Riley backed into Nick and hoped her grandmother hadn't learned how to hurl lightning bolts from her eyeballs.

"You will both be in attendance. You will dress appropriately. And you will not put your tongues in each other's mouths in the presence of your family," Elanora announced, pointing a bejeweled finger at them.

Riley's arms came up like a shield just in case. "We'll be there," she promised.

"Seven o'clock," Elanora said stiffly. "Come, dog. You will walk me out."

Burt, who had given no indication of understanding much of the English language besides *what's that smell?* and *ice cream,* loped over to the terrifying woman and led the way out.

Riley collapsed back against Nick's broad chest.

"Well, that was terrifying. Can she see through walls? How did she know I was feeling you up?"

"You're Nick Santiago. Of course you were feeling me up."

They stared at the open door for another minute. Elanora Basil had an uncanny ability to kill moods.

"We need a new apartment. One with a moat," he decided.

"Let's see if Fred left us any fajitas," she suggested.

They headed into the kitchen to examine the remains of their dinner.

"By the way," she said, "I decided I'm going to help Weber on the case."

Nick blew out a breath. "I had a feeling you were going to say that."

"Looks as if my powers are rubbing off on you," Riley said cheerily.

"I wish something else of yours was rubbing off on me."

5

I forbid it," Nick announced.

"Excuse me?" Riley opened one eye and frowned at him from the pillow next to his.

Despite the fact that the new bed was a thousand times more comfortable than the old one they'd shared, he'd spent half the night awake, thinking about relationships and corpses in closets.

"I'm your boyfriend, and as such, I forbid you from working with Weber on a case." There were relationship rules. Even *he* knew that. Hell, those rules were the reason he'd never settled into a monogamous deal before. But being able to tell someone else what to do was starting to look like a pretty big pro.

Now both of her eyes were open, and there was a fire in them. "You can't do that."

"I just did." He figured it was smart to lead with confidence. Maybe she wouldn't realize he had no idea what he was doing. What the fuck was he thinking? Of course she would know. She was psychic.

She pulled the comforter over her head. "Ugh. Let's talk about this when it's not dawn."

"No need to talk about this," he insisted, yanking the blanket back. "You're not doing it. I've decided."

She shoved a hand through her hair, pushing it off her face. "Listen. I'm trying to cut you some slack here, but you can't just forbid me from doing something."

"Am I allowed to go out and sleep with someone else?"

She glared sleepily at him. "No!"

"Neither are you. See? That's how this works."

She groaned. "If I'm going to get a relationship lecture from Nick Santiago, I'm going to need coffee."

"Look. You're a good girl. Remember?" he said, trying a new tactic. "You want to make other people happy. Make me happy, Thorn. Don't take this case."

She sat up. "I don't know whether to be appalled or impressed that you're pushing my buttons like this."

The skinny strap of her tank top slipped off her shoulder, distracting him. "Definitely go with impressed," he urged, lifting up on his elbow to study her.

"I appreciate that you're trying to protect me," she began.

"You're welcome." He ran his finger under the wayward strap.

"Nick!"

"You matter, Thorn. The last time you got mixed up in something like this, it almost got you killed. I can't deal with that. Ergo, you're not doing it."

He didn't feel the need to tell her that he'd yet to sleep the whole way through the night since the last *incident* because he woke up to make sure she was still next to him, still breathing. That instead of showing her the investigative ropes like he'd promised, he'd shoved her into an office administration job to keep her as far away from bad guys as possible.

He'd fucked up the whole "guardian" thing once already and had paid the price. This time around, he wasn't taking any chances.

She blew out a breath that ended on a long groan. "I don't like disappointing you. And I *still* don't want this talking-to-people-and-solving-murders deal to be my thing."

35

"Great. Then don't."

"*But* my scary grandmother is right. I have a responsibility to do something with this...this..." She waved a hand in the air.

"So get a booth at a carnival and tell fortunes."

"I don't know a lot about the North American Psychics Guild, but I think they'd be deeply offended by that."

He took her hand and brought her knuckles to his mouth. "I don't want you in danger. Ever. Again."

She softened, then shoved his head into the pillow. "I appreciate that. But unless you're willing to open up and discuss specifics and how what happened in that fountain relates to what happened to Beth—"

Every muscle in his body tensed. It was like having an orgasm, only painful instead of awesome.

"There's nothing to talk about," he insisted. "Besides, you're psychic. Aren't you in my head poking around all day?"

She looked appalled. "No! I'm not poking around in your thick head all day. That would be unethical. Yes, I can pick up on your *feelings*. But anyone with an ounce of empathy could do that."

Things weren't going in the right direction.

Kicking the covers back, she swung her legs over the side of the bed. He reached for her, snagging the waistband of her sleep shorts. But before he could drag her back to him, she shimmied out of them, dazzling him with her bare ass.

"I still have a security camera out there," he reminded her as she circumnavigated the bed.

The bottomless woman of his dreams flipped him the bird and stalked out into the hall.

He flopped back on the mattress with a sigh. "That went well."

The ol' "cop shop" hadn't changed much since Nick's days there, he noted as he held the door for a pissed-off-looking wife and her hungover husband. The wife gave him the once-over and a bright smile that he returned with a wink.

He waved to the officer on the phone behind the plexiglass partition and pointed toward the door to the bullpen.

"Weber?" he mouthed.

The officer nodded, and Nick flashed a salute as he headed inside.

The building was old, and so were the furnishings. It smelled like stale coffee and industrial cleaner. The faded linoleum floors had been covered with a budget-level commercial carpet. The windows still sported the dingy film that persevered through the cleaning crew's best efforts.

Phones rang. Conversations rumbled. A rainbow of perps waited their turn for processing.

He almost missed it.

Almost.

He spotted Weber at his desk, crammed into the corner between the old file cabinets and the restroom. The man was wearing yet another tie from his endless collection, and since it was early, he'd yet to roll up the sleeves of his wrinkle-free shirt. He had his cell phone cradled between his shoulder and his ear and was typing, the keys on his ancient keyboard clicking loud enough that he kept having to ask the caller to repeat themselves.

Nick's old desk was occupied by a new detective. The young Asian woman wore a dark suit and the shine of idealism.

"Nicky Santiago." Sergeant Mabel Jones, a good cop and a nice ex-girlfriend, appeared at his elbow. She was short and curvy, with dark skin and thick hair she'd tamed into a low bun for the day. "Surprised you didn't get struck by lightning walking in here. You're not gonna headbutt anyone, are you?"

Nick glanced in Weber's direction. The detective held up a finger.

"I can't promise anything, Jonesy," Nick said. "But I might make an effort if you share one of the good K-cups you keep stashed in your bottom drawer."

She pursed her lips, pretending to consider the offer. "Fine. As long as you make me one too."

"Deal."

He commandeered the coffee maker and went to work on two cups while former coworkers swung by to lay odds on whether he was asking for his job back or taking another swing at his old partner.

Nick delivered Mabel's coffee before taking the chair in front of Weber's desk.

"You look like you're on vacation," his ex-partner noted, hanging up the phone.

Nick glanced down at his shorts and T-shirt. He'd come straight from the gym after he'd attempted to work out his frustrations via a few hundred reps and four miles on the treadmill. "You look like you're choking to death on regulations," he shot back.

"You miss it," Weber guessed, shuffling papers.

"Like hell."

"You here to rough me up again?"

Nick took a hit of coffee. "I can't. Jonesy gave me the good coffee. I have to behave."

"You know I wouldn't ask her if it wasn't important," Weber said, cutting to the chase as he shuffled files and sticky notes.

"Riley's going to say yes."

"Already did. I'm picking her up in twenty to revisit the scene and interview the husband again."

Nick felt his nostrils flare. His girl worked fast when she was pissed off. "I don't want her doing this."

"You made that abundantly clear during your temper tantrum yesterday."

"She got shot."

"She threw herself in the line of fire to make sure a bullet hit you in the ass and not the head," Weber pointed out. "She handled herself better than some of us do in a firefight."

Nick shook his head. "I don't *want* her to have to handle herself in a firefight. She had to throw a gun at that fuck because she didn't know how to shoot one. She's not trained for this shit."

"All I'm asking is for her to tag along on a few interviews and look over the case file," Weber reminded him.

"You're asking her to find a killer. Don't make it sound like you're having her swing by the grocery store for pork rinds."

Weber steepled his fingers. "I've never seen you this worked up over a girl before, Santiago."

"She's not just *a* girl. She's *my* girl."

"Can't say I blame you. Sure is easy on the eyes."

Nick slammed his cup down on the desk, sending coffee sloshing over the rim.

"Down boy," Weber said with a shit-eating grin. "I'm just returning the favor of pissing you off. This is what it was like with Beth."

Nick clenched his teeth. They'd been through hell together, and it hadn't gone well for their friendship. They hadn't talked about her since Nick's last day on the force. Before...everything, Weber's little sister and Nick had acted out a flirtation that had her older brother's blood pressure spiking every time they were in a room together.

"I was just messing with you, man. It was harmless. I wouldn't have taken your sister out. There are rules."

"You don't do rules."

"Yeah, well, even when I try to do them, I don't get them right," Nick complained.

Weber waited.

"When you're in a relationship, isn't part of the fun being able to tell the other person what they can and can't do?"

"Yeah, when you're the woman."

"Oh, come on. Don't give me that. You're telling me that Riley has the right to tell me not to pick up pretty girls at the bar, but I can't forbid her from working a homicide?"

"That's exactly what I'm telling you, brother."

"Fuck. That's not fair."

"You can forbid her from picking up guys in bars. But

unless you two agree on it, neither one of you can tell the other one what jobs to take. I thought you already learned that with Nature Girls."

Without his knowledge, Riley had gotten herself a job as a server at a seedy bar that Nick was watching to get to the owner. She'd pranced around in a miniskirt and belly-baring shirt, serving up cheap booze to the dregs of Harrisburg society to get him information.

He'd thrown multiple temper tantrums over it.

Nick groaned. "This is bullshit. It's for her own good."

"Try explaining that to her?" Weber asked.

"Yes."

His ex-partner stood and shrugged into his suit jacket. "Did you? Or did you just tell her how it was?"

"What's the difference?"

Weber grinned. "Man, I gotta tell you it feels good to see you being an idiot up close and in person again."

"Bite me."

Weber rose and nodded toward the door, and Nick followed him.

"Look. All I'm saying is women are more inclined to listen to your Neanderthal demands if you can give them a good reason for it. If you can make a compelling case."

"So either I pour my heart out to her like a big dumb baby or I give her veto rights over my work life?" Nick summarized.

Weber slapped him on the shoulder. "Now you're getting it."

"This is why I didn't want to do this shit," Nick complained as they stepped outside into the blistering August heat.

The pavement sizzled, and cicadas buzzed menacingly from the trees on the street.

"But you're doing it, and you're doing it for her. She must be pretty special."

Nick sighed. "She is. Which is why I'm here. You let her get within a city block of trouble, and I will break your face into so many pieces you'll need a transplant."

"Message received. I'll be careful with your girl, Nicky. Make sure you do the same."

They crossed the lot to Weber's shitty department-issue cruiser.

"She wanted to talk about it," Nick said.

Weber shot him a bland look. "Women tend to like to talk about things."

"What do you know about women?"

"A hell of a lot more than you. I was married."

"And how did that work out?"

"You know how it worked out since you were my best man and you helped me move out, asshole."

Reminding his friend about his own idiocy made Nick feel better about his own. "She wants to talk about Beth," he said finally.

Weber's eyes sharpened. "Does she know something? Has she seen anything?"

Nick shook his head. "No. And I haven't asked her to look. And you're not going to either. I don't want to put her in that position."

Weber scratched the back of his head. "I get it. Maybe it's better we don't know anyway."

Nick glanced back toward the building where haggard cops, devastated families, victims, and perpetrators intersected. Sometimes it was better being left with hope instead of answers.

"Speaking of Beth, I need the case file."

Weber eyed him blandly. "You know I can't do that."

"Bullshit. Mine got burnt to a crisp when your bad cop buddies torched my place."

"I can't just hand over department files to a civilian."

Nick rolled his head back. "Fine. Then copy yours. I know you've got a file and a board at home."

"She was my sister," Weber pointed out.

"And you're practically my brother. I want the file."

"Fine. I'll get you a copy."

Nick nodded. "Appreciate it."

Weber slipped on a pair of aviators and climbed behind the wheel. "Now do me a favor. Wish your girl luck today so she isn't too busy worrying about her stupid boyfriend's bad attitude to get a read on the husband."

"Yeah, yeah," Nick muttered and pulled out his phone.

6

Bianca Hornberger's neighborhood didn't look like the kind of place where people got murdered. It looked more like the place where bar mitzvahs and expensive political fundraisers with tiny appetizers were hosted. The cul-de-sac was peppered with oversize houses with things like pool houses and outdoor kitchens. The only people visible outside were the ones paid to make the yards and pools look nice.

The Hornberger house was an enormous white brick two-story with a circular driveway and a fountain that featured spitting dolphins.

"Cozy," Riley quipped as Weber shut off the engine.

"Wait until you see the inside," he said.

They got out of the car, and the Pennsylvania humidity instantly added a full two inches of frizz to Riley's hair.

She smoothed damp palms over her pants, then remembered she wasn't supposed to look nervous. She was a civilian consultant with a hot boyfriend and a cute dog, thank you very much. No longer a beleaguered proofreader barely scraping by who had nothing better to do than stalk her ex-husband's new fiancée online.

"Ready?" he asked, slipping his sunglasses into his front pocket.

She nodded. She'd sat with Gabe that morning, working through nearly an hour of psychic exercises that left her feeling open. Open enough to know that Weber's mind was going a mile a minute with thoughts that included the case, Nick, and Beth. The man's brain was very crowded. "Is there anything I should know first?" she asked.

"The vic was alone in the house when it happened. Everything minus the cause of death makes it look like a robbery gone wrong. The security footage was wiped in a thirty-five-minute window. All the computers and tablets in the house were taken, including the victim's phone." He looked at her as they walked up the drive. "If you need anything in there, like if you want to be alone in the room, just give me the sign."

"Sign? What sign?" she asked, worried that she'd missed a cop-talk handbook. Did she have a special sign language to learn? Was that how bad guys could nod at their henchmen and the henchmen knew the boss wanted them to escort the good guy to his death, not that they wanted a cappuccino or their car detailed?

Weber grinned. "Relax. Just nod. I'll get it."

Riley nodded, then stopped. "That wasn't a real nod yet. I mean, that was a real nod, but not a code nod. Maybe we should have a code word?"

Weber put a hand on her shoulder. "You'll be fine. Don't be nervous. You're not a person of interest this time around. So don't panic and yell, 'Cabbage casserole.' I'm just looking for anything you can pick up on that I'm missing."

"Do you think the husband did it?" She wasn't sure if she had the stomach to face another murderer so soon after her first run-in with one.

"I'd rather not taint your impression with my own. Come on, partner. Let's go scare a nerd."

———

Teddy Hornberger was already scared. And sad. And…a little something that almost felt like relieved. It was an info dump of impressions from her spirit guides that made Riley's head spin.

He was in his early forties and had the physique of a regular gymgoer. For some reason, that seemed a little off to her. He had thinning blond hair and a healthy tan that didn't disguise the dark circles under his eyes.

Not sleeping well. Though she couldn't blame him, considering his wife had been murdered in their home just days before.

"Detective Weber, do you have any news?" Teddy asked, taking off his glasses and wiping them on his *Mandalorian* T-shirt.

"Mr. Hornberger, this is my associate Riley. She's helping us with the investigation. We wanted to walk through the crime scene again and ask you a few follow-up questions."

"Oh, uh, sure. Should I have a lawyer present?" he asked, looking like a five-year-old who just got put in the corner by their favorite kindergarten teacher.

"Strictly routine," Riley promised. "I'm very sorry for your loss."

He tried to smile back at her, but his face crumpled. "I'm sorry," he said on a shuddering sob. "It's just been a tough time."

If this guy killed his wife, she would run out and get a face tattoo.

"I can't imagine," she sympathized.

"Do you mind if we come inside?" Weber asked.

Teddy shook his head and stepped back from the door to let them in.

While Teddy blew his nose noisily, Riley looked around. The foyer had a barrel roll brick ceiling and offered a direct line of sight to a huge fireplace in the living area. The white couch was made up as a bed. She wondered if Teddy had been sleeping there.

Above the fireplace was a large black-and-white photo of a very much alive Bianca Hornberger in a huge wedding dress. She was standing in the foreground with a bridal party of fifteen standing far enough behind her that no faces could be made out.

Front and center, just where she always wanted to be.

The Bianca in the portrait looked more natural than the one from the crime scene photos. She had the ability to smile. Her boobs were smaller. And her hair was less horse's mane and more perky cheerleader at the prom.

There were other photos, Riley noticed, tucked onto shelves and framed on the pale pink walls. A young family. Babies turning into toddlers. Toddlers into kids. An energetic little boy and a chubby girl with a sweet smile. Once the kids hit a certain age, the photos changed. There were more of the son turning into an athlete. But the daughter seemed to all but disappear. The one constant was Bianca, who appeared in every single photo sporting miniskirts and a tanning-bed tan.

Teddy finished blowing his nose and wiped the tear fog from his glasses before leading them off the main living space to a set of double doors behind crisscrossed police tape.

"Do you want me to come in with you?" he squeaked.

Weber looked at Riley. She shook her head. "That's not necessary. We just want to have a quick look around, and then I'll be back out to talk to you."

Teddy looked relieved. "Okay."

Weber held the tape up, and Riley ducked under his arm, stepping onto a cloud of white carpet.

The bedroom looked like it had been designed for a princess. The walls were a pinky cream with fancy trim and not one but two crystal chandeliers. The canopy bed was buried under blush-pink bedding with pillows piled high. Little specks in the carpet caught the light and sparkled. There were three full-size mirrors in the room.

The wall space that wasn't occupied by mirrors appeared to be an homage to the new and improved Bianca. Racy boudoir pictures and duck-lipped selfies on canvas adorned the walls. There wasn't a single picture of Teddy, the kids, or any other family.

This was the Bianca show.

"Bathroom's through there," Weber said, pointing at another set of double doors. "Closet's in there."

He handed her a pair of gloves, and she took her time putting them on. When she couldn't stall anymore, Riley swallowed hard and approached the open doorway cautiously. She wished she would have brought Gabe or Burt along for support. Even Nick, though she was still mad at him.

She hoped she wouldn't puke on the snowy white carpet. That would be unfortunate.

"I can come in with you," Weber offered.

"That would be good," she said with relief. "Just so you know, sometimes when I do this, I barf. And I had a blueberry smoothie for breakfast."

He held up a finger and headed into the bathroom. He returned with a trash can. "All set."

"Thanks." He really wasn't the ass that Nick made him out to be. "Okay. Let's do this."

The closet was the size of Riley and Nick's entire apartment. One long wall featured all luxury-brand casual clothes. Designer leggings. Labeled sweatshirts. About a hundred crop tops. The opposite wall was open shelving for bags and shoes. Along the back hung jeans and dresses. The victim obviously had expensive taste. And a cleaning crew. The closet was immaculate. Not a dust bunny to be found.

"What does the husband do again?" she asked, picking up a pair of stilettos with crystal spikes down the heels. There were a few flakes of glitter on the otherwise unblemished sole.

"Software guy. Runs a development company in Hershey," Weber said with the trash can at the ready.

She brought the crime scene photos to mind and positioned herself where the body had been found. There was no telltale carpet stain of death, but she felt a little shiver run up her spine when she stepped onto the spot.

"Did the victim work?"

"Nah. Stay-at-home mom. But she was starting her own YouTube channel. She has a studio set up in the guest bedroom."

Weber's voice faded away, and the closet disappeared as Riley found herself standing amid puffy pink and blue clouds.

"Welcome to my channel!" a perky, squeaky voice announced from somewhere beyond the ether. "I'm Bianca, and I'm here to tell you how to get everything you deserve."

The clouds began to part, and Riley's stomach dropped like she was careening down the first hill of a roller coaster. Then suddenly she wasn't moving.

"But, baaaaaaabe," Alive Bianca said, her fingers clasped under her chin. It looked like a dangerous gesture since her nails were very long and very sharp. "I neeeeed the surgery. The last conference I went to, all the girls agreed that bigger boobs mean bigger follower counts."

"I still don't understand why you care so much what a bunch of strangers think about you and your body," Vision Teddy said wearily. He was shrugging out of a designer button-down.

"It's important to me, babe. I want my voice to be heard. I have things to say. I can help people live their best lives. Just like I helped you," Bianca crooned. "Remember how chubby and pale you used to be before me?" She walked her talon-like nails up his bare chest, and Riley worried about puncture wounds.

Teddy reached into the square foot of closet storage he'd been allotted and produced a T-shirt with a narwhal on it. He dragged it on over his head. Riley could feel his resignation. "It's just a lot of money for that surgery. And didn't the last surgeon say there were significant risks if you went any bigger?"

"Ew, babe. Don't wear that. It's disgusting. Put it in the trash, and wear one of the golf shirts I got you." She shoved a shirt at him.

"I can't relax in that. I just want to sit on the couch and watch a movie with the kids. They don't care what I wear."

"We have an image to project," Bianca insisted. "What if I take a selfie of family movie night and my followers are turned off by that rag?" Her face did a weird scrunching thing, and Riley realized Bianca was attempting to wrinkle her nose.

Teddy reached for his wife and grabbed her hands. "I don't care about your follower count. I think your boobs are already too big. You had to stop wearing all your six-inch heels because you tip over. I miss the old you. What happened to the girl who brought Chinese takeout over and stayed up all night with me watching The Matrix movies?"

Bianca's eye roll was dramatic and practiced. "Babe. I've evolved. And you're evolving too." She poked him in the stomach. "Remember what those thirty extra pounds looked like down here. You were such a fluffy little nerd. And now look at you. Muscles. Tan. Contacts."

"Hair plugs. Dry eyes. And I miss carbs," he argued. "And I worry what kind of an effect your attitude is having on our daughter. She needs a mom, not a model. And I'm not working this hard just so you can turn yourself into some doll for a bunch of strangers."

Bianca booped him on the nose and shoved the golf shirt into his hands. "No. You're working this hard to provide the best life for our family. Now, put that shirt on and these shorts. And you can hold the reflector for my photo shoot."

"I don't even know who you are anymore," Teddy whispered.

"I'm the best version of me, silly."

The clouds were closing again, and Riley felt like she was being sucked through one of those bank drive-thru tubes.

She found herself back in the closet. The momentum of her head trip had her tipping to the side, falling into a section of club wear. Strong hands righted her and pushed her down to the carpet. The trash can appeared in her line of vision, and she managed a wobbly smile.

"I'm good," she promised, waving it away. "Just a little dizzy."

"That was... What the hell was that?" Weber asked, sinking down on the floor next to her.

"That was a vision. Why? What did I look like while it was happening?"

"Your nose kept twitching, but your eyes stayed open and were glazed over. Like you were in a boring class and had totally checked out."

"I was still in the closet. But I was watching Teddy and Bianca."

"Did he do it? No. No way. That's the kind of guy who sets humane mousetraps and shoos spiders outside."

"I didn't see her die," she said, feeling a bit relieved. "But I did see them arguing. She wanted bigger boobs." The dizziness began to fade, and she surveyed the closet from her seated position. She spotted the golf shirt Bianca had tried to force on Teddy on the floor in the corner.

"Bigger? I didn't know they made them bigger."

"Bigger boobs mean a bigger online following."

"Maybe one of her followers killed her?" Weber mused.

"How big of a following are we talking?"

"Twenty thousand."

"Twenty thousand people wanted to watch her tell them how to marry rich and get plastic surgery?"

"Over half of them were fake accounts. We found the purchases on her credit card statements."

"You can buy pretend followers?"

"What can I say?" Weber shrugged. "It's a fucked-up world. Everyone's got an opinion and an audience."

———

They found Teddy in the kitchen, staring vacantly into a bowl.

"Mr. Hornberger?" Riley said.

He jolted, sending milk and Marshmallow Munchies across the pink marble countertop.

"Do you have a few minutes to talk?"

"Uh, yeah. Sure. Sorry. Call me Teddy." He swirled a hot-pink dish towel through the mess and dumped it all in the sink.

"Teddy. Do you know if your wife had any problems with people who followed her on social media?"

He shoved his glasses up his nose. "Nothing out of the ordinary. I mean, there's trolls everywhere. But she just chalked it up to jealousy."

"Did she make a lot of people jealous?" Weber asked.

Teddy shrugged miserably. "I mean, she was beautiful."

"And had a doting husband," Riley added.

He looked around the kitchen at the white enamel fridge, the coral cabinets. "Maybe a little too doting. I just wanted her to be happy."

"So you aren't aware of any threats made against her from people online?"

He shook his head. "Honestly, she isn't one to be intimidated. My wife has…had strong opinions and enjoyed voicing them. Loudly." He winced. "I'm sorry. I shouldn't have said that. I didn't mean…"

"It's okay," Riley said. "Every bit of accurate information you can give us helps."

He nodded. "Yeah. Okay. Thanks. I just can't believe she's gone. I don't know who would have wanted to hurt her. I don't know what we're going to do without her."

"Assessment?" Weber asked as they headed down the walkway to his car. A beige sedan cruised past slowly before parking in front of a mailbox embedded in a fancy brick pillar.

"He's sad and scared that she's dead. But he's also a little relieved."

The detective's eyebrows lifted. "Relieved?"

"He wanted to make her happy, but it was never enough. Every inch he gave, she needed another mile. Another cosmetic procedure. He was a means to an end, and by the time he realized it, he was too in love with her to get out."

"I did a cursory glance at her channel. It's…painful to watch someone twirl their hair and talk about finding the right three-hundred-dollar jeans. But I didn't come across any overtly threatening comments."

"I can do some digging into Bianca's social media," Riley volunteered. "I excel at cyberstalking. I mean, the legal kind," she corrected quickly.

7

Larry Rupley's town house was two short blocks from the Bogdanovich mansion they called home. It was a bland beige unit in the middle of two other identically bland beige units. Nick swung Riley's Jeep into a parking spot in the lot and accepted the folder she passed him.

Burt the dog shoved his wrecking ball head between the seats and scowled through the windshield at the row of buildings as if to say, "This isn't lunch."

"Lunch is next, buddy," Nick promised the dog, ruffling his ears.

He shot Riley a glance. She'd been quiet since she'd returned unharmed—good news for Weber's face—from the interview with the dead woman's husband.

"You sure you're up for this? A homicide in the morning and a missing person in the afternoon seems like a lot for someone used to proofreading portable toilet schematics."

She looked at him and raised an eyebrow over her sunglasses. "Pellet stoves, smart-ass. And restroom partitions."

He grinned and gave her knee an affectionate squeeze. Being called a smart-ass meant she wasn't holding any grudges from their argument that morning. Either him telling her what to do wasn't that bad of an infraction or she was used to much worse shit from her turd of an ex-husband. As long as it meant she wasn't harboring a grudge against him, he was happy.

"Living the dream, baby," he said. "Let's go find ourselves a missing Larry."

They got out of the Jeep. Burt trotted along behind them, pausing to lift his leg on a fire hydrant. Three concrete steps led to Larry's front door.

"This place looks like where divorced men go to learn to fend for themselves," Riley noted as she pulled on the latex gloves he handed her. She'd changed out of summer civilian consultant casual into what Nick liked to think of as hot girl casual. Cute cutoffs, sandals, and a blue tank with a scoop neck that showed just enough cleavage to catch his eye every time he looked at her. She'd pulled her hair back from her face in a cute ponytail after complaining about humidity helmet. Why women ever thought big hair was a bad thing, he'd never understand.

He raised his fist and knocked.

"Wouldn't it be weird if he answered the door?" she mused, looking around at the other identical empty stoops and boring tan front doors.

Burt nosed his way between them and cocked his head.

Nick tried the doorbell next, and when no one answered, he produced the key Shelley had given him. "Let's hope he's not in the middle of an orgy," he said, opening the door. "After you."

"After that image?" Riley shook her head.

He stepped inside over a small pile of mail located directly under the mail slot in the door.

Sparsely furnished was being kind. There was a sagging couch on one off-white wall. It faced a new TV with about two dozen cords running to and from it. The coffee table looked like a trash day sidewalk find. It had two gaming controllers on it and a wallet.

"Mr. Rupley? Are you home?" he called. "Larry?"

Burt echoed with a questioning bark and went snuffling into the kitchen. There was no response.

"Feels empty," Riley said.

"Let's start digging."

Burt pawed at the carpet in the dining area.

"Not literally, buddy," Nick warned him. The dog looked embarrassed.

"So what exactly are we looking for?" Riley asked, sounding eager as she opened the coat closet. "Is there a PI checklist for tossing a stranger's place?"

"We're looking for a couple of things. Clues as to how Rupley lives, how he spends his time, and who he's spending it with. Then we're looking for anything out of the ordinary. What prescriptions is he on? Does he have a pot or porn stash? What's he hiding, and how good is he at hiding it?"

She nodded thoughtfully.

Speaking of hiding things. "Can I borrow your phone to take pictures?" he asked. "I left mine in the Jeep."

"Sure." She handed it over and opened the coat closet to peer inside.

Nick kept his attention on her as he deftly changed a few settings before opening the camera. He wasn't going to feel guilty about it. Not when he was doing it for her own good, he decided.

Nefarious overprotective boyfriend task complete, he flipped the wallet from the coffee table open and found Larry's driver's license, a few credit cards, $42 in cash, and a grocery store club card. No condoms. No slivers of paper with mysterious phone numbers or addresses. He pulled everything out and took a picture of the contents lined up on the coffee table.

There was no art, no framed photos, no plants in the living space. Dirty socks and two pairs of khakis were balled up in a pile next to the front door. Larry Rupley appeared to be a door pants dropper just like Nick's uncle Ricardo. Unlike Uncle Rico, Larry didn't have an Aunt Fotoula picking up his laundry.

The combined kitchen and dining space was too small for

any real function other than warming up frozen burritos for one. The appliances were "apartment-size" and over a decade old. There was a small folding table with a padded top in the middle of the room. There were no chairs, but it held a small mound of unopened packages and envelopes. Larry was apparently the kind of guy who was used to his wife keeping up with the house and the mail.

Nick riffled through the mail, finding mostly junk and Amazon packages.

It looked as though Larry took his meals either on the couch or standing up in the kitchen.

Beyond the table was a sliding glass door that opened out onto a deck so small it could only house a grill. And not a big manly grill but one of the portable charcoal kinds. Off the deck was what Nick guessed was considered a "backyard." It was fenced in for privacy, but given the fact that it was eight feet by eight feet, it felt more like an outdoor prison cell.

Larry had done nothing with his eight feet of backyard.

"Anything interesting?" he asked Riley when he came back in. She'd been combing through the kitchen trash.

She shook her head, nose wrinkled. "Old K-cups and moldy takeout leftovers. No address to a secret cabin in the woods where he meets his cult buddies for a full moon ritual."

Burt found two bowls on the floor and wolfed down the kibble before slurping up the water.

"Guy's got a cat," Nick observed, nudging the pantry door open wider to find a bag of cat food sitting on top of a litter box.

"Here, kitty kitty," Riley called. Burt's ears perked up, but no feline appeared. "Looks like he was on the TV dinner and beer diet." She held up a frozen entrée. "Guy goes from a wife and four kids to living alone and eating Dr. Diet Salisbury steak."

"No pictures. No effort to make 'Dad's place' homey for the kids. Pants dropped at the door. Maybe he liked it better this way?" Nick guessed.

He returned to the living room and peered inside the coat closet. There was a sweatshirt and three coats hanging up. Beneath them were two pairs of loafers and an empty space.

"See anything suspicious yet?"

He shook his head. "No packing lists or plane tickets. No suspicious pools of blood. No ransom notes. Let's check upstairs."

Burt bounded up the carpeted stairs in front of them.

"I swear he understands English," she said, following the dog up to the second floor.

Upstairs they found two bedrooms of equal size and a small bathroom. One bedroom had two sets of bunk beds crammed against the walls. There were no sheets on the mattresses.

Larry's bedroom had a full-size bed with no headboard, one pillow, and bedding that looked as though he'd picked it up from a discount bin. The closet held no secrets and very few clothes. A few T-shirts, a pair of jeans, a couple pairs of athletic shorts, and tank tops were crumpled on the floor. There was a phone charger plugged into the wall under the window, the smallest flat-screen Nick had ever seen perched on the rickety, nearly empty dresser, and a bottle of lotion on the floor next to the bed.

Larry Rupley's life was depressing as fuck.

He followed Riley into the bathroom.

"Hmm," she said, looking at the pile of dirty underwear on the linoleum floor.

"Bring back memories?" he asked. Her former neighbor Dickie had a history of dropping his underwear in the shared bathroom. At least he had before he'd gotten himself murdered.

"I'm betting Larry doesn't have a pair of salad tongs and a disgruntled woman to pick them up," she joked.

Nick eyed the empty roll of toilet paper on the floor and opened the linen closet. No wife to buy Larry toilet paper or more than one towel. He wondered how much effort Larry would have had to make to avoid the divorce. And how much of a lazy son of bitch the guy had to be to not be willing to make it.

"This place is depressing me," Riley said with a sigh as she popped open the medicine cabinet. "And apparently Larry." She tossed a bottle of prescription pills at him. Antidepressants. He emptied it on the off-white vanity top and counted the pills, checking the refill date on the bottle.

"Here's one for cholesterol," she said, handing him another.

He did the same with the second bottle.

"If he's good about taking his pills, he's about five days behind on both. They were both filled on the same day."

"Five days fits the timeline of when Shelley said he stopped responding to the kids' texts and calls."

Nick snapped pictures of the pills, the bathroom, and the rest of the upstairs, and then they returned to the first floor. Burt was lounging on the couch.

His long tail whipped against the cushion when he saw them.

"So what are we seeing or not seeing?" Nick prompted.

"He left his wallet and car keys," Riley said. "But I don't see a phone or a house key. So it looks like he was only planning on being gone for a short time. Or maybe that's how he wanted it to look."

"Shelley said he owed her child support, and there's a couple of past due notices in that stack of mail. Maybe Larry got too far behind and decided to skip out on everything. People of the deadbeat variety do it all the time."

She frowned. "Yeah, but he's got two race bibs on the fridge for 5Ks, and there was a space in the coat closet between his work shoes. It kind of looks like he went for a run and never came back."

"But then there's the cat," he pointed out.

"What about it?"

"We didn't see one."

"Cats hide. It could be lurking in the shadows, plotting Burt's untimely demise," she said.

"There was food in the bowl. What cat goes five days without eating all its food?"

"So maybe someone's feeding it?"

"And maybe that someone knows where Larry went," he said.

She eyed him with what looked like a combination of respect and lust. "Impressive."

"Yeah. I get that a lot," he said, rubbing his knuckles on his shirt. "Let's refill the cat dishes and go knock on some doors."

She headed toward the kitchen, then stopped. "Antidepressants. A depressing house. Being away from his family. You don't think he did something…"

"Like jump off a bridge?" He shrugged. "Coulda been a heart attack. Coulda been a mugging. A hit-and-run. An overdose. Or maybe he met a hot girl at a bar and crashed at her place for a few days."

"What does it say about his life when the only explanations for his disappearance are that he died, had a secret drug problem, or shacked up with a hot girl?" she said dryly.

"Maybe our pal Larry here staged his own disappearance and moved to a nice tropical island. You never know."

Riley's nose twitched.

"What?" he asked.

"Huh?" she asked, blinking at him.

"Your nose twitched. What are you seeing?"

She shrugged. "It's more like a feeling. Like it feels like he had every intention of coming back. But I'm not getting anything clear. I think I burned up my psychic quota in the dead lady's closet."

Nick reached for her and gave her shoulders a rub. "Did you see anything when you were with Weber?"

"I had a vision in the victim's closet. Not the murder or anything. But kind of a glimpse into her life. I didn't barf, but I still kind of scared Weber when I went all weak in the knees."

He didn't care for the idea of his girlfriend going weak in the knees around another guy.

"I think I have to build up my psychic endurance or something. I'm out of shape."

"Don't let your grandmother hear you say that tonight," he warned. "She seems like the kind of lady who'll force you into psychic boot camp in a sweat lodge in Thailand."

Riley grimaced. "I think that's why she's here."

"I'll keep the scary lady away from you," he promised, dropping a kiss on the top of her head. "Come on, Thorn. Let's see what the neighbors have to say."

No one answered the door on either side of Larry's place. But the third door opened to a short muscle-bound guy with a midlife crisis earring and a fresh tattoo on his overinflated bicep. He was short enough for it to possibly be a problem. He either had a nice tan or some Italian or Latino genes and smelled like he'd invested in a body spray company. Nick hazarded a guess that the shiny sports car in the lot belonged to this guy.

"You selling something?" the guy asked hopefully. His gaze landed on Riley and lit up. Pretty girl radar. "You can come in or whatever."

"Thanks," she said. "I'm Riley, and this is Nick."

"Come in! Come in! I'm Roy. Holy crap. Is that a lion?"

Burt regally trotted past Roy.

"We think he's a dog, but he thinks he's a person," Riley explained.

Roy laughed like it was the funniest joke he'd ever heard, and Nick could smell the desperation wafting under the cloud of body spray.

"We're looking for your neighbor Larry. He lives two doors down."

Roy's living room had been converted into a home gym. There were dumbbells lined up neatly on the carpet, and a weight bench doubled as a coffee table. A whiteboard with exercises and reps hung on the wall next to the front window.

"You work out," Riley said, stating the obvious.

Roy lit up like the Rockefeller Center Christmas tree. "Yeah," he said, his head bobbing. "I started getting into lifting. No big deal. My wife—er, *ex*-wife—said I was getting kind of soft. Well, joke's on her now." His head continued bobbing long after the sentence was complete. "Do you guys want something to drink? I was just about to make a protein shake," he said, jerking his thumb toward a kitchen virtually identical to Larry's.

Nick wondered how often residents got drunk and accidentally ended up in someone else's town house.

"I'm good, but thanks for offering," Riley said with a sweet smile.

Roy ate it up. "Have a seat. I've got some prosciutto and cheese in the fridge. It was gonna be my lunch, but I can share."

"We're good, buddy. Thanks," Nick insisted. "About Larry Rupley. Do you know him?"

Roy was back to bobbing his head. "Sure. Yeah. Sure. Big dude. Runs. I've been trying to talk him into lifting with me. I'm getting up there with my maxes. Need a spotter." Head bob.

"Do you know where he is?" Riley asked.

"Who? Larry?"

Nick blew out an exasperated breath. "Yeah, Larry. Do you know where he is? No one's been able to get a hold of him for a couple of days."

Head bob. "Yeah. No. Did you try his work?"

"That's our next stop if you can't help us."

"I can help! I can totally help," Roy insisted, looking panicked at the thought of being left alone with his muscly loneliness again.

"When's the last time you saw Larry?" Riley asked.

"Um. Okay. Let me think," he said. The veins on his neck were standing out, and Nick worried that thinking might put too much strain on the guy's nervous system. "Uh. So like last Saturday, a bunch of us—the ones that didn't have their kids for the weekend—got together in the parking lot for a kind of tailgate. We grilled up some burgers. Drank some beers. Did some push-ups."

He flexed and looked expectantly at Riley like he was about to offer her tickets to the gun show.

She smiled encouragingly. "That sounds like fun."

Nick thought her lie sounded very convincing.

"Yeah. It's cool. Most of us here, we've got a lot in common. With divorce and shit. Uh, sorry. Stuff."

"Was Larry at the tailgate on Saturday?" Nick asked, trying to steer Roy back on course.

"Oh, yeah. Of course. I mean, he wasn't doing push-ups. But he was definitely there."

"How did he seem?" Riley asked.

"Seem?" Roy apparently had never heard the word.

"Did he seem like he was happy it was the weekend? Was he upset or stressed out about anything?"

"Oh." Head bob. "Yeah. No. I don't know. Men don't, like, talk about our feelings and shit. Stuff. Sorry. Right, Mick?"

"Nick. So you're not sure if he was in a good mood or a bad mood," Nick clarified.

Roy frowned but continued to bob his head. "He seemed like he was in an okay mood. He said he didn't want to eat too much because he was heading out for a run later."

"Did you see him leave for the run?" Nick asked.

"Uh. No. Is Larry okay?" Roy asked, finally realizing it was weird to have strangers in his house asking questions about a man he hadn't seen in almost a week.

"Do you know who's been feeding Larry's cat?" Riley asked. "Mr. Pickles?"

Nick covered his laugh with a cough. "Uh, yeah, Mr. Pickles."

"Larry feeds him."

Riley's smile was starting to show strain around the edges.

"You've been a big help," Nick lied. "Here's my card. If you think of anything else, give me a call."

"Yeah. Sure." Head bob. "Do you have a card?" Roy asked Riley.

"No. She doesn't," Nick snapped.

"Oh. Okay. So if I want to talk to you, I'll just get a hold of Rick."

"Nick," Nick repeated.

"Oh. Okay. Right."

They got back in the Jeep. Roy was still watching them and waving from his front door.

"And that's why you talk about your feelings," Riley said, waving back.

"Yeah, yeah. Come on, Thorn. I'll take you to lunch."

8

U h. What errands do you have here?" Riley eyed the squat concrete building in front of them.

The sign above the double glass doors read BIG JOHNNY'S GUNS in red, white, and blue.

"Consider it employee training," Nick said, cutting the engine.

They'd gone to lunch, then dropped off Burt at the mansion so he could supervise Fred and Mr. Willicott as they went back to the drawing board for the ramp. Riley had planned to watch a few of Bianca Hornberger's 4EvaYoungBitchez videos on YouTube when Nick had insisted she join him for an errand. She'd thought it was code for car sex. She was wrong.

"You're going to teach me to shoot?" she asked, perking up. This was the first sign that he was actually going to show her the ropes of investigation. Up until this point, he'd seemed hell-bent on barricading her behind an impenetrable wall of paperwork.

"I'm going to teach you how to safely and responsibly handle a gun," he corrected, climbing out from behind the wheel and opening the back door. He picked up a large black bag and slung the strap over his shoulder. Then he took her hand. "Come on. I'll introduce you to Johnny."

Big Johnny's Guns had concrete floors, neat displays of ammo, tactical accessories, and the kind of people Riley had imagined would hang out at a gun shop before five p.m. on a weekday. The kind who wore a lot of camo and carried visible weapons on their belts.

Hastily, she silently ordered her spirit guides not to let any stray thoughts through unless they were important. She didn't want to accidentally end up inside anyone's head here. Her spiritual garage doors closed on the pretty pastel clouds, leaving her with the relative peace of her own thoughts.

Pop. Pop. Pop.

The muffled sound of gunfire made her flinch.

"Is it weird that I feel *less* safe surrounded by a bunch of people carrying guns?" she whispered, edging closer to Nick.

"That's how they make everyone feel," he assured her with a wink.

He led her to a counter in the back where two guys with holsters on their hips were doubled over watching what sounded like ultimate fail videos on a phone. Behind them, security monitors streamed footage from the indoor range.

Nick dropped the bag on the floor and threw an arm around her shoulders.

"Nicky Santiago."

A tall round woman with broad shoulders and graying hair scraped back in a ponytail appeared through a door behind the counter. She was wearing khaki pants and a khaki vest over a Lenny Kravitz T-shirt. There was a rotund black Lab on her heels.

"Johnny," Nick said.

"Haven't seen your face around here in a while," Johnny said.

"Been busy."

"Yeah, caught that bit about the mayor." If she had any opinions on the gunfight they'd been part of in downtown Harrisburg, Johnny kept her opinions to herself.

Pop. Pop. Pop.

Riley jumped.

Johnny gave her a once-over and a raised eyebrow. "Brought a newbie with you?"

Nick leaned an elbow on the counter, perfectly at home with the gunfire and the bearded gun-toting crowd. "Yeah, this is Riley. Riley, Johnny," he said. "We're gonna need a lane and some targets."

Johnny elbowed the guys away from the cash register. "You're the one from the fountain. The psychic," she said, shooting her another look.

Riley really needed to start wearing a hat and sunglasses, she decided.

Pop. Pop. Pop.

"Uh, yeah," she said weakly. She braced for the typical reaction. "*What number am I thinking of?*" Insinuations about scamming people at carnivals.

"Heard you threw a gun at the mayor."

Riley winced. "Yep."

Johnny leveled Nick with a look. "Shoulda brought her in a long time ago."

"Yeah, yeah. We're here now. Can we have a lane?" He released Riley to give the Lab that had wandered out to sniff them a good scruffing. The dog leaned into Riley's leg and looked up at her with mournful doggy eyes as if to say everything would be just fine. She stroked his silky ears and didn't even flinch when someone fired off another few rounds on the range.

"Lane seven," Johnny said, licking her thumb and peeling off several targets from a stack. "What are you shooting today?"

Nick listed off several words and letter-number combos that sounded more like code than names of firearms.

They turned over their IDs and signed waivers with language that reactivated Riley's nerves. And then Johnny was directing them toward a door marked INDOOR RANGE. Nick pulled her to a stop before the door and unzipped his bag. He slipped a pair of large headphones over her ears. He grinned. "You ready, Thorn?"

His voice came through the speakers sounding tinny and far away.

She nodded. "Yeah. Teach me stuff."

"Don't let her quit 'til she's got a good target," Johnny called after them. Nick tossed a salute in her direction and led the way into the vestibule.

The gunfire was louder between the two doors, even with the hearing protection. Riley followed him through the second door and into a long room. At the far end of the range was a middle-aged dad with—judging from the delighted squeals— two teenage daughters. Two lanes down was an elderly Black man in a golf shirt and shorts loading a pearl-handle revolver. Each lane had vertical partitions and a waist-high counter. Nick hefted his bag onto the counter and unloaded two serious-looking handguns, several boxes of bullets, and two pairs of safety glasses.

"Okay, Thorn, let's get you comfortable with a gun."

He proceeded to provide a concise tutorial on firearm mechanics and responsible handling. Riley did her best to absorb the information. He handed her one of the guns—a Glock if she remembered correctly—and coached her on loading the magazine and racking the slide. They worked on her stance and grip for a few minutes. Then he had her release the magazine and rack the slide again, expelling the chambered bullet. He had her do it until the magazine was empty, then made her reload it with all the bullets.

Professor Nick had her repeat this exercise until her fingers hurt.

"They make it look so easy in movies," she complained.

"They make getting shot look easier too," he pointed out.

Thanks to personal experience, Riley had taken to calling bullshit whenever characters on screen got shot and managed to continue performing heroic feats of strength.

"My fingers are numb."

"Then I guess it's time to shoot. I'll go first. Watch my stance and be impressed."

He clipped one of the paper targets onto the return arm and sent it out five yards. Flashing her a cocky grin over his shoulder, he picked up the Glock and fired off six shots in rapid succession. Riley jumped each time he fired.

He put the gun down and hit the recall button.

"Jeez! Did you even hit anything?" she asked dryly.

"See for yourself."

The man with the revolver whistled. "That's some nice shooting, sonny."

Nick gave him the nod, then looked at her expectantly.

There were six neat holes clustered in the dead center of the target.

She blinked. "Wow. You really *are* good at everything."

He preened. "Yes. Yes, I am. Now, let's see what you've got."

She wiped her damp palms on the back of her shorts and carefully inserted the magazine into the pistol. It took her two tries before she racked the slide properly, and by then, her heart was pounding in her chest. Someone in another lane fired off a shot that made her jump.

"Now you're going to bring the gun up in both hands like you practiced, take a deep breath, and pull the trigger," Nick instructed.

It couldn't be that hard, right? The two teen girls at the end of the range were making Swiss cheese out of their target.

She pointed the gun at the fresh target, took a deep breath, and squeezed the trigger.

She yelped and jerked her elbows when the weapon fired. The shot rang in her ears, and her body tightened reflexively as the gun kicked in her grip.

"Oh my God. I hit it!"

"Yeah, baby. If we ever need anyone to shoot the outside of a bad guy's knees, you'll be the one to take the shot," Nick said with affection, eyeing the hole at the bottom left of the target.

So she hadn't hit the silhouette. But she *had* at least hit the paper.

"Keep going," he encouraged her.

She did as she was told and slowly fired off the other rounds, yelping each time she squeezed the trigger.

He took the empty gun out of her hands and recalled the target. She'd managed to wing the right shoulder, pierce the silhouette's ear, and completely missed the paper for her last three shots.

"Where exactly were you aiming for?" he asked.

Riley tapped the unblemished center circle on the target. "I suck at this, don't I?"

He grinned. "Not going to lie. The terrified squeaking is adorable."

"I can't help it. I'm respectfully petrified."

"Pulling the trigger *should* be scary. You need to be aware of the consequences of every shot you take."

"That's not making me less nervous." One lesson and she already felt defeated.

"Look at me, Thorn. No one is ever any good at this the first time out. It takes practice. Just like your psychic stuff, right? You have to train to get better until it's as natural as a reflex."

She felt a little niggle of guilt in her chest. He had a point. Which meant that her grandmother wasn't exactly wrong. She hadn't been a dutiful student. Since the incident earlier in the summer, she'd been spending most of her days with her spiritual garage doors down, just enjoying being a regular person for a change. In the past few weeks, she and Gabe had spent more time going for ice cream and brunch than they had flexing her clairvoyance muscles.

She hadn't just fallen off the wagon. She'd willingly hurled herself under its wheels. And that was irresponsible, especially since she'd volunteered to help Weber with his case.

Riley blew out a sigh. "You know what one of the most depressing things about being an adult is?"

He clipped a new target to the arm and sent it down range. "What?"

"I always thought at some point I'd be the best version of

myself and that things would come easier then. But nothing is easy. There is no best self. It's all just hard work and sweaty, painful practice."

Nick ruffled her hair. "Poor little Riley Thorn. That's why you gotta make the practice fun."

"How do you do that?" she asked glumly.

"We'll start here." There was a gleam in his eyes behind the safety glasses.

Soon, she saw why. He came up behind her, caging her between the counter and his own body. She could feel every inch of his hard, delicious front where it pressed against her back.

"Pick up your gun, Thorn," he said. She could hear the smile in his voice.

"Uh, okay." She did as he instructed.

"Good girl. Now, load it and chamber a round."

She slapped the magazine into the pistol and managed to rack the slide on the first try. "Now what?" she asked, feeling anticipation mix with nerves. Everything felt better with Nick Santiago pressed up against her.

"Now we do it together." His hands gripped her hips, holding her against him. "Pull the trigger, Thorn. Practice makes awesome."

9

The house at 69 Dogwood Street in Camp Hill looked just like any of the other sedate brick homes on their summer-scorched grass lots. But appearances were deceiving.

"Okay," Riley said, turning around in her seat to look at the rest of the vehicle's occupants. "Is everyone familiar with the plan?"

Gabe nodded. "We are to attend Thorn family dinner."

"And?" she prodded.

Fred's toupeed head popped up in her line of sight. For reasons she couldn't fathom, her eighty-something-year-old roommate had decided to join them at her parents' house for God knows what her mother was going to serve.

"After an appropriate amount of time, we make an excuse and leave."

Burt gave an agreeable grumble from the back of Nick's SUV. Gabe and Fred nodded solemnly.

"Great. Don't let your guards down in there. My grand-mother is a terrifying woman and always has an ulterior motive," she warned them.

"Chicken or tacos after this?" Nick asked as he turned off the car.

"Yes."

They piled out of the SUV and strolled up the walk. A welcoming *moo* came from the backyard.

"That's my dad's spite cow," Riley explained to Fred. "He got it to annoy the lady next door."

Chelsea Strump's house was an immaculate two-story with a front porch she never sat on because she hated all her neighbors. Her lawn was the only one on the street that still bore any resemblance to actual grass. August in Pennsylvania was hell on landscaping.

"No tarot readings. No second helpings. We get in and get out," Riley reminded them as they trooped up the porch steps.

"Aww," Fred whined. His toupee was on sideways. The part ran from ear to ear like an equator.

"Let's get this over with." Riley sighed, squeezing Nick's hand for courage. Her grip was weak from the gun range. But Nick had stayed true to his word. He hadn't let her quit until she'd hit the target with all six shots. Sure, they'd been all over the freaking place. But it still counted, and she actually felt proud of the effort. Proud enough that she was sure she could handle anything Elanora doled out at dinner.

She gave a cursory knock and then opened the door.

It was eerily silent inside.

"Hello?" she called.

There was a beat of silence, and then her grandmother's voice came from the kitchen. "You will join us in the kitchen."

Burt sniffed the air with suspicion. Riley did the same. "Do you smell that?" she asked Nick.

"I don't smell anything," he said.

"Me either. No cabbage. No quinoa. I don't smell dinner."

"Maybe it's fresh vegetables and green juice," he whispered back as they cautiously approached the kitchen.

Burt trotted ahead, tongue lolling out of the side of his mouth. He stopped in his tracks at the doorway to the kitchen and backed into Nick's legs.

"What's the matter, buddy?" Nick asked.

"Oh boy," Riley said under her breath.

Her entire family was seated around the table. Elanora was at the head in her father's chair. Roger was seated at the foot. His hands were fisted on the table as if they held invisible utensils. Blossom sat on her mother's right. Riley's sister, Wander, was on Elanora's left. Wander's three daughters—Rain, River, and Janet—were pouting at a child-size table in front of the sliding doors that led to the backyard. Daisy the cow was on the deck, pressing her wet nose against the door.

"Moo!"

It sounded like a warning.

"You're late," Elanora said. "And you brought an extra guest. That's incredibly rude."

Fred poked his head around Riley's shoulder and waved. "I heard there was an attractive single lady who might need some flirtation." He whipped out a tube of breath spray and doused his mouth suggestively.

Riley fought back the urge to barf.

"Uh, where's dinner?" she asked.

Wander's brown eyes were telegraphing an emergency SOS to her. But it got interrupted when she spotted Gabe. Wander went all gooey and smiley.

"You will all sit," her grandmother ordered. "But since there are too many of you, one must join the children." She said the word *children* like it was a synonym for *demons*.

"Dibs," Nick said, pressing a kiss to Riley's cheek.

"Traitor," she whispered after him.

Riley let Gabe have the seat next to Wander while Fred dragged a chair around and stuffed it into the corner between Elanora and Blossom.

"Now what?" Riley asked. If they weren't eating, she and her little entourage could get out of here faster than she thought.

"Because my family and those they hold company with have become such lazy gluttons, we will be participating in a silent fast," Elanora announced.

"Sounds like fun, sexy lady," Fred said, adding a mouth click and a wink.

Riley's stomach let out a plaintive growl.

Burt barked.

Daisy mooed again from the deck.

"Nick, you mind letting Burt out to play with Daisy?" Roger asked from the foot of the table, still clinging to his invisible cutlery. "She's feeling left out."

"Sure." Nick uncurled himself from the kids' table and opened the door. Burt joyfully romped outside, most likely to tell his cow friend how weird their humans were.

From her vantage point, Riley watched the cow and pony-size dog play chase around the overgrown yard.

"We will begin our hour-long silence. If anyone utters a word, we will start over. The silence begins now," Elanora said, ringing a tiny bell.

The tone hung in the air until Riley's stomach growled over it. She shrugged when her grandmother glowered in her direction.

An hour of sitting and staring at each other. And not eating. *Great.*

While Nick made faces at her nieces and Burt and Daisy sprinted around in circles outside, Riley tried not to make eye contact with anyone.

"Need to ask Rye Bread if there's a safe way to google getting rid of mother-in-laws."

Awesome. Now she was picking up on her father's thoughts.

She gave herself a few minutes to wonder if it was *mother-in-laws* or *mothers-in-law*. Until she was distracted by some R-rated thoughts that were coming from the direction of the kids' table. Her cheeks flamed pink when Nick shot her a look that told her exactly what they were having for dessert that night.

Her grandmother cleared her throat imperiously, and with a guilty conscience, Riley looked past Nick to where Daisy was rubbing up against the fence, scratching an itch on her hind quarters. Burt followed suit, and the fence wobbled dangerously.

She opened her mouth to say something until a sharp kick landed against her shin. Her mother looked her dead in the eye.

Geez. Fine. If the fence fell down, it fell down. It wasn't her fence, and her parents were the ones who would have to deal with the consequences.

Next to her, Gabe was statue-still. Eyes open and unblinking. He was sweating profusely.

Her father was glaring at Elanora like he wanted to stab her with his invisible knife and fork.

Someone farted. Her money was on Fred.

Cabbage casserole would have been a godsend in comparison to this disaster.

With no place else to escape, Riley closed her eyes and called up her spirit guides. "Hey, guys. It's me. Is there anything you want to show me for the next, ohhhhh, fifty-five minutes or so?"

The pink and blue clouds slowly swirled into her mind's eye. They pulsed with warm light, and she allowed herself to relax into them. Maybe she could take a psychic nap on these things, she mused, squishing a cloud between her hands.

"Do you have anything to show me regarding Bianca Hornberger or Larry Rupley?" she asked the clouds.

They pulsed again and then slowly began to rotate like a tropical storm with her as the eye.

When the clouds parted, she saw nothing but sparkling particles. Like a craft store had imploded during a scrapbooking tutorial. She blinked, trying to clear her vision, but there was only more sparkle. Glittering in a rainbow of colors.

"Okay. This is fun. But I don't know what this means," she told the clouds.

In response, she felt a gust of air against her face and the stinging of tiny particles hitting her skin.

"Are you saying I need to schedule a microdermabrasion?" Her friend Jasmine was big on facials and was always trying to get her to go along.

Again, she felt the whoosh of air and the blast of tiny shards of something dusting her skin. This time, though, it was accompanied by a blast of heat. She shook her head. "Sorry, guys. I'm not getting what this is. What else do you have?"

It took a beat, but she saw Nick standing in Larry's living room holding a phone. *Her* phone. Vision Nick glanced toward the kitchen, and Riley realized he was making sure she was occupied.

"Is he snooping on my phone?" she asked, more confused than appalled. Nick wasn't the secretly-read-text-messages kind of guy.

She couldn't see what he was doing, but she felt a grim kind of purpose pumping off him. Like it was something he felt he had to do. Something he knew she wouldn't like. He glanced up again in Vision Riley's direction, and she felt something else. A fierce protectiveness swept through her, followed by a softening, a warmth. Something like, well, *like*...only more. It made her palms sweat. Her pulse accelerated.

Was Nick Santiago in love with her? Was that what she was feeling? And what the hell had he done with her phone?

The doorbell interrupted her psychic epiphany and yanked her back into her body. Her parents exchanged a glance, but neither of them moved to answer it. They had less than ten minutes left on the clock, and Riley sensed the collective agreement to murder anyone who opened their trap now.

The visitor gave up on the bell and pounded on the door. "I know you're in there!"

Her father's face flushed a reddish purple.

Chelsea Strump was pounding on the front door with something to complain about. Not standing up and yelling at her went against Roger's very DNA.

Chelsea pounded again. "Your disturbing menagerie of illegal livestock is going to knock that fence down, and if one splinter falls on my side of the property line, you can bet I'll be on the phone with my attorney so fast it'll make your heads spin!"

Blossom's face turned an unnatural shade of red. Wander's daughters squirmed in their chairs, trying not to giggle as Nick silently mimicked the irate neighbor. Elanora remained completely impassive.

Roger's nostrils flared so wide Riley could have inserted salt and pepper shakers in them.

There was another pound followed by what sounded like a kick. "Answer this door, you weirdos!" Chelsea howled.

Blossom gripped Roger's hand when it looked like he was about to rip the table in half.

Finally, things went quiet again, and Riley envisioned Chelsea stomping back to her house.

Someone at the table farted again.

"Oops. Tooted again. Good thing it was silent!"

That was definitely Fred.

She tuned him out and tried to focus her attention on Wander. Hers was the safest mind to read at the table. Her sister was the kind of person who didn't even *think* mean things, let alone say them. Apparently, Wander wasn't thinking about anything other than how much she liked sitting next to Gabe. It was sweet…and dangerous given their proximity to Elanora's disapproval.

Riley's stomach growled again, drawing a disgruntled glare from her grandmother. Riley gave up being psychic and urged the minute hand on the clock above the sink to tick faster.

Daisy and Burt took turns nosing a large exercise ball around the backyard until Burt accidentally bit it too hard and it deflated. Daisy let out a mournful moo.

Finally her grandmother raised her stupid bell and rang it.

"That was a barely adequate attempt," Elanora announced, and Riley sagged back in her chair.

Wander blew out a breath from somewhere on the other side of the wall of Gabe's large torso.

"Mommy, can we have some tofu nuggets now?" Janet, the youngest, begged from the kids' table.

Nick turned and locked eyes with her. Riley felt…a lot of things. Most of them were obscured by hunger. But girlish giddiness and middle-aged suspicion ranked in second and third place.

"I gotta get to someplace that ain't here," Roger announced, jumping up from his chair.

"So, sweetheart. What's your sign?" Fred asked Elanora.

Nick stood up and let Burt back into the house.

"That was lovely, Mom," Blossom said through gritted teeth.

"Don't patronize me," Elanora announced. "Tomorrow, you will join me for an intensive spiritual training session that will cleanse your souls of laziness and discipline your minds. We begin at six a.m."

"Six in the morning?" Riley swallowed hard.

Her grandmother leveled her with a stare. "Do you have an issue with that?"

"Yes." Riley nodded vigorously.

"I do not care. You will be there, or I will drag you from your bed."

"Sounds great," Riley said dryly.

"Gabe," Wander said softly. "The girls and I would love it if you'd join us tonight. We're making kombucha."

Gabe opened his mouth, hearts in his eyes. But the cloud of doom cut him off.

"Gabriel doesn't have time to socialize," Elanora cut in. "He has much to make up for since detouring from his quest."

Wander dipped her head, disappointment radiating from her.

Elanora pushed her chair back and rose. "I am retiring for the night."

"Need any help with your nightgown?" Fred offered hopefully.

"Not from a man with so little control over his digestive system," she said and swept out of the room.

"Dad didn't go next door to murder the neighbor, did he?" Riley asked, standing up.

Blossom poked her head out of the fridge, a bottle of wine held to her lips. "No. We have a plan."

"You have a plan to murder your next-door neighbor?" Nick asked. He put his hands on Riley's shoulders and dropped his chin to the top of her head.

"Of course not," Blossom assured him. "That whackadoo isn't conserving her water. She's got those sprinklers running in the middle of the night for hours during a drought. Can you believe that? Roger's gonna get footage of it and report her to the municipality. Does anyone else want wine?"

10

Crickets chirped maniacally in the sweltering dark as Nick took the dog outside for a quick game of fetch and one last pee. From his vantage point on the edge of the parking lot, it looked as though every light in the mansion was on. No one over the age of eighty seemed capable of turning off a light or locking a door.

Or building a ramp. The project was on its third week and was still nothing more than a pile of lumber and meatball sub wrappers.

Burt bounded out of the thigh-high weeds of the property next door, a stick clutched in his mouth instead of the Frisbee Nick had thrown. It was their tradition. He threw a fetch-approved dog toy, and Burt returned with something else.

Burt spit out the stick at his feet and trembled with joy.

Nick picked up the limb, gave it a toss into the overgrowth, and thought about how weird life was.

Earlier this year, he was assuring his aunt Fotoula that he preferred being single while she pinched his cheek and told him about a "nice girl" who worked in her accounting office. Now, he was living with a nice girl who *he* picked out without any arm-twisting, in one of the big houses he'd passed thousands of times as a kid, wondering what kind of people lived behind iron gates and manicured lawns.

Front Street in Harrisburg was home to several fancy-ass mansions with river views and large lots. For decades, they'd housed wealthy families before the rich had moved out of the city, leaving their homes behind to be turned into commercial offices for lawyers and associations. Several of the buildings had seen better days. A few of them—like the Tudor nightmare next door—needed a bulldozer.

He looked up to the third floor, where a responsible number of lights were on. Riley Thorn was the responsible sort. And for some reason, he liked that about her.

Burt bounded back, this time clutching a six-foot stretch of orange safety netting in his mouth.

"I don't even want to know where that came from," Nick decided. A slow breeze chose that moment to lazily stir the air, bringing with it the scent of something rotting. "Ah, Harrisburg, you old charmer. Come on, Burt."

They headed back inside via the front door, and each separated to follow through with another nightly ritual. Nick checked the doors and windows to make sure they were locked while Burt wandered off to sniff around the kitchen for crumbs and the occasional floor pizza.

He was just about to hit the stairs when he heard a wheeze and a pained, "One hundred forty-six."

Curious, he found Gabe's door ajar.

When the man had shown up earlier that summer—a big buff stranger claiming to be there to help Riley—the boy-crazy Lily had rented him a room on the spot. It was a parlor of some sort. Like the rest of the house, it was crammed full of a few generations of paraphernalia.

Gabe's bed was a sofa with a single pillow and bedsheet. It looked like it would only hold the man's upper torso. His wardrobe of black gym clothes was folded and stacked neatly on top of some sort of old dressing room vanity next to a black marble fireplace. The man himself was suspended upside down from a metal rig set up in front of the bow window.

"One hundred forty-seven. One hundred forty-eight." Gabe fought gravity and curled his body into a sit-up with each count. There was a puddle of sweat beneath him on an exercise mat.

"Uh, you doing okay there, Mount Olympus?" Nick asked.

Gabe's mouth pinched in a firm line. "No. I am not well. Thank you for asking."

Ah, hell.

They hadn't exactly been best pals. Not with Nick discovering how much he liked a certain resident psychic and Gabe's fawning adoration over Riley. But the guy was basically an oversize teddy bear who had Riley's best interests at heart. It was hard to keep hating him.

"You want to come down here and talk about it?" Nick offered.

To his surprise, Gabe neatly executed a skin-the-cat flip and landed with a *sploosh* in his own sweat puddle.

"I would very much like that," the sweaty giant said.

Crap.

Gabe wiped a bath towel over his brow. It looked like a regular-size sweat towel in the man's dinner plate–size hands. "Elanora is disappointed in me," he announced.

"Elanora seems like she's disappointed in a lot of people," Nick observed. *Like the entire human race.*

Gabe shook his head, sending sweat in a 360-degree radius. "It is my fault that Riley was in danger. I was distracted by my infatuation with…ice cream. Riley could have ceased existing, and it would have been my fault."

Nick was fairly certain Gabe wasn't really talking about ice cream.

"Listen, big guy," he said, clasping Gabe's sweaty shoulder. He removed his hand and wiped his palm on his T-shirt. "Riley's safety is not on you. It's on me. If anyone failed her, it was me, not you."

"But I am here to guide her. Instead, I allowed myself to be distracted by earthly enjoyments."

Definitely not talking about ice cream.

A life without "earthly enjoyment" sounded like a shitty, boring existence.

"Look, Gabe. I don't know what your relationship with Elanora is or what your relationship with Riley is supposed to be. But you've got to cut yourself some slack. You're only human. You *are* human, aren't you?"

Gabe dropped to the floor and assumed the push-up position.

"One. Elanora is my spiritual patron. Two. I repay her generosity by taking on roles she specifies for me. Three."

"And training Riley to open up to her powers was one of those roles."

"Four. Yes. But my role was to guide her *safely*."

"Riley pulled a fast one on all of us by sneaking out to try to rescue Jasmine on her own. It won't happen again. I won't let it. Moving forward, you can guard her spiritually. But I'm guarding her body."

Gabe looked thoughtful while he executed several more push-ups. "I do not know if Elanora would find that arrangement acceptable," he said finally.

"Does Scary Grandma Lady pay you?" Nick asked.

Gabe paused. "Of course not." He said it as if getting paid to do work was the most ridiculous thing in the world.

"Seriously? Then where does your money come from?"

"Nine. The universe provides."

"I notice you didn't answer the Are-you-human? question."

"Ten. We are all human in our own way."

Nick rolled his eyes. "You sound like a fortune cookie." It made him think about the fluffy, lazy divorced Larry Rupley who hadn't bothered putting forth any effort until it was too late. On a sigh, he dropped to the floor next to Gabe. "One," he said, executing a push-up.

"Eleven," Gabe said, now dripping sweat onto a new spot on the floor.

"Two. You do know there's a difference between having a job and having a life, right? Three."

"Twelve. I do not understand," Gabe said, swiping a hand over his sweaty brow while completing a one-handed push-up.

"Fourteen. I mean, no boss gets to dictate how you live your life. That's your choice. You get to decide. Twenty-three. It's kinda your fault if you give someone else the right to make your decisions for you," Nick said.

Gabe paused in a textbook plank, beads of sweat forming glistening rivers of sweat on his bulging biceps and forearms. "Is this true, or are you setting me up for some elaborate and embarrassing prank?"

Nick grinned. "I can see how you'd think that, but I'm being serious. You get to decide who you spend time with and what dairy products you consume by the gallon. Twenty-seven."

"I do?" Bewildered, Gabe looked at him from the plank.

"Of course you do. You're probably human. You're an adult. You wanna make out with ice cream every night? You pick the flavor. It's up to you to figure out what you want and whether to go after it. Whether the thing you want is worth the consequences of having it." Nick banged out three push-ups in rapid succession. "Thirty-eight. Thirty-nine. Forty."

"You are making an intriguing point. I must consider it."

"Thanks, buddy. Fifty-two. Listen, another thing I learned the hard way. You're not responsible for other people's choices. Sixty-three. Riley was the one who stupidly decided to try to solve the problem on her own. You aren't responsible for that. One hundred."

"Many of the things you say are nonsensical. Yet now you are providing real wisdom," Gabe observed with a frown.

"Yeah, I'm a complex guy," Nick said, rolling over and executing a sit-up. "One."

"I would never have guessed. Perhaps Elanora's silent fast opened your mind?" Gabe guessed.

Nick snorted. "Not eating and not talking didn't teach me a damn thing. I've got the whole life-experience thing going for me," he explained. "Two. You know, learning through living. Seven."

Gabe frowned thoughtfully. "Learning through living. Have you ever considered becoming a spiritual coach? I feel I have much to learn from you."

"Fifteen. Stick with me, big guy. I'll show you how to enjoy the world. Twenty."

"A world with ice cream?" Gabe asked, his arms shaking from the plank.

"Twenty-four. A world with ice cream and pretty girls who like you a lot."

Gabe smiled shyly. "I like this world you speak of."

"Me too, Mount Rushmore. Me too."

Bro time over, Nick took the stairs two at a time. It was time to do some living of his own. On the third floor, he kicked the door open, startling Riley into dropping a piece of fried chicken on the floor.

"What the hell, Santiago?" she grumbled, picking up the chicken.

"You. Shirt off," he said, pointing at her as he yanked his phone out of the back pocket of his jeans.

"You caveman," she said. "Why are you all sweaty?"

She was chewing on her bottom lip. A definite sign that she was turned on and trying not to be.

"If you're not naked by the time I finish this text, I will rip the clothing from your body, Thorn."

Her eyes widened. "Seriously?"

"Deadly," he promised.

"Who are you texting?" she asked, dragging her shirt over her head.

"Everyone."

Nick: For the next hour, unless there is a fire or a life-threatening medical emergency, everyone is forbidden from entering the third floor, allowing access to anyone who wants access to the third floor, calling, texting, shouting for, or emailing any resident of the third floor. Starting now.

He shucked his jeans and left them where they fell.

Mrs. Penny: Sounds like the whippersnappers are getting it on.
Fred: Riley, I think you have my favorite chopsticks. I'll be up in a minute to get them.
Nick: Fred, if you step one foot up here, I will duct-tape you to the lift chair. You can wait for your chopsticks.
Lily: Oh my! Do you need any of my flavored massage oils? The Tahitian vanilla tastes just like ice cream.
Nick: Thanks and definitely not.
Mr. Willicott: There's a third floor? What's up there?
Mrs. Penny: An orgy.
Fred: We should have a new code word.
Lily: What a great idea! A sexy code word, and whenever any of us use it, someone has to have sex with us!
Mrs. Penny: For God's sake, woman. I need to see your prescriptions. I think your doc put you on the wrong hormones.

Nick threw the dead bolt, hooked the door chain, and dragged his T-shirt over his head. He hurled it in the direction of the couch and advanced toward Riley.

She was naked from head to toe. It was his favorite look on her. She put the chicken down and braced for impact.

"If your batty grandmother thinks she can convince you to get rid of me, she's gonna be very disappointed," he said, boosting her up and wrapping her legs around his waist.

"Uh-huh. Okay," she said, sealing her mouth to his.

And there it was. That weird swoopy tickle in his torso. It was a new, disconcerting kind of emotional vertigo. And he was going to embrace the shit out of it.

"Ready to test out the table?" He kissed a trail down her

throat and hissed out a breath when her nails bit into his back.

"Oh yeah."

He slid her onto the table and pushed her knees apart, wishing he had the restraint to show a little finesse. But he'd been denied too many times today.

"Condom?" she asked breathlessly.

He grinned and jutted his chin toward the decorative cookie jar thing in the center of the table. "Look inside."

She raised an eyebrow and bowed back, reaching for the jar. "Seriously? A condom stash centerpiece?"

He snatched the foil packet out of her hand. "You got a problem with that?"

Her lips were parted, eyelids heavy. "I have no problem," she panted.

"Good, because both nightstands are stocked, and that book on the coffee table is hollow inside."

Riley sighed. "You're so hot when you're prepared."

He was this close to making her say his name in that breathy, anxious way when the piercing sound of the smoke detector rang out.

"Are you kidding me right now?" he snarled.

"Hey, Nick." Mrs. Penny's voice echoed from her bullhorn over the incessant beeping. "There's a fire in the kitchen. Willicott microwaved a burrito in the tinfoil again."

"We need a new place to live," he muttered, reaching for his pants.

11

P athetic."

Something hard and pointy jabbed Riley in the rib as she tried to suck humid air into her lungs.

"My grandmother could have outrun you on her one hundredth birthday." Elanora sniffed in derision and slammed her walking stick into the ground. "And she was missing her right leg from the knee down."

Riley rolled over onto her stomach and accidentally sucked a blade of grass up her nose. "What...does...running... sprints...have...to do with...being...psychic?"

Ten feet away, Gabe vomited gracefully behind a tree. His wind sprints had been half a mile long.

The sun was up, and the early morning swelter was accessorized by the obnoxious buzzing of cicadas. It was too early for the bumper-to-bumper rush-hour commuters. But there were plenty of joggers loping past and shooting sympathetic glances their way. She was too tired to block out their thoughts.

"That old lady reminds me of Sister Gertrude from junior high."

"I can't believe I wasted a bikini wax on that guy."

"Did I just run through Justin's fart cloud? God, what did he eat?"

"I do not need to explain my teachings to you," Elanora announced.

"No, but it would be nice," Riley wheezed.

The thick breeze stirred, bringing with it a scent so bad Riley had to take another whiff just to verify that it was indeed the worst thing she'd ever smelled. Burt, however, seemed to enjoy smelling rotting, half-cooked roadkill and nosed the air for more.

She wondered if it was the fart cloud from the jogger and if he'd had his intestinal tract looked at.

Burt snuffled off onto the overgrown lot where knee-high dried grass and dying trees dotted the unkempt surface. In the center of the land that nature had given up on reclaiming was a Tudor-style home that had once probably not been an eyesore. Abandoned for the past decade, it squatted on the land under a coat of peeling paint and boarded-up windows.

The For Sale sign had been there as long as Riley had lived next door.

"Burt, come back here," she called.

The dog lifted his head, then looked back and forth between her and the house, debating.

"Now, please."

Reluctantly, the dog trotted back to her side, and she leaned on him to regain her feet.

It still smelled like something earthy and gross but fainter now. In central Pennsylvania, bad smells were quite common. Between paper mills and mushroom farms, breezes always carried with them a hint of something awful.

"You will complete twenty push-ups. Now," her grandmother announced, returning to her folding chair and sitting primly.

Burt wandered over and collapsed in the shadow of Evil Elanora, tongue lolling in the grass. He'd survived two of the ten wind sprints Evil Elanora had forced on Riley.

Apparently burning off physical energy honed the mind… or some bullshit like that. Riley was too dehydrated and nauseated to remember.

"Why are you limping? Basil women don't limp," her grandmother complained.

"I slipped on a flaming burrito while running for a fire extinguisher."

Judging by the pinched look on the older woman's face, she should have kept that tidbit to herself.

Between burrito accidents and psychic preseason, Riley might have to see if Nick's cousin Brian had a spare wheelchair she could borrow for a few days.

Her sister, Wander, appeared before her, looking like she'd just stepped off the set of a yoga photo shoot. Her long braids were pulled up on top of her head in a high tail. She wore a cropped tank and yoga shorts, both in a dusky purple. The natural glow of her brown skin glistened like she'd been dusted by a bronzer fairy. It was how Wander sweated. Riley, on the other hand, looked as if someone had tossed her in the river and dragged her back out by the hair. Wander was lucky she was a nice person in addition to inheriting so much gorgeousness from her biological father, otherwise her sweaty big sister would have been able to work up the energy to hate her.

"How was your five-mile run?" Elanora asked solicitously.

"Lovely. The river walk really opens my heart chakra in the mornings." Wander took a dainty sip from her matching water bottle. Riley eyed the bottle and fantasized about stealing it and running away to hide in her shower.

"Can you guys keep it down?" Blossom complained from the shade of a pine tree just off the mansion's parking lot. "I'm trying to tai chi my ass off over here."

She was getting dangerously close to Burt's favorite pooping spot, but Riley was too breathless to vocalize a warning.

"Push-ups. Now," Elanora insisted, waving her walking stick at them.

Riley was going to find the person who gave her that stick and then beat them with it.

Gabe had finished vomiting and joined Wander and Riley on the ground.

"One," they groaned as a group. "Two."

The back door of the mansion swung open, and Burt jumped up to greet Nick. Riley's unsatiated lady parts paid close attention as he strolled toward her looking like a lust-fueled mirage in gym clothes and sunglasses.

"Heading to the gym. Thought you could use some water," he said, handing her a man-size thermos.

"My hero," she gasped and popped the top. She tilted her head back and let the water rush out into her mouth and down over her face and neck.

Nick chuckled and ruffled her hair. "Later, Thorn."

She responded with a gulping noise.

"You're looking domineering today, Elanora," he said with a wink and a flash of dueling dimples.

"I am aware." Her grandmother was dressed for the weather in lightweight ebony pants, a sleeveless midnight tunic, and a black and more black scarf wound around her head. She was wearing a chunky amethyst necklace and five rings.

Nick left and Burt flopped back on the ground and immediately fell asleep.

"Now that your bodies have been purged," Elanora began, shooting a judgmental look in Gabe's direction, "it is time to cultivate the mind. You are each here because you have a special gift that you have selfishly ignored."

Burt rolled over in his sleep and gave an adorable little grumble.

Riley felt a surge of maternal *aww*.

Elanora spared the dog a glare, then continued. "We will now begin our meditation to prime our minds for the benevolence of our spirit guides."

Riley raised her hand. "Question."

Her grandmother's nostrils flared. Apparently questions weren't a welcome addition to psychic boot camp.

"Does everyone have the same spirit guides? Or do we all have different ones? And why don't they speak the same language as we do? Why can't they just say, '*Hey, your neighbor's husband is planning to murder her with a shovel*'?"

"Excellent question, sweetie," Blossom said, reaching over to squeeze her hand. Her mother's hair had exploded to three times its normal circumference in the humidity.

"No. It is not. It is a stupid question."

"Mom." Blossom sighed.

"You should already know these things. I don't know what Gabriel has been doing in your company for the past two months, but apparently it did not involve teaching you anything."

"Gabe has been a great friend," Riley said, jumping to the man's defense.

"It's true," Wander insisted. "He's been a wonderful addition to the family."

"Gabe is a delight to us all. He's so tall he barely needs a stepladder to get into the cabinet in the kitchen," Blossom added.

"Gabriel is not here to be a friend or a family member or a cabinet opener," Elanora said, briskly snapping open a black lace fan. "He is here to teach you to master your gifts, to be an example of a life of service. He is here to toughen you up and rid you of your laziness, not be corrupted by you."

Riley felt that the statement was directed mostly at her.

"Mom, I love you, but sometimes you're a real buzzkill," Blossom said.

"Buzzes are meant to be killed. Basil women are destined for a life of service. It seems as if you've all forgotten that." Elanora's steely gaze flicked to Riley. "Except for those of you who never bothered learning it in the first place."

Riley sighed. "Okay, Grandmother. We get it. We suck. We're lazy. We're squandering our gifts. Let's get this over with. What do you want us to do?" Movement in the parlor window caught her eye, and she spotted Mrs. Penny with a pair of binoculars trained on them.

Elanora hinged forward in her chair and fixed her with a cool stare. "I want you to recognize what a distinction it is to be born into this family, this legacy. I want you to honor your gifts through hard work and selfless service."

91

"And I wanted to have sex with my boyfriend and sleep in today, but we don't always get what we want," Riley pointed out, feeling surly.

"Let's meet in the middle and agree that we would all like to improve on our gifts," Wander the peacemaker suggested.

"All in favor say, 'Aye,'" Blossom said.

"Aye," everyone but Elanora said.

Riley's grandmother rolled her eyes. "This is *not* a democracy."

"Mussolini," Riley coughed into her hand.

Blossom elbowed her and hissed, "I'm the one who has to live with her. Can you please try not to piss her off? I'm already down to my last jug of dandelion wine."

"Sorry."

"We will begin our practice by stepping into our spiritual state and then exiting," Elanora announced. "We must master showing up as our best selves in order to do our best work."

"That is very wise," Gabe said.

"No one likes an ass-kisser, Gabriel," Elanora said.

Sheesh. Riley didn't know which one of them was more in the doghouse: her for disrespecting her family heritage or Gabe for discovering ice cream.

"You will all close your eyes now," her grandmother announced. "Approach your spiritual mental space with intention."

The only thing Riley wanted to approach with intention was a shower.

Then she thought about dog crap. They really needed to be better about picking it up. Especially if they were going to be boot camping in the middle of Burt's toilet.

"Return to the mortal realm," Elanora ordered.

Riley realized she'd never left it. *Oops.*

"Now, return. Treat it like opening a door and stepping into a room. With one breath, you are here, and in the next, you have moved on to a different plane."

Plane. Plain. Plain...potato chips. Mmm. Snacks. Nick

Santiago covered in Jelly Krimpets and Middleswarth Potato Chips. *Yummy.*

"Resist the baser urges of your squirrel-like mind, and step through the door," Elanora ordered.

Reluctantly, Riley set aside her snack fantasies. They'd sit here until the end of time if her grandmother caught whiff of the fact that she wasn't taking this seriously. She took a reluctant breath and willed the cotton candy clouds to appear.

"Now, exit your spiritual space, and return to the present."

The clouds that had just materialized disappeared like a balloon popping, and Riley wobbled in her seated position. She felt like she did in Wander's flow yoga classes, two steps and a half-dozen breaths behind everyone else.

"Go back again," Elanora insisted.

By the fifth forced exit from the land of pastel puffiness, Riley was dizzy and listing into her mother. When she'd once again made peace with the earth's gravitational forces, she raised her hand. "Can we take a break? I'm getting spiritual vertigo."

"Rest is for the weak," Elanora snapped.

"I'm okay with being weak if it means I get five minutes to remember gravity," Riley said, opening one eye.

Her grandmother was sipping a very large Bloody Mary that had appeared out of nowhere. "If you are incapable of performing the exercises like everyone else, then you are excused. Just don't complain to me when your powers take control of your life rather than the other way around. Mark my words, Riley Thorn. You *will* regret it."

The joke was on her grandmother—Riley *already* regretted it.

But she stayed put anyway. Her mean old-lady grandmother had the vaguest of points. There was no point in dabbling in being psychic. Either she learned to control her gifts or she let them control her.

Elanora met her gaze and gave a stiff nod. "Again."

———

Riley lost all sense of time as the summer sun and humidity battled it out to ruin the day for humans. Burt had long since retreated into the house, following the scents of bacon and coffee.

They'd graduated from spiritual touch-and-gos to intense focus exercises that involved clutching sharp crystals and sniffing incense that smelled like dried crap and moldy berries to heighten the clarity of their spiritual senses.

"It's odd. I keep getting the distinct whiff of death and roses," Wander said, sounding like she was underwater somewhere. She had a psychic snoot that could sniff out things like a dead aunt's favorite perfume or what a student had for dinner last night.

Riley wished she was the one with the sniff-a-voyant nose. Her sister would be a much better psychic than she was.

Somewhere in the middle of memorizing a very long Latin mantra, Riley felt herself slipping into the cotton candy world like a kid on a slide in a McDonald's playground.

She found herself blinking at the puffy colorful clouds. "Uh, did you guys need something?"

The clouds pulsed with light, and she heard faraway whispers layered over the drone of her grandmother's voice.

She squinted through the fluffy fog, hoping for a glimpse of Bianca Hornberger or Larry Rupley. Neither was there. Instead, Riley found another man. A stranger to her. He was chunky and Caucasian, the kind of pale that made her think of vitamin D deficiencies. His straggly hair was tied back in a ponytail. His shorts were stained, and his T-shirt and socks were holey. And dirty.

Riley caught a whiff of something musty and unpleasant.

There was a vibe there. Aggressive disdain, she decided. As if he'd never agreed with anything that had happened to him in his entire life.

Was he connected to the wealthy, plastic Bianca? Or did he have something to do with Larry's disappearance?

The clouds pulsed again, and she felt her vision self

levitating over the Susquehanna River. She tried to look down to make sure her body was still there, but instead she was drawn back to the grungy stranger.

"Okay. So Needs to Do Laundry Guy disappointed with life and the West Shore," she summarized. The clouds lit up as if she'd solved a *Wheel of Fortune* puzzle. "Great. So how is he related to Bianca? Or Larry?"

There was no immediate response.

"Look, guys, if he's not related, I need to focus on one puzzle at a time. Well, okay, two. I need to find out who killed Bianca Barbie, or it would be nice if you could tell me where Larry went."

A silver cord materialized, encircling the man's waist.

"Okay. Did the stranger have lap band surgery?"

The cord projected into the air. Riley followed it as it arched across the river and traveled above the city.

"Well, hell," she said.

The cord ended around a hovering Bianca Hornberger, who looked annoyed by the inconvenience.

"So the stranger and Bianca are somehow linked," Riley said.

Images flashed before her, speeding up as they went. Bianca in her closet, admiring herself in the mirror. Stiletto shoes that had never been worn. Large sneakers hitting the pavement in a slow rhythm, labored breath coming in short, heavy bursts. She saw Front Street and the Bogdanovich mansion. Then the imagery flickered again, and she was looking at Grumpy Guy suspended over the town of Enola on the other side of the river. The stranger didn't seem to find any levity in his levitation. He was flipping her the bird. The faces of Nick, Jasmine, Griffin Gentry, and Detective Weber flipped before her eyes like cards shuffling. Riley felt a rush of air, and the world around her exploded into sparkles.

She flinched as she felt the needlelike, sparkling shards embed themselves in her skin.

"That is *not* the kind of expression one should have when

performing a reading. That is the kind of face one makes when constipated," her grandmother's disembodied voice complained from somewhere outside the sparkly beyond.

"She only makes that face when it's an intense vision. See? Her nose is twitching," Blossom said from somewhere far away.

"Well, she looks ridiculous."

Riley felt herself falling, falling, falling. Just before she hit the ground, she felt a jolt as she was yanked back into her own body for a jarring landing.

When she came to, she found herself facedown in Gabe's lap.

"Sorry," she said, scrambling away from the man's crotch. She got to her feet, her joints feeling too loose to properly support her.

"Well? What did you see?" Elanora demanded.

"I have to find Detective Weber," she announced and then ran for the house.

12

R iley whipped her Jeep into a parking space directly in front of Little Amps, the hipster coffee haven on Green Street that she'd been avoiding. In all her years guzzling caffeine from this place, she'd never once snagged such a prime parking spot. Maybe it was a sign that she could officially return as a regular.

It wasn't until she'd unclipped her seat belt that she realized her spirit guides had nudged her here. She hadn't texted or called to ask Detective Weber where he was or if she could meet him. She'd simply "seen" him having coffee and got in the car.

"*You're really getting the hang of this psychic thing,*" Uncle Jimmy's voice from the beyond said in her head.

Her dad's brother had died a few years earlier. Riley had inherited his Jeep *and* his ghost.

"Thanks, Jimmy," she said. "Just don't tell Grandma that or she'll drag me out of bed even earlier."

She climbed out and stuffed the keys in her still soggy shorts. She probably should have changed. Showered. She sniffed an armpit and regretted it instantly.

Riley burst through the door woman-on-a-mission style and spotted Weber at a table in front of a window with an attractive older woman. He glanced up as she approached and was on his feet by the time she got to the table.

"What the hell happened to you?" he asked, giving her the once-over.

Riley looked down. She looked like she'd just wandered through a car wash.

"Grandma's boot camp," she said, waving away his concern. "I got something. Bianca Hornberger isn't your only victim."

Weber took her arm. "What makes you say that?"

"I've got a *where*. At least I think. But I don't have a *who* or a *how*, unless people can be killed by sparkling explosions."

"I'm gonna need you to start at the beginning."

"This looks like official business." Weber's coffee mate gave Riley a look usually reserved for barefoot people on sidewalks asking for change. "I should go."

She looked like the kind of woman who disapproved of a lot of things and demanded that her grocery store stock exotic organic produce. Her hair was cut in a sleek, stylish bob. She wore gray linen pants and an expensive-looking ivory tank.

"I'm sorry for interrupting. And for looking like this," Riley said, waving a hand over her sweaty torso.

"You two do know each other, don't you?" Weber asked, looking confused.

Riley and the woman eyed each other. "No," they said together.

But just as the word left her mouth, Riley was smacked in the face with a cotton candy vision of the woman, younger and softer, bouncing a drooling, dimpled baby on her lap. *"Who is mama's little flirt? Is Nicky mama's little flirt?"*

Well, hell.

"Mrs. Santiago?" Riley choked on the name.

"*Dr.* Santiago," the woman said, extending a hand for a perfunctory hand shake. Her grip was firm and her palm cool against Riley's shaky, sweaty one.

"Marie, you haven't met Riley yet?" Weber asked, looking like the cat that ate an entire branch of canaries.

Marie's eyes widened in horror. "Why would I have?"

Oh, boy.

"Riley is Nick's girlfriend. They live together. Didn't he tell you?" Weber asked smugly.

Marie's gaze flew back to Riley.

"This must be a joke."

"It's not," Riley said.

"I beg your pardon?"

"It's not a joke. Nick and I are...dating."

"I never implied I thought it was a joke," Marie insisted.

Great. Now she was reading the mind of her boyfriend's mother, who had no idea she existed. "Of course not. I'm sorry for presuming," Riley said. "It's so nice to meet you. I've heard a lot about you from Nick." That was a big fat lie. He'd mentioned his parents in vague terms, as in he acknowledged that he had some. She had a brief recollection of him saying something about them being on a cruise. But clearly, they'd gotten off the boat.

Marie picked up her very nice purse and slung it over her shoulder. "Well, it seems I'll be paying my son a visit. I assume he's working or at least pretending to today?"

Riley didn't know how to answer, so she just nodded.

"Do you have the address of his new office?" Weber asked with a smug grin.

Nick's mother pursed her lips. "Apparently not."

"I'll write it down for you," Riley offered. She patted her pockets and realized she had nothing but her car keys and phone on her.

"No need. It's the big three-story Victorian on Front Street," Weber volunteered. "Watch out for the roommates."

"Yes, well, it was good to see you again, Kellen." Marie turned to look at Riley again. "It was...interesting meeting you, Miley."

"Riley," she corrected.

"Yes. Well."

They watched Marie leave, shoulders back, sunglasses on. She strode out to a glossy BMW parked across the street.

"Nicky's in trouble," Weber sang under his breath.

"That was *not* how I planned to meet his parents," Riley groaned, flopping into the chair Marie had vacated.

"You're not going to ruin my fun and give him a heads-up, are you?" Weber asked.

She snorted. "Please. We've been living together and he still hasn't gotten around to mentioning it to his family? He gets what he gets."

"In that case, let me buy you a drink."

"Make it cold and sugary," she said.

Weber returned with a jar of cold brew flavored liberally with caramel and sweet cream. "So now that you've helped me ruin Nick's day, what had you running here straight from Boot Camp for Grannies?"

"It wasn't a boot camp *for* grannies. It was a boot camp my grandmother was running. Never mind. Forget about that part. And yes, I am aware how crazy this sounds. But you're just going to have to deal with it."

"Consider it dealt with."

"Good. I had this vision of Bianca alive in her closet, and then I was ripped out of the closet and flying across the river."

Weber watched her closely.

She took a gulp of coffee and swiped the back of her hand over her mouth.

"Then I see this guy kind of hovering above Enola. I think it was symbolic? Like psychic GPS. I don't think he was thrown from a plane. Anyway, here's where it gets weird."

"Oh, it hasn't gotten weird yet?" Weber teased.

"Need I remind you that it's your fault I'm here?"

"Apologies."

"You know, men who say that don't know how to apologize."

Riley grinned as Jasmine Patel—best friend, family/elder law attorney, and Indian American bombshell—pulled up a chair. "Hey! What are you doing here?"

Jasmine plunked down a black coffee. "I just finished an

appointment with a couple on Maclay Street. What the hell happened to you?"

"Oh, you know. My grandmother is in town and insisted on torturing me with a psychic boot camp, and then I came here to tell Detective Weber about a vision I had about a case he's working and ended up finding him having coffee with Nick's mom, who had no idea her son was dating anyone, let alone living with someone."

"So the usual then," Jasmine said. She turned to Weber and raised an eyebrow. "Why were you having coffee with Nick's mom?"

Riley frowned. "Yeah. Why?"

"Are you having an affair with Nick's mom, Detective Assface?"

"No, I'm not sleeping with Marie, and I really don't think I have an assface," Weber scoffed.

Jasmine pinned him with a look. "You have the face that I tell you you have."

Her best friend apparently hadn't quite forgiven the detective for labeling Riley a person of interest in the recent murder of her across-the-hall neighbor, Dickie. Jasmine's fierce loyalty was Riley's favorite character trait. That and her ability to hold copious amounts of alcohol.

"Are you trying to arrest my friend again?" Jasmine demanded. "Because if you are, I'll have your badge." She stabbed the table with a shiny red fingernail.

Weber leaned in. "Not as long as she stays on the right side of the law. And I'd like to see you try."

Riley snapped her fingers between their faces to end the glaring contest. "Guys. Can we focus on the exploding shiny dead guy?"

Jasmine wrinkled her nose. "Ew. What?"

Riley ran through her explanation quickly between slurps of cold brew. "Then he just exploded into sparkles. Oh, and he was wearing this Confederate flag shirt that said something like, Stomp My Flag, I'll Stomp Your Ass.

"Husky guy? Looks like he and the shower weren't on speaking terms?" Jasmine asked.

Riley frowned. "Yeah. Thinning hair on top but a ponytail down the back."

"Titus Strubinger. He died in his mom's basement two weeks ago."

"How in the hell do you know that?" Weber demanded.

Jasmine's thumbs moved efficiently over her phone screen. "Here."

Riley's eyes widened. "That's him!" It was an obituary in the *Patriot News* for Titus Strubinger, age forty-nine, from Enola, Pennsylvania.

Weber leaned in to take a look. "Died at home," he read. "How did you know about this?"

"Attorney-client privilege," Jasmine announced smugly.

"Strubinger was your client?" he pressed.

"No. But his mother is."

"What were you helping her with?"

"Get a warrant."

"How did he die?" he asked.

"Heart attack," she said. "His mom found him in the basement a few days after he'd kicked the bucket."

Two dead bodies linked by her spirit guides. It couldn't be a coincidence, Riley mused.

"I guess lawyers aren't completely useless," Weber quipped.

Riley pushed her chair back to avoid the line of fire.

"At least I knew my friend here wasn't a murderer, *idiot*," Jasmine spat out.

"You know what, *ma'am*? This is official police business," Weber said. "Maybe you should go back to trying to get old folks to name you in their wills."

"Don't you *ma'am* me. I am an elder law attorney, you smug son of a—"

"Is that an elderly mime?" Riley strained to look at the front window where a short roundish woman with a cane and a beret had been until she'd been lassoed by an invisible rope. There was something eerily familiar about her.

"Oh. Em. Gee. It's you!" The high-pitched squeal coming

from behind Riley brought their conversation to a screeching halt.

Riley didn't have time to duck the incoming body as it collided with hers. Within a second, a barista with pink hair and a nose stud had her in a headlock.

"Gah," Riley croaked, flailing her arms.

"You're Riley Thorn!" the girl squealed. "You saved my life."

"Oh shit," Jasmine muttered under her breath.

"Help. Me," Riley rasped.

"Okay, honey. Let's let Ms. Thorn breathe for a second," Jasmine suggested, unwinding the girl's arms from Riley's neck.

Every eye in the café was on them.

"Sorry! I was just so excited. I never thought I'd get the opportunity to say thank you," the girl said, fanning her face as her eyes filled with tears. "So thank you from the bottom of my heart. Not only did you find my cancer, I also met a really cute nurse, and we're totally dating now!"

"Uh, you're welcome?" Riley slumped lower in her chair.

Earlier in the summer, Riley had been cursed with a message from the barista's great-grandmother Ida about the girl's lymph nodes. Turned out Ida was onto something. After Riley reluctantly passed on the message, the barista was diagnosed with thyroid cancer, and the story of the mysterious woman with the message from beyond made the local news.

"This is the psychic who saved me, you guys," the girl announced, going in for another hug.

Spontaneous applause broke out around the café, and Riley felt her face turn ketchup red. The patrons started to crowd around their table.

"Just smile and wave," Jasmine advised without moving her lips.

"Let's get out of here," Weber said, picking up on the vibe of the crowd.

"Hey, psychic! What number am I thinking of?"

"Did you get my letter about my gerbil, Ms. Thorn?"

shouted a woman in a maxi dress. "I just need to know if he blames me for the cat eating him!"

"Yeah, I'm going to need you to let go of my friend's neck," Jasmine told the barista, who was sobbing into Riley's shoulder.

Together, Jasmine and Weber led her toward the door.

She felt like a celebrity on the verge of a nervous breakdown with a half-dozen cell phones recording her while coffee drinkers young and old hurled questions at her.

"Should I quit my job to start a lip balm business?"

"Who really killed JFK?"

She was definitely never coming back here.

Riley's Jeep was surrounded by people.

"Leave it," Weber advised. "You can come back for it when they're not so caffeinated and excitable. Step away from the psychic, people!"

13

Titus Strubinger's house was squished between two other homes of the same approximate size and shape. His was painted an avocado green and had metal awnings over every window. Apparently natural light had been considered a bad thing in 1970s architecture.

Weber raised his hand to knock, but Riley grabbed his arm. "Wait, what are we going to say? 'We're sorry, but we think your son was connected to a murder victim'?"

"I was thinking something more like, 'We have a few questions about your son.'"

"Oh. Okay. That's probably better," she agreed.

Nervously, she patted her hair. She'd done her best to scrape it back into some semblance of a ponytail in Weber's car. But she couldn't do anything about the rest of her rumpled, sweaty self.

Weber's knock sounded official and made her anxious.

It took almost a full minute before the front door creaked open, and they found themselves looking down. Way down. The woman peering at them through round tinted lenses didn't even clock in at five feet tall. She was wearing a velvet smoking jacket, distressed jeans, and white sneakers. Her gray hair was wrapped tightly in curlers.

"Mrs. Strubinger? I'm Detective Kellen Weber with the Harrisburg Police. I have a few questions regarding your son."

"Some detective. My son's dead," she announced gruffly.

"I'm aware of that," Weber said.

Mrs. Strubinger gave Riley a suspicious once-over. "She with you?"

Weber turned up the charm. "She's a civilian consultant."

"Looks like trouble." The woman leaned forward and sniffed. "Smells like it too."

"I had a busy morning," Riley said defensively.

"Might as well come in as long as you don't stay long. I need to get to bed."

"Thank you," Weber said.

They followed the woman inside. The house was small but tidy. The small living room was taken up almost completely by a drum kit.

"Was your son a musician?" Weber asked, eyeing the drums.

Mrs. Strubinger snorted. "That lump of misery wouldn't know a backbeat from a click track. I'm the drummer. The gig last night went late. I just got home."

Riley was impressed.

"Mrs. Strubinger," Weber began again.

"Call me Sticks."

"Okay. Sticks, we were wondering if your son knew this woman." Weber produced a picture of a—thankfully—alive Bianca Hornberger.

Sticks slid her glasses off the top of her head and squinted through them at the photo and then snorted. "If you think she looks like the kind of person my son would know, you must not be very good at your job."

"He gets that a lot," Riley quipped.

The detective shot her a har-har look.

"You'd take one look at his bedroom and know those two never had anything in common," Sticks boasted. "What's this about? Did Plastic Petula there say my son was an ass to her? Because she wouldn't be the first. Guess now she might be the last."

"Did your son have problems with many people?" Riley asked.

"Titus hated everyone," Sticks said, fishing a vape pen out of the pocket of her robe. "He was about to get fired from the Game Emporium. You know how much of an ass you have to be to get fired by those special-brownie-eating gamers?"

Riley guessed a really big one.

"Would you mind if we looked at his room?" Riley asked.

The woman shrugged. "What do I care? Help yourself. But know this: that misogynistic idiot lived like a pig in a sty, expecting me to clean up after him. He wasn't raised that way, but every nest has a bad egg, if you get what I'm sayin'."

She led the way into the kitchen with yellow linoleum floors and cabinets painted robin's-egg blue.

"Titus lived down there," Sticks said, gesturing at a battered door next to the refrigerator. "Haven't touched a thing since they carted his lard ass out on a gurney through the Bilco doors. I took no responsibility for his mess when he was alive. Don't much feel like dealing with it now that he keeled over from that heart attack."

Weber reached into the dingy stairwell and flicked on the light switch. A bare bulb cast a yellow glow down the narrow wooden steps.

"Ladies first?" he offered.

Riley shook her head. "Uh-uh."

Weber took the lead, and she followed, closing the door behind them. The stairs were rickety and stained from years of foot traffic.

"I don't know. This isn't looking good, Miss Cleo," he said.

"Do *not* let my grandmother hear you say that."

Riley was no longer the worst smelling thing in the house.

Titus's "room" smelled like a decade of stale farts. Her sister's psychic snoot would have a field day in it.

It was a standard basement with block walls, a concrete floor, low ceilings, and a whole lot of junk.

Come on, spirit guides. Mama needs a win.

"Well, I guess you got one thing right," Weber noted,

pulling a small flashlight out of his pocket. He trained it into the darkness.

Everything glittered.

Everything.

The floor, the walls, every moldy basement object sparkled like a certain Disney fairy had exploded.

"This place looks like a strip club that gives out staph infections," she said.

In the corner was a worn couch that sagged in the middle from excessive amounts of well-proportioned ass. It faced a large TV on a crappy faux wood console. The doors were open, revealing a tangled mess of wires, a few remotes, and loose batteries but nothing else of consequence.

Next to it was a rumpled twin bed. Posters of greased-up women in bikinis sitting on sports cars adorned the walls.

There was a phone charger plugged into an extension cord next to a twin mattress covered with rumpled, sparkly sheets. Small mountains of dirty laundry landscaped the concrete floor between similar mounds of trash. Riley counted fourteen shipping boxes in just one corner.

It all sparkled.

"This doesn't look like the room of a guy who likes to craft," she said, taking the gloves Weber handed her.

"What do your spirit guides think a moldy basement bombed with glitter has to do with our DB across the river?" the detective wondered.

Bombed with glitter.

The cotton candy clouds lit up like Times Square, and Riley thought she heard the sound of slot machines spitting out their bounty.

"Holy shit. I think I've got something," she said.

"What? A tetanus infection?" Weber asked.

She jogged to the stairs and took them two at a time, her legs screaming from that morning's aerobic torture. By the time she made it to the main floor, she was out of breath and barely able to stand.

She found Mrs. Strubinger in the kitchen pouring whiskey into a large mug of coffee and eating a piece of cold pizza.

"Sticks, did your son get glitter bombed?"

Sticks rolled her eyes heavenward. "It came in the mail, and the idiot opened it, thinking it was something he drunk ordered. I told him to clean it up. Every stupid sparkle. It looked like a craft store and a nudie bar exploded. But no, Titus just left it like that. He'd been leaving a trail of sparkly crap everywhere he went for two weeks like a middle-aged, cross-dressing Disney fairy with diabetes."

Weber joined them in the kitchen.

"Titus got a glitter bomb in the mail two weeks ago," Riley explained.

"A glitter bomb?" He frowned.

"There were a few flakes of glitter in Bianca Hornberger's closet." He shot her a look that said she was reaching. But she pointed at him. "Call Bianca's husband, and ask him if she got a similar package."

With a shrug, Weber excused himself.

"What's all this about?" Sticks asked over the rim of her mug.

"Is there a possibility that your son didn't die of a heart attack?" Riley asked.

The woman shrugged. "How the hell should I know? I'm no doctor. He had high blood pressure, high cholesterol, uncontrolled diabetes, and a bad fucking attitude. Between you and me, he hated anyone who wasn't a middle-aged white guy who felt wronged by the world."

"That's a lot of people to hate," Riley observed.

"Titus was an opinionated asshole. Someone always had it better or easier than him. Or someone was trying to take what was rightfully his. Got that from his father," she said. "I mean, who hates shortbread cookies and Tom Hanks?"

Monsters.

"Titus. That's who," Sticks barreled on. "If there was an opinion to be had on something, he had a loud, unpopular one. If he saw a news story about a color-blind kid seeing color for the first time, he'd bitch about society supporting the weak. When the neighbors put up a BLACK LIVES MATTER sign, he pissed on their grass and parked his pickup in front of their house with a Confederate flag flying from the tailgate before the whole thing got repossessed. If he thinks I'm paying for a funeral that no one's going to come to, he's a dumbass. He can rot at the morgue for all I care."

Titus Strubinger sounded like a real dick.

Weber reappeared in the doorway and waved her over.

"Well?" she asked.

"Our East Shore DB got a glitter bomb in the mail two weeks before her death. She opened it in the bedroom. Husband said it took the cleaning crew two days to get it all cleaned up. I've got a team headed over there now to bag and tag every speck of glitter they can find. Another one will be here soon to go through the crime scene."

"Looks like your civilian consultant really pulled through," Riley gloated.

"Yeah, yeah. You get a gold star. Guess what else?" he said.

"What?"

"Unless our pal Sticks went downstairs and collected them, our guy Titus is also missing some electronics. His phone and gaming consoles weren't down there."

"That doesn't smell like a coincidence to me," Riley prodded.

"Yeah, yeah. Good job," he said with a grin. "We need that body."

"Good news for you. Titus is still lying on a slab because Sticks didn't claim his body."

"Lucky for us."

"We don't have to, like, go pick him up ourselves, do we?" Riley asked.

"Yes, Cleo. We drive down to the morgue and just throw him in the back seat."

"I think you're being sarcastic right now, but I'm not totally sure. This is my first civilian consultant gig."

"We're not responsible for body transpo," he promised.

"Thank God."

Weber turned his attention to the drummer drinking whiskey out of a coffee mug. "Sticks, do you know if your son kept the package from that glitter bomb?"

14

Nick yanked back the shower curtain, startling a scream out of Riley.

She beaned him with a bottle of conditioner. "What the hell are you doing scaring the crap out of me like that?" she demanded, dunking her head under the water to wash the soap out of her eyes.

His annoyance temporarily took a back seat to appreciation of his girlfriend's wet, naked body.

"Stop staring at my boobs. You haven't earned the right to appreciate them."

"What the hell are *you* doing roaming all over the state, and why the fuck are you covered in glitter?"

"Dammit!" She groaned and scrubbed vigorously at her skin.

He reached in and shut off the water. "If you tell me you went undercover at some strip joint, I will—"

While he took a beat to think of a good threat, Riley stepped haughtily out of the tub. She snatched a towel off the hook and wrapped it under her armpits. She had flecks of glitter across her collarbones and on her chin. "What'll you do? Tell your *mother*?"

Oops. He'd forgotten that one was going to bite him in the ass. His mother had strolled into his office, lip curled in disdain as she had to climb around junk just to get close enough to passive-aggressively tell him she was so "happy" he was finally settling down with a "complete stranger." Then she'd insinuated that he must have been too busy being a terrible son to remember to tell his parents anything about his life.

Nick had pointed out that if she cared enough to ask him where he was living and with who, he would have been happy to tell her.

She'd said, "With whom," and clicked out of the house on judgmental stilettos.

"Okay. I know it looks bad, but I can explain," he insisted.

Riley grabbed a second towel and wrapped her hair up in it.

He admired the efficiency of it and wondered how women managed to get out of the tub with that much water in their hair and still not leave behind the tsunami men did on the floor.

"Fine. I fucked up. I didn't tell my parents about you. I'm *sorry*," he said a bit more aggressively than he'd intended.

She marched around him to the vanity. "Well, I suppose it's better than, 'Apologies.'"

Nick's eyes narrowed. "Wait. Why aren't you mad?"

Her eyes met his in the mirror. "How do you know I'm not mad?"

"My balls are still attached, and this is a ball-dismembering offense."

Her lips quirked. "I wouldn't have told my parents if I were you either."

"Why the hell not?"

"Wait. Are *you* mad at *me* for not being mad at you?"

"Maybe. I don't know." Relationships were confusing.

Riley spun around and slapped a hand to his face, squeezing his cheeks together. "You're sooo cute when you're confused and pissed off."

"Thorn," he said in the most threatening tone he could muster with duck lips.

"Santiago."

"Why aren't you mad?"

"Oh, come on. What were you supposed to do? Call them up and say, 'Hi, Mom and Dad. I'm seeing someone. She's a psychic, and she talks to dead people. She got me shot last month in the fountain, and she lives with a bunch of old weirdos who fart all the time and can't remember the Wi-Fi password. What's new with you?'"

For once in his life, Nick Santiago found himself speechless.

"I don't blame you. But if I *were* you, I'd be tearing open the shower curtain of your detective pal, since he's the one who told her who I was."

He shook his head to dislodge the image of Weber in the shower. The man probably used a loofah. "Hang on. I can only deal with one issue at a time. I'll murder Weber later. Are you saying you're not mad at me for not telling my parents that I'm living with you because you're psychic?"

"Your mom doesn't look like the type to believe in psychics," she said as if that answered everything.

"My mom doesn't believe in a lot of things, including tipping housekeeping staff in hotels. What does that have to do with me telling her about you?"

Riley reached for her moisturizer.

"Please. No one wants to tell their parents they're dating a psychic who was plastered all over the news for getting their son shot."

He was not liking this whole psychic-second-class-citizen attitude from her.

"You are going to regret this big time," he warned, fishing his phone out of his back pocket.

"What are you doing?"

"Calling my mother."

She stopped rubbing lotion onto her shapely legs. "Why?"

"Yeah. Hi, Mom," Nick said when his mother's voicemail

picked up. "I've changed my mind. Riley and I will be over for dinner tomorrow night. I can't wait for everyone to meet her." He disconnected and crossed his arms. "Happy now?"

"No! Why would you do that? Your mom already thinks I'm a disheveled, sweaty mess. And *then* I accidentally read her mind, which she did not like at all."

He advanced on her until she was pinned up against the vanity. "I didn't tell them about you for two reasons. One, they were on a month-long cruise when we met and got shot. And two, my family is a bunch of weirdos."

Riley placed a hand on his chest. "We just had a silent fast at my parents' house last night, and this morning my grandmother poked me with a walking stick until I fell on the ground. There's no way your family could possibly be weirder."

"Baby, tomorrow night, you'll see how that's possible." He dipped his fingers into the space between her breasts. "Now, tell me why you were roaming all over the East and West Shores and where the hell you left your Jeep."

"I was with Weber," she said.

"Yeah. I got that much from my mother."

"Get ready to raise the weirdo bar then," she grumbled. "I had a vision during my grandmother's Psychic Hunger Games this morning. I made the connection to another possible victim."

She filled him in while she brushed her wet hair and pouted over the flecks of glitter sparkling on her skin.

"That's impressive, Thorn." He reached into her cleavage and released the towel to the floor.

"Uh, thanks?"

"So where's your Jeep?" His hands skimmed over her naked hips, and her eyelids went heavy.

"Oh. I kind of left it in the middle of a human stampede on Green Street."

He chuckled and enjoyed the feel of goose bumps as they cropped up on her skin where he touched her. "Of course you did."

"Help me get it later?" she asked, wetting her lips.

"Anything for you, Thorn." He kissed her and breathed in her sigh of surrender like it was oxygen. His hands had just begun their journey higher when a loud screech interrupted them.

"Santiago, the po-po is here to see you." Mrs. Penny's artificially amplified voice rattled the door.

He dropped his forehead to Riley's. "Who gave that woman a bullhorn?"

"She bought it on eBay to protest whales."

On a sigh, Nick rewrapped Riley and stomped into the hall. He looked down the stairwell to the first floor and spotted Mrs. Penny standing at the foot of the stairs.

"Thanks for the message," he yelled dryly.

"You're welcome," she announced through the bullhorn.

Riley appeared next to him in a bathrobe. "Is she dressed like a mime?"

Mrs. Penny was indeed dressed as a mime with a black-and-white-striped shirt, a beret, and white face paint. Nick sighed. He was going to have to go over the definition of *invisible* again.

Weber stepped into view. He held out his hand to the elderly mime. Mrs. Penny reluctantly handed over the bullhorn.

"Don't get bacon grease on it," she said.

"Get some clothes on, Thorn. We've got work to do," Weber said into the bullhorn.

"We need to move out of this circus," Riley muttered under her breath.

"You didn't have to tag along," Weber complained as Nick opened the back door of the cruiser for Riley.

"Oh, but I did since you're poaching yet another employee of mine," he insisted. As soon as his old buddy was behind the wheel, Nick slugged him in the arm.

"Ow! Dick. What was that for?"

"That's for introducing my mother to my girlfriend." Nick punched him again in the same spot. "And that's for making me take Riley to dinner at my parents' tomorrow night."

"That's what adults in relationships do, jackass. They introduce their attractive psychic girlfriends to their parents." Weber threw an elbow that caught Nick in the chest, which was sore from last night's impromptu workout with Gabe.

Riley leaned onto the divider between the front and back seats. "Excuse me. If you two are going to wrestle the whole way there, I think Nick should ride back here."

Nick threw one last jab to Weber's ribs as he pulled out onto Front Street.

Without looking, his ex-partner shoved Nick's face against the window.

"Gentlemen!"

"Sorry," they said in unison.

"Why are you having coffee with my mother anyway?" Nick asked.

Weber shrugged. "We get together from time to time."

"If you tell me you're having an affair with her, I'm going to shave your eyebrows and half of your head."

Weber grinned smugly. "Your mom thinks of me as the son she never had. I'm the good one," he assured Riley in the rearview mirror.

"Mmm. I can tell," she said.

Nick rolled his eyes and directed Weber across the river to Brian's street in Camp Hill.

"Brian and Josie live here?" Riley asked with a legitimate amount of skepticism.

It was a little brick bungalow on a quiet street two blocks back from the main drag. There were flower boxes on the railing of the wheelchair ramp.

Nick liked to think that the house was like his cousin. Respectable and good-looking on the outside, but inside, it was a den of debauchery.

Between Brian's tech toys, Josie's collection of antique

weaponry, and the room with the sex swing, the freak flags flew proudly behind closed doors.

"They like to keep a low profile," he explained, opening the door for Riley.

Weber popped the trunk and produced two cardboard boxes labeled *Evidence* and followed them.

Nick rapped his knuckles preemptively on the front door before keying in the code and opening the door. "Get your pants on, kids. The boss is here," he called.

A steel-toed boot flew down the hallway and landed with a meaty thump on the hardwood floor.

Riley flinched, but Nick pulled her inside and enjoyed the sensory overwhelm that a first-time visitor experienced in Josie and Brian's living room. The house was much like the couple. They didn't exactly make sense together, but man, was it entertaining.

One wall was dominated by a huge flat-screen surrounded by four smaller screens. A long, low cabinet beneath Screen-o-Rama housed every kind of entertainment equipment known to man, including the latest and greatest gaming systems and a state-of-the-art karaoke system with Auto-Tune. The whole room was wired with speakers that shook the entire house during televised mixed martial arts fights.

The opposite wall displayed Josie's collection of katanas and throwing knives. Nick had been present the time Josie's cousin Ling got hammered and threw a knife at her soon-to-be ex-boyfriend for grabbing the ass of their other cousin Cleo. Ling had missed. So Josie made her come back every day for two weeks to improve her aim.

"Someone better be dead." Josie stomped into the room and glared at them. Her black hair was pulled up in a high ponytail. She was wearing a short slinky robe over what appeared to be nothing else.

"We can come back later," Riley said, looking everywhere but at the studded leather collar that accented Josie's neck tattoos.

"No. We can't," Weber insisted. "Sorry for the interruption, but we've got official police business."

Nick's cousin Brian appeared, wheeling into the living room with a goofy smile on his face. He was shirtless but wearing pants. His blond hair was standing up on end in tufts, and his glasses were askew. "We're kind of in the middle of... stuff, man."

"Yeah. You're interrupting my ovulation," Josie said, blowing Brian a kiss that seemed both affectionate and threatening.

"You're gonna have a lot of babyproofing to do in here," Nick mused, admiring Josie's newest throwing spear.

"Not if you guys don't let us get back to business," Brian complained.

"Believe me, I have nothing but empathy for your interrupted sex," Nick assured his cousin. "But this douchebag who's secretly dating my mom has a proposition for you."

Brian peered in the detective's direction. "Man, I was in the middle of a much better proposition."

"You can get back to that as soon as you hear me out," Weber promised. "I need your help with a case."

"It'll cost you," said Josie, always a mercenary. She drummed black fingernails against her biceps. "We're making babies here. Babies are expensive."

"I'm authorized to hire you as a civilian consultant. Our digital forensics unit is backlogged by three months. We can't wait that long. We need to figure out how two deaths are connected."

"Both homicides?" Brian asked.

Weber nodded. "One death was officially ruled a homicide. The other is now under investigation. Body was picked up from the morgue. We need a link besides the fact that your cousin's psychic girlfriend says the deaths are related."

"Don't forget the glitter bombs," Riley added, looking up from Josie's brass knuckles display. "Both victims received glitter bombs in the mail within two weeks of their deaths."

Brian adjusted his glasses and grinned at Riley. "Let me

guess. Your nose twitched, and now you need something tangible."

"Something that won't get laughed out of court," she told him.

Nick squeezed her hand.

"Let's talk downstairs," Brian suggested.

"You have thirty minutes," Josie warned. "After that, I don't care if we have an audience."

Brian grinned at his wife. "You got it, babe."

They followed Brian to the back of the house, where he opened a door to reveal the cleverly disguised elevator.

The basement of the bungalow was a Tony Stark–style lair that had even Weber salivating. There was a workstation with six monitors in one corner, a movie screen and projector, a bar, two arcade games, and a sauna off the bathroom.

Nick had serious lair envy.

"Show me what you've got," Brian said, wheeling over to the workstation.

Weber followed and unloaded the contents of the boxes on the long low countertop. "Personal electronics were stolen from both scenes," he explained. "No phones, tablets, laptops. Victim two was a part-time assistant manager over at the Game Emporium, and when I stopped by to ask the staff some questions, they said our victim hung out in the back office on the store laptop." He handed over a laptop covered in gaming stickers.

"So you want me to work my magic to figure out what Dead Guy was doing online all day?" Brian clarified.

Weber slid two case folders across the counter. "Bonus points if you can connect dead body number one to dead body number two."

Brian opened both folders. "Sounds fun. I'm in. For my usual fee, of course."

"Usual fee?" Nick demanded.

His cousin shrugged. "I've done a little freelancing for the boys in blue over the years."

Nick's eyes narrowed. "My mom. My cousin. Was my whole family seeing you behind my back?" he complained.

Weber held up his hands. "Hey, man. I only go to your dad's poker games once a month. And I haven't seen your sister since last week when I took Esmeralda for mani-pedis. I can't help it if your entire family likes me better."

Nick glanced down at Weber's hands just to make sure he was kidding about the manicure thing, then flipped him off.

Riley looked at him in surprise. "You really do have a niece named Esmeralda?"

"I wouldn't lie about that, Thorn," he said with a wink.

"I don't want to rain on anyone's baby-making parade, but this is a top priority," Mr. All Business cut in.

Nick decided he needed to limit Riley's time with Weber before the guy turned her back into a workaholic with an allergy to fun.

"I heard that," Josie called menacingly from upstairs.

Weber flinched. "We'll see ourselves out. Do you have a back door down here? One that doesn't funnel us past your angry wife?"

Brian pointed them toward a door.

Nick squeezed Riley's hand. "I'll meet you at the car. I need a sec with Brian."

She nodded, waved to his cousin, and left.

"How's the ramp construction coming?" Brian asked. "Can't wait to see the new digs."

"The new *temporary* digs," Nick corrected. "The ramp is in its ninth rebuild. I'm giving them one more chance, and then I'm hiring it out. And trust me, you can wait."

His cousin grinned. "As you can see, Josie and I have no problem working from home."

"Yeah, I got that."

"So. Got a problem with me freelancing, coz?" Brian asked, looking like he didn't particularly care. Nick got no respect.

"No. But I do like the idea of you being involved so you can help keep eyes on Riley."

"You worried?"

Nick shrugged. "I don't like her being wrapped up in another case after the way the last one went down."

Brian nodded. "Can't say I blame you. How *is* the extra hole in your ass these days?"

Nick's surgical scar had healed into the shape of a perfect heart.

"It's fine. Everything's fine." At least that was what he kept telling himself, hoping that sooner or later, the panic he felt every time he didn't know exactly where Riley was would fade. "But I don't want her anywhere near trouble again. So if you see Weber or Riley or anyone putting her in a situation that could go south, I wanna know about it."

"You got it, coz."

Nick nodded. "Good. Now, go impregnate your wife before she stabs someone."

15

Does this show too much boob?"

Nick whipped around so fast Riley worried he'd given himself whiplash. But then whiplash would mean a trip to urgent care and missing Santiago family dinner. *Gee. Darn.*

There was a beat of silence as his gaze traveled from her heeled sandals to her smoky eyes—thank you, Ulta eye shadow palette. Then he carefully put his beer down on the coffee table, turned off the TV, and headed toward her.

She took a step back and then another one. Before she knew it, her back was against the door, and Nick was pinning her there with his hard body.

He'd showered, but he was wearing jeans and a T-shirt. Her green sundress with the definitely too low neckline was obviously overkill.

"See, that tells me it's too much boob," she complained.

His hand came up to cup her breast. "You say that like it's a bad thing."

"I'm trying to make a good impression with your parents, not entice their son to maul me in the middle of dinner."

"Thorn, baby, I'm the only one in that room whose opinion matters, and I like the dress."

"Your opinion is *not* the only one that matters," Riley scoffed. "I made a terrible impression on your mother."

He brought his other hand to her other breast and squeezed, sending delicious shocks spiraling through her system. "Nowhere to go but up."

"You're saying that because they have to love you. It's in their DNA."

"Why does it matter if they like you or not?" he asked, his thumbs doing wicked things to her nipples through her bra.

"That's a ridiculous question. They're your family. Of course it matters if they like me."

"I'm not following."

"That's because your hands are on my boobs, and you lose the power of thought," she said, pushing his hands away.

"What were we talking about?"

"Nick!"

He grinned, and she was temporarily blinded by dimples.

"Look, all I'm saying is you're my girlfriend. You're coming home with me and getting into my bed tonight. Their opinion has no effect on that."

"You don't mind dating a girl who your parents could hate?" Riley clarified. It was a sentiment that went against her good girl nature.

His lecherous expression made her knees go weak. "Thorn, my family's disapproval would make you even hotter in my eyes."

"That is so seventeen-year-old girl of you," she complained.

He lowered his head, and she shivered as his mouth skimmed over her throat.

"If you give me a hickey before dinner with your parents, I will be very unhappy with you."

His teeth grazed her skin, and she poked him in the belly. Or, rather, the rock-hard abs.

"Have you been working out?" she breathed.

"A guy's gotta make an effort," he said. His tongue darted out to drag over her bare shoulder.

"So you don't care if your parents like me or not," she pressed.

"Not in the slightest. Now if they're rude to you, *then* I've got a problem. Words will be had. Dishes thrown. But no matter what, tonight ends the same way it was always going to end."

"How's that?"

"With me inside you."

"Gah." Her knees gave up the fight against gravity, and she slid several inches down the door before he caught her.

"Now let's get this over with so we can come back here and I can find out exactly what you've got on underneath that dress."

She was wearing sensible, no-line briefs.

"Will you excuse me for a minute? I need to change... something."

———

The Santiago residence was a large contemporary home perched on the hill in the Floribunda Heights neighborhood, or, as Riley called it, Where the Rich People Live. Thanks to tall hedges and immaculate landscaping, it was almost impossible to see the house from the street. All Riley saw were glimpses of dark gray wood and glass.

"Wow," she said when Nick parked at the front door. "Did you grow up here?"

"Nah. My parents bought this after my sister and I graduated and moved out. Bought all new furniture too, since we weren't around to ruin nice stuff anymore. They were counting down the days."

"That's...nice?"

"I'm telling you, my parents' seal of approval is nothing to strive for," he insisted.

"Do you guys not get along?"

He shook his head. "Nothing like that. We just don't get each other. They want me to be someone they understand, and I don't care. Makes family get-togethers fun."

They got out of his SUV, and Riley yelped when he gave the top of her dress a little tug to expose more cleavage.

She slapped his hands away.

"Come on, Thorn. Give me something to enjoy during the thinly veiled parental disappointment portion of the evening."

"You are such an ass—"

The front door opened, and Riley, still trying to contain her breasts, was met with two questioning gazes. Marie Santiago looked much the same as the last time Riley had seen her. Vaguely disgusted. The man standing next to her was definitely Nick's dad. His skin was darker. His silver hair was slicked back, and he had a great mustache. But he had the Santiago dimples and testosterone geysering out of his pores like a nice cologne.

"Your girl got a bee down her dress or something, Nicky?" he asked.

"Hi, Dad. Mom," Nick said, taking Riley's hand and dragging her inside.

After making sure she wasn't flashing nipple, Riley allowed herself to check out her surroundings. The interior of the house was just as confusing and modern as the exterior.

"Aren't you going to introduce us?" Nick's mother asked.

"You've already met while on a date with my ex-partner. But okay, if we're making it official. Riley Thorn, this is my mother, Marie, and my father, Miguel."

Marie scoffed. "I wasn't on a date with Kellen," she insisted, gesturing with her wineglass.

"What's her name?" Miguel demanded loudly.

"Riley," Nick shouted. He turned back to her. "He's hard of hearing and stubborn as hell. He won't get hearing aids, so if you want to have him do anything besides smile and nod, you have to scream."

"Is this why you're so comfortable with my roommates?" Riley whispered.

He tugged her into his side and gave her waist a squeeze. Marie choked on her wine.

"Are you a fan of modern architecture, Charlie?" Miguel asked a few decibels louder than necessary.

"Riley, Dad. Not Charlie," Nick yelled.

"Huh?"

"It's okay. I can be Charlie," Riley insisted.

"No, you can't."

After another minute of exchanged shouts and some spelling, Miguel got the message.

"So what do you think of the house, Riley?" he barked.

"It's very…dark," she observed.

"Too much sunlight is damaging to the skin," Marie sniffed, and she studied Riley's pores for evidence of a subpar skin care regimen.

"All this shouting is giving me a headache."

They all turned to look at the woman who appeared in the foyer. She wore a pantsuit and had her light hair scraped back in a tight no-nonsense bun. She had frown lines from what looked like years of life's constant disappointments. Judging by how thin and pointy she was, Riley guessed maybe she was just constantly hungry.

"Your brother was just introducing us to his…friend," Marie said to the hungry woman.

"My *girlfriend*," Nick corrected. "We live together."

Nick's sister sent a fine mist of red wine into the air. "You? A girlfriend? Ha!"

"Honestly, Carmela," their mother said.

"This is why we can't have nice things," Miguel muttered, producing a handkerchief from his back pocket and bending down to clean up the wine spit. "I told you we shoulda moved to Florida, Marie."

Riley rolled her lips together and tried not to laugh. Maybe Nick hadn't been exaggerating when he said his family was weird.

"Riley, this is my sister, Carmela. Carm, my girlfriend, Riley."

Carmela's frown lines deepened. "You look familiar," she said accusingly.

"I'm sorry?" It sounded to Riley like Carmela was expecting an apology for that.

"Riley's been in the news this summer," Nick said.

Really not wanting that particular topic to come up, she stepped on his foot.

He grunted but got the message. "Ow, okay. So who's playing bartender?"

"Carmela, get your brother and his friend a drink," Marie ordered.

"Girlfriend," Nick cut in.

"Tell him to get his own damn drink," Carmela snapped back. "Or is your favorite kid too good to pour himself a glass of wine?"

"Shoulda moved to Florida," Miguel muttered to the floor.

Somewhere, a bell chimed.

Miguel straightened from his obsessive floor polishing. "That'll be the pork tenderloin." He bustled off in the direction of the chiming.

Marie sighed. "The man can't hear a word we say, but an oven timer goes off, and he's suddenly got Superman ears."

"Let's get this over with," Nick said cheerfully, steering Riley by the shoulders.

Instead of the kitchen, where the majority of the Thorn family socializing happened, Nick led her into a formal dining room with a large window overlooking the river and Harrisburg's skyline.

She was so wowed by the view, she didn't notice the other occupants of the room until it was too late.

"Riley?"

Shit. In the past two months, she'd learned it was a very bad thing when strangers already knew her name when she walked into a room.

She turned away from the glass and felt her jaw open so far she worried it might hit the very expensive rug under her feet. "Andy?"

Andy Pendleton—tall, cute fellow Shippensburg alumnus,

and fondly remembered college ex-boyfriend—stood next to the table with a beer in his hand. He had glasses now and looked as if he used actual grooming products in his curly hair. But he still had the same charming grin.

"You look… Wow. It's been a while," he said.

"You two know each other?" Nick asked. His brow was furrowed as he mentally marched toward the inevitable conclusion.

"We dated," Andy announced.

"In college," Riley added.

"You dated my brother-in-law?" Nick looked as if he couldn't decide whether to swallow his tongue or punch the guy in his parents' dining room.

"The good old days," Andy said with a nostalgic grin, completely oblivious to Nick's discomfort. "Remember homecoming?"

Riley felt the color flooding her cheeks. "All except the streaking. That's still buried in a tequila haze."

"You two slept together?" Nick croaked.

She patted him on the back. She'd gotten used to running into women who had shared his bed at some point since he lost his virginity at sixteen. Even her mother's second cousin had apparently taught him a thing or two when he was eighteen.

People had pasts. Nick just had a more active past than most.

Now that the tables were turned, it was actually kind of funny.

"Here." Carmela appeared and thrust wineglasses at Riley and Nick without enthusiasm.

Nick chugged his down, took the glass from Riley, drank hers as well, then handed both glasses back to his sister. "More."

"Get it yourself, lush."

"I'm not leaving these two alone in a room together."

"They're not alone. I'm here, and so is Esmeralda."

For the first time, Riley noticed the young girl sitting at the table and quietly reading a book that looked like it was half her size. She had the thick dark Santiago hair, Carmela's frown, and Andy's chin and freckles. The girl looked up from her tome and eyed the adults. "Can you keep it down? I'm almost finished with this chapter."

"She's very advanced for her age," Carmela insisted with a defensiveness that made Riley wonder if someone in the room had suggested otherwise.

"I can see that," Riley said agreeably. "What are you reading?"

"A collection of works by Patrick Henry."

"Our girl is really into history," Andy said proudly, ruffling his daughter's hair.

"Takes after her dad," Riley said, remembering Andy's constant barrage of historical trivia in college.

"How many times?" Nick asked.

"How many times what?" Andy asked.

"How many times did you sleep with my girlfriend?"

Carmela blinked. "You slept with Nicky's girlfriend?"

"We dated. In college," Riley cut in hastily.

Esmeralda had gone back to reading.

Carmela looked at the wineglasses. "I'm getting another bottle."

"You really do look great, Rye," Andy said, giving her a fond once-over.

Nick reached over and hiked up the neckline of her dress.

"Nick," Riley hissed.

"Oh good. You remember my name."

"Excuse us for a minute," she said, dragging him into the hall. She chose a door at random, found an empty powder room, and pushed him inside. "What is *wrong* with you? *I'm* supposed to be the embarrassment tonight. Not you."

He looked green and twitchy.

"You and my brother-in-law. Naked. More than once."

"It was a long time ago. Neither one of us was a virgin when we met," she reminded him.

He paused midpace and swiped both hands down his face.

"Oh my God. There are others?" Whirling around, he turned on the faucet in the sink and shoved his face under it.

"Take a breath before you pass out," she suggested, dragging him out from under the spray and handing him a towel.

"What is this feeling?" he demanded, tugging at his shirt like it was too tight. "It's horrible. I feel nauseous and sweaty, and I just want to punch Andy in his fucking face. No one besides my sister wants to punch that guy in the face. He's too agreeable. What's happening to me?"

She chewed on her lip for a second. "Maybe you're jealous?"

"Maybe *you're* jealous," he shot back. "Sorry. Reflex. This isn't your fault. Of course you have a past. I just never thought about how it would feel to meet your past."

She took his face in her hands and held him still. "Look at me."

"I can't. I'm looking at your boobs, which look amazing in that dress, and now there's another guy remembering your boobs in my parents' dining room." He tried to rearrange her dress again, and when that didn't work, he tried pushing her breasts deeper into the garment.

She took a step back and slapped his hands away. "You met Griffin and didn't have this kind of reaction."

"Griffin Gentry is a short whiny asshole who screwed you over. You'd never go back to that prepubescent turd, and he's too stupid to know how badly he fucked up." He was referring to her spray-tanned news anchor ex-husband and the lawsuit he'd filed and won against her after she broke his nose with their wedding picture when she caught him in their bed with a twentysomething weather girl named Bella Goodshine.

Not only had Nick punched Griffin in the face on camera, he'd also managed to get him to drop the settlement so she no longer had to write her cheating ex a check every month. Nick had been tight-lipped on the how, and Riley decided it was better if she didn't know all the details.

"Thorn, baby, is this how you feel when we run into someone I…"

131

"Slept with?" she suggested.

"Oh my God. I made you go get coffee with me and Jonesy. Thorn, you should have told me this is physical torture. I had no idea. I would never—"

She held up her hands. "Maybe you had no idea because you don't still have feelings for the legion of women you went to bed with."

"Of course I don't have feelings for them!"

"And I don't have feelings for Andy."

He took a breath and let it out. "Okay. That's good. I can work with that. Maybe I don't need to murder him with a salad fork and throw his body in the Susquehanna."

"That's probably a good thing, because I think your sister can take you."

"She's terrifying," he agreed. "You're sure you don't have feelings for him?" Nick asked, sliding his hands up and down her waist.

"Feelings? No. Fond memories? Yes."

He closed his eyes and growled. "Great. Now I want to kill him again."

She grinned, looping her arms around his neck. "This is sweet. I like that you care."

"I'm glad you find my emotional scarring so entertaining," he grumbled, nuzzling into her neck.

"It's nice to be on the other side of this for a change," she teased.

"This is the last time. We're moving to Canada."

"You've never slept with a Canadian before?"

"My mom's Canadian. I didn't want to take any chances getting it on with a second cousin or something."

"Full disclosure—I dated my neighbor's nephew from Nova Scotia for a summer when he was visiting."

"Canada is out. How about Costa Rica?"

"Costa Rica works."

He cupped her face in his hands. "Just remember who you're here with," he said gruffly.

"Who could ever forget Nick Santiago?" Riley teased, brushing her mouth over his. In true Nick form, he took the kiss to a very dirty place. She was clinging to the vanity for support while his hand worked its way up the skirt of her dress when there was a knock at the door.

"Stop hogging the bathroom. Esmeralda has to wash her hands before dinner," Carmela announced.

"There's nine goddamn sinks in this house," Nick yelled back.

"And she wants to use this one, so get the hell out!"

"Why must my children revert to adolescent behavior when they come to dinner?" Marie lamented loudly from the hallway.

"This is what happens when you have a favorite kid," Carmela said snidely.

"I don't have a favorite. Right now, I don't like either one of you. Andy is my new favorite."

They exited the bathroom and found most of the family in the hall.

Carmela wrinkled her nose. "Oh God. You're not one of those couples that pees together, are you? That's disgusting."

"Bite me, Carm," Nick said, slinging his arm around Riley's shoulders. "Where's the wine?"

16

Dinner was the usual Santiago shit show of bickering, shouting so his father could hear them, and excellent food.

Nick would have enjoyed the familiarity of it, except for the fact that he couldn't stop glaring at his brother-in-law, who couldn't stop smiling at his girlfriend like he knew her and liked her.

Over pork tenderloin and soy-glazed carrots, Andy wrapped up another stupid reminiscence of his time with Riley at Shippensburg University.

"Hilarious that you had sex with my girlfriend," Nick muttered under his breath, gripping his steak knife until his knuckles went white.

Riley elbowed him in the ribs. "Will you please *relax*?" she hissed.

"So, Riley, is it?" Marie cut in. "What is it you do for a living?"

His girlfriend removed her elbow from his torso. "I just started working for Nick a few weeks ago."

"Sleeping with the employees? Really, Nicky?" Carmela sniped.

His sister was a miserable pain in the ass, which normally didn't bother him. But tonight, everything bothered him.

"Speaking of sleeping together—" he began. This time, Riley kicked him in the ankle. He grunted.

"I worked as a proofreader for a few years," she continued. "Before that, I used to work for Channel 50 in the newsroom."

"That Griffin Gentry is a very handsome fellow," Marie said to no one in particular.

"No, he's not," Nick said.

"He is," his mom insisted. "He's so tan and tall, and he has such a deep voice."

Riley hid her laugh behind a cough.

"I assume, given how we met, you also do something for the Harrisburg police," Marie said. "Were you undercover as a sweaty homeless person?"

"Mom," Nick said, pointing his knife at her. "Be nice."

"What?" His mother was all innocence. "I was merely making an educated guess."

"I'm doing some freelance work for Detective Weber," Riley answered, reaching for the wine.

"What could the police need with an unemployed proofreader?" Marie wondered.

"Help me," Riley whispered to Nick over the rim of her wineglass.

"So, Es, make any teachers cry lately?" he asked, changing the subject.

"Only one this week," Esmeralda said, picking up her glass of juice with both hands.

"Es skipped fifth and sixth grade," Nick explained. "She's a teacher's worst nightmare."

"In that she's so much *smarter* than all the other students *and* most of the teachers," Carmela added, lest anyone confuse being smart with being a behavioral problem.

"So how did you two meet?" Andy asked as he shoveled a fork full of meat into his stupid face.

"Nick knocked on my door selling Nature Girl candy."

Esmeralda gave him an owlish look.

He held up his hands. "Easy, slugger. I wasn't really selling candy," he promised his niece. "I was trying to track down Riley's neighbor to serve him papers."

"My son lies for a living," Marie lamented. "Where did we go wrong?"

"By making him your favorite," Carmela shot back.

Nick tossed a hunk of parsley at his sister.

"Don't throw the garnish! You know how expensive parsley is these days?" Miguel shouted. His favorite hobby was complaining about how expensive things were compared to the 1960s. "In my day, grocery stores gave parsley away for free! Now I gotta shell out four bucks for a clump of organic. It's a travesty!"

"You wish I was still a cop like Weber?" Nick asked his mother loud enough that his father heard him.

"A cop is respectable. What you do? Mr. Spy?" Miguel wiggled his hand in the air. "Not so much."

"Nick's a private investigator. He's very respectable," Riley said, coming to his defense.

"Don't bother, Thorn," Nick said.

"Maybe to *you*," Marie said pointedly. "But in this family, we strive to serve our communities."

"Yeah. Mom here serves the community as an executive in a drug company that got sued for the opioid crisis," Nick said.

She waved the insult away. "The good we've done far outweighs the bad," she insisted.

"I run restaurants. I feed hungry people. You wanna tell me I'm not serving my community?" Miguel shouted, barreling his way into the conversation.

"Oh, please. You charge sixty dollars for a plate of oysters," Carmela pointed out. "Don't make it sound like you're slinging soup to the homeless."

"Your mother and I give back! We sponsored that 5K last year."

"It was for diabetes, and you gave every runner a five

136

percent off coupon for caramel flan," Nick shot back. "They probably had to double their insulin doses."

"Leave Dad alone," his sister said, changing sides.

"Stop trying to be the favorite," Nick told her.

"No one is the favorite. You're both equally disappointing," Marie decided.

"Me?" Carmela gasped. "What did I do?"

"You work in real estate development," Miguel pointed out.

"Because you *told* me to get into real estate development like Mom's parents," Carmela said, exasperated.

"How is kicking farmers off their family farms and turning the land into parking lots and strip malls with vape shops giving back to the community and being respectable again?" Nick mused.

"Oh, kiss my ass, Nicky. At least my apartment and office didn't burn to the ground because of my job."

Riley looked dizzy from the swiftly changing alliances.

Nick patted her knee reassuringly and then opened another bottle of wine.

"Let's change the subject, shall we?" Marie said, holding out her glass for a refill.

"So, Riley, what dirt do you have on ol' Nicky here that forced him to move in?" Carmela asked.

"Carm, why don't you eat something and stop being so hangry all the time?" Nick asked, topping off his sister's glass.

"Moving in with a girl and bringing her to family dinner is a first. I assumed there was coercion. Or maybe she's pregnant."

Their mother gasped and made the sign of the cross.

"You haven't set foot in a church in thirty years, Mom," Nick pointed out. "No one's pregnant, and I'm the one who did the coercing. I moved us in together and surprised her."

"I'm just glad you're not still involved with that woman who got you shot," Marie said. "What was she? Some kind of hotline psychic or tarot card reader?" She shuddered dramatically. "Can you imagine?"

Riley's fingers dug into his knee under the table. But he ignored the warning.

"I am still involved with her," he announced. "And she didn't get me shot."

"Watch your mouth at the table, Nicholas!" his dad bellowed.

"He said *shot,* not *shit,'* Pop-Pop," Esmeralda said, coming to her favorite uncle's defense.

"Probably shouldn't be announcing that in front of your girlfriend, dummy," Carmela sneered.

"Riley is clairvoyant," he said.

"Ah, hell," Riley muttered under her breath.

"Thorn, you can't honestly care what these lunatics think after this," Nick told her.

She sighed. "My mom is the tarot reader, and my aunt is the hotline psychic. My grandmother is a famous medium, and I'm somewhere in the middle."

"Sidekick? Who's got a sidekick?" Miguel demanded.

"Not *sidekick. Psychic*!" Carmela shouted.

"Who's psychic?" Miguel scoffed.

"No one is," Marie chided. "But Nick's friend Riley thinks she is." She twirled a finger around her ear in the universal sign for *cuckoo.*

"She doesn't *think* she is, Mom. She is."

"Wait a minute." Andy shoved his glasses up his nose. "This sounds vaguely familiar."

"My family doesn't watch the news," Nick explained.

"Ever?" Riley asked.

"Just Griffin Gentry in the mornings. He and that Bella Goodshine are so cute together," Marie crooned.

"A psychic," Carmela said. "My friend Trina went to one in Virginia after her mother died. Do you know her?"

"Your friend's mother or the psychic?" Riley asked.

"The psychic. She ripped off my friend to the tune of four hundred dollars and said her mother was finally at peace."

"Trina is an asshole. Maybe her mother was finally at peace," Nick said.

Carmela snorted. "That woman was hell on wheels her entire life. Death wasn't going to change that."

"Do you talk to dead people?" Esmeralda asked Riley.

She shrugged, then nodded. "Sometimes."

"No, she doesn't, sweetie," Marie insisted. "She just says she does so she can take people's money. No offense."

"Offense taken big time," Nick countered.

"It's fine," Riley insisted.

He shook his head. "Trust me. You don't want to start things off as a doormat."

"Good point."

"When are you going to get yourself a real job, Nicky? Stop playing peeping tom—" Miguel shouted.

"Private eye!" Nick corrected him.

"Whatever," Miguel said. "You come from a long line of hardworking Mexican people. Your great-grandmother came to this country with only fifty thousand dollars to her name. Where is your appreciation for your heritage?"

Riley blinked.

"Dad's great-grandparents were loaded," Nick explained. "He likes to pretend he's a self-made man, but he started his first restaurant with his trust fund. The last time he went to Mexico, it was a five-star all-inclusive resort in Cancun."

"Mexican *Canadian* people," Marie reminded everyone sternly so as not to leave out her side of the family tree.

"Yay, Tim Hortons," Carmela said with an eye roll.

"Riley, are you going back for Alumni Weekend in the fall?" Andy asked. "We could go together."

"Over my dead body," Nick snapped.

"Did you know he was going to say that?" Esmeralda asked her.

"Is it over yet?" Riley rasped.

"Do you see now why I didn't tell them about us?" Nick asked, holding up the bottle of wine.

She shook her head. "I'm the getaway driver. Speaking of which, when are we getting away?"

"The second you're ready."

"Let me finish this pork first. It's amazing," she decided.

He respected her priorities.

They cleaned their plates while his parents argued about whose heritage was more vibrant and Carmela lambasted Andy for not cutting his meat correctly. Esmeralda opened her book and ignored everyone.

Riley leaned over. "I'm sorry about all this."

"About what?"

She gestured around the table.

"This? This is normal," Nick scoffed. "All our family dinners end up like this. You should see us on Thanksgiving."

"*All* your family dinners?"

"That's why we only get together once a quarter. It gives us enough time to forget about why we were fighting."

"Wow. Then I guess you were right," she whispered.

He slid his hand under her hair and rubbed her neck. "Of course I was. About what?"

"Your family is weird."

"Told you. I've been thinking a lot about this in the past hour. I think we should never let our families meet."

She nodded, considering his wisdom. "I think that's an excellent plan. You know where they'd never meet? Costa Rica if we moved there."

"God, you're beautiful," he said. "Now finish your pork so we can go—"

"Don't say it," Riley said, pointing her fork at him.

He grinned.

"Nicky, when you give up on this sleazy investigator thing, you can come work for me," Miguel decided. "I need an assistant manager at the new tapas place."

"You scared the new one off already?" Carmela scoffed.

"It's not my fault kids these days are pampered little wusses! 'Why are you yelling at me, boss? Stop throwing forks at me, boss,'" he mimicked.

"Why don't you at least consider going back to the police

force? Look at the job security Kellen has with all the poor people in the city killing each other," Marie pointed out. "And think of the nice girls you met when you were a cop." She shot a pointed look at Riley.

"You ready yet?" Nick asked her.

"One second." Riley set her wineglass down carefully. "Thank you for a delicious dinner, Santiagos. Miguel, Marie, your blatant disregard of your son's accomplishments, happiness, and well-being is truly terrifying. We'll be going now."

His mother gasped. "Well, I *never*."

"Bye, Riley! It was great to see you again. We'll have to do a double date sometime soon," Andy said enthusiastically.

"What did she say?" Miguel demanded.

"She insinuated that we don't care about our son," Marie bellowed.

"Oh, I don't think she insinuated anything," Nick said, slinging his arm around his girl's shoulders. "Night, folks."

"Night, Uncle Nicky," Esmeralda said without looking up from her book.

Nick grinned the whole way to the front door.

17

I think that went well," Nick said from the passenger seat.

"Did we just come from the same family dinner?" Riley asked as she navigated his parents' street. "I'm a money-grubbing psychic, and you're a sleazy investigator with a wine buzz."

"It's easy to not care about what people think when you've been building a tolerance to it your entire life," he explained.

"Huh. You might actually have a point there." She drummed her fingers against the steering wheel and then let loose the question that had been on the tip of her tongue all night. "So you've really never been jealous before?"

He reached over and brushed her hair back from her face, capturing it at the nape of her neck. "Never. I don't like it."

She bit her lip and shot him a glance when she pulled up to a stop sign. "I kinda did. And I know that makes me sound like a seventh grader looking for drama. But it was nice to know how much you care."

"You *know* how much I care, Thorn." His voice was low and gravelly. "You're a psychic, remember?"

"Don't remind me. And just so you know, I don't go spelunking in your head. Every once in a while, I might accidentally pick up on something. But I try to respect your privacy."

"You do know how much I care, don't you?" he repeated, his other hand sliding the skirt of her dress higher and higher.

"I have a rough idea." Her voice sounded like she was being strangled. Only Nick Santiago could take her from pissed off to turned on in the span of ten seconds.

"Pull over there," he said, nodding toward the dead end of the street before turning his attention back to the thigh he was exposing.

"We are *not* having sex in your parents' neighborhood."

His fingers tightened on her hair. "Pull over."

"I used to make good decisions before I met you," she complained as she took the right turn and parked in front of someone's walled mini estate.

His grin was lethal. "But you have a lot more fun now."

She wanted to argue, but he was releasing her seat belt and turning off the engine.

"You can't be serious," she whispered in the dark.

He guided her hand to his lap, where she found him hard. "Deadly. Do you know how many times we've been interrupted in the last week alone?"

"No."

"Seventeen," he said. "I counted."

"How much testosterone do you have? We just got in a fight with your parents, and you had at least a bottle and a half of wine." Not that she was complaining. A turned-on Nick was one of her favorite kinds of Nicks.

He dragged her across the console and eased his seat back to settle her on his lap. "You about done arguing yet?"

She nodded vigorously when he yanked her hips down to meet his. "Yep. All good."

While he kissed the hell out of her, she felt him fumbling at the middle console. He managed to flip up the lid and produce four condoms.

Breaking the kiss, she eyed the birth control. "I find your level of sexual preparation impressive. But you can't just expect me to climb aboard less than a block from your parents' house."

"You just picked a fight with my family to defend me, knowing that my mother will never forgive or forget. You, Riley 'Tell Me Your Middle Name' Thorn, are a badass. And it's up to me to continue your badass training."

She felt both appalled and proud of herself. "You're a bad influence."

"From where I'm sitting, I'm the best influence. Now, show me your sexy underwear."

His argument was short yet convincing. Which was how she found herself with her boobs in his face when a bright light shone directly into her eyes through the fogged-up passenger window.

"Nick!" she hissed, dragging his head out of her cleavage and pointing at the light.

"Fucking great. We're never having sex again. I just have to accept it."

"Maybe you can worry about a life of celibacy after our arrest?" Riley suggested as she yanked the top of her dress up. He shoved the skirt down, covering his unzipped jeans and erection. It was a breathy moan that escaped her lips when he shifted under her.

"Not helping, Thorn," he groaned. "This fucking excuse for a dress doesn't have enough material. I forbid you from wearing it ever again. Unless it's just the two of us and you want to end up ass up on the dining room table."

"*Forbid* me?" she squeaked.

An official-sounding knock at the glass quickly tabled the argument.

Nick shoved her face into his neck. "Just be quiet and let me handle this."

That was an order she was happy to follow. Riley burrowed closer as he lowered the window.

"Can I help you, officer?"

Oh God. Was public sex a misdemeanor or a felony? Did it count as public sex if there was no penetration? What was the sentence for almost sex in a vehicle?

Riley decided it didn't matter since she was going to die of humiliation right on the spot. The worst part? She'd die without Nick Santiago's penis inside her.

"Evening," a man said. "Got a call of a suspicious vehicle parked in the neighborhood."

Riley hazarded a peek and saw the man in the window was in uniform. Jasmine was going to be so proud.

"What's so suspicious about my vehicle?" Nick asked.

"Well, it could have been how hard it was rocking," the officer mused. "You got some ID on you?"

"I do, but if I reach for it, I'm afraid you're going to get an eyeful. I'm Nick Santiago. My parents live one street over."

"No shit? Nicky Santiago? It's me! Tommy Hobart."

"Tommy? Hey! How you been?"

"Real good. Got this neighborhood security gig. Get to drive around in a golf cart. Me and the boys are heading to Atlantic City next weekend. You wanna come? How's your sister? She still hot? Man, this is just like old times."

Riley decided being a badass did not include having almost sex in front of an audience while making small talk. She bit Nick on the neck.

His fingers jabbed into her butt cheeks in response. "Ah, hey, listen," he said. "What are the chances of you letting me off with a warning?"

Tommy guffawed. "Pretty damn good, seein' as that's the only thing security is allowed to do. Well, that and call the cops."

Riley tensed, then felt Nick's hard-on flex against her. There was something profoundly wrong with his hormones, she decided.

"If it's all right with you, Tommy, I'm going to take my girlfriend home."

"*Girlfriend*?" Tommy scoffed. "No fuckin' way."

"It's true," Nick said, patting her on the ass. "I didn't stand a chance."

"Never thought I'd see the day when Nicky Santiago settles

down. I'm Tommy, by the way. Nick and I went to high school together."

The guard shoved his hand through the open window into Riley's face.

For fuck's sake.

She sat up, accidentally smacked her head on the roof, then took the offered hand. "Nice to meet you, Tommy. I'm Riley." *Indecent exposer and local psychic*, she added silently.

Tommy's eyes got rather large, and Riley noticed they were on her rack. Nick noticed too and tried to yank up the fabric.

"You got good taste, Nicky," Tommy decided. "Now, Riley. Is that with an I-E?" It looked like he was asking her breasts.

"Just an I," Nick answered for them.

Tommy flipped open a notebook and started writing.

"What's that for?" she asked.

"It's for the neighborhood security blotter. Got a newsletter that goes out every week so our hoity-toity residents know we're earning our keep."

Great. Just freaking great.

18

With Riley overseeing ramp construction and binge-watching an obnoxious woman talk about plastic surgery and sports bra hauls on YouTube, Nick headed out to turn over a few more rocks in the Larry Rupley investigation.

He'd made a few calls and visits to known associates on the list Shelley had provided. But so far, no one knew where Larry went. And no one really seemed concerned either.

Larry's neighborhood was more active on a Sunday, he observed. Front doors were open, and neighbors yelled back and forth across the narrow parking area. Three guys were sitting on folding chairs and drinking beers in a parking space. There were dumbbells on the sidewalk in front of Roy's place. A guy in his forties was juggling a baby, a toddler, and a diaper bag the size of a small sedan. The town house opposite Larry's had a sparkly sign on the door that said BRUNCH MAKEOVERS 10 A.M.

He wasn't sure what a brunch makeover was, but it sounded like something he'd hate.

He'd have to ask Riley later what the hell a brunch makeover was when she wasn't watching dead lady videos on living your best life.

Nick let himself into Larry's place and glanced around.

It smelled stale. He picked up the mail on the floor and paged through it on his way into the kitchen. More bills and past due notices. Nothing that conveniently screamed, "Thanks for signing up for a time-share in Orlando."

He added the mail to the stack in the dining room and glanced down at the cat dishes.

On a whim, he dialed Shelley Rupley.

"Stop flinging your sweat all over your brother," she answered.

"Shelley?"

There was a cacophony of noise on her end.

"Nick?" she shouted. "Hang on. Let me get you off Bluetooth." A few seconds later, she came back. "Sorry about that. You caught me in the minivan with the entire squad of children designed to drive me to the brink. Did you find Larry?" She sounded hopeful. And desperate.

"Not yet. I was wondering if you knew anything about his cat?"

"Ugh. Yes. Mr. Relish… Wait. No. Pickles. He adopted that mangy thing right after he moved out. I'm allergic to cats, so we never had one. Okay. Technically, I'm not allergic. I just didn't want to add a litter box to my to-do list."

"You wouldn't know where Mr. Pickles hides, would you? Or if Larry had anyone feed the cat if he went away?"

"Let me ask the kids." The noise level on her end of the call returned to deafening decibels. "Hey! Stop licking your sister. I don't care if she spilled Frosty down her arm. Where does Dad's cat hide when you guys are at his place?"

Nick winced as the noise crescendoed.

It went quiet again abruptly.

"The kids say Mr. Pickles likes to hide under Larry's bed and in the bathtub behind the curtain. They don't know anything about anyone else looking in on the cat. Larry never goes anywhere. He's a cheapskate and a homebody."

"Okay. I appreciate the info. I'll keep looking."

"Wait. Is the cat missing too?" she asked.

"It appears so."

"Then he must have gone somewhere and taken Mr. Pickles with him! Which means my ex-husband faked his own disappearance just so he wouldn't have to take care of his own kids for a weekend. That son of a bitch."

"I'll find him," Nick promised.

"When you do, I'll pay you extra if you break his nose for me," Shelley said.

After he did another run through the apartment, paying special attention to cat hiding places, Nick returned to the kitchen and eyeballed the untouched food dish.

Where was Larry?

Where was Mr. Pickles?

He wasn't sure about cats, but people didn't just disappear. He let himself out and locked the door behind him. The brunch sign across the lot caught his eye again, and then he spotted something even more interesting. With a grin, Nick crossed to the other town house and jabbed the doorbell.

He was turned around and checking the angle when the door opened behind him.

"Well, *hello* there."

The man who answered was immaculately groomed in unwrinkled chinos and a short-sleeved button-down patterned with tiny hammocks and umbrellas. He had a mustache, and his short silvery hair was expertly mussed.

"Hi. I'm Nick."

"I'm Alistair, and I know who you are," the man said with a wink. "You can't keep secrets in this neighborhood. You're Nick Santiago, handsome private investigator looking for Larry."

"Well, I don't have *handsome* listed on my business card, but now I'll consider it. I was wondering if you had a few minutes to answer some questions."

Alistair crossed his arms over his chest. "That depends. How good are you at julienning vegetables?"

Four minutes later, Nick found himself in a stylish kitchen clutching an expensive paring knife and staring at a cutting board of mushrooms and green peppers. Alistair expertly ran his knife through a slice of pepper. "You want each piece to be about a quarter of an inch square. Anything bigger will throw off the texture of the omelets. Now, where was I?"

"You were telling me about the neighborhood."

The man was the kind of witness Nick wished every case had. Nosy *and* chatty.

"Ah. Yes! We bought this unit about ten years ago. Then when the place next door went up for sale, we snapped it up and spent a year renovating to combine them."

"It's nice," Nick said, looking up from the peppers. "Feels like people live here."

The place looked like people with taste lived there. The walls in the kitchen were painted something called aubergine, which according to Alistair made the white cabinets and marble counters pop. There was a tall glass vase of lemons and limes on the island. The room opened into a large sunny dining room with black-and-white photos of Alistair and friends on the walls.

"Flattery will get you the best omelet you've ever had," Alistair promised as he turned on a burner on a range that would have made Nick's dad weep. "The town houses on the other side of the lot are still owned by a real estate company. They're all rentals and tend to attract newly divorced men."

"Like Larry," Nick prompted, running his knife through a green pepper.

"Exactly. Personally, I wasn't surprised that Larry was divorced *or* that he disappeared under mysterious circumstances," Alistair announced.

"Really?"

"Larry was the kind of guy who was divorced for a reason," Alistair said, pulling a stylish clear bin of eggs out of the refrigerator.

"Aren't most?"

"There are the typical reasons like 'he never remembered my birthday' or 'he was basically another child,' and then there are *other* reasons."

"Such as?" Nick wondered if he should be taking notes.

"There was something dark beneath that lumpy surface. I picked up on it right away, of course. My husband, Danny, thought I was being dramatic, which to be fair is the default setting. But I knew there was something off with that guy."

"Off how?" Nick worked his knife through the mushrooms.

"Entitled laziness. The guy couldn't be bothered to put out his own trash cans. They'd just sit there overflowing until one of us took them to the curb. And there they'd sit for days until one of us dragged them back. He never once shoveled his own walk. And when he moved in and Danny and I took him our usual welcome package, he didn't even say thank you *or* return the container from the lemon bars. I told Danny that's the kind of guy who loses a woman because he's too lazy to make an effort."

"Interesting," Nick mused.

Alistair placed two glass bowls next to him and pointed at the peppers and mushrooms. "He's the kind of guy who just wanted to do his thing with the least amount of effort possible. I made a few helpful overtures, but he wasn't interested in self-improvement. He just wanted to eat his takeout and watch TV."

"Do you remember when you saw him last?" Nick asked, scooping the mushrooms and peppers into the matching bowls, feeling like a contestant on a cooking show.

Alistair gazed at the ceiling and stroked two fingers over his mustache. "It was a weekend. Ah! Yes!" He snapped his fingers. "Saturday a week ago. Danny and I were painting the door and trim, and Larry was headed out for a run. Which, knock me over with a feather that Mr. Lazy Ass took up jogging as a hobby. I think it had something to do with his cholesterol or blood pressure."

"Did you see him come back from the run?"

Alistair squinted at the dollop of butter melting in the pan. "I don't think so. My sweaty man radar is pretty finely tuned. I probably would have remembered."

Nick felt a prickle of excitement. "That doorbell you have. How sensitive is the range?"

The man's eyes lit up. "Very. Our daughter installed it. She's a genius with technology. We haven't figured out how to shorten the sensor's range. We ended up turning off our notifications since the camera goes off every time someone walks or drives by. Hell, even Mr. Pickles sitting in the front window would set it off."

Nick felt the hairs on the back of his neck stand up. "When's the last time you noticed Mr. Pickles in the window?"

"Oh, gosh. It's been…" Alistair frowned. "Now that you mention it, I haven't seen that cat all week. Which is odd, because Mr. Pickles practically lives in that window."

"Would you mind if I took a look at your doorbell footage?" Nick asked.

"Do you think we have the last known footage of a missing person?" Alistair sounded thrilled at the possibility.

"It's possible."

"Danny! Get down here!" Alistair yelled.

A moment later, footsteps thundered down the stairs. "What's wrong? Did I get the wrong mushrooms? Do I have enough time to run out for the right ones?"

Danny was still buttoning his shirt when he hit the kitchen. His salt-and-pepper hair was mussed like he'd just gotten out of bed. He was barefoot and extremely tall.

"Did you seriously just wake up?" Alistair demanded, shoving a cup of coffee into his husband's hands.

"I must have fallen back to sleep after you got up," Danny said with a mighty yawn. "What's wrong with the mushrooms?"

"Nothing is wrong with the mushrooms. They're perfection. But our guest here has a special request."

Danny noticed Nick for the first time. Apparently it wasn't that odd to find a strange man in their kitchen on a Sunday morning. "Oh. Of course. Hi…" He trailed off as if searching for Nick's name.

Alistair rolled his eyes. "Relax. This is Nick. You don't know him, so you didn't forget his name."

Danny's shoulders sagged in relief. "Oh, thank God."

"Forgive my husband. He refuses to actually use any helpful mnemonics I've given him for remembering names and faces."

"That's what I have you for," Danny said, pausing his coffee guzzling to drop a kiss on Alistair's cheek.

"Nick is the private investigator Roy was telling us about."

"Roy. Roy. Which one is he? The head bobber or the guy with the car stereo?"

"Head bobber," Nick answered.

"Right. You're looking for that grumpy guy across the street with the cat."

"Larry Rupley," Nick added.

"Yeah. Grumpy guy. Cute cat," Danny mused.

"Nick wants to have a look at the footage from our doorbell. We might be the last people to have seen Larry before he vanished," Alistair said, gripping his husband by the biceps. "Isn't that thrilling?"

"He probably just skipped out on the rent. The landlord was knocking on his door for the last three months looking for rent money," Danny said with another yawn.

"And no one has seen him since," Alistair reminded him.

———

It took nearly half an hour and two more cups of coffee for Danny to backtrack through all the doorbell notifications. Long enough for Alistair to get bored and go back to setting up his omelet station.

Their house was a popular one. The doorbell rang at least three times a day with deliveries and friends dropping by, most of them men asking for wardrobe and relationship advice.

"Alistair does some unofficial community outreach here," Danny explained, peering over Nick's shoulder at the screen.

"He takes our neighbors and fixes them up so they can get back out there as a better version of themselves. Some win back their exes. Some move on to new relationships. Overall, he's got a pretty high success rate."

"Does he get paid for his efforts?" Nick asked.

Danny chuckled as they watched a clip of a UPS driver wander past with what looked like a keg of protein powder. Probably for Roy. "Alistair makes a killing narrating audiobooks for a living. His fixer-upper advice is free."

"I'm providing a service pro bono," Alistair said from the stove. "Most men aren't willing to make any serious changes until they've hit rock bottom and lost everything. We're not the brightest sex on an evolutionary scale."

"What kind of advice do you give a guy when he's starting a new relationship?" Nick asked as Mr. Pickles, a large black-and-white cat, eyed a squirrel scampering down the sidewalk.

"Oh, you know. The usual. Learning to be interested in another human being. Figuring out how to anticipate his or her needs. How to speak their partners' love languages."

"What are love languages?" Nick asked.

"The way people express and accept love."

"What if you speak different languages?"

"You have that terrified deer-in-the-headlights look. You must be in a new relationship," Danny observed. "Oh, look. This is it!"

Nick looked down at the tablet's screen and watched Alistair and Danny discussing brush techniques. Behind them, Larry Rupley, dressed in shorts and a tank top, stepped out onto his stoop. Locking the door behind him, he stowed his keys in a pocket in his shorts and then ignored Alistair's chipper "Hi, neighbor," as he set off.

The time stamp was 11:27 a.m. Saturday.

Bingo.

Eagerly, Nick moved on to the next video. It and the next four were more of Alistair and Danny painting. After that, there was nothing for a few hours until Danny stepped outside and met up with a small group of men on the sidewalk.

"That's our walking group," Danny explained. "Three nights a week, we take turns getting some of our heftier neighbors off the couch and outside for some fresh air."

The next several videos were from the same day. Cars entering and exiting the lot. The walking group returning from their jaunt. Two food deliveries. Mr. Pickles was in the front window for all of it.

Until finally, Nick hit pay dirt.

Night had fallen. The cat was no longer surveying the neighborhood from the window when a figure dressed in dark clothes climbed the steps to Larry's place. The figure dug into their pocket and a moment later let themselves into the house.

"Al, we found something," Danny said in a hushed tone.

Both men peered over Nick's shoulder as he scrolled to the next notification.

"That's definitely not Larry," Alistair observed.

Nick agreed. The figure was a good six inches shorter and significantly less round. "Do you recognize that guy?" he asked them.

They both shrugged. "Are we sure it's a guy?" Danny asked.

"Look at the way he walks. He's not very big. But that's definitely a man," Alistair said with confidence. "He's walking like he's trying to disguise his walk."

"You teach guys to walk?" Nick asked.

"You'd be amazed at what the right walk does for a man's confidence," Danny insisted.

"How do you know if you're walking wrong?" Nick asked.

"You don't until we tell you. Don't worry. We'll make you strut the catwalk before you leave," Alistair told him.

The next video cued up, and they watched as the same dark figure stepped out of the house with his arms full.

"What's he carrying?" Danny asked, leaning further over Nick's shoulder.

"It's got cords hanging off it," Alistair pointed out.

The figure disappeared off-screen and returned minutes later to do the same thing.

"So Larry goes out for a run. Later that night, a different guy shows up, unlocks the door, and helps himself to some electronics," Danny summarized.

The figure returned again and disappeared into the house. When he reappeared on the stoop, he was carrying a large box by a handle on top.

"Oh my God. Is that—"

"Mr. Pickles. Our man in black just took Larry's cat," Nick said.

19

Bianca Hornberger was an asshole.

There were no two ways about it. After spending two hours watching 4evaYoungBitchez videos, Riley was convinced the woman was Satan and had been called back to hell for a management emergency.

Bianca's advice on living one's best life was limited to "Marry rich, and lead your man around by his testicles."

"Like I said before, your most important asset is your body. You need to take care of it so you can use it to encourage your man to give you everything you want," Bianca said on-screen, dressed in a mini romper open to the belly button. She was obsessively stroking her hair extensions—which had earned their own video—like a cat.

"I wasn't blessed with thirty double-G breasts. I bought them." Bianca smirked. "Well, *my husband* bought them. But what's his is mine. Wink!"

Bianca had to say the word *wink,* because not only had the fillers rendered her incapable of completely closing her lips, but she had also lost significant eyelid function. She'd probably spent half of her husband's fortune on eye drops.

Riley covered her face and let out a half scream, half moan.

"What's going on? What happened? Who's screaming?" A disheveled and confused Mrs. Penny popped up over the back of the dusty divan.

Riley yelped. "How long have you been there?"

"Long enough to fall asleep listening to that dummy talk about the importance of balancing your lip fillers with butt implants," Mrs. Penny said with a yawn.

"Is there something I can assist you with?" Gabe asked from the doorway. He was sweating from his morning marathon, and instead of a bowl of ice cream, he held a giant mixing bowl of kale and nuts.

"I thought Dickie was bad. But this lady? She made the nanny stand in for the daughter on the family Christmas card because she didn't lose enough weight to be in it and it was 'affecting her brand.'" Riley shuddered.

"Sometimes people are horrible," Gabe agreed.

"About time you said it," Mrs. Penny said. "I was starting to think you weren't human with your bullshit equanimity and niceness."

"That's a very un-Gabe-like thing for you to say," Riley said, ignoring Mrs. Penny. She *liked* that Gabe was so kind it made him seem not human.

"I am feeling un-Gabe-like," he admitted. "Adrift. Unanchored. Floating without meaning or purpose." He stabbed a piece of kale with uncharacteristic violence.

Oh boy.

Riley scrubbed her hands on her knees. "Hey! How about you teach me how to detox my mental spaces so ghosts like Bianca don't hang out in there and start to rot my brain?"

Gabe loved teaching her stuff.

He shrugged his seventeen-foot-wide shoulders. "I suppose I could attempt to help."

His lack of enthusiasm made her overcompensate. She jumped out of her chair. "It'll be great. You can explain to me again why I can't contact the newly dead like Bianca and Titus."

He looked down at his pile of greenery and frowned. "Is

your feigned enthusiasm for my benefit because I am now pathetic?"

"Gabe, buddy. Why in the world would anyone think you're pathetic? You're smart, kind, handsome—"

"Built like two hot linebackers smashed together," Mrs. Penny added.

The complimentary bullet points were cut off by the window next to the fireplace shattering into a cloud of glass.

Burt woke up under Riley's desk, barked once, then rolled back over and immediately began snoring again.

Fred poked his toupeed head in through the broken window over the protruding two-by-four.

"Ooops! We'll have that fixed in a jiffy. Right after lunch and a nap," he promised before disappearing.

"You're so Zen you can withstand living here," Riley continued, waving a hand toward the destruction. "You're wise and strong. Everyone thinks you're awesome."

Gabe looked at the toes of his sneakers. "Not everyone."

"The people who count the most think you're awesome. I do. My sister does."

At the mention of Wander, he turned into a gigantic marshmallow. "Does Wander really believe that I am an excellent human being?"

"Of course she does," she insisted. "She lights up every time you walk in a room. And why wouldn't she? Don't let anyone make you feel like you are less than totally awesome."

His smile worked its way across his face in a blinding flash of teeth and hope. "Thank you, Riley. You are a good friend."

"I learned from the best," she said. He frowned, and she patted him on the bulging forearm. "I meant you. You're the best."

"You are very kind and thoughtful."

"Let's get out of here, and you can teach me stuff," she yelled over the noise of the leaf blower Mr. Willicott was wielding outside.

She nudged Burt awake, and together the three of them

headed into the kitchen, where they found Lily giggling over a laptop and a plate of scones. The scones were blackened and still smoking.

"Morning, Lily," Riley said. "What are you doing?"

"I'm flirting with a British gentleman in a fan group for *The Crown*. He says he's a duke!"

Riley could only handle so many crises at one time. "Whatever you do, don't give him your Social Security number or any money. We'll talk about this later."

"Wait up. I'm coming with you," Mrs. Penny announced.

"Why?"

Mrs. Penny shrugged. "I want doughnuts."

"Doughnuts?" Gabe and Burt both perked up.

"Okay. I guess we're getting doughnuts."

They all piled into Riley's Jeep and grabbed a dozen doughnuts in the Dunkin' drive-thru, including a Boston Kreme for Uncle Jimmy.

"This is a wonderful day," Gabe said, clutching a doughnut in each hand, powdered sugar dusting his lips and black tank top. Burt licked his chops with his mile-long pink tongue as Mrs. Penny fed him bites of a plain doughnut.

"Do *not* let him eat any of the ones with cream or jelly. He has a very delicate digestive system," Riley warned.

Riley drove them to Italian Lake, a lush chunk of greenery sandwiched between Green and Third Streets.

Their little entourage with doughnuts and dog in tow tromped to a shady copse of trees on the edge of the man-made lake.

A group of sweaty joggers trotted past, and Riley was inundated with their thoughts.

"Greg's shorts are the perfect length on the inner thigh. I wouldn't need nearly as much Body Glide on my thighs if my shorts were that long. Is this what shorts envy feels like?"

"Why does Gary keep staring at my ass?"

"Ugh. If Greg and Gary hook up, I'm finding a new running club."

"We really need to start doing these exercises at home," she muttered.

Mrs. Penny happily slurped her way through an extra-large iced coffee and held Burt's leash while he watched the ducks.

With a six-pack full of sugar, Gabe's mood had drastically improved. Riley was happy to let him guide her through the friendly pink and blue clouds, wielding a psychic bottle of disinfectant and metaphorically scrubbing at any smudges of Bianca's negativity that were left behind. It felt like a spring cleaning for the mind.

Riley had to admit, it wasn't horrible. She made a mental note to talk to Wander about adding it into the yoga studio's meditation class.

She was scrubbing at a particularly sticky spot when her phone rang, yanking her out of Cotton Candy World and depositing her back on the goose-crap-splattered park grass.

"Ooof," she said, falling over on her side.

It was Detective Weber. Apparently civilian consultants didn't get things like days off.

"Don't tell me you have another dead body," she answered.

Two moms with strollers full of kids stopped in their tracks and then spun off in the opposite direction at a fast clip.

"None that you need to worry about," Weber said, sounding tired. "I do, however, have a housekeeper for you to talk to today. I'm up to my elbows in court preparation for a case tomorrow, and I just caught a fatal hit-and-run."

Riley winced. Wading into death all day, every day had to take a toll. She was glad Nick had left that profession behind. Instead of piecing together body parts, he handled legal papers and sat in cars to take pictures of people.

In her opinion, it was a much healthier gig.

"You want *me* to interview a witness?" She gulped.

"I can't get away, and she wants to talk away from the Hornberger house so she doesn't get fired."

"Am I your only option?"

"Thorn. There's no reason to be nervous. I'll let you in on a little secret. You're going to interview a witness as a representative of the Harrisburg PD. You don't have to be worried about impressing her. She's already terrified."

"That's comforting," she said dryly.

"I just need you to get the details of the glitter bomb. When it came. Where she opened it. If there was a note. Where the packaging went. Who cleaned it up."

"Got it. Glitter bomb focus."

"Can you handle this?" Weber asked.

"Yeah." Probably. She'd asked people questions before. How hard could it be with a murder investigation at stake?

"Great. She's at the West Shore Farmers Market working at the pretzel stand. Her name is Marina."

Riley glanced back at her crew. Gabe was still meditating. Mrs. Penny had fallen asleep with her mouth open, and Burt was covered in jelly and powdered sugar.

"Is it okay if I have company?"

"As long as she talks to you and you get me the information, I don't care if you take a naked marching band with you."

A naked marching band. Riley wondered if there might actually be a market for that.

"Okay. I'll do it."

"Great. Send me your notes, and don't do anything embarrassing."

Weber disconnected.

Riley dragged Burt out of the doughnut box. "Guys, we have a pit stop to make," she told her friends.

"Hold still, big guy," Mrs. Penny said, reaching into her backpack and producing an orange vest. She clipped it on Burt, who was immediately terrified of it.

They were in the crowded parking lot of the West Shore Farmers Market. A two-story building home to, well…everything from butcher-fresh turkey burgers to wild-caught salmon in the middle of Lemoyne.

"What purpose does that serve?" Gabe asked, admiring the vest.

"They don't allow pets in there, what with all the raw meat. This way, we can pretend he's in training to be one of those support doggies."

"It says *Public Safety* on it," Riley observed.

"Don't see you coming up with a better idea," Mrs. Penny said.

"Fine. Let's go. Burt, don't destroy anything," Riley warned. "We're going straight to the pretzel stand to interview Marina. Then we're coming back to the Jeep without causing any scenes. Got it?"

"I can't make any promises," Mrs. Penny grumbled.

"Oh my. This fresh produce would make Elanora so happy. She enjoys a daily beet juice," Gabe said, his face lighting up.

"Forget the beets. Look at those freaking cookies." Mrs. Penny pointed at the bakery stand.

Riley sighed. "Fine. You two take Burt and shop *quietly*. I'll interview Marina, and we'll meet back at the Jeep."

The pretzel stand was all the way in the back corner past the Lebanese place and next to the candy stand she prayed Gabe wouldn't spot. Riley followed her nose to the fresh-baked pretzels. It was a stand run by young women in pretty homemade dresses and aprons.

Riley got in line, intending to focus on the witness interview, but by the time she got to the register, her willpower had evaporated.

"May I help you, miss?" the girl behind the register asked.

Miss. It beat the hell out of *ma'am*.

"I'll take a large pretzel and a lemonade. And I'd like to speak to Marina," Riley added as she forked over the cash.

She was directed to a young woman in a flour-dusted apron worn over a pale-blue dress that matched her eyes. Her hair was fashioned into a braided bun.

"Are you Marina?" Riley asked over the plexiglass.

Marina nodded and ducked out of the booth. "Are you Riley Thorn?" she asked, wiping her hands on her apron.

"Yes. Detective Weber sent me to talk to you about Bianca Hornberger."

"Let's speak outside," Marina suggested.

Riley followed her out a side door and into the suffocating summer sunshine. She pulled out her phone. "Do you mind if I record this?"

"Do what you must."

"So, uh, Marina." Riley suddenly felt incapable of conversation. "You work for Bianca Hornberger, is that correct?"

The woman nodded vigorously, her head covering fluttering. "Yes. I was hired as a housekeeper and nanny until Mrs. Hornberger realized that I was not able to produce the kind of photography she needed for her social media presence. Then she hired a nanny slash social media director."

Forgetting the point of the conversation momentarily, Riley frowned. "What does a nanny slash social media director do?"

"Yvette was part of an au pair program from France. She drives the children to and from school and takes pictures of Mrs. Hornberger."

"How old are the kids?" Riley asked.

"Thirteen and fourteen."

"And they still need a nanny?"

Marina looked over both shoulders. "I don't wish to speak ill of the dead."

"Honesty doesn't count as speaking ill. Especially not if it leads us to her killer," Riley promised.

"Mrs. Hornberger was a terrible person. Her husband and children are better off without her." Marina's hand fluttered to her chest. "Oh my. That felt wonderful!"

"Let it all out," Riley advised.

———

Riley's head was spinning as images of Bianca Hornberger reinfested her newly cleaned mental crevices.

"And another thing," Marina said, nearly breathless after

ten minutes of uninterrupted venting. "When Mr. Hornberger put his foot down and said she needed to stop sinking so much money into her channel just to get a few free products, she paid for thousands of fake followers to pretend that she was getting famous so he'd have to let her continue. Yvette said if you look in the comments, you can tell which ones are bots."

As far as Riley was concerned, this interview had just widened the suspect pool to include everyone who'd ever had the misfortune to meet the woman.

Marina sagged against the side of the building. "I feel much better now. I've been holding that in for six years."

"So about the glitter bomb," Riley said, trying to steer them back on course.

A muffled crash came from inside the building, and she sent up a prayer to her spirit guides that her entourage was not involved.

"Oh yes. The glitter bomb. Mrs. Hornberger sends me to the post office every day to check for packages."

Inside, someone shouted something Riley couldn't make out.

"Do you remember what day the package arrived?"

"I believe it was a Tuesday. Yes. Two Tuesdays before she met her maker."

"Were you there when she opened the package?"

Marina nodded. "Yes. On Tuesdays after I go to the post office, I scrub the floors, clean the pool, change the bed linens, iron the draperies on the second floor, and make a home-cooked meal that Mrs. Hornberger could pretend she made."

Riley blinked. "Uh, just a quick clarification, where were you on the day Mrs. Hornberger was murdered?"

"I was at my great-uncle's farm for my cousin's wedding." Marina looked suddenly guilty. "Mrs. Hornberger said I wasn't allowed to attend because she needed me to reorganize her makeup supplies. But Mr. Hornberger took me aside and told me to take the day off and that he'd take care of it."

Riley tried to imagine Teddy Hornberger "taking care of

it." But the image of him cramming a thong down his dead wife's throat just didn't compute. "Okay. So you picked up the package at the post office and brought it to the Hornberger residence. What happened next?"

"Mrs. Hornberger preferred to open all her business-related mail in the bedroom so she could film it. I was scrubbing the deep end of the pool when I heard the explosion and the screaming."

Riley held up a finger. "Hang on. Are you saying there's video of the glitter bomb?"

Marina nodded. "There was. I would not be surprised if Mrs. Hornberger demanded that Yvette delete it."

Riley wondered if Weber's team had recovered any memory cards or if they'd been missing along with the rest of the electronics.

"So the glitter bomb exploded, and what did you do?"

Marina's cheeks flushed red. "I finished cleaning the pool."

Riley didn't quite hide her smile. "And then?"

"When I went inside, there was red glitter everywhere. Mrs. Hornberger was standing in the middle of her bedroom screaming. There was glitter in her mouth, and she kept spitting it out. It was magnificent."

Riley could see it. The short sharp burst and the instant hurricane of glitter exploding into the air. The shrill scream. The flapping of bejeweled hands. *What is this? I don't understand! This isn't a free sample of moisturizer!*

"I called a cleaning crew, and they arrived an hour later. It took them two days to clean it all up, and she still made them come back the next week because she kept finding glitter in new places like the refrigerator and the garage."

"What happened to the package the glitter bomb came in?"

"The cleaning crew disposed of it."

There was more shouting coming from inside the farmers market now.

"Do you recall a return address or anything special about the packaging?" Riley asked.

Marina shook her head. "I'm sorry, no."

Behind them, a woman with a stroller and a crying toddler barreled through the door into the parking lot.

"Thank you for your time," Riley said quickly. "If I have any other questions, how can I reach you?"

The woman gave her a funny look and reached into her apron pocket. She produced a cell phone. "You may call me."

"Oh, right. Of course. If I have any more questions, I'll call you."

The shrill sound of the fire alarm cut them off.

Riley had a bad feeling about this. "I'd better get back inside—"

The door burst open again, and Mrs. Penny charged through it. She had a smoothie in one hand and Burt's leash in the other. Burt's public safety vest was now around his waist, and he had a length of bratwurst clutched in his mouth. Gabe followed with a bag of vegetables, a plate of tacos, and half an apple pie in his arms.

Customers and vendors poured out of the building after them.

"Let's hit the road before the five-oh show up," Mrs. Penny called as she hustled toward the Jeep.

"I don't even want to know," Riley said when they got in the Jeep.

"Floor it," Mrs. Penny shouted from the passenger seat.

Riley peeled out of the parking lot just as sirens split the air.

"What is that smell, and why is it lingering?" The Jeep's roof was on, but she'd unzipped the windows for full ventilation. Still, the stench clung to the interior.

"I think it's your four-legged friend back there," Mrs. Penny said, slurping on her smoothie. "Might have been the pizza he stole off that toddler."

"It could have been the bowl of pho," Gabe guessed.

"Why did you guys feed my dog pizza and pho and bratwurst?" Riley lamented.

"Hey, don't look at us," Mrs. Penny said. "Burt was the one who jumped over the counter at the taco place."

"They did not seem pleased," Gabe announced, taking a bite out of the pie.

Riley's phone rang, and she punched the speaker button.

"Where are you, and why do I hear sirens?" Nick snarled.

"We just left the farmers market," Riley said, slipping down a side street just in case.

"The farmers market on the police scanner?"

"I'm not sure," she fibbed.

Mrs. Penny leaned over. "Relax, Santiago. She's with me. Everything's fine. We can outrun the bacon."

It was hard to understand Nick's response. It sounded like garbled Donald Duck–style swearing and muttered comments that shouldn't be repeated in polite company.

"Hey, at least she didn't leave the Jeep at the scene of the crime this time."

20

Nick glared at the Jeep and its occupants when Riley pulled into the mansion's parking lot.

"What do you have to say for yourselves?" he demanded when they piled out of the vehicle. Burt launched himself at him and slurped Nick right across the face.

"Whoa. Look who got all duded up," Mrs. Penny said.

Nick suddenly felt self-conscious. "I'm not 'duded up.'"

"You didn't leave the house looking like that this morning," Riley said, giving him the once-over. "Is that a new shirt?"

He pulled at the collar of his short-sleeved button-down. Alistair and Danny had insisted it was the right cut for him, but now he felt like he was being strangled. "No," he lied.

"Are those boat shoes?" she asked.

He felt like kicking them off in the direction of the dumpster and changing back into gym clothes. Except for maybe the shorts. He really did like the shorts. They were a dark gray and made out of that moisture-wicking crap golfers liked. According to Alistair, they could be crumpled up under the bed for two weeks and still never wrinkle. "I don't know. Maybe."

"You look good," she said.

"Good enough to eat," Mrs. Penny agreed as she sauntered past him toward the house.

"Jesus. What is that smell?" Nick said, shoving his nose into the crook of his elbow.

"Burt got into some people food," Riley said with a sigh.

"A lot of people food," Gabe announced. The man had taco sauce and lettuce on his shirt and a slab of apple pie in his hand.

"Why are you so grumpy about looking good?" Riley asked.

"I'm not grumpy," Nick grumbled. "Come on. Let's go."

He took her hand and dragged her back to the Jeep.

"Where are we going? I have to write up my report for Weber," she complained.

"Need I remind you that *I'm* your boss. Weber's just the middle manager I loaned you to."

"Fine, *boss*. Where are we going?"

"We're paying a visit to a couple of Larry Rupley's coworkers. Your coconspirators can stay here and walk Burt until all that food comes out."

Mrs. Penny stomped her foot in her orthopedic shoe. "You're no fun, Santiago."

"It would be my honor," Gabe said before shoving the last taco in his mouth in one bite.

"Got any more work for me?" Mrs. Penny asked.

Nick felt the weight of Riley's gaze on him.

He narrowed his eyes at Mrs. Penny. The woman couldn't keep a secret to save anyone's life. "I don't have any more *errands* to run," he said pointedly.

The woman brushed her finger over her nose. "Read you loud and clear, boss."

"Mrs. Penny, if you don't have anything to do, you could check out Bianca's YouTube channel and scroll through the comments. Maybe someone there wanted to do her harm," Riley suggested.

"I'm on it. All I need is a laptop, a sandwich, and four martinis."

Riley ruffled Burt's ears. "You be a good boy and poop a lot outside before we get back. Okay?"

Burt licked her face.

"Ugh. He smells like pho."

"Oh yeah. I forgot he ate half a bowl after he knocked down the guy who bought it," Mrs. Penny said.

Nick could feel the muscle under his eye twitching. Before he met Riley, his eye muscles had never twitched. "Let's go, Thorn."

———

"Why *do* you look so good?" Riley asked him as they headed north on Route 83, leaving the city in the rearview mirror.

"You make it sound like I never look good," Nick complained. Alistair had failed to mention the attention putting effort into his appearance would garner. "What am I? Some unwashed, hideous troll?"

She snorted. "You know you're hot. Quit being weird about it. I just want to know why you're extra hot."

Extra hot. Maybe he wouldn't toss the shirt and shoes in the dumpster.

"I'm not being weird. You're the one who tried to burn down a farmers market."

"I was just trying to be nice to Gabe and do a favor for Weber, and the situation spiraled out of control."

"Maybe next time try being nice in a way that doesn't get the cops called," he suggested.

"I'll do my best. How did it go over at Rupley's? Did you find the cat?"

"Even better." He filled her in on the video doorbell shenanigans and the neighbors.

"Oh my God. You got Alistaired!" she said in delight.

"You say that like it's a thing."

"It's totally a thing. He's a legend with the single male population. One of the guys I worked with at SHART got a divorce and spent six months moping around until someone introduced him to Alistair. Next thing you know, he's wearing shirts without coffee stains, growing a beard, and styling his hair. His wife took him back, and he quit his job so they could travel the country in an Airstream."

"We wouldn't survive Burt's farts in an Airstream."

"I think you can look good and hang on to your present living situation," she told him.

He picked up her hand and brushed a kiss over her knuckles. "You look good too."

She looked down at her shorts and tank top. "Not Alistair good."

———

Cindy McShillens lived in a beige Cape Cod on a hill that would have overlooked the river if it weren't for the nudie bars and sketchy massage parlor blocking the view. Duncannon, Pennsylvania, was known for its plethora of strip clubs and She's somebody's daughter billboards.

"How did you know we were in trouble today?" Riley asked as he signaled the turn into the McShillenses' driveway.

"Call it boyfriend's intuition."

"Maybe my psychic powers are rubbing off on you," she teased.

The woman who answered the door was short, Black, and dressed in bike shorts and a T-shirt that said Coffee First. She had a toddler on her hip and two scruffy mutts with wagging tails at her ankles. "You two don't look like my grocery delivery," she observed.

"Mrs. McShillens, I'm Nick Santiago, private investigator. I have a few questions for you about your coworker Larry Rupley."

"Ugh. That guy. Come on in," she said, stepping back from the door. The dogs bulleted into the yard to sniff the Jeep's tires.

"Is it the groceries, babe?" a man called from the back of the house.

"No! It's a PI who wants to talk about that asshole from work."

"Asshole!" the toddler chirped. Her dark hair was styled

into a series of perky pigtails that bounced when she shook her head.

"Dammit. I forgot you started repeating everything I say," Cindy groaned. "Don't say that word, Maxine."

"Asshole," the toddler said amicably and stretched her chubby arms out to Nick.

"Here. Maybe you can teach her some stranger danger," Cindy said, handing Maxine over to him and leading the way into the house.

Arms full of kid, Nick glanced at Riley and saw her nose twitch. "You okay?" he asked. "You picking up on something about Larry?"

Riley turned bright red and shook her head. "Nope. Nothing about Larry."

"Sure you're all right?" he pressed as the little girl squished his cheeks between her hands. He made a fish face, and she let out a belly laugh.

"I'm fine. Totally fine. Nothing is wrong," Riley insisted before tripping over a tricycle in the hallway.

"Yeah, you look fine," he observed. She looked like she was about to faint.

"Oh, bite me," she grumbled under her breath.

"Bite me, asshole," Maxine chirped.

"Way to go, Thorn."

"Come on back to the kitchen," Cindy said. "There's coffee and cookies there."

"Coooookie, asshole!" the little girl said with a giggle when they stepped into a sunny kitchen that looked like a dirty dish bomb had gone off.

"That's my husband, Jim," Cindy said, pointing at the huge man handwashing baby bottles and wearing an actual baby. "Excuse the mess. Our dishwasher broke three days ago."

They made the introductions and sat down at the round oak table in the kitchen.

"We have a few questions about your coworker Larry," Nick said, getting down to business.

Cindy shook her head. "That guy. You know he just stopped showing up for work right in the middle of a big project? I had to work late every day last week, and I went into the office for four hours yesterday."

Maxine didn't like being left out of the conversation. She stood up in his lap, grabbed his face, and yelled, "Hi!"

"Hi."

"Babe, can you grab Maxine before she devours the PI's face?" Cindy asked.

"On it," Jim said, juggling both baby and toddler and disappearing into the family room.

"How long did you work with Larry?" Nick asked.

"Couple of weeks. I was on the hiring committee, and we were desperate. I didn't like how spotty his résumé was or what some of his former supervisors had to say about him. But like I said, we were desperate, and he was the only candidate the temp agency sent us. I wasn't exactly surprised when he flaked on us."

"When did you see him last?"

"Friday a week ago."

"Did he call off on Monday?" Nick asked.

"Nope. He was a no-show. Didn't answer his phone or his emails. Hasn't even logged in to the network to submit his time card."

"Any idea where he'd go?"

"Me?" Cindy gestured around the kitchen with its sink full of breakfast dishes and the crowded calendar on the refrigerator. "I don't have the time to keep tabs on a guy I didn't want to hire in the first place."

"Did anyone else have any issues with him?" Nick asked.

Maxine charged into the room, dragging a stuffed pink octopus behind her. She launched herself at Riley, who—in Nick's estimation—handled her like an expert.

"You look familiar," Cindy said to Riley.

Riley grimaced as she juggled the toddler and octopus on her lap. "Uh, I get that a lot."

"Pussy!"

The adults in the room stopped and stared at Maxine as the toddler whacked Riley in the face with the octopus.

"Pussy," she said again.

"Babe, I told you we never should have laughed the first time she said it," Cindy called to her husband, who was dealing with whatever disaster had befallen the family room.

"That's a very nice octopus," Riley told Maxine. The little girl seemed satisfied with that assessment and flopped down in Riley's lap.

Cindy cocked her head. "I think I know you from TV. Were you on *The Bachelor*?"

Riley pushed her coffee mug out of the toddler's reach. "Uh, no."

Maxine giggled as Riley jiggled her on her knee.

She'd make a good mom. The thought nearly had Nick falling out of his chair.

Never in his entire thirty-seven years had he once looked at a woman and thought about her parenting potential. Alistair must have scrambled his brains along with his omelet.

Riley shot him a baffled look, and he guessed she'd picked up on his temporary insanity.

"Uh. Back to your coworkers," Nick said, his voice sounding strangled. "Was there anyone else at the office who had a beef with Larry?"

Cindy frowned, still looking at Riley. "No one really liked the guy. He was still in his probationary period, and his review was coming up. Spoiler alert: he was going to get a warning about how much time he was spending online *not* doing work-related stuff. Did we meet at a Chamber of Commerce mixer?" she asked Riley.

"I don't think so," Riley said. Maxine was now drumming on the table with her chubby little hands. "Was Larry online a lot?"

"According to his logs, the man was all over the internet doing everything but work. Porn. News. eBay." Cindy's eyes widened. "Oh. My. God. You're Riley Thorn!"

Riley was shaking her head, but Cindy had already jumped up from her chair.

"Babe! Get in here! The psychic from the news is in *our* kitchen!"

"What psychic?" Jim called back.

"The one from the fountain at the capitol! You know, the one who did that Facebook Live of the mayor trying to murder her?" Cindy clasped her hands in front of her. "Oh my gosh, Ms. Thorn. This is an honor. Can I get you more coffee? Do you know how my grandfather died? Have you ever predicted winning lottery numbers? Is Maxine ever going to grow out of her biting phase?"

The toddler chose that moment to stand up in Riley's lap and attempt a swan dive. Nick lunged, but Riley had enough wits about her to halt the toddler's progress before she face-planted on the linoleum.

Cindy's husband wandered back in with the baby. "What are you yelling about?"

His wife pointed a finger in Riley's face. "She's the psychic! From the whole mayor-fountain-shootout thing."

"That's very exciting," Jim agreed. "But maybe she would be less terrified if you weren't screaming and pointing."

"What? Oh, right. Sorry." Cindy plucked Maxine out of Riley's arms. "I got a little excited there."

"It happens all the time," Nick said. "Is there any way you could get me a copy of Larry's browser history?"

Cindy reluctantly dragged her eyes away from Riley. "Right. Yes. Sure."

"Was anyone worried that he just disappeared and stopped answering calls?" Riley asked as Maxine wiggled her way safely to the floor and dashed off, dragging her octopus.

"Not really. He had a history of walking away from jobs. And he's not exactly the kind of guy who you worried about once he wasn't right in front of you."

The kind of guy who no one cared about if he went missing.

"We appreciate your time today," Nick said, getting up from the table.

Riley followed suit, shooting out of her chair as if her cute ass were on fire. "It was nice meeting you," she told Cindy.

"Oh no! Do you really have to go? I have so many questions! Are you doing private contracting now? Did the police ever apologize to you for thinking you had something to do with your neighbor's murder? Did it hurt when you got shot?"

Nick put a hand on Riley's shoulder and flashed a double-dimple smile meant to confuse and dazzle. "Sorry, Mrs. McShillens, but we've got to get going. Riley has a lot of important psychic stuff to do today."

Riley nodded. "Yeah. Psychic stuff. A whole lot of it."

He steered her toward the front door, Cindy and Maxine on their heels.

"Wait till I tell the girls that Riley Thorn was in my house. Do you have some kind of hotline I can call if I need psychic help? Or maybe an email address?"

Nick towed Riley out the front door and onto the porch. "Hurry it up, Thorn."

But she dug her heels in and paused.

"Your grandfather died skydiving," Riley said.

"Oh. My. God. How did you know?"

"She's psychic, Cin," Jim reminded his wife.

"Ooh! Wait! Can I get a picture?" Cindy held her cell phone aloft. "Please, please, please?"

"Uh, sure," Riley said in resignation.

Cindy thrust her phone at Nick and wrapped her arms around Riley, squeezing her much like her daughter holding the octopus.

"Thank you for the information. You've been very helpful," Nick said. He handed the phone back and dragged Riley off the porch. "So?" he said when he got behind the wheel.

"What?" she grumbled, securing her seat belt.

"Does Maxine ever outgrow her biting phase?"

Her lips twitched. "Not before she gets kicked out of two more day cares."

21

R iley stuffed her phone back in her bag.

"Was Weber impressed with your report?" Nick asked.

"He sounded busy." She pulled out a Santiago Investigations hat and put it on. After getting recognized by another stranger, she wasn't taking any chances on the crowded deck of Wormleysburg's favorite riverfront restaurant.

"Investigating homicides for a living will do that. Now, let's go drink some beers and feel smug about our life choices," he said, pulling her toward Dockside Willies.

Inside, she tugged the bill of the hat lower and didn't make eye contact with anyone.

The host led them out onto the deck and slapped menus on a table with a great view of the skeletal remains of the Walnut Street Bridge. The site of their first official kiss.

Riley blinked when Nick pulled out a chair for her.

"You're pulling out my chair for me?"

"I can be gentlemanly," he insisted.

"Alistair really did a number on you, didn't he?" she teased.

"Sit your ass down, Thorn. I'm hungry."

They sat and snapped open the menus. Doughnuts long ago digested by adrenaline, she decided on the sliders and a beer since her day had gone to hell in a handbasket.

Nick leaned back and hooked his foot around the leg of her chair, scooting her closer. "This is nice."

She looked around them. It was hot, but the overhead fans helped stir the humidity around to make it almost tolerable. "Yeah. Beautiful summer weather."

"I meant being here with you," he corrected.

"What's gotten into you?" she asked.

"*Me*? Nothing's gotten into me. Stop asking me why I'm making an effort."

"You're being very attentive and grumpy about it," Riley pointed out.

"Can I take your drink orders?" A harried server who had already sweated through his polo shirt arrived just in time to save Nick from having to answer.

They ordered, and the server left, leaving little beads of sweat on the edge of the table.

"Did you get anything helpful from Cindy?" Riley asked Nick.

He shook his head. "I wasn't expecting to. Just confirmed that Larry was a flake who no one liked. Lazy. Grumpy. Entitled."

She crossed her arms. "I feel like both cases are going nowhere fast. Two dead bodies with nothing in common but the fact that both victims were assholes? And then there's a father of four who up and vanishes before someone steals his cat. How can there be no leads in either case?"

Something was simmering in the back of her head. Something she couldn't see yet. Like an itch she couldn't reach.

"It happens," Nick said. "Every once in a while, a criminal is either really good at what they do or gets really lucky."

"You're leaning toward Larry being dead, aren't you?"

He nodded. "Yeah. He's just not smart enough to disappear on his own."

"It could have been an accident. A hit-and-run while he was out for a jog. Or maybe he had a heart attack? He could be in an ICU under John Doe," she suggested.

He shook his head. "He had a DUI arrest about ten years back. His prints are on file. He would have been identified by now. Besides, someone had to know he wasn't coming back."

"And that someone took his cat."

The server returned with their beers and more sweat.

"I've got Brian running some fancy configurations on the doorbell footage, hoping we come up with some identifying mark that'll lead us in the direction of the guy who stole his cat."

"Do you think the guy who took his cat had something to do with his disappearance?"

Nick nodded. "My gut says yes. Even if the catnapper had his own keys to the place, how else would he have known Larry wasn't there? He didn't ring the bell or knock. He walked straight in."

"Good point." Something tickled at the back of her mind again. "Maybe he was doing it because he didn't want Mr. Pickles to starve?"

"You mean you think a potential murderer knew Rupley had a cat and knew no one would come looking for him for a while?" he pressed.

"Yeah. What if he's one of the neighbors? Neighbors give each other keys all the time. Or maybe he's the landlord?"

"The landlord is a six-foot seven-inch former high school basketball star. I checked up on him, and he was on a Bermuda cruise the week the vic disappeared."

"Have you talked to Weber?"

Nick took a long pull on his beer. "He's got his hands full with your sparkly dead bodies. I filed a missing person report this morning while you were trying to burn down the farmers market."

"That was Mrs. Penny's fault. And maybe a little bit of Burt. Apparently, he jumped the counter at the taco place and tackled a pho customer. I'm pretty sure it was Mrs. Penny who pulled the fire alarm."

"Can't take them anywhere."

She shifted in her seat to make sure no one was eavesdropping. "I'll sit down with Gabe tonight and try to get something out of my spirit guides," she offered. She'd been putting a lot of psychic energy into Weber's case and doing nothing but holding babies and filing paperwork for Nick. "Worst-case scenario, we ask my grandmother."

"Speaking of psychic stuff, what kind of vision did you get at Cindy's place?" he asked.

Riley choked on her beer. She didn't really think he was prepared for what she'd seen...again. The first time she'd had the flash of Nick Santiago holding a little girl with his dimples, she'd chalked it up to insanity. This time around? Well, she had no more excuses. She was seeing the future. Nick's future. And she didn't know if she was part of it.

"Ah, crap. You didn't see me die again, did you? Am I going to have to duct-tape you to the bed to keep you from running off and trying to save my life?"

"No! I saw...something else."

"What?"

She blew out a breath. "I saw you in the future holding a baby with dimples."

It was Nick's turn to choke on his beer.

Other patrons were starting to look at them.

She handed him a napkin. "You're the one who asked."

"Lots of babies have dimples," he pointed out.

She shook her head. "Not Santiago dimples."

He wiped a hand over his nice new shirt. "Huh. Okay. How do you feel about kids?"

"Me?"

"No, the lady in the straw hat behind you. Yes, you, Thorn."

"I guess I like kids."

"Okay. Me too."

"Have you ever thought about having kids?" she pressed.

He shook his head. "Not until you were juggling Maxine with the naughty vocabulary."

Riley felt her face flush. She'd managed to convince herself she'd imagined reading Nick's mind at the kitchen table. "So what are you saying?"

"I'm saying you're the kind of girl who makes a guy start thinking about the future."

"I need another beer," she decided.

He grinned. "Relax, Thorn. We don't have to map out the next twenty years of our lives right now."

"But a family is on the table? With me," she clarified.

"You're really sexy when you're freaking out on the inside," he told her.

"I'm not freaking out. You're freaking out."

"I'm sitting in the sun with my incognito girlfriend enjoying a cold beer. There's nothing to freak out over."

"Spoken like a guy who thinks diapers magically change themselves."

"You wound me, Thorn."

Their food arrived, and they dug in until Nick's phone rang. "Hey, Bri. What've you got for me?"

Riley attacked her sliders and listened to his side of the conversation.

"Okay. She's going to hate that."

"What am I going to hate?" she demanded when he hung up, the slider forgotten in her hand.

"Brian says he didn't have enough to run facial recognition. And it was too dark to get a look for any tattoos or identifying marks."

"So Mr. Pickles's catnapper is still a ghost."

"For now. Brian's running a search on properties that Larry or his family own in case he's holed up in a cabin somewhere."

"What else? What am I going to hate?"

Nick grinned. "He also mentioned that there's a photo of you on Instagram that's getting a lot of attention."

He held out his phone to her.

It was a photo of Riley being smother-hugged by Cindy.

Met a celebrity today! Harrisburg's famous psychic

Riley Thorn! Not only did she know how Grandpa Ryan died (skydiving accident); she's on the case looking for my missing coworker. If anyone has any information on Larry Rupley, contact Riley Thorn directly! But save those marriage proposals, guys. She appears to be taken by a very hot, very dimpled private investigator. #psychic #celebrityencounters #shestallerinperson #dimpledhottie

The picture had four thousand likes already.

"I think I'm going to be sick," she decided, reaching for her second beer.

Her phone rang.

"What is it, Lily?" Riley asked.

"Just calling to deliver your messages. Mr. Winters, or was that Summers? Billy Blanks—do you think he's the real Tae Bo guy? And Ellie Karpinski… Wait. Maybe that was Crapinski. I can't read my handwriting. Oh well. They all say they have information for you, but they'll only share it in return for a psychic reading. I told them you don't get out of bed for less than a thousand dollars, and they all hung up."

"Uh, thanks?" Riley said. She shoved her hand into her hair, dislodging the hat.

"Nick's business phone has been ringing off the hook for the last hour, so I had Mr. Willicott start answering it since he and Fred finished the ramp this morning. What should I tell them?"

"Tell who?" Riley groaned.

"Everyone who keeps calling. What are your rates for a reading? How serious are you and Nick? I told them I wouldn't be surprised if you elope soon. You'll take me along, won't you? I've always wanted to be a bridesmaid."

"Lily, do me a favor, and just leave the phones off the hook for now."

"But how will I tell everyone I'm your executive assistant then?"

Riley banged her head on the table. "Just leave the phones off the hook, and Nick and I will take care of it when we get home."

"Okey-dokey! Oh, I accidentally let Burt eat a bowl of spaghetti and meatballs."

Riley hung up.

"What's with the face? You look like the world just burned down," Nick observed.

She looked down at her plate. "Would it be wrong to turn this into a liquid lunch?"

"That's never wrong," he assured her.

"The mansion landline and your office phone have been ringing off the hook since Big Mouth Cindy posted the picture. Fred and Willicott apparently finished the wheelchair ramp. Oh, and Lily fed Burt a bowl of spaghetti."

"Let's just stay here and drink for the rest of the day. When we're done, we'll call a Lyft, throw our phones in the river, go to the airport, and fly to Costa Rica."

"You have never been more attractive than you are right now," Riley decided.

"It's the shoes," he said.

Her phone rang again, and with an eye roll, Riley answered. "Hi, Mom."

"Sweetie, I hate to do this, but I have an emergency. I need you to come over as soon as you can."

"Is everything okay? Did Grandma give Dad a heart attack?"

"Your father is fine."

"No, I'm not!" Roger bellowed in the background. "You Thorn women are driving me batty!"

"Don't listen to him. We just have a situation with your grandmother."

"An emergency situation?" Riley clarified. "As in first responders are on their way?"

"No. Don't be silly. No one's bleeding or turning blue."

"So then it's just a regular situation?"

"Just get over here as soon as possible," Blossom begged. "Please, Riley. I don't ask for much."

"Yes, you do. You ask for stuff all the time."

"For the love of Goddess, do not make me use your middle name!"

"Nick and I will be there in fifteen minutes," Riley said and hung up. He looked at her expectantly. "Costa Rica will have to wait."

"Who did your grandmother kill?"

"No one yet. But my mother seems to think we're needed at the house immediately. She almost broke out my middle name, which means it might not be a severed limb, but it is serious."

"When are you going to tell me your middle name?" he asked.

"Only when it's absolutely necessary."

Nick stuffed the rest of his burger in his mouth and made the universal check sign to the server across the deck.

Riley was in the middle of guzzling the remainder of her beer when a very pretty server with long black hair and pink tips sauntered up to the table.

"Nicky Santiago," she purred.

Nick jumped out of his chair so fast it tipped over backward. "Ah, God. Okay. Riley, this is Twyla. Twyla and I dated very briefly," he said, wrestling his wallet out of his pocket.

"*Very* briefly. As soon as he heard I was ready to settle down, get married, have kids, this one was out the door," Twyla said with a laugh, jerking her thumb affectionately in his direction.

Riley noted she had a wedding band on her left hand and a picture of a kid in her order notebook. "It's nice to meet you," she told Twyla.

"Yeah. Nice to see you again. This is my girlfriend, Riley. We'd stay and chat, but we're leaving the country," Nick said, dragging Riley to her feet.

"Bye, Twyla."

22

When Nick pulled up in front of Riley's parents' house, they found Roger in the front yard, spraying Daisy the cow with a garden hose.

"Okay. Let's agree that our families are equally weird," he said.

"We'll probably miss them when we're drinking in the Costa Rican rain forest," Riley mused. They got out of the vehicle. "What's the big emergency, Dad?" she called.

But he didn't respond. Nick noticed he was wearing headphones. Just a man, some music, and his cow. Roger Thorn was a simple man.

With an eye roll and several muttered four-letter words, Riley led the way onto the porch and in through the front door.

"Mom," she bellowed.

Blossom appeared at the top of the stairs. She was wearing a flowy tunic over an equally flowy skirt. Both were embroidered with a pattern that looked suspiciously like female anatomy. She had a dusty cardboard box in her hands and a cigarette in her mouth.

"It's about time!" Blossom announced.

Riley gasped. "Are you smoking?"

"Of course not. Don't be ridiculous," Blossom lied, stomping down the stairs and shoving the box at Nick. "Hi, Nick. It's nice to see you. Can I borrow your strong arms for a second?"

"Mom, if you called us over here just to get Nick to move some furniture again—"

But Blossom was already rounding the corner, heading toward the sunporch, where she did her tarot readings.

Nick peeked into the box and found dozens of white pillar candles, all with a fine coat of dust on the wax.

He put it down next to the front door and followed the women.

"Why is Dad hosing down Daisy?" Riley asked.

"Your father and that cow." Blossom tsked. "Daisy has cow dandruff, and her constant scratching on the fence has Chelsea in a tizzy. Your father is using special cow dandruff shampoo on her to stop his precious heifer from itching."

"Is that the big emergency?"

Blossom stubbed the cigarette out in an incense burner. "No, of course not. Nick, be a dear and reach into the top shelf of this closet and get all those boxes down for me?"

"What's with the headphones?" Riley asked.

"It was the only way I could get Roger to agree not to leave until my mother goes home. Noise-canceling headphones. He's been wearing them twenty-four seven."

Nick dragged a chair into the closet and went to work unloading the top shelf while Riley interrogated her mother.

"What is going on?" Riley demanded.

"Oh. You know your grandmother. She lives to hurl my life into chaos," Blossom said.

He pulled the first box down. It was labeled *Cloaks*. The second box was labeled *Event Crystals*.

"Are these what you're looking for?" he asked, setting the boxes on the rug.

"Yes! Thank you, Nick. You are such a big help."

"Mom, why is Nick getting your demonstration supplies down?"

Riley's voice was getting higher and tighter.

"Your grandmother has decided that the best way to repair our family's reputation in the eyes of the guild is to host a public séance."

Riley's gasp had Nick checking the doorway for a gun-wielding maniac.

"No!"

"Yes. Tonight."

"No!"

"At your place since ours isn't big enough, and she felt that Wander's studio decor was too 'reassuring.' Whatever the hell that means."

Riley looked like she was about to collapse, so Nick guided her to the couch and pushed her down.

Blossom dug through the box of cloaks, muttering to herself. "Aha! Here it is." She tossed a black filmy hunk of material to Riley. It hit her in the chest and fell on her lap.

"What. Are. You. Doing?"

Nick had never heard that particular tone from Riley before. Sure, she'd yelled at him plenty. And he was quite fond of the noises she made when he was inside her. But this sounded flat and a little scary.

"It's your outfit for tonight. All the Basil women are required to attend and participate."

Riley collapsed against the couch. "This is insane! How is Grandmother communing with the dead in front of my neighbors going to fix our 'image problem'?" she demanded, using air quotes.

"Well, maybe it's because she 'also invited' a couple of guild representatives and a handful of 'journalists,'" Blossom shot back.

The woman clearly didn't understand how air quotes worked.

"Journalists?" Riley's voice had entered the pitch that made dogs start howling. Daisy mooed outside.

"Everything all right in there?" Roger bellowed from the window.

"Oh, go back to washing your cow!" Blossom yelled with a flutter of her hands.

"Mom, I'm not doing this. I don't want any more media attention."

"I know you don't, sweetie. But I don't know what to tell you," Blossom said, opening the box of crystals and taking inventory. "Riley has performance anxiety," she explained to Nick.

"It's not performance anxiety!"

"When the girls were little, we spent a week with my mother in her free-thinkers spiritualist camp, and she enrolled Riley and Wander in a talent showcase."

"Kill me now," Riley said, pinching the bridge of her nose.

"Wander got up and was able to sniff out an entire week's worth of dinners the senior guild member had. But poor Riley. You can understand why she's been so hesitant to use her powers when her vision broke up her father and me."

Nick felt like some kind of reaction was required, so he nodded.

"Anyway, the poor kid froze and just stood there on stage like a robot."

"They threw cabbage at me," Riley whispered.

He squeezed her hand and decided that the Thorns may have just edged out the Santiagos in the Weirdness World Cup.

"It was for good luck," Blossom insisted. "Cabbage wards off bad spirits."

"Well, consider me a bad spirit because it warded me off. You can't make me do this." Riley's big brown eyes settled on Nick and pleaded with him.

"We'll figure this out, Thorn. I promise."

"It won't be anything like the talent show," Blossom assured her. "There's no stage. All we're going to do is sit around a table and call up a few dead people, do a few tarot readings, and then listen to a dozen or so speeches. In front of an audience and half a dozen journalists."

"N-O."

Blossom shrugged. "Your grandmother insists. So you can take it up with her."

Riley's eyes narrowed, and her nose twitched. "What else aren't you telling me?"

Her mother avoided her gaze and handed Nick the box of crystals. "Do me a favor and put these by the front door so you can take them home with you."

"Sure," Nick said.

"You're a good son-in-law," Blossom said, patting him on the cheek.

"He's not your son-in-law, and he's also not your pack mule," Riley argued.

"You know that your father and I are fine if you two decide to get married legally or not. It's a very personal decision."

Nick left his open-mouthed girlfriend gaping at her mother and took the box to the front door.

"You did *not* just say that!" Riley screeched moments later.

He ran back into the room. "Everything all right?"

Riley had a pillow and was holding it over her face. "I'm going to kill my grandmother." The words were muffled, but he caught them loud and clear.

He pulled the pillow away from her face, then on instinct checked to make sure she wasn't carrying any weapons.

"She's just kidding, Nick," Blossom said, looking not entirely sure. "She just had a little shock. That's all. How about some tea, Riley? You like tea."

"I hate tea. I want alcohol," Riley said, her face white.

"I'll get the hooch," Blossom said. "Try to get her to lie down in the TV room."

Nick led Riley to the couch he'd personally helped move the first time he'd met her parents, and pushed her down. "What's wrong, baby? What did your mean grandma do now?"

"B-B-Bella."

"Bella? What's a bella?" he asked.

"G-Goodshine."

"Channel 50 is sending their weather girl, Bella Goodshine,

to cover the séance," Blossom said, shoving a bottle into Riley's hands before lighting up another cigarette. "Apparently she's branching out into fluff pieces instead of just storm systems and ruining my daughter's marriage."

Riley took a hit from the bottle and snatched the cigarette from her mother. She took a long drag and coughed out a cloud of smoke.

Nick took the bottle from her in case it was flammable.

"Does anyone smell smoke in there?" Roger yelled from the front porch.

Blossom stole the cigarette and dunked it in a flower vase.

"No!" mother and daughter shouted together as they frantically fanned the air.

"Weird. Imma take Daisy for a walk around the block," he bellowed back.

"I can't just perform for a crowd, Mom," Riley groaned.

"I know!"

"And I can't not perform with my ex-husband's future wife sitting there judging me."

"I know!" Blossom wailed.

"Everybody calm down," Nick ordered. The Basil-Thorn women turned their gazes on him, and he held up his palms. "Before you kill me, hear me out. What if Elanora gets her séance, but it gets interrupted?"

"By what? A swarm of locusts and a farting dog?" Riley asked.

Someone pounded on the front door. "For Pete's sake, Roger. The door is unlocked," Blossom snarled, whipping it open.

The skinny, nosy next-door neighbor stomped inside waving official-looking documents.

"You went too far this time, Thorns!"

Riley bounded to her feet and made Nick fear for the neighbor's life.

"*Not now, Chelsea!*" Riley snarled, grabbing the woman by the shoulders and shoving her back out the door. "Go ruin

191

some other neighbor's life for ten fucking minutes. How about Mr. Abbott? I hear he's going through radiation treatments. Maybe you should complain to him about the parking habits of his home health aides."

"We have regulations *for a reason*," Chelsea snipped. She had a head of blond helmet hair and was dressed in a pink blouse and white pants.

"*You* violated those regulations by using too much water to keep your stupid grass green! So turn your hoity-toity tight ass around and *get off my property*," Blossom shouted.

"You should probably go," Nick advised, stepping into the terrifying territory also known as the physical space between three very upset women.

"You haven't heard the last of me," Chelsea howled.

"You sound like a Marvel movie villain," Blossom shrieked, peering over Nick's shoulder.

He slammed the door shut and threw the dead bolt just in case.

Both women took several deep, cleansing breaths.

"I apologize for my outburst," Blossom said finally after accessing some kind of internal well of Zen. "What were you saying about an interruption, Nick?"

"How about a power outage?"

"Oh, come *on*!" Blossom snapped, apparently having lost touch with the well of Zen. "I say this with love, but we'll be lighting about a hundred candles. We don't need electricity, you handsome idiot."

"Mom," Riley chastised.

Blossom winced. "I'm very sorry. I'm a little stressed out."

"I understand," Nick said. "But you know what you do need?"

Riley reached for the bottle again, and he held it out of reach.

"What? What do we need?" Blossom demanded. "Enough alcohol to drink ourselves stupid?"

"Yes, but more importantly, *air-conditioning*."

Riley stopped reaching for the bottle.

"A hot August night, all those people crammed inside around open flames with no air-conditioning?" Nick painted them a picture.

"I take back the *idiot* comment," Blossom said. "You're a diabolical dimpled genius."

"You'd sabotage an HVAC system for me?" Riley whispered.

"Baby, you know I would."

"That is the sweetest, most underhanded, biggest grand gesture any man has ever made for me," she decided.

"Are you forgetting about the time I saved your life?" he teased.

She shook her head. "No, I am not."

"Oh, crap," Blossom interrupted. "Nick, did I mention that my mother needs you to pick up two of her guild friends at the train station tonight?"

23

It was nine million degrees in the mansion. Nick had worked his magic on the air-conditioning before leaving to pick up her grandmother's associates at the train station, and the effects were sweat lodge-y. Burt was soaking up the air-conditioning with her father, who was babysitting his granddaughters.

Riley embraced the heat. With every degree the temperature rose, it became less and less likely that she would have to face Bella freaking Goodshine.

There was a low rumble of voices coming from the front of the house, where strangers and journalists were gathering. She'd prayed to every deity she could think of to cover her bases. The séance couldn't happen.

"I look ridiculous," Riley complained to the mirror they'd hauled out of Lily's room and propped against the kitchen table. The second and third floors were too hot to be inhabited, so they'd turned the kitchen into a dressing room.

She'd gone with a short black dress for airflow purposes and topped it with the gauzy black cloak her mother had forced on her.

"I think you look witchy and very attractive," Wander countered with her trademark sisterly support.

Riley's beautiful sister looked annoyingly cool in a similar style cloak. Wander had paired it with a long, flowing black skirt and a belly-baring tank. She looked like she'd just stepped off a yoga mat and was on her way to a jazz club.

"No. *You* look witchy and attractive," Riley said accusingly. "I look like I'm about to drown in my own sweat. Wait. Why do you look so cool?"

Wander grinned and opened the freezer door. "Here." She handed Riley a pair of chilled underwear.

"Seriously? You're wearing frozen underwear?"

"A little trick I learned after childbirth," Wander explained.

"These are mine," Riley said, recognizing the tacos on the thong.

"I know. I put them in the freezer for you when you were getting dressed. Put them on."

Skeptical but desperate, Riley stepped into the pantry and traded out sweaty briefs for an icy thong. "Wow. That helps."

"Hello, Wander. It is lovely to see you again." Gabe's deep baritone carried into the pantry. Riley stuffed her underwear behind a dusty box of penis-shaped pasta and quickly rearranged her dress.

"Hello, Gabe. You look…good."

Wander was never one to lose her Zen, so seeing her get tongue-tied around the gigantic teddy bear was adorable.

"I would have hoped to find you in meditation," Elanora, ruiner of all fun, snapped.

Gabe and Wander both apologized profusely. Those two were taking the whole honor-your-elders thing a little too far.

"Come out of there at once, Riley," her grandmother ordered.

Apparently Elanora Basil's powers extended to seeing through walls.

"What were you doing in there? Snacking on processed garbage?"

"Putting on frozen underwear."

Elanora's gaze pinned her like a dead bug with a needle through its thorax.

"You will not embarrass or disappoint me tonight."

It was not a request.

"Your guests have arrived," Nick said, appearing in the doorway like a sexy hero.

"I trust you brought them here in one piece," her grandmother enunciated sternly.

"No. There was a horrible accident, so I scooped up all the body parts and threw them in the trunk."

Gabe looked like he was going to faint. Wander looked like she might actually laugh.

But Riley's grandmother merely stared him down.

"There's this thing called sarcasm—"

"Your sense of humor is appalling."

"You're *welcome*, Elanora. It was my pleasure. Oh no. No. Put your money away. I wouldn't dream of asking for gas money to run your errands. It's my *honor* to pick up your weird friends instead of being here to give my girlfriend moral support for the dog and pony show you're insisting on parading her in."

She was in love with him. He'd taken a bullet for her, punched her ex-husband in the face for her, and now he was calling out her grandmother on her bullying. Nick Santiago was the goddamn love of her life.

"Your girlfriend has wasted enough of her life hiding from who she is."

Nick crossed his arms and rubbed his chin as if he were seriously considering her words. "Have you ever considered— hear me out—allowing people to exercise free will?"

"Free will is wasted on the weak and spineless," Elanora snapped.

"You should consider putting that in your Christmas cards," he suggested.

"Why is it so warm in here tonight, Nicholas?" she demanded.

Gabe whimpered.

Nick shrugged. "August in Pennsylvania. Probably too much for the air-conditioning to keep up with," he said, all innocence.

Riley was impressed. Most people started croaking like frogs when they tried to lie to Elanora's face.

Her grandmother drew in a stern breath and turned to face the rest of them. "You will *not* disappoint me."

"About that," Riley began. "I don't want to do this. And I'm an adult, and you can't force me to do it."

Elanora's eyes narrowed, the crinkles on her face sharpening scarily. "You have a responsibility to this family and to the guild. You will do this, and you will do it well."

"I don't think you're hearing me," Riley insisted, noting that Gabe was pressed against the wall as if he hoped to be absorbed into the mint-green cabinets.

"What I am hearing is my granddaughter, who possesses supreme powers and has wasted her entire life hiding from them like a coward, *still* doesn't want the world to know that she is special. I speak for all the Basil women who came before me when I say you are a disappointment to all who cultivated their gifts and shared them with the world. I insist that you stop your willful ignorance and step into who you were meant to be instead of clinging to the average disappointment you strive to be."

Elanora vanished into the hallway in a swirl of black. Riley sagged against the pantry door. "Um, ow." She felt like she'd actually been stabbed by some sort of spiritual guilt dagger.

Wander and Gabe were no longer making moony eyes at each other or eye contact with her.

"Damn, baby. Your grandma is mean," Nick observed as he approached. "But at least you look good."

"Thanks," Riley said. He pressed a kiss to her sweaty forehead.

"Yo." Josie, Nick's "muscle" and cousin-in-law, appeared in the doorway. She was wearing black bike shorts, a fitted tank top that said ANTISOCIAL BUTTERFLY, and a fanny pack probably full of knives and brass knuckles. Her jet-black hair was tied in a high ponytail, making her look like an evil cheerleader.

"What are you doing here?" Riley demanded. She didn't need any more witnesses to her humiliation if the air-conditioning scheme failed.

"Oh, I wouldn't miss this for the world," Josie said with a rare smile. "Besides, Brian's got something for you on the case. He's trying out the new ramp."

"Let's talk in the office," Nick said, taking Riley's hand. He led her toward the front of the house, where Elanora was greeting her guests.

"That's who you picked up?" Riley hissed under her breath.

The guy was built like one of those inflatable arm-waving things car dealerships seemed to like. Tall and entirely too bendy. He was so white he practically glowed. His long straw-colored hair was pulled back in a man bun, but not a hot one. He was wearing a three-piece suit the color of grape jelly. The woman next to him was of medium height and medium build. She had darker skin and jet-black hair, and she wore a stylish pair of flowy pants under a bright green tunic. She looked annoyed.

Two camera crews were busy setting up in opposite corners of the parlor, where all the furniture had been moved out except for a large round table and a few dozen mismatched chairs for the audience.

Riley shivered despite the temperature.

"You okay?" Nick asked.

"Where did all the furniture go?" she wondered out loud. But if Nick answered, she didn't hear him. Her attention was captured by Bella Goodshine in a Barbie-pink pencil skirt and white sheath top. She was taking a series of puckered-lip selfies in front of the séance table.

It was one thing to see the woman on a TV screen or her carefully curated Instagram account. It was another to see the woman Riley's husband had left her for in the flesh.

Riley dug her fingers into Nick's arm and decided now was as good a time as any to run away to Costa Rica.

But it was too late. Bella looked up, and her vacant gaze

landed on them. "I know you!" she said, mincing over to them on pink patent-leather heels. She threw her arms around Nick in a full-boob contact hug.

"Dear God. Please tell me you didn't," Riley said, feeling faint. Little dots were floating in front of her eyes.

Nick extricated himself from the weather girl's grasp. "I swear on my life, *no*."

"Oh, thank God," she muttered.

"You're a fan of my fiancé," Bella bubbled. "I remember when you came to our house for his autograph."

It was Riley's turn to choke.

"I'll explain that later," he promised.

Bella turned to Riley with a glossy pink smile. "Hi, I'm Bella Goodshine, Channel 50's weather girl! It's going to be a humid one tomorrow."

"I know who you are," Riley said, standing stiffly, arms at her sides, as Bella hugged her. "I met you when you were naked and kneeling in front of my husband."

Bella pulled back and cocked her head. Her expression was thoughtful.

"Griffin," Riley prompted. "Griffin Gentry cheated on me with you in my bedroom."

"Ohhhhh! Riley!" Bella said as if Riley told her they'd met at a Taylor Swift concert. "It's so nice to see you again. I guess I should say thanks for your husband!"

Nick grabbed Riley by the waist.

"You are so welcome," Riley said through clenched teeth.

"Easy, tiger," he said, dragging her into the hall.

"Things like this don't happen to normal people," she complained. "We're all going to sweat to death just so my grandmother can prove we're respectable psychics, not even caring that she is literally going to ruin my life."

"Just keep picturing umbrella drinks in Costa Rica," he suggested, towing her into the music room.

Without warning, they both tumbled over backward, ending in a heap on the floor.

"What the hell, Santiago?" Riley grumbled under his sweaty body.

"What the hell is right."

She looked up. "So *that's* where all the parlor furniture went." They were staring at a wall of stuff. The fainting couch and wingback armchair from the parlor were shoved just inside the doorway, and three occasional tables were stacked atop an old trunk. Beyond was a tangle of rolled-up rugs, Mrs. Penny's bar, two hutches, and the organ bench.

"Uh. Marco?" Brian's voice came from somewhere on the opposite side of the room.

"Polo," Riley called back as Nick hauled her to her feet.

"We need a new fucking office," he muttered under his breath.

"You guys are going to have to come to us unless you want us to Tarzan and Jane it across Mount Yard Sale," Josie said from somewhere beyond the wall of crap.

"Hang on. We'll climb over," Nick said gamely.

Riley stopped him and shook her head. "I'm not dressed for rock climbing. We'll meet them outside."

They skulked back into the hallway around sweaty strangers. Wander and Gabe were lighting several dozen candles in the parlor around the video equipment.

"Wow. That feels almost refreshing," Riley said, airing out her armpits in the humid, thick air on the front porch.

"It's ninety-three degrees inside," Nick said proudly. "There's no way your grandmother is going to go through with it."

She hoped he was right.

They found Brian and Josie in the yard, eyeing what Riley could only assume was the finished "ramp."

"You've *got* to be kidding me."

Behind her, Nick was muttering a lot of f-words and something about rainforests.

After weeks of work, the two stooges had propped a pair of two-by-sixes side by side over a half-crushed traffic barrel, forming a kind of lopsided teeter-totter that led to the end of the porch where they'd hacked off the railing.

"Figured it was safer on the ground," Brian observed.

Nick jumped to the ground, then turned to chivalrously lift Riley off the porch.

"Knock knock." Weber wandered around from the back parking lot to join them. His only concession to the heat was the rolled-up sleeves of his button-down. "Nice outfit, Miss Cleo," he said.

"I hate my life," Riley muttered.

"Here's something else you'll hate. No video cards were recovered from the Hornbergers'. So if the glitter bomb was recorded, the killer took the evidence with him."

He was right. Riley did hate that. Dead ends sucked.

Brian cleared his throat. "Ladies and gentlemen, I've called you all here tonight to reveal a murder."

Josie gasped theatrically.

"What have you got for us, Brian?" Weber asked.

Brian held out his hand, and Josie produced his laptop from a bag on the back of his wheelchair. "The coroner's report had some interesting notes," he began, firing up the computer.

"Wait. How did *you* get the report? I haven't even seen it yet," Weber demanded.

Brian cracked his knuckles. "It's not my fault county security is garbage. The report is still in draft. But it looks like cause of death was digitalis toxicity."

"Strubinger was poisoned?" Nick asked.

"Technically, yes. Digitalis is a drug used to treat certain heart conditions," Brian lectured.

"So maybe he accidentally took more than he was prescribed," Weber argued.

"Except Titus Strubinger didn't have a prescription for digoxin," Josie pointed out smugly.

"Common garden plants like foxglove and oleander contain chemicals similar to digitalis and are poisonous to humans," Brian continued.

Weber sighed. "So what you're saying is the murder weapon could be growing in anyone's backyard?"

"Essentially. But that's not the most interesting part." Brian's fingers flew across the keyboard, and he turned the screen around to face them. "Four weeks ago, user GunsNAmmoMurica made this comment on a video on Channel 50's YouTube channel."

Riley leaned in. "'I hope you die alone in your mother's basement, and no one cares,'" she read aloud. "Wow. Friendly guy."

"So are you telling me that this GunsNAmmo guy is our killer?" Weber asked.

"Nope," Josie said with a sassy swing of her ponytail.

"Those are the words of our victim," Brian said triumphantly.

"Either this guy predicted his own death, or someone decided to give him a taste of his own medicine," Josie announced.

"Tell me you got this information legally," Weber said, tugging on his tie.

"Everything except the coroner's report, which, by the way, they're holding because they're pissed at you," Brian told Weber cheerfully. "Anyway, you have a copy of my report in your email. Here's a hard copy with screenshots of some of our victim's more creative online insults."

He handed over a thick pack of papers.

Riley peered over Weber's shoulder.

"Guy was a straight-up troll," Josie said.

"With atrocious spelling," Riley observed.

"Seems like he spent a lot of time on Channel 50's social media being a dick," Nick noted.

"Wait. Go back," Riley said, holding a hand to her nose.

Weber paged backward, and she stabbed a finger at one of the screenshots of a news story about a clothing drive for a homeless shelter shared to Channel 50's Facebook page.

"Well, I'll be damned," Weber said.

"RealBarbie: 'I'd rather choke on my La Perla than let my

kids wear hand-me-downs. What kind of pathetic parent can't buy their children brand-name clothing? Ugh. Who are these people, and why are we letting them in our towns and schools? I don't know about you, but I'll be keeping my money and my clothes,'" Riley read.

"She sounds nice," Josie said dryly.

"That's someone who comments on all Bianca Hornberger's content agreeing with everything she said," Riley told her.

Weber crossed his arms and rubbed his chin. "Coincidence?"

"Could be," Riley admitted with a shrug.

"Your nose is twitching," Nick pointed out. "It's no coincidence."

"Two online assholes end up dead in ways they or other followers predicted while insulting others," Brian mused.

"It's pretty fucking poetic," Josie said.

"Just because they were assholes didn't mean they deserved to die," Riley pointed out.

"Weeell..." Brian said, flipping the pages of the report and pointing to another comment.

Weber looked green. "Jesus. On an obituary?"

Riley held up her hands. "I don't want to know. I already had to bleach my brain once today."

"Looks like we're heading to Channel 50 tomorrow," Weber decided.

"You can handle that one by yourself," Riley said.

"Didn't you used to work there?" Josie asked.

Riley attempted to shoot lady daggers out of her eyeballs at Josie. "Yes. And my ex-husband and his perky, practically teenage fiancée still do."

"Then you're the perfect person to accompany me. You'll already know most of the people there and can give me all the pertinent background," Weber said smugly.

"To be clear, you want me to go back to the place that fired me because my husband was having an affair with the weather girl? An affair that everyone but me knew about?"

"Look on the bright side, Riley. Maybe Gentry's the killer, and you'll get to help put him behind bars."

She rolled her eyes. "Griffin wouldn't ruin his manicure by folding laundry. He's not going to asphyxiate a woman and then stuff a thong down her throat."

"Come on. I'll let you play bad cop," Weber said, dangling that little nugget in front of her.

She turned to look at Nick. "Remember that plan from earlier?" she asked.

"Just tell me where your passport is, and I'll pack for you," he promised.

The tinkling of a bell echoed eerily from within the house.

"Shit. I have to go. You guys should definitely stay out here and keep discussing this," Riley said. She scooted around them and headed for the front of the house. Nick caught her at the porch steps. They were alone. Crickets chirped in the dark as he drew her into his chest.

"You're going to be fine, Thorn. It's a thousand degrees in there. As soon as everyone is gathered, no one will last five minutes in that room."

"Keep talking," she said as her heart raced.

He did more than that. His hand skimmed over her stomach to her hip and then her thigh. He reached under her dress and trailed his fingers higher over her leg.

"Gah," she said as her thighs trembled.

"In half an hour, you and I are going skinny-dipping in the river while the house cools off," he predicted.

"Are you seriously heading to third base with a coven of weirdos on the other side of the door?" she whispered.

"I told you I liked your outfit," he said, teasing even higher with his fingers. "Do I want to know why your thong is cold?"

"Don't ask."

"Hey, sweetie."

Riley jumped away from Nick at the sound of her mother's voice.

"Sorry to interrupt your third base. But it's time to start," Blossom said apologetically.

24

Minutes later, Riley found herself seated at the round table with her sister, her grandmother, and her mother, sweating profusely and wondering exactly how her life had come to this. They were bathed in the light of way too many open flames for a summer night with no air-conditioning. Red lights on the video cameras winked, taunting her with the reminder that she was about to embarrass herself not just in front of her family and friends but also her ex-husband's new fiancée and the greater Harrisburg area.

It was ninety-four degrees in the room, yet when Elanora had commanded them all to sit, they followed orders like a bunch of sweaty sheep. No one dared speak up.

The opening remarks had been short and not sweet. Elanora had stoically addressed their dehydrated audience with an explanation of her family's "gifts" and how they used those gifts to serve.

Gabe's pores were so efficient at sweating that a fine mist was rising from his dark skin where he stood in the corner waiting for Elanora to give him an order.

The rest of the audience was a mix of bored journalists and the overly excited public, including her neighbors. Mrs. Penny was drinking a martini in one corner next to Lily, who was fluttering an oversize Spanish lace fan in front of her shiny face. Mr. Willicott sat with his back to the action and facing a wall while Fred kept scooting his chair closer to Elanora.

Bella sat pretty and perky on a chair in the front row and made faces at her cameraman like she was a kindergartner.

Weber stood against the wall, looking relaxed with his arms crossed. But Riley could feel some kind of anxious energy emanating from him. Nick was next to him. The two painted quite the attractive picture in humid candlelight. And one of them was all hers.

Wander nudged her under the table, and Riley realized she'd missed a cue. Her grandmother's talon-like hand was reaching for hers. The feathers in Elanora's hair were long and checkered, swooping backward and nearly tickling Gabe's broad chest.

"Sorry," Riley murmured. She took Wander's and Elanora's hands with her own sweaty palms and pretended she was somewhere else doing anything else in the world. Her forearms were already stuck to the table. She'd probably lose a layer of skin peeling them off.

"Maybe we should reschedule for a cooler evening, Mom?" Blossom suggested. Riley vowed to give her mother the best Christmas and Mother's Day presents.

Relief rippled through the crowd as brows were mopped.

"We will now begin," Elanora announced, ignoring the perfectly reasonable suggestion and closing her eyes. The hope was snuffed out all around them, and the temperature felt like it had risen another five degrees. Riley shot Nick a look.

He shrugged and mouthed, "You've got this."

She did not have this.

She couldn't parade herself in front of cameras and whip out a party trick to make people believe she was a respectable psychic. Hell, regular people didn't know what a respectable psychic was.

The candle flames barely flickered in the thick, still air. The lights in the room seemed to get lower, and a whisper stirred up in the audience. They got brighter and then flicked on and off as Bella gasped audibly.

Elanora opened one judgmental eye.

"Mrs. Penny!" Riley hissed.

The woman shrugged and stepped away from the light switch. "What? I was just adding atmosphere."

"We do not require your atmosphere," Elanora said. "The spirits bring their own. We will now open ourselves to the souls who have passed on." She squeezed Riley's hand in a crushing grip, and Riley reluctantly closed her eyes.

Okay. Fine. What's up, spirit guides? Any chance you could set off the carbon monoxide detectors and get me out of this?

The pastel clouds came into focus in her mind. Unfortunately, it wasn't any cooler in her vision place. The clouds seemed to be pooling and melting like ice cream in thick colorful drips.

"Sorry about the heat, guys," Vision Riley explained to the clouds. "I was really hoping to give you guys a night off."

Her grandmother began to speak somewhere far away.

"There is a man here who has something to say. I'm getting an *H* and an unprecedented amount of body hair."

Vision Riley smirked at the idea of her ornery grandmother "getting an unprecedented amount of body hair." Maybe Elanora would be less terrifying with a nice mustache, she mused.

There was a faraway gasp, and a woman tearfully said the name: "Harold?"

Riley listened as Elanora relayed Harold's lawn fertilizing process to his widow. The woman had probably come in hopes that Harold would express his love from beyond the grave. Instead, he was lecturing her on lawn care. Sometimes it was better not to get the messages from beyond.

"I'm getting a scent of lemons. Very clean," Wander said, her voice rising in the room. "Furniture polish."

"Oh my God. It's Aunt Esther!" someone in the crowd announced.

Great. What the hell was Riley supposed to do? Sit here and hope a dead loved one popped into her head?

Beth.

The name popped into her head, and Riley tensed. The last thing she needed was the spirit of Weber's little sister making her presence known in front of both her big brother and Nick.

"No Beth," Riley instructed her spirit guides. The dripping clouds pulsed once, and Riley realized it wasn't a spirit trying to get through. It was Nick and Weber standing side by side and thinking about the same woman. There was a kind of intensity pumping out of them. A controlled desperation for answers.

Of course she was curious about what had happened to the girl. But neither Nick nor Weber had ever asked her to *look*. And if she were being honest with herself, she didn't want to carry that kind of psychic baggage on her own.

She was overheating. The clouds were getting bigger and brighter, sucking her in and suffocating her. She could feel the heavy dampness on her skin. Fighting off the panic, she tried to close the spiritual garage door on her boyfriend's brain, but she was so disoriented. So hot.

And there was something else in the clouds with her now. Someone else.

With a queasy drop and a hard jolt, Riley found herself back in Bianca Hornberger's closet, staring at a glittery ghost.

"Bianca," Vision Riley gasped.

"Yes, I'd like to speak to your manager," Vision Bianca announced, studying her fingernails for any flaws. She was dressed as she had been in the crime scene photos. There was a plastic bag next to her.

"Excuse me?"

Bianca coughed delicately into her hand. Then, with a barely discernible frown thanks to the fillers, she reached into her mouth. Like a magician yanking flags out of his throat, Bianca produced a very expensive-looking thong. "Ew! This is not okay!" she snapped. "I have a complaint, and I'm not going anywhere until I speak to the manager."

"I don't know if I have a manager," Riley admitted. "Maybe you should talk to my grandmother. She's the scary lady next to me talking about body hair and lawn fertilizer."

"I want a refund," Bianca announced, fluttering her inch-long lashes in what Riley could only assume was a sign of an impending hissy fit.

"A refund for what?"

"For life. *Duh.* It was just starting to get good. I was building my brand. I was expanding my following. I had tickets to the Start Leveling Up Today conference. And now I'm just supposed to accept that it's all over?" she scoffed. "I was this close to getting everything I deserve, and some weird creeper in my closet is going to end it all? I don't think so!"

"Weird creeper. Can you describe him?"

"Ew, no. Not until I get a refund or a do-over or whatever it is you people do around here." Bianca glanced around them at the clouds encircling the closet. "God. Who is your decorator? A glue-sniffing preschooler?"

"How about I get my grandmother, and you can tell her how disappointed you are with your experience?" Riley suggested. She didn't know if that was something she could actually do. And inviting Elanora into her head seemed like it could present its own host of problems. But Riley wasn't equipped to interview a murder victim as a witness.

"Deal with it yourself." Elanora's voice came through like it was on a high school intercom.

Okay. Fine. Thanks, Grandma.

"Uh, okay. So you're unhappy your life got cut short," Riley said, scrambling for a topic that could lead back to the murder.

"I already said that. Now do something about it."

"I don't think I can unmurder someone." She sensed something or someone else in the closet and got up to paw through the hanging clothes.

"Stop touching my club wear, and figure out a way to bring me back. Now!" Bianca demanded.

The presence didn't feel murdery. In fact, it felt just the opposite. Calm, cool, strong. *Familiar.*

"Gabe?" Riley whispered.

Vision Bianca kicked her heels against the carpet and let out a bloodcurdling shriek.

"Ah! God! What the hell?" Riley stuffed her fingers in her ears. "Who's the preschooler now?"

Bianca abruptly stopped her tantrum and frowned. "Why aren't you doing what I want you to do?"

"Because you're acting like an entitled brat. I don't want to do things for entitled brats."

"But...but this *always* works. It's how I got the Porsche even though stupid Teddy complained that it didn't have any room for the kids. It's also how I got the Land Rover for the nanny so she could drive the kids around. *And* it's how I got these." Bianca hefted her unwieldy breasts in her hands.

"I guess it doesn't work in the hereafter," Riley said. "Do you know the person who killed you? Maybe you could haunt him?"

"Why would I waste my time haunting a loser?"

"So you did know him?"

"God! Why are you so obsessed with him?" Bianca demanded, picking at a hair extension and plucking the ends of it. "Oh my God! I'm not going to get to go to Miami for fall break! Death is the worst!"

"Bianca, who did this to you?" Riley decided she was going to demand a medal from Weber. This was going above and beyond for a psychic civilian consultant.

"I don't know. Some guy. He was in my closet when I got home from the tanning salon. No, wait, the lash salon. Whatever. He was just standing there, and I was like, 'Who the hell are you?' and he was like, 'Karma.' And then I was like, 'Karma? That's a stupid name.' And he was like, 'You haven't learned anything.' And then I don't know what happened.

Now I don't get to go to Miami, and I already bought half my outfits."

"Wow. That's a lot to unpack. Aren't you a little old for fall break?"

Bianca screamed shrilly. "Don't say that word!"

"What word? *Break?*"

"*Old!*" The busty ghost clamped her hands over her ears. "I'm never getting old! You can't make me!"

"I don't think you can get old now that you're dead," Riley observed.

That perked up Vision Bianca. "That's true. Maybe this isn't all bad. But I still need to go back. I miss everyone there."

"I'm sure your family misses you too," Riley lied.

"Ugh. Not them. They're so basic. My husband is too busy nerding out over whatever he does for a living. My daughter loves carbs—can you imagine? And my son is okay. But the older he gets, the older he makes me look. I miss my *followers.*" Her hair toss stirred a breeze in the vision closet.

Riley was sweating all the liquid out of her body into a puddle on the closet carpet.

"You want to come back to life because you miss your followers?"

"They're the ones who get me. They pay attention to me. They ask me about my makeup and clothes. We're like family."

"I thought you bought most of your followers and they were fake accounts."

"Well, yeah, but *other* people don't know that. Besides, my fake followers were real where it counts. Flattering me in the comment section."

"Did you know Titus Strubinger?"

"Gross. That's a terrible name. No. I don't or didn't or whatever."

"What about GunsNAmmoMurica?"

Bianca shrugged her slim shoulders. Only one of her breasts rose. "You're boring me."

"Okay. How about RealBarbie?"

"Uh, duh. That's me."

"You're RealBarbie?" Riley clarified.

"Are you stupid, or does being so unattractive make you hard of hearing?"

"You created fake profiles on YouTube and Facebook just to comment on all your own stuff."

"Oh. Em. Gee. You're so boring. It's called *social proof.* Look it up."

"I know what social proof is," Riley said. She felt oddly woozy and hoped she wasn't going to die in the closet with the ghost of an idiot.

"Then you should know that it's important to set up your own fake accounts so you can leave the kinds of reactions you want from other followers. You're grooming your audience to give you the right kind of attention, stupid."

"You had entire conversations in the comment sections with yourself?"

"Who else is going to be as interesting?"

Dear God. Riley needed a gallon of water, a cold shower, and a new identity. "Did you also use the same username on Channel 50's website?" she pressed.

"Sometimes. It depends on who I was logged in as."

"You left some really mean comments," Riley pointed out.

"I can't help that I was born a lion and everyone else was born sheep." Vision Bianca was back to examining her nails. "God, I hope this death place has good salons. I need a lash refill, like, yesterday."

"So this guy who was waiting for you in your closet. He knew you, but you didn't know him?"

"Why do you keep harping on him?"

"Oh, I don't know. Maybe to stop him from killing other people?"

Bianca snorted. "What do I care if he kills someone else? I'm already dead."

Riley was exhausted, and a headache was interfering with her concentration. She had one last Hail Mary to try. "Well,

I hope you were at least killed by a good-looking murderer. There's nothing worse than being murdered by an ugly guy."

"Oh my God. You're right. It goes totally against my brand that I was unfairly killed by an uggo. Like, I would never have dated him. I'd be as tall as him in my six-inch heels. And his face. Ick! He just had a regular boring face. There was literally nothing interesting about him."

"Was he white? Did he have any tattoos? Did he tell you his name?"

"He was white. But not a tan white. Like poor person white."

"What's poor person white?"

"Someone who doesn't have a pool or take vacations," Bianca said as if it were obvious.

"How old was he?"

"I don't know. And you're boring me."

Riley felt like her energy was evaporating out of her. There was a weird faraway noise like a distant crowd muttering.

She felt a hard tug, and then she was being catapulted backward.

"Hey! Where are you going? Bring me back a Starbucks!" Bianca called.

"Thorn. Baby, come on. Wake up."

"Nick?" she croaked.

"That's a good girl. Open those beautiful brown eyes for me."

With great effort, Riley pried one eyelid up and then the other. Nick's handsome face came into focus.

"There's my girl. Where did you go?"

"Where are we?" she rasped, trying to look around.

"On the floor in the parlor."

"Please tell me the cameras aren't rolling."

His dimples nearly blinded her. "No cameras. About a minute into the show, both cameras overheated. Then you and Gabe fainted. Your grandmother called it a night."

She tried to sit up, but Nick pressed her back down, and

she realized she was cradled in his lap. It was nice. She managed to turn her head to see Wander and Lily plying the prone Gabe with water and damp towels for his forehead.

As if sensing her attention, Gabe turned his head in Wander's lap and smiled at Riley.

"You okay, Gabe?" she asked.

"I am wonderful," he said with a happy sigh.

Riley made a note to talk to Gabe about how he ended up in the closet with her and Bianca the Boobed.

"You had me worried, Thorn," Nick said, drawing her attention. "I thought you got psychically kidnapped or something." He brushed her hair away from her face.

"I was kind of held hostage by a moron."

"Oh good. She's awake." Riley's mother came into her line of sight. "Here, sweetie. I brought you some water."

"Thanks, Mom."

"I'm sorry for making you do this, Riley," Blossom said. "If it's any consolation, your grandmother was not humiliated."

Not humiliated. It was a gold star and a thumbs-up.

"It's fine." Riley drained the glass, spilling half of it on herself. "And she should be impressed. I interviewed a vapid murder victim." She winced and looked up at Nick. "I realize how weird that sounds, and if it's too much, I don't blame you for running off to Costa Rica by yourself."

"Never a dull moment with you, Thorn. Why would I want to walk away from that adventure?" he said, rewarding her with dimples.

She managed a weak smile before rolling over to barf under the table.

"Baby." He sighed, holding her hair back.

"I need a shower, a sports drink, and a conversation with Weber."

25

C hannel 50's broadcast studio was housed in an unattractive building on Sixth Street in Harrisburg near the rumbling railroad tracks. Riley winced as memories of her years there punched her in the face when Weber pulled his cruiser into the rear parking lot next to the dumpster.

She was still feeling raw and wobbly over the whole conversation-with-a-corpse thing and sweating out three pounds of water weight.

Being forced to literally walk back into her past less than twelve hours later seemed like lemon juice on top of a dozen paper cuts.

"Come on, Cleo," Weber said, looking annoyingly handsome and confident behind his aviators. "You'll be fine."

"I am not accepting that nickname," she groused, getting out of the car.

The humidity blasted her as soon as her shoes hit the asphalt.

She'd taken a little—okay, a lot—of extra care with her appearance today. Not because she was trying to impress anyone named Griffin "Stupidface" Gentry but because she'd left these offices humiliated. This was an opportunity to give them a different last memory of her.

Weber led the way around the building to the front door, where the frigid air-conditioning met them like a French kiss from a polar bear.

The waiting room was a vanilla box with one plate-glass window emblazoned with Channel 50's logo. Life-size cutouts of the morning and evening news anchors formed a creepy wall of talent. She shuddered when she spotted Griffin's, which had obviously been blown up larger than life-size since it was over six feet tall and had regular-size feet. Less than half of the dozen chairs scattered around the room's perimeter were occupied.

"I really need this job." The thought seemed to be coming from a thirtysomething white brunette in a cheap suit. She was jiggling her foot so hard her shoe fell off.

"Man, this place is depressing." This from the Asian woman two chairs down in the gauzy summer blouse. "I'd need a lot of alcohol in my life to walk through this door every day. Maybe I should fake a family emergency?"

There was another person tucked into the corner holding up a newspaper. Purple hair peeked over the masthead.

Weber badged the guy at the front desk, and less than a minute later, an overly eager staffer named Hudson appeared to lead them directly to the studio.

They arrived in time to see morning news anchor Griffin Gentry chortling with an area chef over crepes in the kitchen studio.

The set was looking a little dated, but the studio beyond it was downright decrepit. Paint peeled off the walls. The cleaner-resistant mold still dotted the baseboards above the concrete floor. Cables snaked between cameras and sound equipment held together with duct tape. Camera two now had two fans on it to keep it from overheating.

It looked like the years had not been kind to Channel 50, Riley noted.

"And we're out," a member of the crew yelled.

"I appreciate this opportunity," the chef said, beaming at Griffin. "This means so much to my restaurant."

"Yeah, whatever. Makeup! I need more bronzer," Griffin bellowed, losing his boyish for-the-cameras grin. He hopped down from his box and made a beeline for the makeup artist.

Weber hid a laugh with a cough. "Was he—"

Riley nodded. "Oh yeah. He does all his interviews on a booster box."

"He looks like an overgrown preschooler who got in his mother's spray tanner," Weber observed.

"Don't I know it. Come on. The news director is over there," she said, pointing to a man in a rumpled short-sleeved plaid shirt that was two sizes too big. His khakis hadn't seen the hot side of an iron in at least a month. "His name is Chris Yang. He's been with Channel 50 for at least ten years. If anyone on the staff is getting threats, he'll know."

They picked their way around camera equipment and fraying cords to where Chris paced with a coffee in hand and a phone to his ear.

"I don't care if she's hungover. Put some eye drops in her and get her to fucking smile on camera for sixty seconds," he said before disconnecting.

"Chris Yang?" Weber asked.

"Yeah. One sec." Chris held up a finger and called up an app on his phone to record a note. "Remind me to look into local rehab clinics. Also remind me to stop hiring twenty-two-year-old country club girls who serve Malcolm Gentry cocktails." Memo recorded, he stowed his phone in the cargo pocket of his khakis. "We're in the middle of a show. You can sign up for a tour at the front desk."

Weber produced his badge. "I'm Detective Weber with homicide. I have a few questions for you."

Chris's eyes bulged, and his breath expelled in a nervous laugh. "Me? Ha. Questions from a homicide detective? Come on. This is some joke, right? Did Clarence in advertising put you up to this?"

"Two dead bodies are no joke," Weber said sternly.

"Well, shit. Yeah. Sure. Am I a suspect? Wait, you wouldn't

tell me if I was. Listen, I've got fifteen more minutes of the morning show. You mind hanging out in the sound booth?"

"That's fine," Weber said.

"Holy shit." Chris's gaze finally landed on Riley. "I know you!"

They'd interacted on an almost daily basis when she'd been a lowly copywriter here. He damn well better know her.

"Hey, Chris," Riley said in what she hoped was a cool, professional tone.

"I didn't recognize you since you're not dyed blue and bleeding from a bullet wound."

Oh, right. The fountain shooting. The news crew had shown up within minutes of the gunfight and Mrs. Penny's attempt at vehicular manslaughter. Well, it was better than being known as Griffin's pathetic ex-wife, she supposed.

"Are you finally here for an interview?" Chris snatched the clipboard away from the hovering production assistant and glared at it. "I swear to Christ if they tried to sneak this into the shooting schedule without talking to me—"

"Riley's here in an official capacity," Weber explained.

"Back from break in thirty," someone warned.

Griffin dragged himself away from a bronzer brush and plopped down at the news desk.

"Nice of you to join us," Valerie, the co-anchor, said dryly.

Griffin scrunched up his face. "Nice of you to join us," he mimicked.

Riley noticed his foundation cracking in several places and the satisfied look Valerie flashed the camera.

"You're working with the cops?" Chris demanded, ushering them toward the sound booth. "Is this a big case? Does that mean the department is employing psychics? Do you have time for an on-camera?"

"Live in ten…nine…"

He didn't wait for an answer before shoving them both inside the sound studio and shutting the door.

There were fewer people manning the booth than when

she'd worked here. The equipment was the same and looking a lot worse for wear. Buttons were broken. Bulbs hadn't been replaced. The sound engineer was balanced on three wheels of a chair because the fourth was missing.

The news business was significantly less glamorous than TV and movies made it look. It was just one of adulthood's many disappointments.

Riley tucked herself into the corner and tried to stay out of the way.

"Welcome back, Harrisburg! We'll leave you with one last look at the weather," Valerie said cheerfully on camera.

If I have to work here for one more year, I am going to throw myself off a bridge.

Riley jumped at the stray thought, and then another one swooped through her head.

It'll all be over soon.

I'd like to headbutt that Gentry weasel right in the face.

Riley had wanted to shut her spiritual garage doors for the day so she could recuperate in peace, but the whole point of her being a psychic civilian consultant was the psychic thing.

Glancing around, she couldn't figure out who she'd intercepted the thoughts from. It was like an invisible cloak of depression clung to the entire studio staff.

She grunted and watched Griffin Gentry pretend to become a real boy on camera.

"Let's head over to our beautiful weather girl, Bella Goodshine," Griffin said, flashing his unnaturally white teeth at the camera. "Bella, what have you got for us today?"

The cameras cut to Bella dressed in another low-cut pink blouse. Her thick blond hair was styled in curls the size of sausage links. "Well, handsome, I've got *heart eyes* for you today!" Bella chirped, making a heart with her fingers and holding them up to her face. "And a chance of severe thunderstorms with possible hail damage!"

Valerie mimed vomiting under the desk. Riley decided she liked her immensely.

"That's all for today. Have a great Monday, Harrisburg," Valerie said to the camera.

"From our family to yours, have a Channel 50 day," Griffin said, throwing his trademark wink and salute at the camera.

"Go fuck yourself."

That last thought sounded like it came from several minds at the same time.

"And we're out," someone on the floor announced.

Chris opened the door with a loud creak and waved them out.

They followed him through a set of metal doors down a windowless corridor past the restrooms.

The corridor opened up into a dingy room of cubicles where sales, advertising, and a handful of copywriters claimed space. It looked as though the room had barely survived some kind of roof leak. Several ceiling tiles were missing, and the ones that remained were stained a dirty brown.

Chris jiggled the handle on a door in the corner and gave it a kick to open it.

"Welcome to my humble abode," he said.

Technically it was a corner office, but the only appealing feature of the block-walled windowless room was that it was far enough downwind from the restrooms that it didn't smell like sewage from the problematic plumbing.

Chris sat behind a desk that was covered in papers, bobble-heads, and enough family photos it seemed as though he was worried about forgetting what his wife and kids looked like.

"Have a seat," he said, gesturing at the two vinyl chairs across from him.

They sat and Weber produced two photos. "Do you know Bianca Hornberger or Titus Strubinger?" he asked, handing over the pictures.

Chris held them up side by side and frowned. "Hornberger's the corpse in the closet, right?"

"That's correct," Weber said.

Riley wasn't surprised. Chris had made local news his life.

He could recite the names of every murder victim in the city for the last twenty years.

"This guy isn't ringing a bell. Sure looks like the cheerful sort."

Riley peeked at the photo. Strubinger was dressed in camo pants and a DON'T TREAD ON ME T-shirt decorated with a myriad of stains. He had a bushy beard, unruly hair, and a scowl.

"He dead too?" Chris asked.

Weber nodded. "Both victims appear to have been active on Channel 50's website and social media accounts."

"Active how?"

"They were both vocal on articles and posts with these usernames," Weber said, sliding another piece of paper across the desk. "Both express aggressive points of view."

"'You're a horrible mother for allowing your child to attend public school. What did you think was going to happen? Of course he was going to choke on the subpar lunch in the cafeteria. I hope you choke and die on your next meal,'" Chris read out loud. "Yeah, that sounds about right for our comments."

"That was Bianca Hornberger on an article about a student saving another student's life with the Heimlich maneuver," Weber said.

Chris moved on to the next. "'The United States of 'Merica wasn't founded to cater to women. It was built for and by white men. It's time we remember our heritage and remind the rest that they are here to serve.'" He chuckled. "This guy sounds like he's the type who lives in his mother's basement."

"Where were you on the night of August second?" Weber asked.

Chris's eyebrows scaled his forehead. "Oh, shit. He really did live with his mom? I swear I didn't know that because I murdered him. You just get a feel for the kind of people—and I use that term loosely—who think their opinions are required on everything that happens in the world."

"Where were you on the night of August second?" Weber repeated.

Chris dropped the photos as if they were scorpions and dug out a planner.

"Looks like I was here in the editing room until about six. I headed out to my son's soccer scrimmage. Grabbed some Popeyes in the drive-thru on my way back here to shoot some promos until ten. Then I went home, drank two beers, and fell asleep on the couch with my wife watching *Outlander*."

Weber didn't say anything. And sweat broke out on Chris's forehead.

"How about during the day on August seventh?" Riley probed, getting in on the fun.

She sensed Weber's approval.

"I was here. I'm always here," Chris said, gesturing around him at the general chaos. "I would have been in the studio from five a.m. to ten a.m. Then it was a normal workday until about six p.m."

"Okay," Weber said.

"Okay 'I believe you' okay, or okay 'I'm getting an arrest warrant'?" Chris asked.

"Okay, your alibis can easily be verified," Weber said. "Moving on. Have any of your staff received any threats recently?"

Chris opened his hands. "We're the news, man. Everyone hates us." He gestured at the printout of comments. "We get this shit all day, every day. Give someone even the pretense of anonymity, and they turn into a horrible human being. I wouldn't be surprised if my nana was online threatening the pope."

"What about strange packages in the mail?" Riley asked.

Chris laughed. "Strange how?" He pointed at her. "You know how it is. You worked here. Griffin gets at least two pairs of underwear a week from stalkers with no taste. Bella gets marriage proposals and jewelry and free clothes from her admiring fans. We had two suspicious boxes that we had to call the cops on in the last month alone. One ended up being a damaged shipment of dry shampoo for makeup. The other, some yahoo bagged up baking soda and mailed it in with a note claiming we'd just been 'poisoned by Amtrak.'"

This time when Chris laughed, it was the sound of a man who had gotten used to being close to the edge.

"But no gag packages?" Riley pressed, wondering just what had happened at Channel 50 since she'd left to make things even worse.

"What kind of gag packages? Like those bags of gummy candy shaped like dicks?" he asked.

"That's need-to-know," Weber told him. "We'd like to talk to some of your staff. Any of them who have been the target of online threats. Anyone who deals with your online accounts."

Chris glanced down at his clipboard, then tossed it over his shoulder. "Sure. Why not? Who needs to stick to a schedule? Fuck." He picked up his desk phone. "Hudson, can you make a coffee run? You guys want anything?"

———

Riley: Just wanted to take this opportunity to thank you for hiring me so I don't have to work in moldy, soul-sucking hellholes anymore.
Nick: Going well, huh?
Riley: I feel my soul dying from proximity.
Nick: I'll breathe some life into your "soul" later. And by "soul" I mean your pants. Heading out to check on a cabin Rupley's second cousin has upriver.
Riley: My pants and I look forward to it. Think you'll find Rupley there?
Nick: Nope. But I'm taking your Jeep so Uncle Jimmy can smell the fish air.

26

"Cold brew with cream?"

Riley accepted the to-go cup from the skinny, gawky Hudson. He was somewhere between hipster and nerd with oversize glasses, tight pants, and visible socks.

"Thanks," she said.

"No problem. All part of the job," he said chipperly before bebopping out the door of the conference room.

Ahhhh, to be young and naive again, she thought.

"This is Chance Banks, one of Channel 50's attorneys," Chris said, introducing a middle-aged white guy with silver wings at his temples and a two-thousand-dollar suit. "He'll be sitting in on the interviews."

Chance Banks smelled like money and too much expensive cologne. But Riley didn't mind since it helped cover the musty mystery odor emanating from the carpet.

Her nose twitched, and she saw herself during psychic boot camp, Burt bounding through the tall grass, the sweet stench of rotting roadkill and garbage wafting through the air.

And then she was back in the conference room with frayed carpet and duct-taped chairs.

"First up is Valerie Edmonds, morning show anchor," Chris said.

Valerie swept into the room in gym clothes, her face now makeup-free, her dark hair pulled back in a low ponytail. She didn't know either victim and never read online comments, which Riley felt was a healthy rule to have.

"Look, I'm a Black woman on the morning news who takes herself seriously and doesn't dress like a sex doll. Of course I get threats," she said.

"Most of them are misspelled and max out at around fifth grade grammar," Chris added. "Any threats our team deems as serious, we pass on to the local authorities."

"How many threats do you pass on?" Riley asked.

Chris squinted at the ceiling. "Not a ton. Maybe only eight or nine a week."

"Has anything ever come out of the investigations into the threats?" Weber asked.

"You tell me. From where I sit, it looks like the only thing that gets any action are statements that get passed on to the Secret Service. If you're a regular person talking shit about another regular person, you can say just about anything you want online without repercussions until someone gets a lawyer involved."

"It's not hard to figure out who these people are and where they live," Chance pointed out. "But most of the individuals misbehaving online don't have anything worth suing over. It usually comes down to whether it's worth pursuing legal action."

Well, that was depressing.

Weber ran through a few more standard questions before excusing Valerie.

"Next up is Armand Papadakis," Chris said, consulting his clipboard.

Riley remembered Armand from her days at Channel 50. He was the mail room supervisor who always had a smile on his face and a pack of Twizzlers in his shirt pocket.

But the man who stomped into the room with a plunger in one hand was not smiling.

"This better be a surprise birthday party with cake," he said.

"We don't do staff birthday parties anymore because of budget cuts," Chris reminded him. "Happy birthday."

Armand slapped the plunger down on the table, making a gross slurping noise. "Then what the hell is more important than a blocked-up toilet?"

"Aren't you the mail room supervisor?" Riley asked.

"Yes. And then I also became the head custodian and the person in charge of ordering garbage for the vending machines in the break room." He sat down next to the plunger.

"There have been some budget cuts around here," Chris explained. "We've all had to make adjustments."

"That is a dirty lie. Weasel Face and that high-pressure system he's marrying got big fat raises. The rest of us got screwed."

Chris pulled a bottle of Pepto Bismol out of his cargo pants and guzzled it.

"Now I mop up dog piss after the adoption segments and watch people turn into Russian spy robots online," Armand continued.

"He means bots," Chris cut in.

Armand was on a roll now. "You know the guy at the front desk? He answers the phones, writes copy for the six o'clock news, and styles hair for *Wake Up Harrisburg*. He bartends on the weekends just to afford his rent."

"What happened around here?" Riley asked.

"Griffin Gentry had his daddy negotiate a sweet contract extension that cost us ten full-time jobs and our entire maintenance budget," Chris explained.

"Things are falling apart so quickly in this building that one of these days, the entire place is going to collapse in on itself. And when it does, I'm going to set whatever's left on fire," Armand announced.

"I'd advise you both not to discuss the station's financial situation or any future arson plans with law enforcement," the attorney said without looking up from his game of *Candy Crush*.

Armand suddenly looked guilty. "If this is about who took a poop in Mr. Gentry's convertible, I want a lawyer," he announced.

"It's about murder, not poop. And there is a lawyer," Chris pointed out.

"Mr. Papadakis," Weber began, trying to wrestle back control of the conversation. "Are you aware of any strange packages being delivered to the studio?"

"I took a pay cut to scrub urinals, sort mail, and monitor the Book Face and small blue bird accounts. Now you want me to guess what's inside every package that gets delivered?" Armand was rightfully outraged.

"He means Twitter," Chris added helpfully.

"Mr. Papadakis, if anyone at the station receives a prank package, we need to know about it," Weber said, sliding a business card across the table.

Armand glared at the card. "I'll add it to my list of responsibilities. Now if you'll excuse me, I have urinal cakes to replace."

"Who's next?" Weber asked.

"Hi!" a breathy voice chirped.

"Kill me now," Riley muttered under her breath as Bella minced into the room on five-inch stilettos that probably cost more than two months' worth of Armand's salary.

"Bella, have a seat. These nice people have a few questions for you," Chris said as though he were addressing a preschooler.

Instead of sitting, Bella pranced around the table and hugged Weber. "I remember *you* from the séance last night. You looked *so* broody!" She booped him on the nose, and Riley choked on her cold brew. Bella turned to Riley and held out her arms. "Hi! I'm Bella."

"Seriously?"

"Oh, for fuck's sake," Chris muttered, covering his eyes.

"Ms. Goodshine, I believe you've already met Riley Thorn," Weber said.

"A few times," Riley muttered.

"Ms. Thorn, why don't you go follow up on that thing,"

Weber said, nodding pointedly toward the door. "Away from here."

Message received. "Yeah. Sure. I can do that." She avoided Bella's huggy arms and hurried from the room.

She made it all the way to the ladies' restroom before she let out the screech of frustration that had been building in her throat. She landed a kick to the trash can under the sink. It was already dented, and it made her wonder how many employees came in here just to kick out their own frustrations.

Her phone rang. It was Jasmine.

"Tell me we're day drinking today," her best friend demanded with no preamble.

"I thought I was supposed to be the psychic, but you just read my mind," Riley said.

"Look at you, making psychic jokes."

Riley eyed the abused trash can. "Yeah. Good for me. Why do *you* need prenoon alcohol?"

"I just eviscerated a *disgusting excuse for a grandson* in court."

Based on the way she shouted part of the sentence, Riley guessed her friend was leaving the courthouse at the same time as the opposing party.

"Nice. Maybe consider not smashing up his car, okay?" When Griffin had won his civil suit against Riley for breaking his nose with their wedding photo upon walking in on him and a naked Bella Goodshine, Jasmine had left the courthouse and driven right into Griffin's car, which was parked in a handicapped space.

"That's why we're day drinking. So you can prevent me from smashing up his *stupid face!* When can you get to my place? I'll start the margaritas."

"I'm at Channel 50 right now."

There was a beat of ominous silence. "Why in the name of tequila are you there? Wait! Is Griffin dead?"

"No. At least not yet. I'm here on official police business."

"Well, wrap it up and get your ass over here. We're having a Rasmine day drinking extravaganza so we can forget about people being *selfish, tiny-dicked assholes!*"

Riley disconnected and decided she felt good enough to rejoin the interviews. At least until she made it into the hallway.

"Well, well, well. If it isn't my ex-wife."

Riley turned slowly and found Griffin giving her a lecherous once-over.

"What do you want, Griffin?" she asked warily.

"Did her boobs get bigger?"

Gross. Her ex-husband was openly admiring her breasts. She suddenly wanted to get Armand a birthday cake for pooping in his car.

"Stop staring at my boobs."

He held up his hands. "I'm a soon-to-be-married man."

"You were a married man when you did a lot more than stare at Bella's ta-tas."

"Riley, I explained it all. I'm a man. Men are visual creatures. We see an attractive woman, and there's no point in fighting centuries of DNA. You just need to accept it."

"Not all men are like that, you unevolved amoeba."

He scoffed. "Of course we are. Anyone who says different just hasn't been caught yet."

"You're an ass."

"Speaking of asses, yours looks great in those pants. Have you been doing squats?"

"My boobs and my ass and everything in between are no longer a concern of yours. Unless you want my boyfriend to punch you in the face on camera again."

Griffin pouted. "I'm giving you a compliment. Why can't women accept a heartfelt compliment anymore? In this day and age, I'd like to see someone more oppressed than a—"

"Finish that sentence, and I'll make sure you regret it."

"Look. There's no reason we have to be at war. You're happy. I'm happy. We don't have to be enemies."

"You want to be *friends*?" Riley nearly choked on the word.

He threw back his head and laughed. "Ah, silly girl. No. Unless you're talking about friends with benefits."

She crossed her arms to keep herself from slapping him across his stupid face. "Friends with benefits?" she repeated.

"Just because our marriage didn't work out doesn't mean we can't have an arrangement." He danced his dainty fingers up her arm to her shoulder.

The thoughts of simpletons always came through loud and clear.

Griffin was imagining her naked.

Riley took his hand in hers and flashed a fake smile. He took it as a good sign and stepped closer, wetting his lips.

"Griffin?" Riley said sweetly.

"Yes?"

"If you ever touch me again, I'll rip your fingers off and stuff them so far up your nose, you'll need a surgeon to remove them."

He recoiled. "There's no need for threats. Not when I was making a generous offer."

"My ex-husband who cheated on me with a mutual coworker, then got me fired and sued me for justifiably breaking his nose, offered to have an affair with me," Riley said loudly enough that several heads in the cubicle farm turned in their direction. "That's not a generous offer."

Griffin was so used to attention and getting away with things that he didn't bother trying to shush her.

"Oh, come on, Riley. We were good together. Don't you remember? I remember. I miss it. I miss us. Well, not being married to you. That was terrible. You really had some unreasonable expectations." He laughed. "But I miss that thing you used to do with your tongue—"

She didn't slap him. But she did grab him by the necktie and drag him closer.

"I find your aggression attractive," he croaked. "Pull harder."

"Listen closely, you no-talent, couldn't-deliver-an-orgasm-if-your-life-depended-on-it turd waffle. If you *ever* talk to me that way again, I will scamper on over to your bubbly bride-to-be and tell her everything. Then I'll help her hire a lawyer to ruin your life."

"Hi, sweetie!"

"Bella, baby!" Griffin rasped, extricating himself from Riley's grip. His face was bright red. "How long have you been standing there?"

Bella's foot-long lashes batted hard enough to stir up a breeze in the hallway. "I have no idea," she giggled. "How long have *you* been standing here?"

Riley suddenly needed to be literally anywhere else in the world. She physically could not survive sharing the same space with these two.

"Mr. Gentry," Weber said, appearing in the door. "We'd like a few minutes of your time." He glanced in Riley's direction, then shook his head. *"Go away, Thorn. I don't have time for another murder."*

"I'll wait in the lobby," she said and stormed off.

She entered the lobby under a full head of steam and stopped in her tracks.

"Mrs. Penny?"

The newspaper flapped back up to cover her neighbor's face.

"I can see you behind the sports section," Riley said dryly.

Reluctantly, Mrs. Penny dropped the paper. "How'd you know it was me?"

"Because I saw your purple hair. And your face. What are you doing here?"

"Who? Me?" The woman pointed at herself.

"Yes, you. And why are you dressed in a suit?"

Mrs. Penny was wearing a pin-striped pantsuit with thick shoulder pads and brass buttons on the double-breasted jacket. Her orthopedic shoes were patent leather.

"Maybe I'm applying for a job," the woman sniffed.

Riley's nose twitched. "Or maybe you're following me."

"No fair using your Jedi mind tricks on me!"

"Do you two mind taking this outside?" the guy at the

231

front desk hissed, covering the mouthpiece of the desk phone. Riley could hear someone on the other end yelling.

"Sure. Sorry. Let's go, Stabby McGee."

Mrs. Penny hefted herself out of the chair and hobbled out the door behind Riley.

"How long have you been following me, and why?"

Mrs. Penny nudged the soggy remains of a sandwich with her cane and pouted. "I want credit for all the times I've followed you and didn't get busted. It's not fair surveilling a psychic."

It hit Riley then. "Nick hired you to follow me."

"Don't get your granny panties in a twist. The guy's just being a little overprotective since the whole shooting thing." Her neighbor hooked the bread crust with her cane and tossed it into the street. A pair of fat pigeons descended on the sandwich.

"You've been following me since Mayor Flemming?" Riley shrieked.

The startled pigeons flew away in a cloud of feathers and poop.

"Maybe," the old woman said stubbornly. "It's not the only thing I've been doing. Nick's no dummy. No one looks at the old lady feeding the birds. He used me on a couple of surveillance gigs. I only follow you around when Santiago's not with you."

A few brave pigeons returned to the sandwich.

Riley rubbed her temples. "Is this how he knew I was in the middle of a mob scene at the coffee shop?"

"Well, that and he's been tracking your phone."

"He's been *what?*" This time, the pigeons didn't bother flying away.

"What? Lots of people do it. My grandson's parents track his to make sure he's not skipping school and smoking doobies behind the Hot Topic anymore."

"Yeah, because he's a minor and they're his parents," Riley shouted. "I'm a grown woman, and my boyfriend is stalking me."

"He prefers to think of it as protecting you. Stalking carries some hefty fines and possible jail time," Mrs. Penny explained.

"So you do what? Follow me around and report back to him?"

She shrugged, watching a pigeon fight break out over a piece of old cheese. "Pretty much. Gotta say, for a young gal who looks the way you do and has the whole psychic thing going for her, your life is pretty boring."

Riley was offended. "Excuse me! I got shot and caught several bad guys this summer. That's not boring."

Mrs. Penny held up her hands. "I'm only saying. You land yourself a guy like Nicky Santiago, and you eat early-bird dinner with a bunch of senior citizens every night. You two are acting like the old people in the house."

Riley grabbed her neighbor by the synthetic lapels. "Is he bored? Has he said he's bored? Does he want more excitement?"

Mrs. Penny pushed her hands away. "Relax, cray-cray. I'm saying you both act like old fogies. Hell, if I were five years younger and had the joint mobility of my thirties and a guy like Santiago? I'd be installing a sex swing in the living room. If you catch my drift."

Mrs. Penny's drift was not subtle.

"Ew."

"Youth is wasted on the stupid. So where we going next?"

"*We* are going nowhere. *You* are going home."

Mrs. Penny looked at her watch. "No can do. The boss man paid me for four hours today. And now that you know about me, I can ride with you."

"I am not happy about this."

"I'll be sure to note that in my report."

"Wait here," Riley told Mrs. Penny when they returned to the uneven air-conditioning of the lobby. She headed back into the bowels of the building and stepped into the first empty office she found. She dialed the front desk. "Excuse me," Riley said. "The older woman in the lobby seems a little...off. I'm worried that she might be diabetic or maybe confused. She said she's interviewing for a job, but she's in her eighties and keeps muttering to herself."

"Thanks for the information. She probably just wandered away from Golden Years Day Care down the block," the receptionist said. "I'll call the authorities."

"Great! Thanks," Riley said and hung up.

"What was that about?" Weber asked when she stepped back into the hallway.

"Oh, just taking care of some old business," Riley said.

27

J asmine Patel lived in a swanky two-bedroom condo with kick-ass views of the city and a rooftop garden.

Jasmine was waiting on the sidewalk with a blender pitcher of margaritas when Weber pulled his cruiser up to the curb.

"That counts as an open container, Ms. Patel," he said when Riley exited the vehicle.

"So arrest me, Detective," Jasmine shot back.

"Don't tempt me."

She sent him a look that would have incinerated a lesser man but only resulted in a cocky grin from the cop.

"Bye," Jasmine snapped.

Weber threw them both a snappy little salute before accelerating away from the curb.

"Show-off," Jasmine muttered under her breath before turning to Riley. She wiggled the blender. "How did it go?"

"We basically wasted an entire morning interviewing people who know nothing about anything and reopening several of my emotional scars."

"Then let's show this tequila who the bad bitches are."

Jasmine's fourth floor condo was modern yet feminine. The floor-to-ceiling windows delivered a damn good view of downtown Harrisburg, flooding the concrete floors with sunlight. Two white couches with deep cushions and a dozen colorful throw pillows faced each other in front of the short horizontal gas fireplace.

"How does someone with such good taste in interior design keep picking such terrible guys to date?" Riley wondered.

Jasmine handed her a large mason jar with a metal straw. The jar was filled to the brim with margarita mix.

"It's the Patel women's curse."

"But your dad is awesome," Riley pointed out, taking a hefty gulp and letting the icy alcohol soothe her tight throat.

"All Basil-Thorn women are psychic. And all Patel women have to get several horrible men out of their systems before they find the one."

"How many more do you think you have to go through before your system's reset?" Riley teased.

Jasmine stuck out her tongue and flopped down on one of the couches. "At least a half dozen more. Sticks Strubinger introduced me to her band's bass player, and we have a date to go to the drag races next weekend. I can already tell it's going to end horribly." She blew out a breath that puffed her silky black bangs straight up. The hair fell back into uniform perfection across her brow.

"How do you do that?" Riley took her preferred spot on the opposite couch, kicking off her shoes and digging her toes into the thick, fluffy rug.

"Do what?"

"How does your hair just magically fall back into place like that? Is it some kind of secret product? Is it an Indian thing? Or are you just ridiculously gifted at grooming?"

Jasmine's eyes widened over her jar of margarita. "Oooh! Let's do a hair makeover on you!"

Riley groaned. "Why can't I just have naturally great hair that does what it's supposed to? Why does it have to be an eighteen-step process to get it to look okay for public consumption?"

"Girl, no one has naturally great hair. No one can roll out of bed, run a brush through it, and look selfie-worthy. Everyone needs to make an effort. It's not just you."

Riley plucked at a strand of what she'd always considered to be "meh" brown hair and thought about Bella's sixty pounds of extensions.

"Do you think I'd look good with blond extensions?"

"No. But some glossy chestnut highlights and some fake lashes would be the bomb."

"How many pitchers did you have before I got here?" Riley wondered.

"Only one. Come on. Let's go see the magic I can work."

Some women collected T-shirts with hilarious sayings. Some collected shoes or bags or recipes on Pinterest that they'd never actually make.

Jasmine collected beauty products.

"Every time I come in here, I feel like I'm walking into an Ulta," Riley said, peeking into a vanity drawer in the white marble bathroom and finding a few dozen eye shadow palettes.

"First things first," Jasmine said, all business now. "What look are we going for?"

Riley thought about it while slurping down margarita. Her best friend liked to theme her makeovers with oddly specific visions. "Bella Goodshine just reintroduced herself to me for the second time in twelve hours because she didn't recognize me from that time I caught her having sex with my stupid husband and broke his nose with our wedding portrait. And then I found out that my hot PI boyfriend has been tracking my phone and having me followed."

Jasmine puckered her lips. "So unforgettable badass bombshell babes out to surgically remove his balls?"

That sounded good.

"Griffin Gentry is a pig, and you keep puckering wrong," Jasmine insisted, squishing Riley's cheeks between her fingers so she could dust blush or bronzer or something over her cheeks. Even drunk, her friend's makeup application was perfection.

"How am I puckering wrong?"

"You're trying to do a closed-mouthed duck lip. You need an open-mouth duck lip to show off the hollows of your cheeks."

"Are all women born knowing this?" Riley asked, closing one eye to see her reflection more clearly and practicing the open- and closed-mouthed duck lips.

"Why do you keep thinking there's some kind of natural aptitude surrounding hair and cosmetics? It takes damn hard work to look damn good."

"I would counter that you were blessed with magical beauty genes and therefore don't have to work hard to look like a cover model," Riley insisted. "Ha! Counter!" She slapped the marble vanity top. "I'm punny."

"I forget how weird you get about stupid puns when you're drunk," Jasmine complained.

"I have an intoxicating sense of humor." Riley snorted at her own joke and got margarita up her nose.

Her phone rang on the counter, and she ignored it.

"It's Nick again," Jasmine said, reading the screen. "Have you had enough tequila to tell him that he's a big sexy idiot and you never want to see him again so he goes out and buys you something expensive?"

"There's not enough tequila in the world for me to put into words how mad I am at him for hiring my elderly neighbor to dress up like a mime and the cast from *Working Girl* to follow me."

Jasmine put down the bronzer brush and picked up her jar of margarita. "You're right. You should definitely not speak to him for at least six months."

"I love you, but we both know I can't take relationship advice from you."

"This is true," Jasmine agreed.

"I wouldn't be surprised if he shows up here since he's also tracking my phone. And here I was trying to respect his privacy by not snooping around in his head. I knew he was still freaked out about that whole fountain thing. But I expected him to talk to me like a regular human being, not have me followed!"

"Well, there's your first mistake. Men are not regular human beings."

"Hey! *You're* beautiful," Riley said, pointing a tube of foundation at her friend. "I bet you've had lots of stalkers. How do you handle them?"

"The nice ones I threaten with legal jargon."

Riley's phone rang again. She picked it up and held it out. "Threaten Nick with legal jargon!"

Jasmine shook her head and reached for the mascara. "Not yet. He's only called three times. He deserves to stew through at least thirteen missed calls."

"You know what's *the worst*?" Riley said.

"Worse than your eighty-year-old neighbor dressing up like a mime to follow you around?"

"I find out all this *after* another vision of him holding a little girl with dimples like his."

"Uh-oh. You had a daddy vision about Nick?" Jasmine said.

Riley nodded with her straw in her mouth. "Yup. And let me tell you, he is a stupidly hot dad."

"Was it your kid?"

She shrugged and knocked a bottle of makeup remover to the floor. "Dunno. I just saw Nick and Dimple Kid and backed away. I'm not ready to think about serious stuff like that. We just started dating."

"You guys are living together," Jasmine pointed out. "It's already serious."

"Yeah, but what if I'm seeing him with someone else's kid? What if he dumps me for someone else to make beautiful babies? Or what if I'm dead and he makes babies with someone else? Or what if Dimple Kid is my Dimple Kid, which means I forgave Nick for being a complete and total overprotective idiot?"

"This requires more alcohol," Jasmine decided.

"Agreed. Maybe we should go out? I have double vision, but both of me look really good," Riley said, studying herself in the mirror.

"Of course both of you do! Because you're both beautiful," Jasmine insisted.

"Let's go to the Millworks. We can be beautiful in the beer garden."

"Oooh. They have those really good deviled eggs."

"What should we wear for the deviled eggs?" Riley asked.

This time, Jasmine's phone rang.

Riley peered at the screen. "That's Nick's number. Now he's stalking you."

Jasmine set her margarita down with a snap and grabbed her phone. She stabbed at the speaker button. "Listen to me, Nicholas Santiago. You owe my friend a big apology and some serious groveling."

Riley gave her a double thumbs-up.

"Jasmine, let me talk to—"

"No! I am Ms. Thorn's attorney, and you will talk to *me*. You were an asshole to my friend and client."

"Jasmine—"

"I hear you talking. I do not hear you listening."

"I love it when you're mean," Riley whispered.

"Fine. What do you want me to do?"

"I want you to think about how Riley felt today when she found her blue-haired neighbor—"

"Purple," Riley interrupted.

"What?" Jasmine looked at her.

"Mrs. Penny's hair is purple."

"Riley, if you can hear me—"

"Shut up, Nick!" Riley and Jasmine shouted together.

"Think about how Riley felt after being humiliated by her ex-husband and his fiancée."

"*Humiliated* is kind of a strong word," Riley complained. "It's too victim-y."

"*Annoyed* by her ex-husband and his fiancée," Jasmine amended.

Riley gave her another thumbs-up, then chased the straw of her margarita around the jar with her mouth.

"Prepositioned by her creepy ex-husband—"

"Griffin did what?" Nick's shout bounced off the marble and echoed in Jasmine's shower.

"*Prepositioned* her," Jasmine enunciated.

"You better not mean *propositioned*, or that little shitbag is going to need a proctologist to remove my foot from his ass."

"Not five minutes later, Riley discovers that her boyfriend has so little trust in her he's not only having her followed; he's tracking her phone. How do you think my client feels?"

"Throw some jargon at him," Riley hissed, lying down on the bench in the walk-in shower.

"Don't mess up your hair, babe. We're going out."

"Where are you going?" Nick demanded.

"I don't have to tell you anything, habeas corpus," Jasmine growled.

"Yay! Jargon!"

"You had my client followed into a professional situation, and it hindered her ability to do her job. How do you plead to these charges?"

"Jasmine, you're a good friend. But I need to talk to Riley," Nick said in that tone he used when he was trying not to explode.

"No. You do not get to talk to Riley today because you're an idiot. You have to earn the right to talk to her."

"Fine. What do I have to do to earn the right?"

"I'll let you know." Jasmine poked her head into the shower. "Let's go eat deviled eggs and flirt with businessmen on their lunch break!"

———

They wisely left Riley's phone at Jasmine's place and walked to Millworks, snagging stools at the bar.

"Do you think my outfit makes me look like a call girl?" Riley wondered, tugging down the hem of the very short skirt she'd borrowed.

Jasmine stopped to consider, then nodded. "Definitely. But an expensive one."

"Okay. That's cool," Riley decided. She spun around on her stool, nearly toppling over. "Look at that. No Nick. No purple-haired neighbor. No creepy, mean grandmother. I think I should move in with you, and we could do this, like, every day."

"Oh my God. Oh my God, Rye! That would be the best thing ever. We could be our own *Sex and the City*."

Riley stuffed a deviled egg into her mouth and started plotting her new Samantha *Sex and the City* wardrobe.

"Riley."

The familiar gravelly rasp behind her nearly had her swallowing the egg whole. "Is that Nick, or am I having a drunk psychic vision?" Riley asked Jasmine.

Jasmine peered over her shoulder. "I think it's Nick because I see him too."

"How did you find us? Are you psychic? Did you insert a tracking chip under my skin?" She started patting herself down when he reached for her.

"Jasmine didn't hang up the phone. I was still on the line when you decided you'd come here for deviled eggs and businessmen."

"Oops," Jasmine said. "Here. Take a picture of us!" She pushed her phone at Nick and threw her arms around Riley. This time, Riley really did fall off her stool. He caught her before she hit the floor and propped her against the bar.

"Can I buy you a drink?" A trim Asian guy in a great suit with even better hair sidled up next to Jasmine, distracting her.

"Read my mind," Nick demanded.

"Wha?" Riley asked, trying to focus on him.

He cupped her chin. "Read my mind, Thorn."

"Why? Are you thinking about my butt too?"

He closed his eyes and let out a breath. "The only way you're going to understand why I did the stupid things I did is if you can actually be in my head. So do it. Go be in my head."

"That's an invasion of privacy." Riley sniffed. "And unlike some others, I respect my partner's privacy." She tried to boop him on the nose Bella-style but missed and poked him in the mouth.

"I invaded your privacy. Now you get to invade mine. That's how relationships work."

"I don't know if I can read your mind with so much tequila swimming through me," she told the Nick on the left.

"Try."

"Ugh. Fine." She closed her eyes. Then opened one. "I don't owe you any favors, you know. I could just tell you to go away until I'm ready to talk to you."

"I know that, and I appreciate that you haven't done that yet even though I deserve it."

With that settled, she closed her eyes again and tried to remember how to be psychic. It took her a few tries, and she got the hiccups, but she finally found herself in the cotton candy place.

"Hey, guys! It's me, Drunk Riley. Nick says I can read his mind. So I guess go ahead and show me whatever is going on in there. I'm guessing it has to do with sex and lawn care."

Either the clouds were spinning or her brain was. It wasn't entirely unpleasant.

This time, the clouds didn't part. There were no visuals partially obscured by pastel fluff. There were only feelings. Adrenaline. The red-hot haze of fury. Heart-pounding fear. Like the first hill of a roller coaster, her stomach dropped, and she felt like she was in a white-knuckled free fall.

There was a flash of blue water, of a man kneeling in the water.

This was what Nick felt when he'd found her under the water in the fountain, a madman's hands on her neck.

Where jail and justice had given Riley the peace she needed, it hadn't been enough for Nick. He wanted more. Needed more.

It was a constant, drumming beat in his blood. *Not again. Not again. Not again.*

Not Riley.

Keep her safe. Any means possible.

I love her.

On the last revelation, she slid right out of the clouds and slumped against the bar. "*That's* what goes on in there?" she slurred, staring at both of him.

"Yeah. All the time."

"I thought it was like, I don't know, football scores and women and beer preferences."

"Very funny, Thorn."

Nick Santiago was a protector. And he thought he'd failed once. He wasn't willing to pay that price again. So he'd assumed responsibility for her safety.

"You know you're not responsible for me," she pointed out, poking him in the chest with her finger. She missed his chest and got him in the neck.

"You're shit-faced by noon because of me."

"Yeah, but also Griffin stupid Gentry. He *propellered* me. As if I would ever consider going anywhere near his penis again."

"I'm going to murder him," Nick announced.

Riley snickered. "You're cute when you're mad. But you shouldn't be mad all the time. It's not good for your internal organs and stuff."

He took a deep breath and blew it out.

"Are you trying to be patient with me?" she whispered.

"Yes."

"That's also very cute. I'm getting less mad at you by the minute. Wait a second. Did your mind tell me you love me?"

He shrugged. "Probably. Because I do."

Jasmine abandoned her businessman and spun around to make a closed-mouthed squeal that drew attention from all corners of the restaurant. "He loooooooves you. He wants to make dimpled babies with yoooooooou."

"Well, they don't have to have dimples. That's not a requirement," Nick said.

"Jas?"

"What?"

"Did Nick Santiago just say he loves me and would be willing to make dimpled babies with me if I wanted to?"

"Yep!"

"And is he also looking super cute but also red like a tomato?" Riley and Jasmine leaned in to examine his face more closely.

"Wow! He is really red. I think he's blushing," Jasmine decided, poking him in the face with her finger.

"Okay. Let's get you two home before you embarrass yourselves instead of me," Nick grumbled, pulling out his wallet.

"He's buying our drinks! That's romantic," Riley said with a lusty sigh.

"Wait. If he loves you, do you love him?" Jasmine asked.

"Of course I do," she scoffed as Nick's head snapped up. "I just didn't want to tell him until he had more time to get comfortable with the idea."

"You should totally tell him now," Jasmine decided.

"But what if he thinks it's because I'm drunk? Like people say a lot of stupid things when they're drunk."

"You mean like five minutes ago when you said you wished Santa Claus was real so you wouldn't have to do your own Christmas shopping?"

Nick rolled his eyes.

Riley shook her head. "That wasn't stupid. That was smart."

He pocketed his credit card, apologized to the bartender, and guided them out of the restaurant.

"We should go do karaoke right now!" Jasmine announced.

"Yes! Nick, can you sing any Spice Girls songs?" Riley asked, leaning heavily against him. She felt much happier than she had just a few minutes ago. Her boyfriend was being an overprotective idiot because he loved her. She'd tell him she loved him when the timing was better and she wasn't burping up tequila.

"If you really loved my best friend, Riley, you would totally learn to sing Spice Girls," Jasmine slurred.

"You're really pretty when you're drunk, Jas."

"So are you, Rye. Like so pretty. Even without all the beautiful makeup."

"Watch your heads, ladies," Nick said, stuffing them both into the back seat of his SUV.

"Let's pretend we're super rich and that Nick is our driver," Jasmine suggested. "What should we call him?"

Riley gave it a significant amount of thought that made her feel sleepy. "How about…umm…Nick!"

"Take us to karaoke, Driver Nick!"

28

Nick nudged the bedroom door open and stepped inside. An episode of Riley's favorite TV show, *Made It Out Alive*, was demonstrating the proper way to stay safe during a livestock stampede. He opened the shades with a satisfying snap.

"Mmmph!" His girlfriend complained from the center of the bed. She had one arm thrown over her face. Her other arm was pinned beneath Burt, who was resting his head on her shoulder, looking at Riley adoringly while his tail wagged against the mattress.

"Morning, sunshine," Nick said cheerfully. "How hungover are you?"

"Oh, God," she rasped. "Is it really morning?"

He grinned as she glared at the sun streaming through the window over the fire escape.

"I'm just messing with you, Thorn. It's still Monday. Coffee or sports drink?"

"Mmm, coffee," she decided, then yawned. Burt took the opportunity to French-kiss her.

"Ew, barf," she groaned but gave the dog a series of noisy kisses on top of his gigantic head.

The thumping increased. "I think our dog is in love with you," Nick observed as he handed over the mug of coffee and put the bottle of Gatorade down on the nightstand.

"Yoo-hoo! Burty boy! Aunt Lily made you a special T-R-E-A-T!" Lily called from downstairs.

Burt's ears perked up, and then he launched himself through the door.

"He has got to be the most spoiled dog on the planet," Riley mused, working her way into a seated position while gulping coffee. She frowned at Nick. "Wait. Are we still fighting?"

"You're really groggy after a nap, aren't you?" he noted.

"I'm not at my sharpest," she admitted, then took another hit of caffeine. "Okay, horrible day at Channel 50—which, by the way, seems to be circling the drain. Someone should just burn that building down. The whole thing is falling apart. Busted Mrs. Penny. Busted you. Drunk makeover. Deviled eggs. You refusing to sing Spice Girls with Jasmine and me in the car. Okay, I don't think anything is missing."

"While you were passed out drunk, I sprang Mrs. Penny from the emergency department," Nick told her. "They didn't believe her when she said she was working undercover for a PI until I showed up."

"Serves you both right." She sniffed and guzzled the sports drink.

"You're a little fuzzy on the part where I told you I loved you—and I'm totally not freaking out yet that you haven't said it back. And then I let you into my head so you could see first-hand what a fucked-up mess I am."

She gave him a small smile. "Oh, right. I must have forgotten that part."

"Well, now you're caught up, and you have thirty minutes to wash the drag show off your face."

She slapped a hand to her face and came away with fake lashes on her middle finger. "Shit."

"Serves you right," he teased and headed for the door. "Now, get ready."

"What am I getting ready for?" she called after him.

"Date night."

"Hey, Nick?"

He stopped in the doorway. "Yeah?"

"I love you too."

"I know," he said with a wink.

Twenty-seven minutes later, Riley made her grand entrance in the re-rearranged parlor in a pair of sexy-as-hell shorts, a silky red tank top, and strappy sandals with heels. Her hair was pulled back in a low tail with a few wispy curls framing her face. She'd managed to scrape off the trowel-load of makeup and looked fresh-faced and only vaguely hungover.

Fred let out a wolf whistle. "Looking good, Riley!"

"You look like a lotus blossom," Gabe announced from the floor where he was in minute nine of his plank.

Mrs. Penny looked up from the report of her "detainment" at the hospital. She had her feet on Gabe's back and a laptop perched in her lap. "You bested me today, Thorn, but it won't happen again."

"Don't mess with me, Penny," Riley shot back with a wink.

Mr. Willicott strolled into the room and looked at Riley. "Who the hell are you?"

She sighed. "I get that a lot more than I should."

"Who's ready for liverwurst?" Lily sang from the hallway.

"Let's go, Thorn," Nick said, steering her toward the front door before the liverwurst fairy could demand they stay. "Penny, you're in charge of Burt. Don't let him eat any people food."

She tossed him a jaunty salute. "You got it, boss."

Nick dragged Riley out onto the porch and down the steps into the humid evening air.

"Where are we going?" she asked with another yawn.

"It's a surprise." He led the way to the Jeep and opened her door for her.

"Wow. This is serious date night treatment," she observed.

"I'm pulling out all the stops tonight, so be prepared to be wowed," he said, sliding behind the wheel. "By the way, check your phone."

She pulled it out of her back pocket and frowned at the screen. "What am I looking for?"

He leaned over her and tapped on an app. "That."

She looked up at him in surprise. "I get to stalk you too?"

"It's only fair. Now we can both be creepy stalkers."

"Are we sure this isn't super unhealthy?" she mused. "I mean, I get the practical applications, but it feels a little wrong to track you wherever you go."

"As long as we're creepy and wrong together," Nick said firmly. He wasn't going to budge on this. It wasn't a trust issue. It was a safety issue, and if he had to quid pro quo this shit to keep Riley safe, that was what he was going to do.

"Okay. I'll give creepy and wrong a shot. Now where are we going, and is food involved?"

Food was most definitely on the menu. Nick drove down an alley and slid into a parking space next to a dumpster.

"VIP parking?" Riley joked.

"This is my dad's restaurant."

She winced. "Isn't it a little soon for us to be inflicting ourselves on your family again?"

He squeezed her knee. "My dad doesn't work Monday nights."

She perked up. "In that case, I'm starving! I haven't had anything since the tequila and eggs."

"I can't believe you didn't need to vomit after that." He took her hand and led her around the building to the front.

Small Plates was a cozy tapas place tucked away on North Street under a red awning. It was his father's newest restaurant. All the tables on the sidewalk were occupied. He pulled Riley inside to the host stand and stopped short.

"Nicky! What the hell are you doing here?" Miguel said with very little enthusiasm behind the host stand.

"What are *you* doing here, Dad? You don't work Mondays."

"What?"

"What are you doing here?" Nick repeated loud enough for the words to carry over the noisy buzz inside.

"This is my restaurant. Why wouldn't I be here?" his father bellowed.

Nick sighed. "It's Monday. You don't work Mondays."

"I do when half the waitstaff and the dishwasher quit on me!" The desk phone rang, and Miguel answered it with a snarl. "What do you want? I'm busy here!"

"I can't imagine why half your staff would quit on you," Nick said dryly.

"They hung up. People have no phone etiquette these days. You shouldn't be here. It hasn't been long enough to get over the hurtful things your girlfriend said after I so graciously fed her."

"Need an expo, Miguel," a harried woman in a long white apron barked as she hauled ass out of the kitchen.

"I'm coming!"

"I'm taking Riley on a date. The service might suck here, but the food is good."

"You're damn right the food is good. But I dunno if you deserve the good food."

Nick blew out a breath and surveyed the restaurant. There were dirty dishes stacked on empty tables and disgruntled-looking customers waiting for food. He'd grown up in kitchens in Harrisburg and knew what was expected. Family lent a hand, even when family was pissed. "Fine. But you owe us a five-course meal plus dessert, and you can't be a dick about anything."

"Three-course and you share a dessert. I can't promise the dick thing."

"Deal," Nick said and turned to Riley. "You ready to earn your supper?"

"I don't even have to wear a skirt that shows off my hoo-ha? Count me in," she said with a grin.

"You can wear one later. For me," he told her.

She blew him a kiss and tackled the closest dirty table with the dish bin.

Nick snagged the ringing phone at the host stand and sent a wink in the direction of all the waiting female patrons. "I'll be right with you folks," he promised.

Working in tandem, he and Riley divided and conquered effortlessly, shifting between front-of-house and back-of-house duties. Tables were cleared, food run, dishes washed, and inconvenienced patrons charmed within an inch of their lives. He'd never had the opportunity to watch Riley on the clock when she was undercover at Nature Girls, but the woman was a natural in a restaurant. She even barked a few orders at his father when Miguel plated the wrong steak. And when his dad asked her if she was going to let the fish sit in the window until it rotted, Riley had responded with a cheery "Bite me, Miguel."

She fit right in.

An hour and a half later, the bulk of the dinner crowd was fed and pleased enough to leave sizable tips.

Finally, Miguel grudgingly pointed them in the direction of a table they'd just cleared. "Your dinner'll be out whenever." He snatched the menus away from them. "You'll get what you get, and that's that."

"The service here is *delightful*," Riley told Nick.

He gave her bare knee a squeeze. "Stay here. I'll go make us some drinks. If you can handle more alcohol."

"I slept off most of it and sweated the rest out here. I'm ready for some hair of the dog."

He ducked behind the bar, nodded to the bartender, and got to work. When he returned to the table, Riley eyed the concoction he handed her.

"Cheers," he said, holding up his glass.

"What are we toasting?"

"You said you loved me. I think that's worth alcohol."

She tapped a finger to her chin thoughtfully. "If I remember correctly, you said it first."

"Of course I did. Because I'm much braver and more manly."

"You also screwed up a lot bigger than I did."

"I'm willing to drink to that," Nick said, touching his glass to hers.

"To us," Riley said.

"To us," he echoed.

"Mmm. What is this?" she asked after her first sip.

"Sangria."

"You're a talented man behind the bar, Nick Santiago."

"I'm talented everywhere. Except maybe in the putting-feelings-into-words portion of life. So let's talk."

She raised her eyebrows. "About what?"

"About all this shit. You've been in my head. Now there's no secrets."

"Alistair," she said.

"How did you know?"

"You're wearing an ironed shirt. I assumed he was involved."

"I may have stopped by his place and briefly mentioned that I'd made a few practically insignificant mistakes."

"You hired an eighty-year-old woman to follow me. That's a little bigger than 'practically insignificant.'"

"Good thing we've moved on from that part."

She snorted.

"Here's some damn calamari and whatever," Miguel said, unceremoniously dropping an artistically plated appetizer onto the table with a crash.

"Thanks, Pop," Nick said. He squeezed lemon over the exquisitely fried calamari before plucking a piece off the plate and feeding it to Riley.

"Oh. My. God. That's good," she purred.

"You're damn right it's good," Miguel huffed and then stomped back to the kitchen.

"Back to talking," Nick prodded.

"Hang on. Between your dad's calamari and your sangria, I'm having a mouth orgasm."

"I'm not sure I'm comfortable with my dad being involved with your orgasm."

She wrinkled her nose in that adorable way of hers and snickered. "Okay. Fine. Back to talking."

"Do you have any questions about whatever you saw when you were drunk spelunking in my head?" He asked his plate the question, not really wanting to make eye contact when he felt so exposed.

"You feel responsible for what happened to Beth," she said.

He shrugged and pulled one of the fried rings apart.

"It's not your fault."

"Is that a prediction or a pep talk?"

"Maybe a little bit of both," she mused. "But the bottom line is you weren't the one to take her. That's who should get the blame."

"I may not have abducted her. But I sure as hell didn't protect her."

"You tried. She didn't make it easy. And I haven't made it easy either."

He rubbed a hand over his forehead. "No, you haven't."

"I think if we had talked like this before, maybe I would have been more sensitive to your feelings."

"I'm not the kind of guy who needs someone to be sensitive to my feelings," he insisted.

"Maybe only in certain limited circumstances," she revised.

He could accept that. "So now you know what you mean to me and how important your safety is to me," Nick said. "And you know if you put yourself in a situation like that again, I'm going to murder you myself."

"That's fair."

"Now it's your turn," he instructed.

"My turn?"

"I told you what I want from you. Now you tell me what you want from me."

She looked at him over the rim of her glass, her brown eyes warm and sparkling. "More," she said.

"More what? Calamari? Sangria?"

"More of everything with you."

Maybe it was the sangria. Or maybe it was the two hundred dollars in tips in his pocket. Or maybe it was the woman who wanted more than he'd ever wanted to give before. Whatever it was, he felt something warm and not at all terrible in his chest.

"Deal."

29

"That was fun," Riley said as they tiptoed up the back stairs of the darkened house.

"It's not over yet," he promised her.

She felt an anticipatory tingle in her lady parts. His hands came to her hips as she navigated the narrow stairs. Her life had changed in so many wild and wonderful ways thanks to Nick. One of those wild and wonderful ways was an adventurous sex life, which she was looking forward to resuming tonight without any interruptions.

When they reached the third floor, Nick put her back to their bedroom door and kissed her long and soft.

"Wow," she whispered breathlessly when he pulled back. "Where did you learn to kiss like that, Santiago?"

"Alistair gave me a few tips," he joked.

Riley laughed against his mouth and let her fingers trail down his chest.

"Wait," he said, catching her hands.

"For what?"

He pointed toward the window. "Follow me." Nick opened the window and stepped out onto the fire escape. "Coming?" He held out his hand to her.

Old Riley would have asked at least half a dozen questions—
What the hell are we doing on a fire escape? Or *When is the last time that thing was inspected?* At the very least, *Have you lost your damn mind? We have a huge bed that we've yet to break in with the horizontal mambo.* But New Riley was open to some reasonable adventures.

She kicked off her sandals and climbed out with him.

"Up you go." He pointed to the metal ladder.

They were already on the third floor. The only "up" was the roof.

"Seriously?"

"Come on, Thorn. Don't tell me you're scared of heights."

"This better be good," she warned him, taking the rungs one at a time. "Oh. Wow. Okay. This is good."

"Of course it is. Minus the whole well-meaning stalking, I'm-killing-this-boyfriend thing," he announced, climbing up behind her.

There was a knee-high spiky iron railing that ran the perimeter of the roof and looked like it was made to impale pigeons. Beyond it, in the center of the flat roof, Riley spotted a nest of blankets and pillows. There was an ice bucket with a couple of beers, and a dozen LED candles flickered to life with a flourish of the remote. A can of bug spray was at the ready next to the blanket.

"Rooftop romance. Not bad, Santiago. Not bad at all."

He turned her in his arms and walked her backward until her bare feet hit blanket. "Best part? No one else in this house can climb up here themselves."

"That is the best part," she whispered, looping her arms around his neck. "Are you sure it's safe?" The roof felt a little mushy under her foot.

"Lily swears up and down she had the roof replaced three years ago. Should be solid," he promised.

Those eyes of his were casting a hormonal spell on her, making her much more interested in getting naked than worrying about structural integrity.

She decided to go with it. He'd made a hell of an effort, and she'd never regretted getting naked with Nick before. What could go wrong?

Her lips found his in the dim flicker of faux candlelight while his hands moved enthusiastically over waist and hips, fingers sliding under the hem of her shirt so he could relieve her of it.

"You're a hell of a girl, Thorn," he murmured against her mouth as crickets chirped, frogs croaked, and old people snored beneath them.

"You're not so bad yourself, Santiago."

They made quick work of shorts, pants, and Nick's shoes. When his body covered hers on the quilt, Riley held him against her.

"God, you feel so good under me," he groaned. "I spend half my day thinking about how it's going to feel to get you there."

"What do you spend the other half of your day thinking about?"

"You on top."

"Perv." She laughed, and he bit her on the shoulder.

His hands found her breasts and proceeded to do wonderful things to them. And when his mouth joined in, Riley bowed against him, ignoring the way the roof flexed against her back.

There were more important things to enjoy. Like the way his touch made her skin burn in delightful ways. Their kisses became more frantic as Nick fumbled for the condoms he'd stashed in a candy dish next to the bug spray.

She smiled against his mouth.

"What?" he rasped.

"I like that you're in as big a hurry as I am."

"I've heard good things about makeup sex," he told her, rolling on the condom and giving her a look that turned her insides to lava.

"Let's give it a go."

She felt the roof flex under her again and went still as Nick lined himself up with her greedy core. "You okay?" he asked, breathing heavily.

Something bit her leg. It wasn't Nick.

She slapped at it just as something else nibbled on her ankle. At the same time, Nick reached around and slapped himself on the ass.

"Did you just—"

"Fucking mosquitoes. Hold still." Ever prepared, he doused them in a cloud of bug spray.

"Better than the mayflies," Riley decided.

Every year, the riverfront exploded in what looked like a blizzard. But instead of fluffy little snowflakes, the white stuff blotting out the sky was the disgusting exoskeletons of mayflies.

He gave them one last blast with the can of bug spray and then tossed it over his shoulder. It landed with a thunk and rolled much farther and faster than it should have on a flat surface.

"Who fixed the roof? It doesn't look like they did a very good job." She had a sudden vision of two idiots with ropes tied around their waists haphazardly nailing boards over a gaping hole.

"Forget the roof, Thorn. I'm about to levitate you off it," Nick promised with cocky dimples.

His erection twitched between them, and Riley immediately dismissed the idiots in her head.

She took his face in her hands. "I had fun tonight."

"Yeah? Even though dinner was a bust?"

"It wasn't a bust. You got to impress your dad and me. And I made over a hundred dollars in tips."

He looked down at her with a softness around the eyes that she'd never seen before. "I love you, Thorn."

With a wicked grin and a squeeze of his very firm ass, Riley winked. "I know."

With that, he thrust into her, and all smugness vanished as she remembered exactly who was in charge.

"How do you make tab B fit into slot A so damn good?" she groaned.

"God, baby. I can feel you locked down over every fucking inch."

They didn't have to be quiet. Didn't have to keep the headboard from knocking into the wall. Didn't have to make sure Burt the dog wasn't staring at them creepily. On the roof under the August moon, they were free to bang each other into oblivion.

Riley moaned. "This is the best idea you've ever had."

"No, it isn't, Thorn," he said through clenched teeth. "You are."

Damn. Nick was ready to teach a master class in rooftop romance.

They moved in sync toward a common goal: pleasure. With every thrust, every heaved breath, every drop of sweat, Riley felt closer and closer to him.

She felt those delicious little muscles that had been ignored for far too long before Nick quicken around him.

He growled against her neck. "I feel you, baby. I know you're ready to let go. I'm with you."

There was a groan that seemed to come from neither of them. And then she was coming. Nick went rigid above her. She gripped him with her thighs and surrendered to the free fall as their bodies did what Nick told them to. She was halfway through the orgasm of a lifetime when she realized the fall wasn't just metaphorical. They landed, still joined, with a bone-jarring thump crossways on their bed in a pile of candles, condoms, and roofing debris.

"Jesus Christ," Nick groaned.

"Did you just—"

"I fucked you through the roof. Are you okay?"

Riley brushed plaster dust off his face. Her bra hung from the gaping hole in the ceiling, which now afforded an unrestricted view of the starry sky. Burt looked up from his dog bed and gave a questioning *boof.*

"Hi, buddy," she said. She did a body scan, but everything seemed more interested in reporting with orgasm feedback. "I think so. Are you okay?"

"Yeah. I landed pretty hard on you. Or in you," he pointed out.

"I'm okay," she assured him, wondering if vaginas could bruise.

He spit out a cloud of dust. "What the hell is this? Drywall?"

Burt jumped up on the bed to investigate just as the bedroom door swung open. "I told you I heard an alien spaceship land on the roof," Mr. Willicott said, poking the gun-toting Mrs. Penny in the shoulder.

Mrs. Penny accidentally fired the gun into an undamaged part of the ceiling. More plaster fell down. "Whoops."

Gabe walked in and immediately turned his back on the tableau. "I am unsure how I can be of assistance in this circumstance."

"Good for you kids, practicing safe sex," Lily said, plucking a condom wrapper off the lampshade on the nightstand.

Fred huffed and puffed into view. His hastily applied toupee was on inside out. "What happened? What did I miss?"

"Nick and Riley are having sex," Lily announced. "You must not have anchored your sex swing to a stud." Then she giggled and whispered, "Stud."

"Why the hell do we end up with an audience every time?" Riley hissed at Nick. Her face was flaming with embarrassment.

"Baby, we're so damn good everyone wants a ticket."

To add insult to injury, a mosquito chose that moment to bite her under the eye. Nick slapped it for her.

"Ow!"

"Did you see that?" Lily whispered in delight. "They're into some really kinky stuff. I can't wait to tell my pottery class."

"My mother is in your pottery class," Riley groaned.

"Stop making noises like that, Thorn," Nick gritted out in a whisper. She felt him flex inside her.

"You have got to be kidding me. Isn't there anything that affects your libido?"

"Penny, get me a towel and Riley's robe from the bathroom. Everyone else out!"

"Lily, who the hell replaced the roof? It should still be under warranty, right?" Riley asked, trying not to focus on the fact that Nick was inside her and they were both naked while carrying on a conversation with their audience.

Fred threw his muscly arm around Willicott's shoulders. "That'd be the dream team here. Can you believe she was going to hire a couple of professionals? Ha!"

30

Riley woke with a crick in her neck and a naked man sprawled facedown on the rug next to the fireplace. A quick look at the butt and she identified it as belonging to Nick.

"Ugh," she groaned. "Wake up and put your shorts back on before—"

Too late.

"Good morning, lovebirds," Lily twittered as she sashayed into the room. "Oh my. You are a lucky girl getting to put your hands on a patootie like that."

Nick was a night stripper, meaning if he went to bed wearing clothes, he woke up wearing nothing.

Riley tossed a blanket over his ass and nudged him with her foot. "Rise and shine."

"Mmph. I had the weirdest dream last night that we were having sex and—"

Lily was hanging on his every word, glassy-eyed with desire…or maybe cataracts. Riley couldn't tell from this angle.

"Shut up, Nick. It wasn't a dream, and you're naked on the parlor floor."

"Is Lily staring at my ass?" he asked.

"Yep."

"I brought you two breakfast in bed," Lily said proudly. She dropped the tray on Mrs. Penny's cocktail bar. "We have coffee, toast, and eggs."

"Thanks, Lily," Riley said, stretching her arms and yawning. The green velour divan was not the most comfortable place to sleep, but the soreness she felt in her nether region had nothing to do with the lumpy furniture.

"I'll call the roofers," Nick volunteered, shimmying into his shorts.

"Oh, you don't need to do that," Lily said with a dismissive wave. "I have two strapping fellows just raring to get back up there."

"No," Riley said.

"Absolutely not," Nick said at the same time.

"Lily, some jobs are best left to the professionals," Riley told her landlady.

"They are going to be so disappointed. They were talking about starting their own company, you know."

Nick stood up and stretched. Lily stared at his bare torso and continued to pour the coffee long after the cup overflowed.

Riley cleared her throat and took the coffeepot from her neighbor.

"Thanks, Lily."

"It's my pleasure." Lily put a distinctly gross emphasis on the word *pleasure*.

"Who's ready for breakfast?" Riley yawned when Lily left the room.

Burt's head popped up from the ancient recliner he'd confiscated last night.

"This body is not meant to sleep on the floor," Nick groaned.

"Yeah? Well, this body isn't meant to fall through a roof with a penis inside it." The more awake she became, the less vague the soreness in her lady part region got. Nick flashed her the dimples, but she shook her head. "No. It's too early for charm. Drink your coffee eggs," she said, handing him the plate of soggy breakfast.

"Why do you get the noncoffee eggs?" he pouted.

"Because my upper body didn't cast a spell on Lily," Riley said. She cocked her head to study him. "Are you getting more ripped?"

He seemed somehow bigger and leaner. He'd never been a slouch in the muscles department, but there was definitely something going on with his upper body. Even his tattoos seemed bigger.

As any man would, Nick flexed. "You like what you see?"

"Put the gun show away," Mrs. Penny grumbled as she stalked into the room. She poked him in the chest with her cane.

"Is that any way to speak to your boss?" Riley asked, taking a bite of toast.

"What's my assignment today?"

"You're taking a gun safety class," Nick told her.

"I don't need a stinking safety class!"

"You shot out a ceiling last night. And two months ago, you blew out Lily's bedroom door when you thought Riley was an intruder."

"She used the code. We were under a cabbage casserole," Mrs. Penny insisted.

"I've been thinking—" Fred appeared and seemed to be midconversation. He'd gone with his Justin Bieber toupee this morning. "We need a new code word."

Mrs. Penny's beady eyes lit up behind her thick prescription lenses. "Good thinking."

"A code word for what?" Riley asked. "No one's broken in here in weeks."

"That's not a safety record I'd brag about," Nick pointed out.

"A code word so I don't come running to investigate a noise with a loaded Beretta," Mrs. Penny explained.

"We weren't in any condition to send out a text before you came upstairs and tried to shoot us," Riley said. But Mrs. Penny and Fred already had their heads together over possible code words.

"Good morning," Gabe said, appearing in the doorway.

"Are your muscles getting bigger too?" Riley asked, cocking her head.

Lily jumped out from behind Gabe and wrapped her hands around one beefy bicep. "Ooooh! They are!"

"Are you two working out together or something?" Riley asked.

Nick shrugged. "Maybe we did some push-ups or whatever."

"Nick is very bad at counting repetitions. But he puts forth a reasonable effort to hone his body," Gabe announced.

"I need more coffee for this," Riley decided, taking Nick's plate from him and pouring some into her cup.

"I'll make more coffee and eggs if someone brings in the packages from the porch," Lily said, scampering back to the kitchen.

"I'll get the packages," Riley said.

She stepped out onto the porch and eyed the stack of deliveries. Between Mrs. Penny, Lily, and Nick, the residents of the house were on a first-name basis with the UPS, FedEx, and Amazon drivers. Lily had also ranked each of the driver's butts on a scale involving firmness and shape.

It took her two trips to bring everything inside. As expected, most of the packages were addressed to the other residents. But there was a small square-shaped package with her name on it. The return label said it was from Make Better Choices. "Hey, Burt. I think your organic dog treats from Etsy are here," she said, bringing the box into the parlor.

The dog rolled out of his chair gracelessly and trotted over to her.

"Organic dog treats?" Nick asked, scratching his bare chest.

"Wander recommended them for his digestive issues."

"That dog's farts can strip the paint off a car," Mrs. Penny observed. She flopped down on the divan and helped herself to Riley's toast.

The doorbell rang, and Gabe raced to the front door. He returned with a dozen doughnuts and opened the box. "You do not have power over me, doughnuts," he said.

Burt lost interest in organic dog treats and tip-tapped over to Gabe.

"Do *not* give him any doughnuts," Riley warned Gabe.

But the man was busy performing mountain climbers over the open box of pastries with swift exhalations of breath that blew powdered sugar into Burt's face.

"Leave them," she told the dog sternly.

Burt pouted and settled for licking the sugar off his muzzle.

Riley grabbed a pair of scissors off the parlor's writing desk and sliced open the box.

"Who's ready for a special tr—"

The word was cut off by an explosive pop and a cloud of sparkle.

There was a deadly silence as every color of glitter rained down.

"What the fuck?" Nick choked.

"Oh my God." Riley coughed as glitter invaded her nose and mouth.

Gabe, still sweating through mountain climbers, was coated in a thick layer of sparkle as if he were some kind of personal training fairy.

"Give me the fucking box," Nick ordered.

Blindly, Riley felt around until her hands made contact with the box.

"What in the rainbow swirl hell happened in here?" Fred demanded.

"Oooooh! Did we get glitter bombed?" Lily asked from the doorway.

"Am I dead? Is this hell?"

The question came from Mrs. Penny on the divan. Her glasses were obscured by glitter.

"You're not dead, Mrs. Penny," Riley assured her.

"How would you know? What if you're dead too?"

The woman had a point.

Riley coughed again, sending a small cloud of glitter back into the air.

Everything was covered. Walls, ceiling, floor, furniture, dog, doughnuts.

Nick, glitter clinging to his eyelashes, glared at the box.

"Is it him? Is it the same guy?" she asked, trying to peer over his shoulder.

"I don't know," he growled. "But it's addressed to you."

She didn't like his tone of voice. It sounded like he was about ready to murder someone.

"Why? I don't get it. I'm not an asshole online. Unless there's some other random connection we haven't figured out."

"You were asking questions about online assholes," he pointed out.

He swiped the glitter off his phone screen and took it and the box out onto the front porch, leaving a trail of glitter behind him.

Riley heard him on the phone. "I need you to get over here now. And bring that guy I hate. Yeah, that one."

Lily lay down on the floor and swept her arms back and forth. "Look at me! I'm making a glitter angel!"

31

Nick walked down the line, eyeing each sweaty, sparkly person in front of him. "One of our own has become the target of a murderer," he said.

"Sir, yes, sir," Lily said with a salute and a saucy wink. She'd changed out of her nightgown and into camo bike shorts and matching tank top that showed off her blinding, vitamin D–deficient arms.

Riley made a note to check Lily's vitamins to make sure she was getting enough.

"You're old. You're soft. You're confused," Nick continued, stopping in front of Mr. Willicott, who was attending the day's festivities in a tuxedo jacket and boxers. "You're in danger."

"I'd like to see you try," Willicott announced. Glitter sparkled in his graying short-cropped hair.

"That's why I've got the ol' Beretta," Mrs. Penny said next to him. She patted her hip, then frowned and looked down at her empty holster. "Well, crap. Now where did I leave it?"

Riley felt her lips twitch and tried to cover it, but Nick caught her. He stopped inches in front of her. "Do *not* smile, Thorn. None of this is funny. You've been targeted, and it's time for you all to learn how to take safety precautions."

"Boring!" Willicott shouted.

"Yeah, we want to learn how to wrestle attackers into submission," Lily said from the other end of the line.

"And make booby traps!" Fred yelled.

Nick gritted his teeth, and Riley winced. He was sweating glitter. The humidity closing in on them made the parking lot an oven.

Detective Weber had arrived on the scene with a couple of uniforms and a forensics expert. They'd taken the bomb packaging and glitter samples back to the lab. After a little manly side conference, both Nick and Weber had looked rather grim.

She got it.

A glitter bomb tied her to the other two victims and set a clock in motion. Both victims had been dead within two weeks of receiving the packages.

"It's hot. Can't we fight bad guys inside in the air-conditioning?" Mrs. Penny complained.

Gabe was the only one not talking back. He stood with his back straight, his eyes staring at some unseen, faraway object.

"What the hell is that?" Riley asked as a vehicle pulled into the lot.

It screeched to a halt in front of them, and Josie jumped to the ground. "Regulation Humvee," she announced.

The driver swaggered over to stand next to her. He was shorter than Nick and barrel-chested. He had a mustache perched over unsmiling lips. "Santiago," he said with an arrogant nod.

"Canon," Nick acknowledged grudgingly. He turned back to his motley crew. "Welcome to self-defense boot camp, ladies and gentlemen."

Everyone but Gabe and Riley cheered.

———

Half an hour later, no one was cheering, and everyone was sweating.

"I have glitter in my dentures," Fred complained. "Can I go brush it out?"

"Do you think you'll have time in a firefight to call a time-out and brush your dentures?" Canon responded.

The guy came across like an unhinged drill sergeant.

"I guess it depends on what a firefight is," Fred mused.

"Wrong! Show me the moves again."

"Stab. Poke. Swipe. Stab. Poke. Swipe," the over-eighty crowd shouted, wielding canes and walking sticks.

"Is this absolutely necessary?" Riley huffed, putting her boxing-glove-encased hands on her knees and trying to catch her breath.

Nick lowered the pad she'd been assaulting for the last five minutes and glared at her. "Do not ask me that, Thorn. I wanted to handcuff you to me and get on a plane, but instead I'm teaching you how to defend yourself."

"Gee, thanks."

"Not that you'll ever be alone again. I'll be there when you shower. When you work. When you sleep. When you're peeing."

She shook her head vehemently. "No way. I draw the line there. If you want this relationship to work, we're putting off the peeing in front of each other as long as possible," she insisted.

"I will be there when you go to yoga," he continued. "When you visit your scary grandmother. From now on, think of me as a pissed-off appendage."

She took a breath and blew it out again. "I'm not going to point out that I think you're overreacting."

"Good."

"But I *am* going to point out that you have cases of your own to solve. How are you going to track down Larry Rupley if you're busy watching me shower?"

"Don't worry about the logistics. I'll take care of those. Now, get back on that mat with Josie, and prove that you can escape a rear naked choke hold so I can sleep at night."

"That sounds like you want us to get naked and wrestle

around. Are you sure this is self-defense and not some male fantasy?"

He growled at her, and she wisely decided to do as she was told.

"Just stay away from my vagina," Riley warned Josie when she stepped on the mat they'd unloaded from the back of the Humvee. "It got a workout last night."

"Nice job, Nicky," Josie said with a rare grin. Which disappeared immediately when her open palm connected with Riley's face.

"Ow!"

"That wasn't hard," Josie scoffed.

"No! You hit the mosquito bite Nick slapped last night."

Josie's eyebrows were the only part of her face that showed interest. "You two are kinkier than I thought. Nice going." She slapped Riley on the other side of her face. "Now, put your damn hands up and block me."

She tried. She swore she was trying. But Josie managed to get her tattooed arm around Riley's neck every time, and Riley couldn't break free.

"My turn," Canon said, gesturing for Josie to step aside. "You don't know me. You won't be worried about hurting me."

Nick was watching them closely with a fierce frown.

"I hate this guy."

She got that loud and clear.

Josie read the situation too. "Go spar with the Great Pyramid," she told Nick and pointed at Gabe.

Riley watched the two men size each other up as they pulled on boxing gloves.

"Since you're such a peaceful flower child, let's start with the basics," Nick said. "A jab is a—"

Gabe's gigantic fist flashed out and sucker punched him right in the nose, snapping Nick's head back.

"Fuck." Nick swiped his forearm under his nose. "Yeah. That's a jab, smart-ass."

Gabe grinned. "I have been wanting to do that for a long time."

"Riley, right?" Canon said, drawing her attention back to the mat.

"Yeah," she said, reluctantly turning away from the hot, sweaty guy show to face Canon. He skimmed in just under six feet tall and was very muscly. His mustache and dark hair were both trimmed with a precision that definitely made her think military.

"Let's start with you in the hold, and we'll work on it step-by-step before working up to full speed."

They got down on the mat, and Riley wrinkled her nose as the breeze carried with it the now familiar disaster of scents from next door. She wondered if Burt had been sneaking out at night to poop at the abandoned mansion.

When Canon's beefy forearm came around her neck, she forgot to worry about Burt's poop.

"I'm applying just enough pressure to make it scary," he explained to her.

"Gah. It's working," she gargled.

He smelled nice. Expensive. She, on the other hand, smelled like she'd forgotten to apply deodorant all summer.

"How come we don't get to wrestle with that cutie?" Lily asked.

"Less flirting. More stabbing," Mrs. Penny ordered, taking the elders through their self-defense moves again.

Canon walked her through a few escape techniques, but as soon as her oxygen was cut off, Riley panicked and started flailing.

After a fourth disastrous attempt, he gave her a break and consulted with Josie.

Riley crawled to the edge of the mat and picked up her water bottle. This scenario reminded her a little too much of being held under the water while another man's hands choked the life out of her.

She felt Nick's gaze on her and gave him a wave a second before Gabe's fist drove into his torso.

Maybe Nick wasn't the only one still freaking out over past events.

"You're not using all your tools," Josie told her as Riley guzzled water.

"What tools do I have left? Whimpering for help?"

Josie flicked her in the forehead. "You're a psychic, dummy. You know what your attacker is going to do before they do it."

Riley blinked. "Can I really do that?"

"I'm not the psychic. But if I had that talent, you can guaran-damn-tee I'd be using it to get inside my opponent's head. If it's a life-or-death situation, you want to use everything you've got at your disposal."

Riley sat with that for a minute and decided it wasn't the worst idea in the world.

She put down the water and climbed back on her feet. "Okay. Let's try this again."

Canon flashed her a grin. "Think you've got me this time?"

"We'll see."

Okay, spirit guides. Mama needs to not get choked out.

This time when Canon wrapped a beefy arm around her neck from behind, she saw cotton candy clouds instead of spots. As he slowly cut off her oxygen, she recalled an episode of *Made It Out Alive* on evading abduction attempts. A teenage girl had been walking home from her tae kwon do class when the abductor tried to drag her into his car and got an ass kicking for his trouble.

Breathless, Riley made herself go limp. When Canon's grip lessened, she reared her head back. He saw the attack coming but couldn't completely dodge the blow. She caught him just under the eye, stunning him enough for him to release her.

She jumped to her feet and did a victory dance. "In your face, attacker!"

He grinned up at her. "Nicely done. But next time, wait to celebrate until after you've run away."

"Solid advice," she said.

He held up a hand, and she moved to help haul him to his feet.

Instead, she found herself flat on her back with Canon

274

straddling her hips. "One more thing, Riley," he said with a quick grin. "Don't help your attacker up."

"Get off her, Canon."

Nick's voice was deadly, and it was coming in hot.

She peeked up in time to see Josie stepping in front of Nick, slapping a hand to his chest. "Be cool, boss."

Canon took his time getting to his feet, most likely to piss Nick off. He held out his hand to Riley, and she took it. But as Canon was pulling her to her feet and glaring at Nick, Riley swept his legs out from under him.

He hit the mat with a laugh. "You're a fast learner, Riley."

"It's my turn," Lily shouted, tottering over to the mat and throwing herself on top of Canon. "Oh no! I seem to have fallen down and can't get up!"

Riley turned her attention to Nick, who was bleeding from the nose. His left eye was swelling. Beyond him, Gabe had a split lip and was grinning. "Why can't you have normal friendships with guys? Why does everything have to be an anti-bromance with you?" Riley asked.

"It's not my fault men are assholes," Nick insisted, pulling up the hem of his shirt to swipe away the blood.

She sighed, enjoying the peek at his torso. "It's really nice of you to do this for us."

"I'm doing it for *you*, Thorn."

"I know."

He nudged her chin up. "Promise me you won't let some half-assed self-defense lesson make you think you're invincible."

"I promise. I also promise I won't go looking for trouble."

He blew out a breath. "That would make me feel better if trouble didn't have such a knack for finding you."

"Good thing I have you," she said, grabbing him by the sweaty shirtfront and yanking him into her.

A happy bark came from the house. Riley and Nick turned and spotted Burt's face in the parlor window.

Crap.

"Lily, I thought you closed the parlor doors?"

"I did!" she said indignantly from the mat where Canon was trying to extricate himself from her surprisingly effective hold. "At least I think I did. Maybe I just thought about it?"

"That pony's all sparkly," Willicott observed. "He's got white stuff all over his face. He a cokehead?"

"Gabe, tell me the doughnuts aren't still on the floor in there," Riley groaned.

But Burt's powdered-sugar-and-glitter face told the story.

Riley jogged to the front porch and let herself in. The parlor doors were wide open, and there were glittery paw prints leading everywhere.

Burt trotted out of the room to her with a doughnut dangling from his mouth.

"We are never going to get your farts under control if you don't stop snarfing down people food," she complained.

An unnatural rumble came from the direction of the dog's intestinal tract. Burt's eyes went wide, and the doughnut fell out of his mouth.

"Oh no. Not in here, mister. You get your glitter behind outside to do your business," she said, pointing to the open door.

Burt bounded for the door, then skidded to a stop. He raced back for the doughnut he'd dropped and pranced outside.

When Riley followed, she found her grandmother glowering at everyone while Burt sniffed around in a circle next to the wrestling mat.

"Hey, Grandmother," Riley said, hoping to land on the woman's good side.

Any normal grandma would ask why everyone was covered in glitter or wonder why several of her housemates were bruised and bleeding. Elanora was not a normal grandma.

She whipped around to study Riley. The pheasant feathers in her hair tickled Fred's nose, and he giggled, then sneezed.

"There are other ways of defending oneself. Brute force is rarely the correct answer." Her eyes flicked to Gabe's split lip and narrowed.

"Look, lady," Nick said. "Your granddaughter is in danger and not from ghosts or dead people. This is a real live threat."

"Then you should want her to have all the tools she requires."

Nick's nostrils flared, and Riley stepped between them just in case her boyfriend did something stupid like try to punch her grandmother or her grandmother tried to murder him with psychic powers.

"You will *all* attend my granddaughter's yoga class and stay for an intensive spiritual defense training."

"Everyone?" Riley repeated, thinking about Mr. Willicott getting confused in corpse pose and dying on the spot.

"It's happening," Josie announced.

All eyes turned to Burt in horror as the dog squatted.

"My God," Canon hissed.

"That ain't natural," Mrs. Penny said, shaking her head.

Burt's poop sparkled festively in the summer sunshine.

Elanora tut-tutted. "Disgraceful."

"All in favor of 'sparkle poo' as our new code word, say aye," Lily called.

"Aye."

32

Nick stopped short when he walked into Wander's yoga studio with his posse of weirdos in tow.

He wasn't exactly a yoga guy. Sure, he was a fan of the tight short-shorts Riley was wearing for the class. But he didn't know what the gong at the front of the room was for. And he sure as hell wasn't expecting to find his mother sitting serenely on a pink mat in the center of the studio.

She glanced in his direction and did a double take.

"Nick?" She looked delighted…and suspicious in gray tights and a high-necked tank. Her hair was pulled back from her face in a bun.

"Mom? I didn't know you did"—he gestured at the colorful tapestries and collection of incense burners—"this stuff."

"I've been coming here every Tuesday for the past two years. Wander is wonderful. I'll introduce you when she gets here."

"Actually, I know her."

She cringed. "Oh God. You didn't sleep with her, did you, Nicky? Because if you did, we're pretending we don't know each other. I'm not giving up this class."

"No, Mom. I didn't sleep with her," he scoffed. "But I am sleeping with her sister."

"Hi, Dr. Santiago." Riley stepped out from behind Nick and waved.

"Oh. It's you." The pre-yoga buzz evaporated from his mother's face.

"It's nice to see you too," Riley said with a fake smile.

His mother turned her back on Riley. "What happened to your face, Nicky? And why are you so sparkly?"

He pushed her hand away as she fussed over him. "Nothing. It's fine, Mom."

"Well, come set up next to me. And stay away from that ridiculous couple in the corner. She's some sort of hippie witch, and her husband is a farmer obsessed with his cow, I believe. Absolutely dreadful people." She shuddered and pointed.

Blossom and Roger Thorn waved cheerfully from the designated dreadful corner.

"You probably shouldn't tell her," Riley suggested.

"Oh, I'm telling her." Nick blew out a breath. "Mom. Meet Riley's parents, Blossom and Roger Thorn. Blossom and Roger, this is my mother, Marie."

Blossom hauled Roger off his mat, and the introductions were made.

"Your son is a lovely human being," Blossom said to his mother.

"Yes, well," Marie said.

"What's with the glitter?" Roger asked, peering at Riley and Nick.

"We got glitter bombed this morning," Riley explained.

Marie's well-maintained eyebrows skyrocketed up her forehead. "Glitter bombed? Is that some kind of euphemism?"

"I wish," Nick said.

"What the hell is the she-devil doing here?" Roger demanded as Elanora swept through the door and frowned at the room.

"Is that Stevie Nicks's mother?" Marie wondered.

Nick helped himself to a mat from one of the shelves and gauged the distance from the door. They were on the second floor, so it was less likely that a threat would come for Riley through the windows, but the door was still a problem. "Mom, move your mat."

"But I always set up here," she complained.

"Humor me and move it over there. Wander's a big fan of novelty. Seeing the world from new perspectives," he said.

"Really?"

"What are you doing?" Riley asked under her breath as he took her mat and spread it out next to his.

"Putting myself between you and the door and my mother and your family."

"Are you expecting a fistfight to break out in the middle of sun salutations?" she asked.

"I'm not taking any chances."

Riley looked down at her phone. "Mrs. Penny texted and said they went through the drive-thru on the way here and they're still waiting on hash browns. They want us to get started without them."

"Josie went home to have sex with Brian."

"I'm starting to think we should have taken their lead," she said.

"Yeah, well, your grandmother scares the shit out of me. And you don't go to Tuesday morning yoga classes. Breaking up your routine is a good idea in case Glitter Guy is watching you."

Riley shivered.

Canon strutted into the room like a rooster, surveying the room and its inhabitants. With a twitch of his mustache, he grabbed a mat and set up directly behind Riley as she bent over to stretch her hamstrings.

Nick bared his teeth.

Canon grinned at him.

"Yeah. Not happening," Nick snapped. He grabbed Riley and her mat and shoved her between her parents.

"What the hell, Nick?"

"Humor me." He returned to his mat and moved it so *he* was directly behind Riley and his ass was in Canon's face.

"Is this spot taken?"

Gabe gestured at the spot between Nick and his mother.

Nick shrugged. "Have at it, Goliath."

His mother's eyes widened as Gabe unfurled his mat and sat. "Hello," she said.

"Hello. I am Gabe. It is a pleasure to enjoy this class with you."

"Hello, Gabe. It's lovely to meet you. I'm Marie. Are you a fan of Wander's?"

Nick couldn't tell if his mother had a bigger crush on the mountain of muscle next to her or Riley's sister.

"Wander is a most wonderful teacher. I enjoy my time with her."

Elanora cleared her throat from the hanging egg chair she'd perched in. She looked like a disapproving ostrich in her nest.

"Give the guy a break, lady," Nick whispered.

Elanora's eyes narrowed, and he felt a prickling sensation all over his body.

"Mom!" Blossom hissed from the front row at the same time that Riley whispered, "Grandmother!"

Fortunately, Elanora's voodoo gaze was interrupted by the arrival of the instructor. "Good morning, everyone," Wander said as she picked her way through the mats to the front of the room. She was wearing cropped tights and an open-back tank that said KINDNESS. Her long braids were pulled back from her face in a high tail.

Gabe sighed forlornly next to Nick.

———

Nick wasn't sure what the fuck chair pose was supposed to feel like, but he was pretty sure it shouldn't be making his quads and traps shake like he was coming off a three-day bout with the flu. Next to him, Gabe held the pose like a fucking statue. The only sign that there was a living, breathing human beneath all that muscle was the steady drops of sweat raining down on the mat.

"Swan dive back down into your forward fold. Feel your hamstrings lengthening. Feel yourself rooting to the mat." Wander's voice soothingly insisted his body do things it wasn't comfortable doing. His hamstrings felt like they were shredding like a piece of lunch meat.

Nick peered between his feet at Canon, who was also sweating profusely, but he didn't appear to be shaking like a goddamn leaf.

He was sweating his way through plank pose when Wander's feet stopped next to his mat.

"Shifting forward into cobra pose," she instructed, straddling his ass with her feet and pulling his shoulders up and back into a position he didn't know he was capable of getting into. "Beautiful extension," she said.

Behind him, Canon snickered. Gabe made moony eyes at her.

In front of him, Riley's ass tempted him from those short shorts as Wander told them to transition to downward-facing dog.

His girlfriend was hot.

He felt the weight of a disapproving stare. This time it wasn't coming from Elanora. It was coming from his own mother busting him as he checked out his own girlfriend.

He shrugged at her and nearly toppled out of downward dog.

Marie rolled her eyes and then got distracted when Gabe's unnaturally large biceps rippled as he opened his arms for one of the warrior poses. It was Nick's turn to shoot a judgmental stare in her direction.

When she shrugged, Wander paused behind her. "Let's drop these shoulders, Marie," she said, adjusting his mother's upper body.

For the rest of the class, Nick kept his attention divided between Riley's ass, the door, and his manly competition. When Wander announced it was time for corpse pose, he almost broke down and cried. Between spending the night on the fucking floor, finding out his girlfriend was the target of a killer, getting sucker punched by Ham Hands, and trying to keep up with stupid Canon in sun salutations, he was in desperate need of a beer, a burger, and a nap with Riley glued to his side.

The scent of hash browns and old people reached his nose, and Nick guessed that Mrs. Penny had arrived with the rest of the neighbors in tow.

It had been a long fucking day, and it wasn't even lunchtime yet. And his gut was telling him his girl was in trouble. Big trouble.

33

I don't know if anyone ever told you this, Nick," Blossom said, approaching them after yoga class. "But your mom's got a real stick up her ass."

Riley spit out the water she'd just swigged down. "Mom!"

"What? I'm only speaking my truth. She comes in here every Tuesday and looks down her nose at us. She doesn't even know that Wander is our daughter!"

"You wouldn't be the first to point out the fact that my mother's ass has no lumber shortage," Nick said.

"Still, that's not a very Blossom-like thing to say about someone," Riley argued.

"Puh-lease. I've been nice as pie to that woman for *two* years."

"Enough chitchat," Elanora announced from the front of the room. She thumped the floor with a sizable staff.

"Who gave mean Granny a stick?" Nick wondered.

"You will all sit. Now," she ordered.

They all did as they were told. Even Roger. Though Riley saw him sneak earbuds into his ears.

Canon took the cushion next to her, and Riley thought she heard Nick growl audibly.

But any testosterone-fueled growls were drowned out by an earsplitting screech as Mrs. Penny dragged a metal chair from the back of the room all the way to the front. Lily, Mr. Willicott, and Fred all did the same.

Elanora glared and waited until the elderly troublemakers were seated and eating their hash browns.

Wander quietly took the floor cushion next to Gabe. Riley noticed that their knees were touching.

"Since you all feel that brute force is the only way to defend yourselves, it is up to me to show you another way. But be warned, this is a grueling training. Not for the weak."

"I'm gonna go find a Blockbuster and rent a movie," Mr. Willicott announced and headed for the door.

Lily jumped out of her chair. "I should help. The last time he went looking for a Blockbuster, we didn't see him for three days."

Blossom raised her hand.

"What?" Elanora snapped, pronouncing every letter in the word, including the *h*.

"I was just wondering what we're protecting ourselves from, Mom."

"Your daughter has been targeted by a murderer."

Blossom turned to Riley. "Oh, come on. Again?"

Riley shrugged. "It's not my fault, Mom."

"It most assuredly is your fault. Predators sense prey," her grandmother announced.

"If we could move beyond the bashing-my-girlfriend phase of the morning, that would be great," Nick snapped.

"Everyone has the gift. Some gifts are smaller than others," Elanora said.

Fred held up his hand. "When you say 'gift,' are you talking about penis size?"

Riley pressed her lips together. She didn't know if it was laughter or barf that wanted to escape, and she wasn't taking any chances.

Her grandmother's withering stare had no effect on Fred. He merely leaned forward and said, "Well? Are you?"

"I am most certainly *not*. I am talking about the gift of clairvoyance."

"Oh." Fred sounded disappointed.

"It is available to each of you so long as you aren't too lazy to work at it."

"Now we're definitely talking about penis size," Fred decided.

To prevent emotional scarring, Riley focused on her dad's head as it bopped from side to side.

"You will pair up for a demonstration. You two"—she pointed to Riley and Gabe—"are a team."

Wander looked longingly in Gabe's direction before Mrs. Penny dragged her chair over. "Looks like it's you and me, Stretch McFlex."

Nick was paired with Canon. "I don't think that's such a good idea," Riley whispered.

"Do not question my judgment, child!" Elanora sealed her edict with a thwack on the floor.

Riley and Gabe shifted on their floor pillows to face each other. "If they start fighting, I might need you to break it up," she said to him.

"I will punch Nick in the face again and sit on Canon," Gabe promised.

"You're a good man, Gabe."

"Silence!"

Riley rolled her eyes.

"For this exercise, you will look deeply into your partner's eyes," Elanora continued.

"That's gonna get awkward fast," Mrs. Penny guessed.

Awkward and deadly with two alpha guys staring each other down.

Gabe stared into Riley's eyes, his brown eyes seeming to burrow their way into her brain, her soul. It was like staring down a golden retriever.

"Now, you will take control of your minds and direct negative, hurtful thoughts at your partner."

"Grandmother, is this necessary?" Wander the peacemaker asked.

"It is absolutely necessary. Begin."

"I hope the old lady chokes on her egg salad today."

"What is up with that old bat dressing up like Stevie Nicks?"

"I said direct your thoughts at your partners, *not* me," Elanora said crisply.

"Come on, Fred. Gimme your best shot," Blossom said, rolling her shoulders.

"What are you looking at, fuckface?" Nick asked Canon.

"A sweaty douchebag," Canon returned.

Riley decided to leave them to her grandmother's wrath and focused on Gabe's face. She couldn't think anything mean about him. It just wasn't possible. He had the same kind of soul as her sister. Open, warm, loving.

"Your hair is not very shiny."

Riley blinked.

Gabe was doing their assignment, and she could hear him loud and clear.

"Yeah? Well, your head is shiny enough for the both of us," she shot back internally.

Gabe flinched as if she'd struck him.

"Sorry."

"No, you must keep going. We must complete the assignment. You're not a tall enough person."

"Gabe. Come on. If you're going to do the assignment, do the assignment. Don't be a scaredy cat."

"I am not a frightened feline. You are the one who does not try hard because you fear failure. Which only serves to limit your experiences in life."

Okay. That one hurt.

"You want to talk about fear? Which one of us is afraid to stand up to a crusty old lady and date my sister?"

"Elanora made me who I am. To disrespect her is unthinkable."

"To accept her word as law means you don't care deeply enough about yourself or my sister to stand up to her."

"At least I am not afraid of the hard work it takes to do good work."

"What kind of work do you do anyway? As far as I know, all you do is hang around eating ice cream and moping after a woman you're too afraid to profess your feelings for."

Gabe's eyes filled with tears, and Riley blinked back her own.

"I am not here to fall in love with Wander. I am here to guide you. Yet I have found it impossible to guide someone who is determined to go nowhere."

Riley's gasp was audible. *"Nowhere? I'm trying! I show up for psychic boot camp. I open myself up to the cotton candy!"*

"Yet you still waste most of your energy wishing you were different."

"Enough!" Elanora's voice rang out. The thwack of the walking stick next to her startled Riley out of her trance of criticism.

She realized that they were sitting in the midst of chaos. Nick and Canon were wrestling. Mrs. Penny was loudly apologizing to Wander, who looked a little shell-shocked.

"I've never even heard some of those words before," Wander whispered.

"Yeah, well, hang out with a few Navy SEALs in Shanghai, and you'd be surprised what language you pick up."

"What do you mean everyone knows it's a toupee?" Fred howled, clutching his Justin Bieber hair.

"Oh, gosh. I'm so sorry, Fred," Blossom said, rubbing her temples.

Elanora got to her feet and crossed stiffly to where Nick was squishing Canon's face into the floor.

She prodded Nick in the ass with the walking stick. Hard.

Canon used the distraction to throw Nick off him.

The entire room felt like backstage during a taping of *The Jerry Springer Show*. Hurt feelings reverberated within the walls.

"Good."

Everyone went silent and stared at Elanora.

Riley and Gabe exchanged a look. *Good* wasn't in the woman's vocabulary.

"I'm sorry. Did you say 'good'?" Blossom asked her mother.

"I did. You all managed to fumble your way through the execution."

"Yay us?" Riley said, heavy on the sarcasm.

"You have each just witnessed how powerful your thoughts are. How you were able to transmit messages to one another by merely using your minds—as lacking as they are—and your eyes."

"What exactly did that prove?" Riley demanded.

"That, to some degree, you each have the ability to read the feelings if not the thoughts of others."

"Damn. Granny's got a point," Canon said quietly.

Wander raised her hand. "Perhaps we should reverse the exercise by thinking loving thoughts about our partners? It would clear the room of any negative vibrations."

"Nonsense. That is an unnecessary waste of time," Elanora sniffed. "This is not a preschool class with sharing time. We are adults. We will move on."

Canon threw an elbow into Nick's ribs and caught a fist in the jaw for his trouble.

"Seriously, can we split those two up?" Riley asked.

Her grandmother pinned her with an imperious look. "Stop worrying about everyone else around you, and focus on yourself."

Jeez. Okay, lady.

"We will move on to the next exercise. Instead of working against each other, you and your partner will work together."

"Work together to do what?" Riley asked.

"The point of this exercise is to boost your own powers by using the energy of another. Gabriel's gift lies in his ability to attach himself to the energy of others. Like a leech."

As annoyed as she was with Gabe's character assassination on her, Riley didn't know how she felt about anyone else dissing him. "A what now?"

"A leech attaches itself to a host and makes the host's blood available to itself. Gabriel can attach himself to your gifts and enhance your energy."

This was weird. Even for a Thorn.

"Okaaaaaaay," Riley said, wondering if her grandmother had broken into Mrs. Penny's Bloody Mary mix.

"You will begin."

"Begin? Begin what? What are we doing?"

"I will follow your lead," Gabe told Riley. "Ask your spirit guides a question, and I will make myself available to aide you in interpreting the answer."

Riley was feeling a bit raw and didn't know if she was ready to forgive and forget. He was her friend. Friends weren't supposed to notice your crappy parts. And if they did, they certainly weren't supposed to throw them in your face.

Her resistance crumbled under the weight of her grand-mother's glare.

"Fine. But what do I ask? I already had a chat with Dead Bianca at the sauna séance."

Her grandmother's eyes narrowed sharply.

"Perhaps find another question for which you do not have the answer," Gabe said cryptically.

"Find out where Larry is," Nick called from behind her.

"Good idea."

"Okay. Let's get this over with."

"That is not the attitude that brings your gifts into sharp focus. That is the attitude of a moping child slamming their bedroom door," Elanora said coldly.

Riley felt her nostrils flaring even as she realized her mean grandmother was right. Just because she didn't *want* to be a psychic didn't give her an excuse for not being the best damn psychic she could be. She made a mental note to consider turning that bit of wisdom into a motivational poster with a kitten.

"Fine. I'm ready to begin," Riley announced.

She closed her eyes and shut out the rest of the room.

Bringing her breath into focus, she called up her admittedly sporadic training and dropped lightly and intentionally back into Cotton Candy World.

"Hello, spirit guides. It's me, Riley."

"I am Gabe."

Gabe was *in* her cotton candy world. She couldn't see him, but she could certainly sense his presence. Steady. Calming. Good. *Familiar.*

Just like the presence she'd felt during her vision with Bianca. "Hey. Were you in my head at the séance too?"

"I was. I should have sought your permission beforehand, but I was concerned for your well-being."

Suddenly, she felt like a jerk for being mad at him. Gabe didn't mean to hurt her on purpose. He'd simply been telling her a truth she needed to hear.

"Thank you for being here, Gabe," she said sincerely.

"You are most welcome, Riley. I am honored."

"Okay, spirit guides. We're here to find out where Larry Rupley is. He disappeared over a week ago, and we need to find him."

The clouds pulsed lazily. She'd learned that the energy in the clouds directly reflected her own energy. And after falling through a roof having sex, sleeping on the lumpiest divan in the history of furniture, getting glitter bombed and boot camped, she was running low on fuel.

But something else was happening. A boost, a rev, a jolt of energy. It was different from a shot of espresso. Smoother and steadier. It was…Gabe.

The man wasn't a leech. He gave rather than took. Anchored rather than disrupted.

The clouds deepened in color and began to part. Riley felt herself being pulled into them, zooming through them, their cool moisture soothing her overheated skin.

"I see something," she announced as the clouds thinned a little more.

It was a tall hefty figure slowly trotting down the sidewalk. One running shoe in front of the other.

"He is running," Vision Gabe observed from somewhere.

"Slowly," Riley added. "He's on the riverfront. Close to our house!" Then suddenly there was a hard tug, and she was no longer watching Larry plod along the riverfront. She was dragged forcibly up and back. "Hey, I can see our house from here!"

A moment later, she was floating above Larry's neighborhood. Her stomach dipped as she plummeted toward his town house like she was on a cosmic roller coaster.

"Continue to breathe deeply," Gabe reminded her.

"I need to start wearing motion sickness patches for this crap," she complained as her vision swayed. One second, she was standing outside Larry's door, and the next, she was passing through it like a ghost.

"Am I a ghost? Am I dead? Did Larry kill me?"

"All is well. Your guides are just moving you through the vision."

To be safe, Riley counted her fingers and toes to make sure they all made it through the door with her.

"They are trying to show you something."

She looked up and saw clouds swirling around the stack of mail on Larry's dining room table. There was a package that seemed to glow brighter than the others. But it wasn't actually glowing.

It was sparkling.

"Oh, shit. Are you seeing what I'm seeing?" Riley whispered.

Gingerly she reached out to pick up the box, which was blinding in its sparkle now.

"Does this box mean something to you?" Vision Gabe asked.

"I think Larry Rupley got a glitter bomb in the mail and never opened it."

34

N ick!"

The panic in Riley's tone had him shoving Canon out of his way and rushing to her side. Her nose was twitching like she was mid-allergy attack.

"What is it? What did you see?"

"I think Larry Rupley got a glitter bomb."

"Fuck! The mail on the table," he said, catching up quickly.

"The return addresses on the packages are all different. You wouldn't have known."

"What's all this fuss?" Elanora demanded.

"Nick's been working on a missing person case. I think it's linked to the homicides Detective Weber is investigating. Which means his missing person isn't missing. He's dead."

"There's only one way to find out," her grandmother announced stiffly.

Riley blinked. "Are you saying—"

"I will consult my spirit guides," Elanora announced. "Gather the candles. The rest of you will shut up. Now."

Nick watched as the Basil-Thorn women gathered candles and crystals from around the room, organizing them around the matriarch. When Elanora was satisfied, she ordered the lights dimmed.

The room went silent, and all eyes focused on her as she arranged her skirts. She closed her eyes, and her lips began to move silently. Like a witch casting an ancient spell.

Riley slid her hand through Nick's as they both watched in fascination. This wasn't the show Elanora had put on at the mansion. This was something different. More raw. And for one aching second, he thought about asking her about Beth.

The tension in the room built as the sky seemed to darken outside.

The first streak of lightning that flickered across the window made him jump.

"Did she do that?" Nick whispered.

Riley shook her head.

Blossom leaned in. "Coincidence. Mom can't control the weather."

"How about Gabe?" he asked.

The man in question was seated just behind Elanora to the right. His eyes were also closed, and he too was muttering something under his breath.

"I mean, are we sure he's human?" Nick asked.

"We're mostly sure. I mean, I think," Riley whispered back.

Blossom leaned in again. "I think he's an extraterrestrial being."

"Who? Gabe?" Mrs. Penny asked. "No way. He's some secret billionaire who roams the earth trying to give away his fortune."

"Do any of you actually know anything about the man?" Nick asked.

Everyone shrugged.

"So you just let him move in with no references or anything?"

Again, they all shrugged.

"To be fair, if he *is* an extraterrestrial, we wouldn't be able to contact his references anyway," Blossom explained.

"Good point," Fred whispered from his cross-legged position on the floor.

There was another jolt of lightning, this one accompanied by an ominous roll of thunder.

"Poor Daisy. She ain't a fan of thunderstorms," Roger complained.

"She'll be fine, dear," Blossom assured him, patting his arm. "She has my nice gardening shed that you ripped apart to turn into a barn."

Elanora's eyes snapped open like cartoon window shades. "Larry Rupley is deceased," she announced.

Heads snapped back to look at her.

"How long? Where is he? How was he killed?" Nick asked.

She held up a wrinkled hand. "The newly dead do not communicate as well as the more experienced dead. He showed me the river. He was running."

"That's what I saw too," Riley agreed.

"Then he showed me a strange pattern. White and brown in thick lines and squares." Elanora held out her palm.

Obediently, Gabe handed over a pen and paper that he'd produced from who the hell knew where.

"He was taken somewhere with this pattern, and his life was ended. Now his soul is free to roam, but his body is still there alone."

She held out the paper between two bejeweled fingers to Nick. He took it and stared at it. "It looks like a game board?"

"I assure you, Mr. Rupley was not having any fun when he was murdered," Elanora said sternly.

Nick started to pace the studio.

"What are you thinking?" Riley asked, catching up with him in the corner. Her nose twitched twice.

"I think you already know."

She winced. "Sorry. I'm still plugged in to the other side or whatever. You want to check Larry's place to confirm the glitter bomb is there, and you want to call Weber."

He nodded and stopped in front of her. "I also want you to go home with your parents."

"But I can help," she said.

"I know you can. Which is why I need you to work with your grandmother on this."

She pouted. "But why can't I go find a dead body with you?"

"Because you and I both know, if you two put your heads together, you will figure out who our killer is. And if you know who he is, we can stop him from coming anywhere near you before your two weeks are up."

"Ugh. Fine. But just know that you're way less sexy when you make sense," she grumbled.

He grabbed her by the front of her tank and kissed her hard.

"Wow," she said, dazed, when he released her. "What was that for?"

"For being my girlfriend. For being a sexy psychic. For wearing those freaking shorts. Take your pick."

"Wow."

"I am weary," Elanora announced. "I would like to go to my daughter's house and enjoy a steak, medium rare, and wine."

"Well, Mom, you're going to have to get a ride and cook your own steak. Roger and I have a couples massage scheduled," Blossom said.

"Riley will take you," Nick told her. "Take the Jeep," he said to Riley, staring down at the piece of paper in his hand. Something niggled in the back of his mind.

Riley paused. "You have a tracker on it, don't you?"

"We can fight about this later. I'll put one on my car too. Then we'll be even."

"You can't presettle a fight," she complained. "Besides, I got glitter bombed today. That means I have two weeks before Glitter Guy comes after me."

"If he sticks to his pattern. Baby, this is for your safety and my peace of mind. Now be a good girl, and don't make me make Weber throw you in a holding cell downtown."

"Fine. But for the record, I'm annoyed with you."

"I can deal with that. Gabe, you're with Riley and Scary Granny."

35

Y ou live in a place like this, don't you?" Nick asked, unlocking Larry Rupley's door while Weber surveyed the street.

"I live in a town house, if that's what you're trying to get at."

"I was going more for soulless bachelor pad with no future."

"Just because you got yourself a girlfriend doesn't put you in a better position than me."

"That's exactly what it means. I'm living with a woman. I'm better than you are."

"Why are we here?" Weber asked, glancing around the living room.

It wasn't messy because Larry didn't own enough to mess up.

Nick led the way into the dining area, yanking a pair of gloves out of his back pocket. "Wait for it," he insisted as he pawed through Larry's mail. The first two packages were from Amazon. The third one was the right size and shape, and the return address said it was from a business called Shape Up. "This," he said, holding the box up triumphantly.

"A box. Congratulations, Santiago. You just broke the case wide open."

"It's a glitter bomb, jackass. At least according to my hot psychic girlfriend."

Now he had the detective's interest. "You're saying your missing person is tied to my two dead bodies?"

"Only one way to find out," Nick said, nodding at the box.

"Very funny, glitter boy. I'll have a uniform take it into the lab." Weber ducked into the living room, already dialing his phone. He returned minutes later. "This better be a glitter bomb. What the hell am I going to put in my report? My ex-partner called with information gleaned from his psychic girlfriend?"

"And her scary grandma," Nick added. "Who drew this when I asked her where the body is."

"Remember the good old days when criminals were too stupid to cover their tracks? I can't believe it's come to consulting psychics to solve murders," Weber complained. "How scary is this grandma, by the way?"

"I keep expecting wings to sprout from between her shoulder blades so she can flap around the room biting people."

"Lemme see this," Weber said, taking the paper from Nick. He cocked his head. "Looks architectural."

"Holy shit." Nick snatched it back and gave it another look. "I know where our dead body is."

———

They cruised past the property on Front Street first. A rusty iron gate blocked the driveway.

"Pull in at my place, and we'll walk over," Nick instructed.

"No, really, PI Obvious? I was planning on ramming the gate and kicking in the front door," Weber said, heavy on the sarcasm.

"Who pissed in your Marshmallow Munchies?" Nick asked.

"Excuse me if I care about getting justice for the victims and their families."

"How much justice are you going to get for three certified assholes?"

Weber slid into the Bogdanovich mansion's parking lot,

and they got out. Almost half an acre of thigh-high weeds and piles of dog shit lay between them and the Tudor-style estate.

Huge oak trees dotted what had once been a lawn. There was a detached three-car garage that matched the same buttery yellow and brown exterior of the main house.

They were halfway to the house, the dead grass and weeds crispy underfoot, when someone called his name.

"Yoo-hoo, Nick!"

They turned around and spotted Lily waving from the parking lot of the mansion. She had Burt on a leash. The dog was actively circling a prime shitting spot.

"If that dog sees a squirrel, that's the end of that tiny old lady," Weber observed.

"Burt's a gentle giant," Nick promised. "He's too lazy to chase anything but an ice cream truck."

He waved at Lily.

She cupped her hands and yelled, "You're at the wrong house!"

"Does she think you don't remember where you live?" Weber asked with a smirk. The joke was on him because he was about six inches away from getting his shiny loafer dipped in glittery dog shit.

"I know, Lily," he called back. "Detective Weber and I are just having a look around."

Burt's head came up at the sound of one of his humans' voices, and he ceased squatting.

"Uh-oh," Weber said as Burt tugged on the leash. "It was nice knowing Lily."

"You can let Burt go, Lily," Nick yelled. "I'll walk him."

Lily gave him an exaggerated thumbs-up and dropped the leash. "I'll make some lovely cucumber sandwiches for you and your handsome detective friend."

"Son of a bitch." Weber looked down at his shit-streaked loafer.

Nick snickered. "I forgot to mention you should probably watch your step."

"I do not miss you being my partner."

"Yeah, you do," Nick said with a smug grin. Burt bounded up to them, grinning goofily, and Nick picked up his leash. "Let's go find a dead body, buddy."

"Don't let that beast contaminate the crime scene."

"So you admit it's a crime scene," Nick said triumphantly as they continued the trek up to the house.

"I admit nothing—"

He would have said more, but the slow summer breeze shifted then, wafting the unmistakable scent of decomposition toward them.

Both men covered their noses, Weber with a handkerchief and Nick with the neck of his sweaty, sparkly T-shirt. Burt lifted his nose and sniffed excitedly.

"Could be roadkill," Weber insisted.

"Decomp and what the hell is that?" Nick asked, taking another sniff. "It smells like someone died on the john in an old lady's house."

"What?"

"You know how old ladies have that dried potpourri crap and those smelly soaps?"

Weber lowered the handkerchief for a second. "Oh, God. That's exactly what it smells like."

The breeze died, leaving them with just the heavy humidity, and they both uncovered their noses.

"I feel like I can still taste it," Nick complained.

"You never could handle the smell of death," his ex-partner reminisced.

"I threw up *one* time!"

"Six times."

"Whatever. How are we getting in there? Is that smell enough to get us in the door?" Nick nodded at the mammoth arched wooden door recessed into the long front porch.

"I have a better idea," Weber said, pulling out his phone and heading in the direction of the For Sale sign.

Ten minutes later, the metal gate creaked open, and a shiny white SUV rolled up the cracked asphalt of the driveway. A tall, lanky woman got out with a big let-me-sell-you-something smile and sunglasses. She wore a purple skirt that showed off long legs and a sleeveless matching tank that showcased nicely muscled arms.

"Gentlemen! You obviously have great taste if you're interested in this property. It's the perfect fixer-upper for a handy couple."

"We're definitely not a couple," Nick said. Burt let out a happy bark and swished his tail in the dead leaves on the driveway as if volunteering to be part of a couple.

"Investors with vision then," she decided. "I'm happy to show you around."

"Are you Haley?" Weber asked, stepping forward to shake her hand.

"I am. And this beautiful riverfront estate could be yours for a bargain-basement price."

Haley was about to be very disappointed.

"I'm Detective Weber, and this is my consultant, Nick. We're investigating a missing person who we think may be connected with this property."

Haley deflated. "Well, hell. You really got my hopes up."

Burt trotted over to her and leaned into her lower body comfortingly.

She blew out a breath and stroked a hand over his gigantic head. "Nice sparkly dog."

"His name is Burt," Nick said, making the introduction.

"Man, I've had this albatross of a mausoleum hanging around my neck for two years. Two years!" She kicked at a pine cone with very pointy shoes.

Burt trotted off to retrieve it.

Haley blew out a sigh. "Badge."

"Excuse me?" Weber asked.

She hooked her fingers. "Let me see your badge, please."

He held it up.

She grimaced. "You're not homicide, are you?" Weber hesitated, and she rolled her eyes. "Just great. Homicide's at my abandoned shithole estate with a sweaty guy and a cadaver dog looking for a 'missing person,'" she said, using air quotes.

"Technically, Burt and I are mostly civilians," Nick put in. "I'm a private investigator."

"And you think your missing person is dead in this house?"

"We can't really say," Weber hedged.

Haley tipped her head back and let out a strangled groan. "If you find a dead body in this house, I am screwed. No one wanted to buy this dump when someone hadn't died in it. What am I gonna do with a corpse?"

"The police usually remove the body for you," Nick offered.

"Yeah, the body, but the stench of death clings to a listing."

"Would you mind opening the place up and letting us have a look around?" Weber asked.

Haley shrugged. "Sure. What do I care? I'll just be stuck with this place until it falls down and gets condemned." She stomped past them onto the front porch and reached for the lockbox. "Some detectives you two are," she said. "The lockbox is broken, and the door's unlocked."

"When were you here last?" Weber asked.

"Three weeks," she said with a shrug. "I had a no-show showing. I got here early, opened the place up, and the guy never showed."

Nick glanced around the porch. "Is that your security camera?" he asked, pointing to a small camera tucked into the eaves of the porch pointing down at the front door.

Haley looked up and frowned. "That's not mine. There's nothing in here worth stealing unless some antique nut wants to steal a big-ass Kelvinator refrigerator installed in 1931."

Nick and Weber shared a look. Three weeks ago meant planning, calculation. It meant the killer had scoped out a kill site right around the time he sent the glitter bomb. If Larry

Rupley's body was inside, it meant the killer had planned and executed three murders. And Riley was next on the list.

"Do you have a name for the potential buyer you were supposed to meet?" Weber asked.

Haley pulled her phone out of her bag and scrolled through her calendar. "Says *Jackson Neudorfer*. He contacted me through the online listing, so it's probably a fake name."

Weber nodded and stepped away, his phone to his ear.

Haley gave the front door a nudge, and it swung open. This time, the breeze wasn't necessary. The smell of death hit them in the face.

"Oh, hell," she groaned and yanked a pack of tissues and a spray bottle of essential oils out of her bag. She doused two tissues and handed one to Nick.

"You don't have to go in there," he said, accepting the tissue. It smelled clean, like eucalyptus and lavender. Better than his own sweaty pits or the decomposing body.

Burt jogged for the door, and Nick stepped on his leash.

"I'm going in," Haley said firmly. "My dad was on the job in Philly for twenty years. I'm more used to this than most. Besides, I know this place like the back of my hand."

Weber returned, pocketing his phone and grabbing his handkerchief again. Together the three humans and one dog stepped inside.

"These are the original marble floors," Haley said, sliding into real estate agent mode. "They were imported from Italy. The ceilings here in the foyer are twenty feet high, and that's all original woodwork. And since you two aren't buying the place, I can tell you they were assholes who made their money on the backs of underpaid, overworked coal miners and steelworkers."

"Wow," Nick said. It was a hell of a space with a big-ass grand staircase curving up and around to the second floor. Rooms opened off both sides of the foyer, and hallways flanked both sides of the staircase. Rooms that had a few pieces of furniture and zero glitter. Rooms that would make a pretty damn nice waiting room and office, Nick couldn't help but notice. Burt looked impressed too. Weber looked grim.

"Depressing, isn't it? The foundation is sound, and the roof is new. An investor with pockets that weren't quite deep enough managed to rewire and replumb most of the house a couple of years ago. But he lost a boatload of cash in a divorce and ended up moving to Santa Fe. He rented it out to a couple of tenants over the years, including some wacky candlemaker," Haley said.

That explained the potpourri smell, Nick decided.

"I'll take the south. You take the north," Weber decided, handing out gloves before unholstering his gun.

"Got it," Nick said, doing the same with his piece, which he'd tucked into the waistband of his shorts. "You might want to wait outside," he told Haley.

She produced a small Glock from her bag. "I'm coming with you," she said firmly. "You'll need my help accessing the secret passage between the servants' quarters and the main floor."

"Don't shoot anyone," Weber called. "I don't want to deal with the paperwork."

Nick jerked his head toward the left. "Let's go. What's the asking price?" he asked.

"The asking price is practically free. That's not the problem. It's the tax liens. The mouse and bat infestation. The fact that no one in their right minds wants an eight-bedroom, ten-bathroom house with two kitchens, neither of which have been updated in a million years. There's not enough parking for it to be an event space. It's too chopped up to be a family home. It's basically the perfect dumping ground for dead bodies."

They cleared the first room on the left. It was a high-ceilinged living room with a fireplace and French doors that opened out onto the wraparound porch. Beyond that was a moody-looking den with wood paneling, an even bigger fireplace, and an entire wall of bookcases. No body, but both rooms looked like they'd make kick-ass offices. Beyond the den was a long skinny room with countertops running the length

304

on both walls. There was an exterior door that led out onto the side porch.

"Is that a ramp?" he asked, peering through the dingy glass.

"Yep," Haley said morosely. "An owner added that in 1993. They were going to turn this place into a bed-and-breakfast until the bats ran them out."

She directed him into the hallway, where they passed a large built-in hutch on the way to the last room on the first floor. It was a huge formal dining room with a high coffered ceiling and built-in hutches on either side of an ornately carved buffet.

The smell had intensified, making it impossible for him to fantasize about using the space as a fancy conference room.

"That secret passage you mentioned. Is it nearby?" Nick asked.

"It's actually a staircase," she said, gesturing for him to follow. Back in the hallway, she stopped in front of the hutch. "You just push here." She pushed one of the trim pieces until it recessed into the wall. With a creak, the entire left side of the hutch popped out of the wall by an inch or two.

The smell was overwhelming.

Nick gestured for Haley and Burt to stand back and gave the cabinet a hard tug. He shoved his gun into the open space and peered into the dark, trying not to gag.

Burt whined.

"Looks like we found our guy," Nick said grimly.

36

The silence in the Jeep was oppressive as Riley navigated across the bridge toward her parents' home on the West Shore. Elanora sat in the passenger seat, clutching her purse in her lap, her face painted in frown lines.

"*Awkward*," Uncle Jimmy sang in her head.

"That was nice of you to help Nick and Weber," Riley ventured.

"One does not use their gifts to be nice. One uses their gifts to be useful," her grandmother snapped.

"*Has anyone ever told her she looks like Grumpy Cat?*" Uncle Jimmy wondered.

"Still. You didn't have to help Nick with his case."

"Getting justice for the dead is a noble pursuit. When one is properly trained," Elanora said pointedly.

"You don't have to be so judgmental all the time, you know," Riley said.

"*You should respect your elders. Even the crabby ones*," Uncle Jimmy chimed in.

"Who is this person who haunts your vehicle?" Elanora asked with a disapproving frown.

"My uncle Jimmy. My dad's brother. You can hear him too?"

"You will leave us in peace," Elanora ordered, presumably to the spirit of her dead uncle.

"Look, I know you like being in charge. But he's *my* uncle, and you can't tell him to leave my Jeep," Riley pointed out.

"You do not need any more distractions in your life. You have been blessed with great gifts that you seem determined to squander."

Riley clenched her teeth. "Just because I don't want to live my life the way you live yours doesn't mean I'm doing it wrong."

"That's precisely what it means," Elanora clipped. "You waste your time 'living your life' while ignoring your duty to hone your gifts, to be of service to this world."

"I'm not interested in only being of service, Grandmother. I am a human being. That means I get to have a life."

"A life," she scoffed. "Look at what you've done to my most promising pupil. Gabe used to be practically inhuman in his focus. His mind was sharp, his body toned. His entire being was dedicated to service. Now he eats ice cream and lusts after my granddaughter. He's soft and useless."

"He's sitting in the back seat," Riley said, glancing at Gabe in the rearview mirror. He looked like someone had just ripped the head off his favorite teddy bear and then drop-kicked it off the roof of a building.

"I do not concern myself with the feelings of others."

"No shit," Riley snapped.

"You will not take that tone with me, young lady."

"I'll take that tone if you've earned that tone. Maybe you're happy being a servant to your gifts, which I doubt, seeing how miserable you are *all the time*. But that's not how I want to live, and it's not how Gabe has to live either. I appreciate your knowledge, what little you've decided to share with me. But you don't get to tell us how to live our lives."

Riley was still fuming when she turned onto her parents' street and almost missed the catastrophe.

"What disaster is this?" Elanora demanded as Riley slammed on her brakes in the middle of the street.

"You have got to be kidding me," Riley groaned.

Her parents' fence was horizontal, crushing an entire row of boxwoods on the Strump side of the property line.

Daisy the spite cow was grazing happily on the buffet of orange zinnias in the middle of the front yard. Chelsea Strump, dressed in pink tennis shorts and a white polo, was standing in front of the cow, screaming bloody murder. Her helmetlike hair didn't budge as she shouted and waved her arms like a deranged marionette.

"You stupid walking hamburger! I'm going to shoot you between the eyes and turn you into a roast!" the woman howled.

Suddenly, Riley felt the swoop in her gut and found herself staring at Chelsea through cotton candy clouds. "Oh, hell," she murmured.

Her vision narrowed on Chelsea until there was a sudden burst of air and glitter rained down.

"You have *got* to be kidding me!" Chelsea Strump, cow-hating neighbor, was apparently Glitter Guy's next target.

Riley fought off her seat belt and jumped out of the Jeep.

"I do not have time for this ridiculousness. I want my steak," Elanora announced, climbing out the other side and stomping toward Riley's parents' house.

"Chelsea!" Riley yelled, running into the yard.

Chelsea responded by turning the hose on her.

"Get off my lawn and take your stupid livestock with you. Unless you want me to butcher it in the front yard!"

"Chelsea, this is very important. Have you been glitter bombed yet?" Riley asked, looping an arm around the cow's thick neck and trying to hip check it out of the flower bed.

"Your illegal family farm is destroying my yard!" Chelsea howled, waving the hose wildly and managing to soak herself in the process. "I have tried to be tolerant. I've tried being polite."

"Really? When?"

Daisy meandered out of the flower bed.

"But you people are the worst! I hate every last one of you, and I hope you all get some kind of incurable disease and die tomorrow!"

If the woman was comfortable saying it to her face, Riley could only imagine what she'd said to people online.

"Stay where you are!" Chelsea screamed, firing the hose over Riley's shoulder.

Gabe took the deluge of water to the face heroically. "May I be of assistance, Riley?" he sputtered.

"I will call the police right now if you don't get off my grass!"

"Good! Yes. Do that," Riley said, deciding she'd rather take her chances explaining things to the local police than having Chelsea get herself murdered. Even if she was an asshole.

Daisy wandered over to the plantings around Chelsea's front porch and helped herself.

"Stop devouring my begonias," Chelsea screeched, dropping the hose and gripping her hair.

Riley pushed at Daisy's sternum, trying to back the cow out of the flower bed to no avail.

"Gabe, give me a hand here," she called, then looked back at Chelsea. "Look! This is really important. Have you received a glitter bomb in the mail?"

Chelsea glared at her. "Is that what your father's next power move is? Well, I can assure you, I won't be opening anything. And I'll be suing your entire family for harassment, property damage, and emotional suffering."

Gabe made clucking noises that had Daisy lifting her head and giving a curious "Moo?"

"Keep doing that," Riley encouraged.

Chelsea flounced into her house without closing the door, most likely to call the cops or to find a cow-size weapon.

Riley abandoned the cow that was trotting after Gabe like a puppy and followed her.

She'd never been in the Strump house before. The front door opened directly into a dark living room with white carpet. There were twin armchairs, both upholstered in a mauve velour, that faced the TV and a white brick fireplace. A long low couch in a dusky pink squatted along one wall decorated with a shrine-like photographic timeline of the Strump family. Both boys had picked colleges on the West Coast, presumably to put as much distance between themselves and their helicoptering mother as possible.

Riley didn't blame them one bit.

Chelsea stormed back into the living room with her cell phone in one hand and a shotgun in the other. "Take off your shoes! I just steam cleaned the carpet, you barnyard animal!"

Riley threw her hands up in the air and kicked off her flip-flops. "Don't shoot!"

"You should have thought of that before you trespassed," the woman snarled. She tried to pump the handle but couldn't do it with her phone in her hand. "Here. Hold this." She thrust the phone at Riley.

Not wanting to get shot, Riley did as she was told.

Chelsea awkwardly pumped the lever. It fell off the gun onto the snow-white carpet. Both women stared down at it.

"Why is the universe against me?" Chelsea wailed. "Why do people like your idiotic parents get to live happily ever after, and I'm the one who suffers? I go to church and tell Reverend Clampeter all about the sins other congregation members commit. I sit on the school board so I can weed out bad seeds in the district. Once I even bought Girl Scout cookies from an Asian scout. Yet I am saddled with Neanderthals for neighbors!"

Riley was getting nudges from her spirit guides at an alarming rate. She was seeing coffee and Channel 50's building followed by one of those psychic explosions. Only this time, there was no glitter.

"Maybe it's more of an attitude problem?" Riley suggested.

Chelsea put down the shotgun, picked up a pink tufted pillow from the couch, and screamed into it.

"Look, I'm sorry about the cow and the damage. I'm sure my parents will work something out with you, but I really need to know if you've gotten any strange packages in the mail or noticed anyone following you—"

"A glitter bomb. How tacky. Your parents know the pride I take in my home. Of *course* they would attack me there. Well, this time, the joke is on them. I'm just going to burn their house down!" Her eyes were wide under her blond helmet of hair. "That's it! I'll just get my mower gas and a lighter, and I won't have to listen to your stupid cow having a conversation with your idiot father ever again. I won't have to smell incense burning or see that disgusting neon sign lit up every Monday, Wednesday, and Saturday!"

Chelsea let out an unhinged high-pitched giggle that made the hair on Riley's neck stand up.

"Maybe arson is going a little far," Riley suggested.

"Maybe arson is going a little far," Chelsea mimicked.

Riley was tempted to walk out the door and let Glitter Guy finish his business. But then she remembered Dickie. She'd made an effort, sort of, to keep her gross neighbor from getting shot, but he'd still ended up dead.

If she wanted to look at herself in the mirror, she probably needed to do her best to save Chelsea's life. Even if the woman was horrible.

"Do you post comments on Channel 50's social media?" Riley asked.

But Chelsea was mid-rage. The woman stomped into the kitchen and started yanking open drawers. The countertops gleamed white. There were no stray fingerprints on the refrigerator door. The dish towels were looped over the oven handle at precise ninety-degree angles.

"Aha!" Chelsea triumphantly produced a long lighter from a drawer filled with birthday candles organized by number.

Riley stepped in front of her. "You can't just burn my parents' house down."

"Why not? Everyone else on this block does whatever the hell they feel like. The Hollenbachs don't mow their lawn until it's four inches high. *Four inches!*" she repeated like it was a personal affront. "Then there's the Hummels, who leave their garbage cans out for twenty-four hours. What is this? A homeless encampment?" The unhinged laughter was back. "Maybe I'll just burn down the entire neighborhood!"

Chelsea barreled into Riley, a woman on a mission.

"Gabe!" Riley yelled.

His hulking form appeared respectfully on the doorstep. "May I come in?" he asked politely. Daisy the cow was nowhere to be seen through Chelsea's open door or front windows.

"Don't you dare set one sweaty foot across that threshold or I'll set you on fire too," Chelsea howled. "You and your bulging muscles and your flawless skin! It's not normal, I tell you!"

"Can you stop threatening everyone for a minute? I think you're in danger and—"

"Of course I'm in danger! I live next door to a hippie circus. It's amazing I'm still alive. Your mother hangs her laundry out to dry in the backyard! Who does that? What kind of monsters raised you?"

Fresh line-dried sheets were the best to crawl between at night, but Riley didn't feel like that information was pertinent to the conversation.

"Now, Chelsea," Riley said, holding up her hands and trying to look nonthreatening.

Gabe did the same thing. Except his eyes rolled back in his head, and for a moment, he stood completely still. And then his gigantic body keeled over face-first onto the carpet.

"Don't you drool on my carpet! I just steam cleaned it yesterday!" Chelsea shrieked.

But Riley's attention was on the figure behind Gabe. The figure holding a now-empty syringe in one hand and a gun in the other. He was glaring at Riley.

"You're ruining everything!" he shouted.

37

Riley stared in shock at Hudson Neudorfer, the affable Channel 50 employee who brought her coffee when she'd gone to the studio with Detective Weber to interview the on-air talent. He was holding a gun.

"Hudson?"

He stepped over Gabe's legs and into the house.

"Of course it's me. You're the psychic. It's why you keep messing up my plans, isn't it? You knew all along!"

She really didn't have it in her to handle two unhinged individuals at the same time.

"I really didn't. I'm not a very good psychic."

"Oh, please. I'm supposed to believe that you just *happened* to show up at Channel 50. You just *happen* to be here when I'm delivering the package. You just *happen* to live next door to one of the murder scenes."

"*That's* what that smell is?" Riley yelped. She felt suddenly nauseated.

"Take your shoes off!" Chelsea yelled.

"She just steam cleaned the carpet," Riley explained.

Hudson glanced down at his sneakers, then back up at Chelsea. "No," he said firmly. "And I hope that I'm tracking mud inside."

She gasped and took an unsteady step back as if he'd struck her. "How dare you," she hissed.

"How dare *I*?" Hudson repeated. "How dare *you*! You are a horrible human being. Do you know how terrible you have to be in order to make my murder list? Pretty freaking terrible, lady."

"I think you're in the wrong house. The terrible people live next door. That's their cow destroying my yard."

"Good! I'm glad your yard is being destroyed just like you've destroyed the lives of other people."

"Uh, Hudson. What did you do to Gabe?" Riley asked, inching closer to her friend. She couldn't tell if he was breathing or not.

"I injected him with a tranquilizer. He'll be fine. But I am not happy that I had to go off plan. You are ruining everything!" He glared at Riley.

"Is this a friend of yours?" Chelsea asked Riley.

"No. I think he's here for you," Riley answered, noticing a small package sitting on Chelsea's welcome mat. "Is that the glitter bomb?" she asked him.

Hudson pointed the gun at her. "It most certainly is. And now it's going to go to waste since I have to kill both of you today," he complained.

"You are *not* setting off a glitter bomb in this house," Chelsea said, putting her hands on her hips.

"Maybe don't antagonize the guy with the gun?" Riley suggested.

"Shoot *her*." Chelsea shoved Riley in front of her. "But take her outside first."

"I don't want to shoot *her*," Hudson said with a stomp of his foot.

Riley thought she saw a flicker of movement in Gabe's trapezius muscles.

"Then why are you waving a gun around in my house?" Chelsea demanded.

"I don't really want to shoot you either. I'm on my lunch

break, damn it! I had much more dramatic plans. But a good vigilante adapts. I'll do what I have to do," he insisted.

This was not good. This was very not good. Nick was going to kill her...if, by some chance, she survived being murdered by Hudson.

Gabe was definitely at least breathing. That was a good thing. But she didn't need him coming out of his tranquilizer and scaring Hudson into shooting them all.

"I'm sorry for ruining your plans," Riley began. "Is there anything I can do to make it up to you?"

"Make it up to me?" Hudson repeated, looking at her like she was the village idiot. "Do you know how long I've been planning this? How meticulous I was with my research and organization? And then you come along, and instead of incapacitating her and throwing her into the mountain lion enclosure at the Hershey Zoo, I have to skip straight to the grand finale *weeks* ahead of schedule."

Oh boy.

"You were going to throw me into the mountain lion enclosure? Why?" Chelsea demanded, with not nearly enough fear in her tone.

"I'm glad you asked," Hudson said, throwing the syringe over his shoulder and pulling a folded sheet of paper out of the back pocket of his neatly pressed khakis. He cleared his throat. "'You're a horrible mother. You deserve to be left for dead and eaten by mountain lions for putting your child in danger.'"

"I stand by my statement," Chelsea sniffed. "A good mother would have driven home and made her husband put gas in the car. She certainly shouldn't have left her baby strapped in while she was pumping gas. Of *course* someone stole her minivan with the baby in it."

"Seriously?" Riley asked Chelsea.

"You see what I'm dealing with?" Hudson said, gesturing toward Chelsea with the gun.

"So you were monitoring the comments?" Riley asked him.

"Armand didn't know a Facebook page from an Instagram

account until I offered to help. I was just being nice. Something all those commenters know nothing about," Hudson explained.

"That's why you want to kill me? Because I posted a completely valid truth online?" Chelsea scoffed. "That's stupid. You're stupid."

"And you're trying to stop me?" Hudson said to Riley.

She shrugged.

"Because I made a comment online," Chelsea repeated, clearly missing the point.

"Because you have no empathy, no regard for your fellow human beings. What about when you told a mother to put her family out of their suffering and kill herself?"

Chelsea rolled her eyes. "Oh, come on. She shouldn't have let her daughter out of her sight. She's a horrible parent. My boys never wandered into a bison enclosure at Zoo America," Chelsea pointed out.

"She was giving CPR to someone's grandfather," Hudson shouted. "He survived, and her daughter was fine!"

Chelsea shrugged. "She's a mother first. It's her duty to never take her eyes off her children. I was just pointing out what we all know. She's a bad mother and deserves public humiliation."

"So you combined the mountain lion mauling and the Zoo America situation into a death sentence," Riley said, spotting Chelsea's cell phone half-buried in the thick carpet.

"Who died and made you judge and jury over mothers?" Hudson said with a humorless little laugh.

"Obviously, I'm a better mother. Look at my boys," Chelsea said, pointing at her photo shrine. "They're perfect. They never needed braces. They were both varsity starters in their sports. They both took attractive young ladies to prom. They had the perfect upbringing, and they're perfect young men."

Hudson used his gun hand to flip the page. He cleared his throat again. "I'm so glad you brought that up. As the perfect mother, you must be aware that your son Henry was arrested twice this year for underage drinking, public intoxication, and urinating on a police officer."

"That's absurd," Chelsea scoffed.

"Your son Elvin has been seeing a therapist with virtually no online security. Twice a week, he goes to an office off-campus and tells Dr. Najimura just how horrible you are."

"You take that back! Neither of my perfect little boys needs therapy! I gave them everything. I am the perfect mother."

"You gave them a suitcase full of neuroses and a complete and total inability to problem solve," Hudson said triumphantly. "Ergo, you are a horrible mother, and you deserve the public humiliation of everyone knowing it."

Riley started to inch her way toward Chelsea's cell phone. If she could call 911, they might be able to survive this.

"I am *not* a horrible mother! I am the best mother in the history of motherhood! I *invented* Elf on the Shelf and gluten-free bake sales! I color coordinated the entire family's Easter outfits every year for the past two decades. I made sure the boys never had a teacher who didn't like them or a grade below a B. When Elvin's soccer team lost the tournament in fifth grade, I sued the soccer organization for poor refereeing and bankrupted the organization!"

"It's like she doesn't even hear what she's saying," Hudson said to Riley.

"I know," Riley sighed, stretching her foot toward the phone's screen.

"And that's why she has to die."

"Hang on," Riley said. Her shoulder blades were starting to scream from holding her hands up for so long. "Just because she's a horrible person doesn't give anyone the right to kill her."

"If I don't kill her, she's just going to keep doing harm. Sooner or later, she's going to hurt someone badly enough that they'll hurt themselves."

She felt a nudge from her spirit guides. There was something important there, but it was hard to focus with a gun in her face.

"I'm stopping this horrible woman from ruining more lives," Hudson said. "*I'm* the hero."

Riley chanced a peek down at the floor and pressed her big toe to the emergency call button on the screen.

"The hero? Please! You're the bad guy, dummy," Chelsea scoffed. "If anyone's the hero in this scenario, it's me. I'm the one who's been wronged and bravely continues to hold my head high."

"You can't tell me you think she's a good person," Hudson said to Riley.

"Oh, I'm definitely not saying that."

"Then *why* are you trying to ruin everything?" he demanded. This time, Gabe's shoulder blades flexed.

"I'm not trying to ruin anything. I'm just trying to do the right thing," Riley insisted. "So why take the victims' electronics?" She needed to buy some time. Enough time for a 911 call to go through, the call to be traced, and Nick to get his sexy ass over here.

"Don't call them victims!"

"Sorry. How about *terrible people*?" she offered.

"I didn't want any obvious ties between the terrible people. One look at any of their browser histories, and any idiot could see they spent the majority of their time insulting people online. So I covered my tracks by covering theirs."

"Smart," Riley said.

"It was until you Scooby-Doo-ed your way into my plan. Now I have to accelerate my timeline, and thanks to you, the next seventeen terrible people on my list get to keep on being assholes," Hudson complained. "That's on you."

"Let's get back to this accelerated timeline thing. What does that mean, exactly?" Riley asked.

"I didn't even get to glitter bomb her," Hudson complained.

"What is it with you people and glitter bombs?" Chelsea demanded.

He rolled his eyes. "The glitter bombs are a two-week warning. The recipient of the bomb has two weeks to clean up their act and start behaving nicely."

"Nicely according to you, Hudson?" Riley asked loud

enough that anyone listening on the phone could hear, hopefully.

Hudson nodded. "I am the official judge, and I monitor each recipient's behavior after the glitter bomb. All any of them would have had to do is stop being horrible. No more mean comments online. No more cutting people off in traffic. No more stealing coworkers' lunches out of the fridge. It's not that hard."

"Wait a second. How many people have you killed?" The seriousness of the situation finally seemed to be sinking in with Chelsea.

"Three so far. You'd be amazed at how many assholes there are out there," he said conversationally. "Not one of them changed their behavior in the slightest. In fact, some of them got even worse. But I guess now we'll never know what you would have done with a warning, Chelsea."

"It sounds like a lot of planning went into this," Riley noted.

"I've been researching and following these jerks for months," Hudson explained. "I have a dossier on each one."

"Maybe you don't have to accelerate anything," Riley said hopefully. "Maybe you can consider this visit to Chelsea Strump's house her two-week notice. And you can sit back and watch to make sure she turns into a nice person."

"I demand my two weeks' notice," Chelsea insisted.

"That's not the way it works. And nice try, Ms. Thorn. But I'm not a crazy person. *She's* the crazy person," Hudson said, pointing the gun menacingly at Chelsea.

"Hudson, maybe you could put the gun down," Riley suggested.

"Moo?" Daisy the cow poked her head in the front door.

"Get out of here, you flea-ridden roadkill," Chelsea screeched.

"She can't even be nice to a cow," Hudson pointed out.

He had a point. Chelsea really was awful.

"Daisy, don't step on—" Riley's warning came too late

as the fleshy cow hoof crushed the package on the welcome mat. There was a muffled pop and a poof, and glitter exploded everywhere. The cow, not used to stepping on exploding boxes, hightailed it off the porch.

Riley spit out a mouthful of glitter.

Chelsea was frozen next to her.

"You okay?" Riley asked.

The woman sucked in a breath and started coughing up glitter.

"You…you…motherfucking assholes!"

Riley had never heard Chelsea swear. The woman considered four-letter words to be the language of disgusting poor people with no education.

"You think you can come into my house and—"

Hudson was remarkably glitter-free from the front, but when he bonked Chelsea on the head with the butt of his gun, Riley saw his back was more sparkly than a disco ball.

"Ow!" Chelsea howled.

Hudson frowned at the gun. "Huh. They make it look a lot easier on TV."

"You stupid son of a bitch. I hope you get testicular cancer, go through treatment, lose your hair, and the day you find out you're in remission, *you get run over by a bus!*"

Bonk.

This time, the blow penetrated Chelsea's seventeen layers of hair spray, and she slumped to the floor next to Gabe.

Hudson sighed, then looked at Riley. "Pick her up and get moving."

"Where are we going?" she asked.

"It's time for the grand finale."

38

"What's your problem?" Weber asked Nick as he slumped in the passenger seat of the cruiser. "You found your missing person. Doesn't that mean you get to take the rest of the week off and drink beer in your underwear?"

Nick frowned at his phone. "Riley's not responding to my texts. She should have made it to her parents' place over an hour ago."

"Maybe Scary Granny abducted her," Weber teased.

"GPS says she's there on her parents' street."

Weber snorted. "You're tracking your girlfriend?"

"It's consensual tracking. She can digitally stalk me too," Nick said defensively.

"I'm sure she's fine. There's a waiting period after the glitter bomb before this guy makes his move. He wouldn't move this fast."

"First, the guy has killed three people that we know of. He's obviously not right in the head. So if he wants to deviate from his fucking timeline, he will. Second, you reminding me that she's being targeted by a nutcase maniac isn't helping. Can't this piece of shit go any faster?"

He hit redial and listened as it rang a few times before going to voicemail.

"Maybe she just left her phone in the car," Weber said. His voice was calm, but Nick noticed that he was accelerating.

"Drive faster," Nick insisted, hitting redial again.

His gut was telling him something was off.

Three minutes later, they turned onto Dogwood Street and screeched to a halt. Riley's Jeep was parked in the middle of the street, doors open, engine on, in front of the neighbor's house.

The fence between the Thorns and the Strumps lay on the ground. Daisy the cow was taking a gigantic cow crap in the middle of the Strumps' driveway.

"Is that cow sparkling?" Weber asked.

"Fuck me." Nick jumped out of the car and pulled his gun. Weber did the same, and together they ran low toward the house. The front door was open. The living room looked like last call at a strip club, with a truckload of glitter. There was one spot on the carpet that was completely clear. A large, Gabe-size spot.

"Goddammit," Nick muttered.

"What the hell happened in here?" Weber asked grimly.

"Call for backup. Riley!" Nick shouted.

But there was no response. The house was empty. Riley was gone.

They cleared the house and returned to the yard to wait for their backup.

"He's got her," Nick said, pacing through a bed of already half-crushed flowers.

"Whose cow is this?" Weber asked as the glittery Daisy gave him an affectionate headbutt in the gut.

"Nicholas."

Nick jumped, and Weber let out a girly yelp of surprise.

Elanora seemed to have materialized on the ruined lawn out of nowhere.

"You will take me to my granddaughter," she announced.

"Love to, lady, but I don't know where she is," Nick snarled.

She held up a pale wrinkled hand. "You will find her and take me to her. She's in danger."

"Gee, you think?" he snapped.

"There is no time for sarcasm, young man."

Weber's phone rang. "What have you got?" he barked.

Nick's phone rang. He stabbed at the screen. "Now's not a great time, Penny."

"No shit, Sherlock," Mrs. Penny said, obviously not having received Elanora's memo on sarcasm. "Seeing as how we've got a code sparkle poo."

"What are you babbling about?"

"Your girlfriend just got dragged into Channel 50's studio by a gun-toting lunatic. It's definitely a code sparkle poo."

He tensed. "How do you know that?"

"You pay me to follow your girlfriend. I follow your girlfriend," she said. "I followed her to her parents', saw the whole thing go down. Bad guy showed up to leave a package and ended up tranqing Gabe and abducting Riley and that helmet-headed hyena who lives next door. I've got Gabe with me. He's a little woozy. We followed your bad guy across the river. Looks like he's planning something pretty big."

Fuck.

"Why are you *just now* calling me?"

"I got so excited I dropped my phone under the seat. My hands were all greased up from hash browns. Just now fished it out."

"I'll be there in ten minutes."

"We're figuring out a way inside," Mrs. Penny said.

"Do not do anything stupid before we get there," Nick shouted into the phone.

He disconnected, and Weber did the same.

"We gotta go to Channel 50," they said in unison.

They jogged back to Weber's cruiser.

"I will join you," Elanora said, appearing next to Weber. Weber jumped and slapped a hand to his chest.

"Fine. Whatever. Get in," Nick said, pushing Weber out of the way. "This time, I'm driving."

He didn't wait for his passengers to close their doors before revving the engine and throwing the car in reverse.

"We'll get to her," Weber promised.

Cold dread settled in Nick's gut. The suspect had deviated from the pattern, which meant anything could happen. And Riley was unarmed and unprotected.

"What did you get?" Nick asked, fishtailing onto the Route 83 on-ramp, lights on and sirens wailing.

"Jackson Neudorfer was a high school junior who committed suicide a few years back. Looks like bullying was involved. Had a little brother named Hudson, who just so happens to work at Channel 50."

"Fuck me," Nick muttered, riding the ass of a pickup truck and laying on his horn.

"Language, Nicholas," Elanora huffed from the back seat.

"Call Mrs. Penny," he said, throwing his phone in Weber's lap. "She's the eyes on the scene. Looks like a hostage situation."

"Great. Just what we need," Weber complained. "The paperwork alone will take weeks. Wait. Is Mrs. Penny the purple-haired fool who ran the ring of vigilantes and smashed her minivan into the fountain?"

"That's the one," Nick said grimly.

"Fuck me. Drive faster."

The cruiser screamed up Sixth Street and came to a halt just inches from the police barricade. Only a handful of cops were on the scene. Nick was already out of the car and running toward the building by the time a uniform started yelling that they couldn't park there. Weber badged them through the barriers, and Elanora followed at a disapproving distance.

"What have we got?" Weber snapped at one of the uniforms.

"Looks like a hostage situation inside. No contact with the suspect yet. Still trying to identify him."

"Hudson Neudorfer," Weber said. "He's an employee. Any idea how many hostages?"

"They were wrapping up the live morning show, so it's a full house in there," one of the officers reported.

Fists clenched at his sides, Nick stared at the hideous building that separated him from Riley. He needed to get inside. He spotted Gabe on the other side of the police barricade, leaning heavily against an SUV.

"Nicholas," Elanora said, appearing at his side.

"Gah! What?"

"Riley will defuse this situation," she announced calmly. "But she'll need your help to do it. You must get inside."

"I'm working on it," he promised.

She nodded grimly and disappeared into the crowd.

"Let him through," Nick snapped at the closest officer and pointed at Gabe.

Gabe headed his way, listing hard to the side.

"You okay there, Titanic?" Nick asked.

"I will be fine," Gabe promised, slurring his words. "It was just a horse tranquilizer."

"Where's Penny?" Nick asked.

Gabe pointed to the building. "Inside."

"Fuck. Show me."

39

This was not how she was going to die, Riley decided. Not sitting on a concrete floor surrounded by idiots. Chelsea was on her right, muttering under her breath about lawyers. On her left, Riley's ex-husband Griffin was rocking in place and whimpering about dry-cleaning fees.

Neither of them was smart enough to know just how much trouble they were all in.

Hudson had strolled right on into the studio as they were preparing for the noon news. Before anyone knew what was happening, he'd put a gun to Griffin's head and told everyone to get on the floor.

They'd gone to an emergency commercial break.

"How long are we going to have to stay like this?" Chelsea demanded. "This lighting is giving me a headache, and I need to make four dozen cupcakes for the marching band bake sale tomorrow."

"That's my chair," Griffin complained when Hudson sat down behind the anchor desk.

"Let the man with the gun sit in your chair," Riley advised.

"Just great," Griffin whined when Hudson lowered the seat. "It's going to take me forever to get it back to the right height."

"Oh, please," Valerie hissed from her position between cameras one and two. "You put it as high as it goes, and we all pretend you're a normal-size human."

"Let's focus on the real problem here," Riley advised. "That guy has killed three people so far, and he has more on his list."

"No one wants to kill me! Everyone loves me," Griffin insisted.

"Not everyone," Riley said pointedly. "Your new contract meant everyone else either lost their jobs or had to take a pay cut."

He waved a dismissive hand. "No one really minded. They were happy to make the sacrifice. Besides, I'm the one who brings the ratings, so I deserve to make more money."

"Have you continued to devolve, or was I really that stupid when I married you?" Riley wondered.

"Personally, I think it was a combination of both," the camera one operator at her feet chimed in.

"Hey, Don," Riley whispered. "Long time, no see."

"How's it going?" the hefty mustachioed man asked.

"So what's he going to do after he's done messing up my chair?" Griffin hissed, tugging at his collar. "You don't think he'll do something terrible like—"

"Kill you? Anything could happen at this point," Riley said.

"*Kill me?*" Griffin croaked. "I was going to say, 'Make me look silly on air.'"

He'd gone from indignantly inconvenienced to anxious. Beads of sweat appeared on his spackled forehead.

Griffin was a nervous sweater. And he was very, very nervous. He looked as if he'd been hosed down in Chelsea's front yard.

"Look. He's one guy with a gun. There's sixteen of us in here. If we attack him in order of least important person to most important person, most of us will survive," Chelsea said.

"Obviously, I'm the most important," Griffin said, latching on to her idea.

"You read things from a teleprompter and wear makeup,"

Chelsea scoffed. "I'm a *mother*. I'm raising the future of our country."

"Your kids are in college," Riley pointed out.

"And they still need their mother! I'm last. Griffin can be next to last," Chelsea conceded.

"Bella should be next to next to last," Griffin decided.

On cue, his fiancée popped up next to him and held out a hand to Riley. "Hi! I'm Bella!"

"I know who you are!" Riley yelled.

Hudson spun around to glare at her.

"Sorry," Riley said. "But she keeps introducing herself to me!"

"Didn't she steal your husband?" Chelsea asked.

"She sure did," Griffin said cheerfully. He was still sweating.

"This must be really awkward for you," Chelsea observed.

"It's not great."

"Don't mind Bella," Griffin said, reaching for Riley's hand. She snatched it away. "She has female face blindness."

"Female face blindness?" Riley repeated.

He nodded. "She only recognizes men. It's a medical condition."

Riley blinked slowly, then shook her head. "I'm not dying here with you people."

"So who should be first in line to attack this guy?" he asked. "I never cared for Armand. I don't like his urinal cake placement."

"Fine. He'll go first," Chelsea decided. "Then maybe that guy over there by the bagels. I don't like his shirt."

"That's Rose. She didn't sign my birthday card this year. Maybe she should go first?"

"You people can't just decide who lives and who dies," Riley hissed. This was what was wrong with the world. People like Griffin and Chelsea, who had overinflated senses of impor-tance, wielding power over others.

As the clock ticked closer and closer to noon, Riley saw Chris Yang get more fidgety.

"What a ratings gold mine. I hope he shoots Griffin on camera."

She flinched, instinctively wanting to tune out his thoughts, then realized it might be the only way she could get them all out of this.

"Will you both shut up? I need to concentrate," she whispered.

Griffin frowned. "Concentrate on what?"

"Just shut up and let me think," Riley snapped.

"No need to get so crabby. If you're wondering why our marriage didn't work out, that right there is a big reason. You yelled at me a lot."

"You deserved it," she growled. "Now, shut up and let me think."

She could hear sirens outside. Sirens meant cops. Cops didn't like to let entire TV studios full of people die. This was good news.

There was a happy humming coming from somewhere. Like someone in the room didn't have a care in the world... or a clue. Riley stole a glance at Bella, who wasn't moving or blinking. She was just sitting there looking like a dazed Disney princess. Either she was some kind of Zen master, or the woman had nothing going on upstairs.

Deciding it really didn't matter at this point, Riley closed her eyes and dropped into the clouds. "Okay, spirit guides. I need some help here. Give me something that will help stop Hudson."

Voices crowded into her head immediately. It was an overwhelming cacophony of anxiety and worries.

"We better be getting overtime for this."

"I can't believe I'm going to die with all these assholes."

"I really wish I wouldn't have had that second helping of Thai food last night. I don't know if this hostage-taker will let me go to the bathroom."

"Thorn, if you can read me, I'm here, and I'm gonna get you out. And then I'm going to yell at you for at least a week."

Relief coursed through her. Nick was there, and he wasn't going to let her die next to her stupid ex-husband.

She sent him a silent thank-you that he probably wouldn't hear and went back to reading the thoughts around her.

Weber was outside, his cop brain grimly scrambling through procedures and logistics.

She pulled back and focused on the thoughts coming from inside the building.

"I don't get paid enough for this shit."

"This goddamn air vent is too tight."

"This is for you, Jackson."

That last thought stood out from the rest. It wasn't colored with anxiety or annoyance. It felt proud, purposeful. She zeroed in on it. "Help me out, guys," she whispered to her spirit guides.

The clouds pulsed, then shifted. Riley found herself peering through the mists into a bedroom. A teenage boy in ripped black jeans lay on the twin bed, staring up at the ceiling as silent tears slipped down his cheeks.

A visceral pain echoed in Riley's chest.

"Jackson?" A younger teen ventured cautiously into the room. "Are you okay?"

"Go away, Hud," Jackson said quietly.

It was a young, nonmurdery Hudson Neudorfer.

"Mom says kids won't be mean forever. Eventually everyone grows up," Hudson said, his voice full of hope.

"Mom's wrong," Jackson whispered.

The clouds closed, like curtains on a stage. And when they parted again, it was to rapid-fire images. Jackson's bedroom. An overturned chair. A rope fashioned around a pull-up bar. Feet dangling. Hudson's cry. "Jackson! No!"

She felt it. The snap. The pain that transformed Hudson Neudorfer from hopeful teen to broken human.

Tears pricked at her eyes as the clouds muddled together again before offering her a peek at something new. The faces of three young lively teens laughing. No. Not laughing. Taunting. One by one, they were all snuffed out like someone extinguishing a candle.

Her blood ran cold as the realization set in. She opened her eyes and stared at Hudson Neudorfer as he calmly unzipped the backpack he'd been carrying and unpacked a few items.

He'd begun his murderous rampage years before, starting with his brother's bullies.

The phone in the sound booth rang. Everyone froze. It continued to ring.

"It's probably the cops," Chris called to Hudson. "Do you want us to answer it?"

Hudson gave Griffin's chair a slow spin, then nodded once. "Put them through on the speaker," he said imperiously.

"This is Detective Kellen Weber with the Harrisburg Police."

Riley blew out a sigh of relief. With Weber and Nick on the scene, they all had a good chance of walking out of here alive.

"Detective Weber. How nice to hear your voice again," Hudson said.

"How are the hostages? Is everyone okay?" Weber asked, his voice calm.

"Everyone is fine. For now," Hudson said ominously.

"Let's talk about it. I'm happy to listen to your demands. We can work with you to make sure no one gets hurt."

"I'm afraid that's not going to work for me," Hudson returned. "You see, I want some of them to get hurt."

There was an instantaneous whispering among the hostages as they debated which hostages Hudson wanted to hurt.

"It doesn't have to go down like that," Weber told him. "We can work this out. Your brother wouldn't want you to do this."

"Ha! Goes to show what you know. You know nothing about my brother. He's been waiting a long time for justice."

"Tell me what you want, Hudson, and we'll start working on it," Weber coaxed.

"I want justice!"

"Justice for your brother?"

"Justice for him and everyone else who's ever been the target of someone like Larry Rupley, Titus Strubinger, and Bianca Hornberger."

"What kind of justice are we talking about? All the folks you just named are dead. They can't go to trial or jail."

"I streamlined the process. And I'll do it again today."

"Uh, excuse me." A production assistant off camera raised her hand. "If we're making demands, I could go for some lunch."

There were rumblings of agreement.

"I could go for pizza."

"We had pizza last night. I want sushi."

"What about some Italian ice?" someone else offered.

"I'm doing Whole30 right now. I need a salad."

Hudson looked around the room. "Fine. Justice and lunch. You got that, Detective?"

"No problem. Send one of the hostages out with your order, and we'll get it delivered."

"Nice try, Detective. I'm not letting anyone go. We're too busy having a *blast*."

Riley felt a nudge at the back of her mind, and her nose twitched.

She glanced at the backpack on the anchor desk, and a sick feeling of dread settled in her gut. The glitter bombs had been homemade. How hard would it be for a motivated Hudson to build an actual bomb?

"It sounds like you have a lot of important things to say," Weber observed.

"And I'll be doing it live during the noon broadcast," Hudson announced. "You can get our lunch order by watching." He made a slashing motion over his throat. It took Chris a good beat to figure out Hudson wanted him to hang up.

"Uh, goodbye," Chris said, disconnecting the call.

"Chris, get out here. I've got some breaking news for the teleprompter," Hudson said, waving a flash drive in his hand.

"Does anyone else want to split a meatball sub?" someone called.

Riley had never seen a live broadcast quite like this one. On one end of the news desk, Griffin Gentry was duct-taped to a chair wearing a sign on his chest that said, GREEDY DOUCHEWEASEL. Chris Yang sat at the opposite end of the desk. His sign said, ASSHOLE ENABLER. Between them sat Hudson. The sports desk was occupied by Chelsea Strump, who had refused to hold up her sign until Hudson had forced Riley at gunpoint to duct-tape it to the woman's head. The duct tape had been overkill, seeing as how the JUDGMENTAL TROLL sign wedged neatly into her helmet of hair. But Riley didn't want to argue with a guy with a gun.

The producer counted, holding his fingers overhead like it was any other live broadcast. The red light turned on.

Nobody moved or spoke. Griffin looked like he was sitting in a sweat lodge.

Hudson cleared his throat. Still no one spoke.

He gave Griffin a swift kick, making him squawk like a disgruntled chicken.

Hudson pointed at the teleprompter.

"Ah! Um, good afternoon, Harrisburg. I'm Griffin Gentry, coming to you with breaking news. I am—" He paused and squinted at the screen. "Hey! That's not nice. I'm not saying that!"

"Oh, but you are," Hudson said, plucking the gun off his lap and holding it to the news anchor's neck. "Read it, Gentry. Read it with feeling."

"I'm Griffin Gentry, and I'm a huge jerk who only cares about looking taller than I really am. I'm five foot nine."

Hudson jammed the gun harder into his flesh. "You're five foot four, you lying little leprechaun. Read. It."

"Erm. Okay. Um, because of my greed, Channel 50 fired nearly a dozen people and gave pay cuts to everyone left. Also, I use my expense account to pay sex workers to call me Big Boy."

There were a few titters from the captive audience. Riley noticed that no one looked overly surprised.

She shot a glance at Bella, who was standing on her usual

mark in front of the weather green screen. She didn't look too bothered by the forced confession. She didn't look…well, anything. She was probably still humming in her head.

"I'm a greedy pig man incapable of caring for anyone other than himself. I'm a mean, selfish man-child, and I don't deserve to live. Over to you, Hudson."

Hudson preened for the camera. "This just in—Griffin Gentry admits to being a selfish asshole."

"We're gonna get so many fucking FCC fines," Chris moaned into his hands.

"And this, Harrisburg, is Chris Yang, news director and professional ass-kisser. Thanks to him, people like Griffin and his father, Malcolm Gentry, whose hobbies include rampant sexual harassment, are rewarded for their behavior with higher salaries and fatter expense accounts. While everyone else pays the price. Say hello, Chris."

"Hi," Chris said through his hands still covering his face.

"Over at sports, we have Chelsea Strump, neighborhood nuisance, tattletale, and internet troll. Say hello, Chelsea," Hudson ordered.

Chelsea crossed her arms in front of her skinny chest. "This is ridiculous. I don't belong here with the rest of these losers."

"On the contrary," Hudson insisted. "You are one of the nastiest commenters on Channel 50's social media accounts. And if you don't admit it right now, I'm going to shoot Griffin."

"What do I care if you shoot him?" she snorted. "I don't care if you shoot everyone in this building. None of them are as good a person as I am."

Hudson flashed the camera a smug I-told-you-so look.

Camera one closed in on him. "You see, Harrisburg, I'm the hero you need. The man willing to not just stand up to the schoolyard bullies but eradicate them. People like these don't learn lessons. They don't change their ways or turn over new leaves. They get more bitter and more dangerous until they need to be cut out of your life like a cancer."

"Oh, please," Chelsea scoffed.

"Unfortunately, my work was interrupted by local psychic Riley Thorn."

Camera two whipped around to zero in on her.

Riley waved weakly.

"If you'll watch the bottom of your screen, these are the rest of the individuals on my murder list, including their infractions. I may not be able to finish the work I started, but that doesn't mean one of you can't step into the role of hero and continue eradicating evil."

Great. Just what the world needed, an unhinged lunatic on TV encouraging other unhinged lunatics to start killing people.

Riley peered at the monitor closest to her and saw a ticker tape running across the bottom of the screen listing names and infractions.

"I encourage you to stay tuned, Harrisburg, for my grand finale," Hudson said, unzipping his backpack. "When I send Channel 50 and its employees to hell where they all belong."

"Oh, shit," Riley breathed.

"That's not good," Valerie agreed as Hudson revealed an improvised explosive device with a countdown clock and important-looking wires.

"Is that some kind of robot kid's toy?" Chelsea asked, wrinkling her nose at the sports desk. "My children were never allowed to play with robotics because circuits are the devil's work."

"It's a bomb, lady," Hudson snarled. "Now, over to Bella Goodshine with the hostage lunch order."

40

Nick hated tight places. But he didn't have much of a choice. He'd shimmied his ass into the air duct that Mrs. Penny had crawled into on the side of the building. He was a man on a mission.

"Don't freak out, Santiago. So the walls are a little close, and you couldn't roll over if your life depended on it. So there isn't any fucking air left in this goddamn tomb. It's no big deal." His pep talk wasn't working. The only thing that kept him moving forward was thinking about Riley somewhere inside, scared out of her wits, waiting for him to save her.

"I'm coming, Thorn. Hang in there," he muttered.

He elbow crawled his way to the first T and, after a beat, crawled into the dark on the right.

His phone vibrated in his pocket, and he nearly dislocated a shoulder digging it out.

"What?"

"Santiago, where the fuck are you?" Weber snarled in his ear.

"I'm a little busy right now," Nick grunted. He was sweating like a greased-up WWE star.

"If you're where I think you are, I'm going to add another

body to the count, and I won't even mind the paperwork," Weber said.

"This is your fault. If you would have let me play delivery guy, I wouldn't have had to stuff my ass into this duct," Nick reminded him.

"Get your ass out here now."

"Climb in here and make me." Nick hung up and started to crawl again but paused when he heard something up ahead.

It sounded like a fart.

Smelled like one too.

"Mrs. Penny?" he called.

"Pipe down!" an elderly voice hissed.

Nick used his nose to turn on the flashlight on his phone and shone it in the direction of the voice.

A pair of orthopedic shoes clogged up the duct ten feet in front of him.

"Are you stuck?"

"No, I'm not stuck, dingus! I'm listening to our friendly neighborhood murderer's live broadcast and waiting for my moment."

"Your moment to what?"

"To jump down onto the news desk, kick him in the face, and then shoot him with my Beretta."

Maybe a highly trained nineteen-year-old parkour athlete with soft bones could execute a plan like that, but not an octogenarian with a cane. He was trapped in an air duct with a delusional woman with gas and a weapon. This was not the day he'd set out to have.

"How exactly are you going to jump down?"

"Haven't figured that part out yet. I'm kinda wedged in here around the hips."

He felt a little light-headed. "So you're stuck?"

"It's not my fault the ducting got smaller."

She was stuck in an air duct with nowhere to go. The very thought of it had Nick scrambling back a foot before he remembered he had a job to do. Little black dots floated before his eyes. If he passed out, Mrs. Penny would definitely die in here.

"I don't know about you, Penny, but I don't want to die like a hamster in a habitat trail."

"Ten-four," she acknowledged. "So what's your plan?"

His plan? He hadn't thought much beyond getting into the building.

Good thing he was Nick-fucking-Santiago, and Nick fucking Santiago was fast on his feet and his belly.

"Here's what we're going to do. I'm going to shimmy up behind you and grab you by the ankles."

"Keep talking."

"I'll pull you backward, and then we'll back out of the tomb and go through the first air return we find."

"Let's find the snack room. I'm hungry, and they're talking about food down there."

"My girlfriend is being held hostage by a rampaging murderer, and you want a snack," he repeated.

"I shoot better when I'm not hungry."

The duct gave a creak beneath him. The duct supports probably weren't designed to hold the weight of two adults.

"You must always be hungry," he grumbled, shimmying closer to the orthopedic shoes in front of him.

"Real funny, boss. Hey, wanna hear something even funnier?"

"Sure. Why not," he said, grabbing her by the ankles and wondering how he was going to get the leverage to pull her backward if he was stretched out flat like a tapeworm.

"Pull my ankles," she said.

Nick gave them a hard tug, and Mrs. Penny let out a loud fart. He smacked his head off the top of the duct. "Ow!"

"Hehe," Mrs. Penny chuckled. "Pull my ankle. Get it?"

"Hilarious. God, you smell like Burt."

"We eat a lot of the same things. Am I unstuck yet?"

"Does it feel like you're unstuck?" He pulled his shirt over his nose for protection and reached for her feet again.

Nick's phone vibrated, and he let go of her ankles. "What?"

"Get the fuck out of there now," Weber enunciated in his scary cop voice.

The duct creaked ominously.

"Listen, I'm doing my best not to get tear-gassed in an air duct while rescuing a civilian."

"There's a fucking bomb in the studio. The captain just had us push the barricades back another block. You need to find a way out. Now."

"I'm not leaving without Riley."

"I had a feeling you'd say that," Weber said, sounding resigned.

"Then why waste the call?"

"We've got someone on the inside. We sent someone in to deliver the food."

"Who?"

"Gabe in disguise."

"You sent the biggest pacifist in the Western Hemisphere into a hostage situation?"

"We had no one else. This Neudorfer kid said no cops. Somehow he got access to the PD's human resources database. Gabe was the only other option."

"What's he going to do? Sit on Neudorfer?"

"We put a wire on him and hid a gun in a carton of Chinese food."

"Are you trying to get him killed?"

"Look, just get your ass into that studio, and get everyone out before that countdown clock starts running."

"Fuck." Nick disconnected the call and banged his forehead off the duct a few times.

"Keep it down back there," Mrs. Penny grumbled. "I'm trying to eavesdrop."

A gunshot rang out beneath them.

He froze, mid- head bang.

"Well, that wasn't good," Mrs. Penny announced.

41

It was amazing the damper a bomb could put on a regular Tuesday. The hostages had gone from grumpy complainers to shivering, sobbing messes. Well, that last part was mostly Griffin.

Riley was inundated with the thoughts of people realizing that they could be facing the last few minutes of their life. It wasn't pretty. But it was poignant, mostly.

"I can't believe the last thing I said to my daughter was, 'You're grounded for failing calculus.' Everyone fails calculus! I failed calculus!"

"Great. My last communication with my husband is going to be a passive-aggressive note on the way he folds bath towels."

"I thought I had more time to be a better person."

"I can't believe I'm going to die with all these assholes."

Riley dodged her way through the incoming thoughts and asked her spirit guides to help push out a message.

"Grandmother, I could really use your help right now," Riley said, sending the message into the clouds.

"You will solve this problem yourself." Elanora's reply echoed off the cotton candy clouds in Riley's head. "The only way you will learn is to do for yourself."

"I appreciate the sink-or-swim technique, but I'm telling you a lot of people are going to die if I sink."

"Then you have no choice but to swim," Elanora said. "Use your gifts and your tools, and fix the situation. You must do what you have no desire to do in order to live."

"Are you serious right now?"

There was no response.

Riley fell out of the clouds with a pop and landed back in her own body.

"Do you need a tissue?"

Riley blinked and realized Bella Goodshine was peering down at her. Her nose twitched again.

"No, thanks," she said.

"Do what you have no desire to do." She stared at the cameras trained on Hudson and the news desk and tried to ignore the sinking feeling in her stomach.

A knock at the studio doors startled her.

"Who is it?" Hudson called pleasantly.

"I am Gabe. I have been entrusted with your food."

Riley covered her eyes for a moment and then opened them. Nope. She was not asleep, having a terrible nightmare. She was wide awake, living one.

"Gabe, I'm going to need you to strip down out there so I can make sure you're not carrying a gun."

"What about the wire I am wearing?"

Riley could hear the internal screams from about a dozen cops.

"An honest delivery guy. This is a treat," Hudson crowed. "You can keep the wire on. But no weapons."

"I understand."

A minute later, Hudson peeked through the door and then opened it the whole way.

"Run!" Chris yelled and sprinted for the emergency exit. *Sprinted* was a kind description for the disjointed shuffle of limbs he displayed.

A gunshot rang out, and Chris crumpled to the ground.

Frightened screams erupted from the rest of the hostages.

"Ow! That hurt!" Chris screeched.

"Relax. I shot you in your foot, not your windpipe." But Hudson's hand was shaking when he pointed the gun around the room. "Anyone else want to run? I've got ten years of experience with first-person cowboy video games. I can hit a spittoon at twenty paces!"

Everyone shook their heads.

"Good. Now get in here, food guy," he said, gesturing toward the door with the gun.

Riley closed her eyes as the lovable Gabe stepped into the studio carrying several bags of to-go food. He was wearing nothing but black briefs and a police wire taped to his chest.

"Oh my," Valerie fanned herself. "I know we're about to die, but thank you, Jesus, for your bounty."

"Everybody line up one at a time and get your food," Hudson said.

Riley got in line behind Floyd the sound engineer.

"Excuse me! Can someone bring me my lobster salad?" Griffin called from his chair.

"I said no onions on my sandwich," Chelsea complained. "I'm not paying for this."

Hudson rolled his eyes. "No one is paying for this because I'm blowing you all up in a few minutes. Eat the goddamn onions."

"Here is your sparkle *pupu* platter," Gabe said, handing Riley a paper carton. "Your *chopsticks* are inside."

Riley blinked. Gabe had just *sparkle poo*-ed her. She suddenly had a good idea just who was stuck in an air vent.

"Thank you," she said and took the carton behind cameras.

While Gabe handed out the rest of the food and Hudson oversaw the chaos, she opened the container and peered inside. There were no chopsticks or Chinese food. But there was a small gun. Covertly, she tucked it into the waistband of her shorts.

Once the food was distributed, Hudson pointed his gun at Gabe. Riley reached behind her, closing her hand over the cold metal.

"Food guy, sit in front of the studio doors. You hear that, cops? If you try to breach the studio, you'll be trampling an innocent, almost-naked delivery guy," Hudson yelled into the wire on Gabe's chest.

"It would be my honor to sit," Gabe announced.

He took his position on the floor in front of the swinging doors, then nodded at Riley.

Apparently, she had her tools. A gun that she could maybe sort of shoot and a guy who could make her more psychic. Well, it was better than nothing.

Now all she had to do was figure out what she had no desire to do and...

"Crap," she whispered.

"Crap what?" Valerie asked. She was eating stromboli with two hands. "Is that countdown clock moving? I can't chew any faster!"

"No. Not yet," Riley said. "I have to go be on TV and try to save the day."

"Shh!" The sound engineer glared at them.

"Nobody cares if there's background noise when we're all going to die, *Floyd*," Riley shot back.

Valerie pointed a piece of stromboli at her. "If you being on TV means I get to go home to my kids and my towel-folding husband, then get your ass up there now," the anchor said.

Riley sighed. "Fine. But I am not happy about this." She rolled up her metaphorical psychic garage doors and gave Gabe a pointed look.

He nodded sagely and closed his eyes.

Hands over her head, she cautiously approached the news desk. "Um, Hudson?"

He stopped in the middle of a monologue about Bianca Hornberger's extensive offenses. "Will you stop ruining things for me?"

"I'm really sorry," she said, edging closer to the desk. "But I think there are some things you need to consider before your grand finale. Things Jackson wants you to know."

Hudson studied her, scrubbing his hairless jaw with the barrel of his gun. "Fine. I'll give you two minutes to change my mind." He gestured to the empty chair at the anchor desk.

"I hope she doesn't realize I nervous peed a little up there."

Gross.

"Sit," Hudson ordered.

Riley checked the chair and, finding no visible puddles, sat.

"Let's have two minutes on the screen," he said to the sound booth. He waited until a timer appeared on-screen, then gestured at her. "You may begin."

"You want to know why I keep showing up and ruining everything, right?"

"I do. Why in the world would anyone want to save these horrible people?"

"Your brother, Jackson, wants to save them, and he's been trying to tell you from the other side."

He snorted. "No, he hasn't."

A cold sweat broke out at the hairline on her neck. The TV lights were hotter than she'd imagined.

"Your brother was bullied in high school," Riley said.

"Yeah. And then he committed suicide. You're wasting your two minutes. You don't know him. You don't know what he wants."

"I know that he was your favorite person on earth. I know that he let you win at video games, and when that girl on your bus told you there was no Santa, he took you aside and told you that the spirit of Santa is in all of us."

"So what? He'd be *happy* that I'm finally punishing the wrongdoers. I've dedicated my entire life to getting him justice."

"There's a difference between justice and revenge, and Jackson doesn't want revenge. He wants you to see the value of each human life." She glanced at Griffin, who was blubbering about how much he was going to miss fresh dry cleaning. "Even the pathetic, terrible ones."

344

"Hmm. Nope. Not buying it."

She felt the nudge in her brain and let the visions come. She saw it all playing out, each scene connected by a silver cord.

"It was a terrible thing that you lost your big brother to bullying. But he's still out there trying to look after you," she said. "Think about it. You killed Larry Rupley in the house next door to mine. You chose the victim and the location. My boyfriend was hired to find Larry. That's a pretty big coincidence, don't you think?"

"If you want to waste your time with rhetorical questions, then sure," Hudson said smugly.

"I was hired by Detective Weber to consult on Bianca's case. I wouldn't have even been here at Channel 50 interviewing people if he hadn't asked me to. Before today, I had never once set foot in Chelsea's house. She just so happens to live next door to my parents, and my dad's cow got loose. What are the odds that I would keep showing up like that in your life over and over again?"

"You're right. It's a sign," he admitted. "A sign that I need to definitely kill you so you don't prevent any future heroes from finishing the work I started!"

"Listen to me. To Jackson. Justice would be letting these people keep on living their miserable lives full of hate and fear. Justice would be allowing their communities to shun them now that you've unveiled them for who they are."

"They're not living miserable lives. They have everything!" Hudson yelled.

She shook her head. "Griffin and Bella have been cheating on each other for their entire relationship. She can't stand the way he touches her, and he hates the sound of her voice. Chris lost his hair and his first marriage to this job. He only sees his kids every other weekend. And Chelsea's sons moved across the country to get away from her. She'll never be a part of their daily lives again."

"Yes, I will! My boys love me! I gave them everything!" Chelsea howled from the sports desk.

The clock was down to ten seconds, and Riley was feeling desperate. "Mr. Pickles!" she said.

"Is she having a nervous breakdown?" Chris whimpered from the floor.

"Not everyone is cut out to be on-air talent," Griffin said.

"After you killed Larry, you went back to his place and rescued his cat, Mr. Pickles, because you knew no one would come looking for Larry for a while, didn't you?"

Hudson shrugged. "I always wanted a cat."

She felt the nudge at her consciousness. "But you couldn't have one because your brother was allergic, wasn't he?"

"It wasn't his fault he turned into a snot rocket around cats," he said defensively.

"What if I tell you that your brother sent you Mr. Pickles? Who is going to feed Mr. Pickles tonight if you don't come home? Think of Mr. Pickles," Riley said.

"First of all, I'm not an idiot. Mr. Pickles has an automatic feeder that will last at least a week. And after I blow up the station, the cops will be all over my apartment. Mr. Pickles will be fine."

The timer had ended on-screen, but Hudson hadn't noticed yet.

"The cops will take Mr. Pickles to a shelter. You know how overcrowded shelters get. What if there's no room for Mr. Pickles? He's innocent. He never hurt anyone. You can't just let him go to a shelter to be put down."

"Poor Mr. Pickles," Chris sobbed from the floor. "My wife will take him! We don't want him to die too."

Hudson pushed his glasses up his nose with the barrel of the gun and grinned. "See? Problem solved. Chris's widow will take him. And guess what, Miss Fancy Psychic? You're out of time."

Ah, hell. She was going to have to do this the hard way.

"Yeah, well, so are you," Riley said, drawing her gun.

42

S orry about that one," Mrs. Penny said.

"God, woman. When we get out of here, you and Burt are both going on a diet," Nick said, trying to breathe through his eyes.

He'd managed to scoot back about two feet when she warned him he was in the blast zone, but there was no escaping the fart in such close quarters.

"Are you calling me fat?" Mrs. Penny demanded.

Before he could answer, the floor of the duct between them erupted as another gunshot rang out.

"Okay, that one wasn't me," his partner in crime insisted.

"Oh, fuck," Nick muttered as metal supports beneath them gave way with a loud creak. With a tremble, the duct split apart at the bullet hole.

"I don't like the sound of that," Mrs. Penny cried as the duct went from a gaseous tomb to a playground slide, hurtling him down and out into a free fall.

He landed awkwardly on something squishy and whiny. It was impossible to see due to the dust cloud. Surprised shrieks rang out.

"Ow! Get off me!" the something whined.

Nick caught a glimpse of unnaturally tanned skin and realized he'd landed on Griffin Gentry, who was duct-taped to a chair behind the anchor desk.

"Look out below!"

Nick's vision cleared just in time to see Mrs. Penny careening backward out of the duct above them.

"This is gonna hurt," he muttered and braced for impact.

The old woman's body hit him square in the gut, and Griffin's anchor chair couldn't handle the added weight. It tipped backward in a pile of bodies.

"Nice of you to drop by."

Nick extricated himself from between Mrs. Penny's generous thighs and spotted Riley performing a rear naked choke hold on one Hudson Neudorfer behind the news desk. The guy's face was the shade of a radish.

He grinned. "I'm impressed, Thorn."

"I learned from the best."

Nick pointed at the ceiling. "Just so you know, this wasn't the plan."

"Gah!" Hudson said.

"Same here," Riley said through gritted teeth. "I can't tell. Is this working?"

"Ow! I think you broke my entire body," Griffin howled.

"Shut up, Griffin," the entire studio yelled in unison.

Mrs. Penny managed a clumsy ninja roll to the side, planting her knee in Griffin's groin before she climbed to her feet.

"Learned...my...lesson," Hudson rasped.

"Are you just saying that because you see little spots floating in front of your eyes?" Riley asked.

"Maybe."

"That's the will to live," she said, releasing him. "Your brother says you're welcome."

Nick tossed his phone to Riley. "Call Weber," he said as he rolled Hudson over on his stomach. "Tell him the hostages will be coming out the side door and to hold their fire."

Riley's eyes widened. "That sounds like it would be better coming from you."

"Make the call, Thorn," he said with a wink. "A badass like you should have no trouble telling the cops to stand down."

"Is it over?"

"Are we going to live?"

"Is there any lobster salad left?"

The hostages were starting to peek over the desk.

"Everybody, form an orderly line, and put your hands on your heads," Nick advised as he patted Hudson down.

"Weber, the hostages are coming out the side entrance. Hold your fire," Riley said.

"Oooh! I'm taking this chicken parm with me," Mrs. Penny announced, snatching a to-go container off the anchor desk. She turned, and Nick watched in slow-motion horror as the thick sole of her orthopedic shoe caught on the cable running to the bomb.

"Noooooooooo."

But it was too late. The clock started a countdown from thirty seconds.

"Everybody out!" Riley shouted.

"Now! Move!" Nick ordered.

Gabe picked up Mrs. Penny and tossed her over one shoulder. He grabbed the associate producer and put her under his other arm and ran like a linebacker for the emergency exit.

Armand scooped up Chris on a dolly and sprinted for the door.

Bella skipped past them, looking like she was lining up for chicken fingers in the cafeteria.

"Wait! Help me! I'm stuck to this chair," Griffin wailed, scooting after her.

"Really tempted to leave him here," Nick said, throwing Hudson over his shoulder.

"I know. But you won't because you're a good person," Riley told him.

"I'm the most important person in this room! Someone has to save me," Griffin wailed.

"I'm not *that* good of a person," Nick insisted.

"Come on, Santiago. I'd like to see you naked again."

"The things I do for you, Thorn."

With that, they ran for the door, Nick carrying Hudson and pushing Griffin in front of him.

The clock glowed brightly in her head as they made it through the emergency exit into the parking lot. "Get back," she yelled as she held the door for Nick.

"Ahhh! This is too bumpy," Griffin complained when the chair wheels hit the parking lot.

"We can't get far enough away with this luggage," Nick said through clenched teeth.

Riley glanced at the dumpster, then back at Nick.

"Good idea," he said.

"Nooooo!" Griffin kicked his feet. "This suit is Indonesian mohair!"

"Better than being buried in it," Riley quipped as she flipped the lid.

Nick tossed Hudson inside, then picked up her ex-husband, office chair and all, and tossed him into the dumpster.

She flipped the lid back down just in time for Nick to grab her and drag her after him in a dead sprint.

"Everybody get d—"

Nick didn't get to finish the warning as the explosion ripped through the building. The blast of the concussion hit Riley in the back, and she felt herself flying.

But Nick never let go of her hand.

She landed hard with all two hundred and thirty pounds of Nick Santiago on top of her. A human shield against the heat and debris. Her own personal hero.

Wrapping her arms around him, she held on tight and buried her face in his shoulder.

A flaming life-size cutout of Griffin sailed overhead before crashing to the asphalt.

Nick grinned down at her. "Come here often?"

Across the parking lot, Gabe stood with Mrs. Penny, who

was poking debris with her cane. Bella was signing autographs for the firefighters.

"Are we alive?" Riley asked.

"You tell me," Nick said, lowering his mouth to hers.

"Get a room," Mrs. Penny shouted from across the parking lot.

"Hello? Is anybody out there?" called a tinny-sounding voice from the dumpster.

43

There was something comforting about the aftermath of a crime, Riley thought as she watched firefighters, paramedics, and cops slowly restore order to Sixth Street.

Channel 75, a rival news channel located just down the block, gleefully reported live from the scene while Chris Yang tried his best to record Bella Goodshine reporting the news on an iPhone while a paramedic bandaged his injured foot. Chelsea was strapped to a gurney while an EMT attempted to remove a stapler that had embedded itself in her hair. Firefighters pulled a still duct-taped Griffin from the dumpster.

The rest of the Channel 50 staff was celebrating being alive and the prospect of getting a new building with drinks at a bar two blocks down.

"No more moldy break room."

"No more stopped-up toilets."

Riley sat half a block back from the barricades to avoid the cameras while Nick gave his statement. She'd already given hers and had taken Weber aside to strongly suggest he look into what had happened to Hudson's brother's high school bullies. He'd find more death and, if he looked beneath the surface, more murder.

Families would get answers to questions they didn't know they had. She wondered if the knowing would do more harm than good. Wondered if a high school bully would have grown into a compassionate adult if given the chance. But Hudson had taken those chances away.

Gabe was next to her, his biceps and shoulders covered in shallow cuts and scrapes from the shrapnel. He was still shirtless, but one of the paramedics had given him scrub pants.

"You did great today, Gabe," Riley said, nudging him with her shoulder.

He beamed down at her. "It was my honor."

"We make a great team."

"It would appear so." He looked at his extra-large hands. "I am sorry for saying you wish to go nowhere. That is not what friends do."

"You may have made a teeny, tiny, practically insignificant point," she admitted. "I have to either embrace this or swear it off. Dabbling is dangerous, and I can't just cherry-pick the good stuff about being psychic and avoid all the bad stuff."

"Am I good stuff or bad stuff?" he asked.

"You're the best stuff," she assured him. "I'm serious. You walked into a hostage situation today on purpose to help. I had to be dragged in at gunpoint. You and Nick make the whole hero thing look so easy. I've got a lot to learn from both of you."

"You believe me to be a hero?" he repeated.

She grinned. "Yeah. I do. And anyone, including Elanora Basil, who says otherwise can fight me."

The man looked as if he'd just been handed an entire litter of sleeping puppies. "Thank you for the gift of your friendship, Riley Thorn."

"You are welcome, Gabe… Hey. What *is* your last name?"

"Gabe!"

Riley and Gabe both looked up as Wander pushed her way through the crowd.

"Are you okay?" she asked, reaching for him and then

dropping her hands to her side. "Are you both okay?" She gestured in Riley's direction.

"Is our heroic friend moment over?" Gabe asked solicitously.

"Yeah, I think so," Riley said.

"Wonderful." He climbed to his feet. "Wander, would you do me the great honor of joining me for ice cream?"

Riley watched her sister's face as it beamed like the sun with a crush on the earth. "Yes, Gabe. A thousand times, yes."

Elanora appeared and fixed Gabe with a piercing gaze. Riley tensed, and Wander looked crestfallen.

But Gabe straightened his shoulders and stared down at her tiny grandmother.

"Elanora, I am escorting Wander to get ice cream," he announced.

Riley blinked and held her breath.

There was silence for a long moment, and then her grandmother nodded curtly. "I trust you both will continue to apply yourselves to your work with diligence regardless of any dalliances with…frozen desserts."

Wander and Gabe shared a wide-eyed look before nodding vigorously. "We will, Grandmother," Wander assured Elanora.

"Then go. Enjoy yourselves." Elanora sounded like she was choking on the words. But it still counted as a blessing.

It might have been the smoking debris still raining down from the sky, but Riley felt a little teary-eyed as she watched her sister and her gentle giant friend walk down the sidewalk hand in hand.

"Well, that was a fine mess."

Riley looked up and found her grandmother staring down at her.

"Yeah. Thanks for the help," she said dryly.

"You will walk with me," Elanora announced.

Too tired to argue, Riley climbed to her feet and followed her grandmother down the alley.

"You did not need my help," the old woman said.

"I did. You could have contacted the spirit of Hudson's

brother much faster than I did. This whole thing could have ended an hour ago. With no explosion, I might add."

"It was your responsibility. You needed to see it through."

"Grandma, this is not some kind of class project. This was life or death."

"And you needed to realize that when it comes to life or death, you can handle situations like this. Maybe not as efficiently or with as much poise and grace as me. But you got everyone out of that building alive. Including your insipid ex-husband."

"That was a team effort," Riley said modestly.

"And you stepped up to be part of that team. Those people got out because of you." Riley's chest was just puffing with pride when her grandmother added, "Unfortunately, the property was destroyed because of you. However, I sense that most of them will get over it quickly."

"So why did you come down here then, if it wasn't to help?" Riley asked in exasperation.

Elanora frowned. "To watch my granddaughter in action, of course. Some grandmothers attend soccer games or debate clubs or homecoming parades. I came to watch you save lives."

"Are you saying you're proud of me?" Riley asked, fishing for praise.

Elanora's lips twitched in their perpetual frown. "Perhaps I did it so I could say, 'I told you so.'"

It was good enough for Riley. "Thank you for the lessons— even the painful ones."

"Do not thank me. It's unseemly."

Riley rolled her eyes. "I guess it would be extra unseemly if I hugged you," she said, opening her arms, knowing full well she was a dirty, smoky, glittery mess.

"Don't be ridiculous," Elanora scoffed. "Now, before I go, I received a message for you from a Bianca."

"Bianca Hornberger?"

"Yes. She wanted me to tell you thank you and she wants a favor."

"That sounds about right."

"She wants you to tell her family she's sorry for being too distracted by the shiny things in life to be present for the important things."

"Wait. Are you sure you got the right Bianca?" Riley asked.

"Death strips away everything we think is important only to reveal what actually is important," Elanora said. "All souls remember their truth once the distortions of life begin to fade."

Riley blinked. "Wow. So even bad people become good souls?"

"Something like that. The important lesson is to not wait for death to make you a good soul. Now, if you will excuse me, I have an important meeting to attend." Elanora paused, then awkwardly patted her on the head before striding off, leaving Riley to stare after her, feeling like she'd just been handed a cosmic lesson, one she didn't know what to do with.

"Hey there, Sexy Sparkle. Got you a souvenir," Nick said from behind her.

Riley turned and admired the view as he approached. He looked heroic with a half-dozen bandages over cuts and burns, his clothing torn and dirty. Luckily for him, the bomb blast seemed to have shaken off most of the glitter.

"Hey there, Hometown Hero."

He held out a piece of cardboard. It looked like a very small pair of shoes. "This is all that's left of your ex's cutout."

Riley laughed and threw Griffin's tiny feet over her shoulder so she could loop her arms around Nick's neck. "Have I told you today that I love you?"

He grinned the full dimpled wattage at her. "Not nearly often enough."

"I love you, Nick Santiago. Thank you for saving my ass once again."

"It's a nice ass. I'm kind of in love with it," he said.

She felt something between them vibrate.

"Is that a phone in your pocket, or did you learn a new trick?"

He fished out her phone and handed it over. "You left this in your Jeep at a crime scene."

Riley glanced at the screen and winced. "Ten missed calls from my mother."

A shiny black car rolled up to the police barricade, and a distinguished-looking man in an expensive suit rolled down the rear window.

"Mr. Gentry," Chris said, abandoning his iPhone reporting.

"Why are we getting scooped on our own explosion?" Malcolm Gentry demanded.

Chris pointed over his shoulder at the smoldering skeleton of the building. "Well, sir, there was a bomb."

"I can see that," Malcolm said crisply. "Why aren't *we* reporting it?"

Chris rubbed his dirty hands over his forehead. "Well, Mr. Gentry, sir. The bomb blew up our building with all our equipment. So there's that."

"I didn't drive down here for excuses. Get a cameraman and a reporter, and get on it."

"Dad!" Griffin waved to his father as a firefighter cut through duct tape around his legs.

"Hi, Daddy!" Bella purred, batting unnaturally long lashes in her soon-to-be father-in-law's direction.

"Man, I do not miss this place," Riley said.

"I like that you're the kind of girl who blows up buildings," Nick said.

"Technically, that was Mrs. Penny," she pointed out.

"Riley! Hey, Riley! I'm going to need you on camera in five minutes," Chris said, waving frantically. "Also, do you have a camera?"

"Not happening, Chris," she told him.

"But—"

"Not happening," she repeated.

"You heard the lady," Nick cut in, glaring at Chris until he scampered off.

"Wow. You didn't even have to punch him in the face."

"I'm heroically bloody and intimidating," he explained. "Let's go grab some lunch, Thorn."

She laughed and looked down. She was a sweaty, glittery, dirty mess. "Like this?"

"Hell yeah, like this. Let's go sit on a deck and get drunk," he said.

"It's a Tuesday and not even—" She glanced down at her watch. "Oh my God. One p.m. This is the longest day of my life."

"Live a little, Thorn," Nick suggested, nuzzling her neck.

"Mmm, you're very convincing," she said as they meandered away from the wreckage of Channel 50.

"By the way, my dad called during this whole fiasco."

"What did he want?" she asked.

"He wants us to come to dinner at the restaurant again."

"To eat or work?"

"Both. Seems he's down a server and a bartender tonight."

After the morning she'd barely survived, Riley didn't feel up to the dinner shift in a busy restaurant.

"I told him we had other plans," Nick told her.

"Oh, thank God."

"He was still willing to pack up a dinner for us to go." He sounded enthusiastic about this.

"Which means what?"

"He likes you. He's welcoming you to the family," he explained as he led her down the block. He was walking with a limp and leaning on her. She liked it.

"What about your mother?"

"She still thinks you're the daughter of a hippie witch and a farmer, so I wouldn't be expecting any hugs from her anytime soon," Nick advised.

"Noted."

"I'm proud of you, Thorn."

"Why is that?"

"You didn't throw a gun at the bad guy this time."

"No. I almost shot you and Mrs. Penny instead."

"Progress."

"Yo! Wait up, boss man," Mrs. Penny called. She was hustling after them as fast as her cane could go. "Where are we going?"

"To get drunk," Nick told her.

"Count me in. My blood alcohol level is dangerously low."

Riley's phone rang.

"Hi, Mom," she said.

"Oh good. You're not dead," her mother said dryly.

44

Their Lyft driver dropped them off in the mansion's parking lot. A drunken Mrs. Penny swayed like a pirate finding her sea legs.

Burt burst through the back door to greet them, running in happy circles.

"Who's my best sparkly boy?" Riley crooned to the dog.

She wasn't drunk. She'd been too tired to put any effort into getting shit-faced. Plus, she'd missed out on the shots Mrs. Penny and Nick were doing due to all the phone calls. Her father. Her sister. Lily called to tell her she saw Griffin Gentry being helped out of a dumpster on TV. Jasmine had called demanding to know why she didn't get an invite to the hostage situation and bombing of Channel 50.

"I think I could give Burt a run for his money. Wink," Nick said, winking with both eyes. He was an adorable drunk. He'd announced to the entire bar that he was in love with Riley Thorn and that he thought she was superhot. Twice. The third time he'd tried it, she kissed him just to shut him up.

The server, a woman who hadn't ever slept with Nick, had brought out a dozen hot wings to celebrate.

So they were dirty, glittery, and sticky. Riley couldn't wait for a nice long shower. And then she remembered the damage upstairs.

While Burt and Nick raced each other around the parking lot, she pulled out her phone.

"Mom, can we come shower at your place? Our bathroom doesn't have a ceiling."

"Sure, sweetie! Come over, and I'll make dinner."

"Is Dad still on a diet?" Riley asked cautiously.

"He is, but this is a special occasion, seeing as how our daughter didn't get murdered today. And your grandmother is leaving to go back to the guild today. How about I make my nondairy mac and cheese, and we open six bottles of wine?"

It was a recipe that required only snacking beforehand rather than an entire drive-thru meal. "That sounds great, Mom. Thanks."

"Nick can help your father put the fence back up."

Riley shot a glance in Nick's direction. He was lying facedown in the tall grass of the neighboring property. "It might take us a little while to get there, and I wouldn't trust Nick with any power tools today."

"I'm gonna keep the party going," Mrs. Penny shouted to them. "Who wants daiquiris?"

Nick raised his hand without lifting his head off the ground.

Burt followed Mrs. Penny into the house, leaving Riley to help Nick up.

"Let's take a walk, pretty lady," he slurred.

"Are you sure you're up for it? If you fall in a doggy land mine, I might not help you back up."

"I'm fit as a fiddle," he announced, dancing a jig in the grass.

"And I'm just going to record this for posterity's sake," Riley told him, cueing up her camera app.

"Let's go. I've got somethin' to show you, Thorn." He grabbed her hand and dragged her toward the neighboring house. "Have you ever been inside this place?" he asked.

She shook her head. "It's been vacant since before I moved in."

Nick tripped on the front porch steps and nearly took a header before he steadied himself.

"You all right there?" she asked.

"Pfft. Course I'm all right. C'mere."

He strolled purposefully to the front door and ducked under the crime scene tape.

"Um, if you think I'm having sex with you at a crime scene, you are sorely mistaken," she pointed out as he fiddled with the lockbox.

With a flourish, he unlocked the door and pushed it open. "Just hear me out, 'kay?"

Riley gagged. "Oh, God. It smells."

"Forget about the smell. Don't think about the dead body I found here this morning. Focus on the marble floor. Look at the woodwork. The cool-ass foy-yay."

"Have you decided to get into real estate?" she asked.

"Look over here at this room. Wouldn't this be a nice office for a sexy girlfriend office manager?" Nick walked into a room off the admittedly cool-ass foyer.

The room was spacious and not filled to the rafters with junk.

"It's very nice," she said, breathing through her tank top.

"Think about it, Thorn."

"Think about what?" she asked.

"More space for Santiago Investigations. More privacy. No weird roommates walking in on us while we have sex. There's a gate on the driveway. Plus, Burt already loves pooping here."

"Are you talking about buying a mansion that someone was murdered in?"

"Forget about the murder part. We can definitely get rid of the smell. And don't think about the bats either. I know a guy."

Riley turtled her head into her shoulders as she looked up, expecting to see an entire colony of bats on the ceiling.

"What would we do with all this space? Wouldn't it make more sense to rent another storefront and live above it?" she asked.

"Yes, it would. But what's the fun in making sense? This place is here, and thanks to my new partner, I've got some additional financing."

"Who's your new partner?"

"Shh! It's a secret! Mrs. Penny is a *silent* partner."

"Oh, well, there's no way *that* can go horribly wrong," she said dryly.

"Don't be responsible and logical right now," Nick told her. "Think about opening the gate and driving up to your very own mansion in your fancy… What's your dream car?"

She shrugged. "I don't know. A bigger SUV, I guess?"

"Boring. Imagine driving up to your very own mansion in your fancy Porsche convertible."

"So we're entering the delusions-of-grandeur part of happy hour. Okay. Good to know."

"Gotta dream big, Thorn. Otherwise, you're not dreaming. You're just planning."

"I can't tell if that was deeply philosophical or total bullshit."

"Imagine a life where you don't have to reconnect someone's phone to the Wi-Fi every day. Where you don't have to close the bathroom door when you're peeing."

"Yeah, I'm still going to do that no matter where I live."

He sighed. "I have so much to teach you." He gestured wildly. "This is the kind of place that has Christmas mornings and weekend barbecues. Lazy Sunday sex and snoring dogs."

The kinds of moments that had turned into photo shoots at Bianca's house. Leave it to Nick Santiago to inherently know the meaning of life. "Did you hit your head when you fell out of the air vent?" she teased.

"Yes. Yes, I did."

"That explains a lot."

He shook his head and then tipped over, catching himself on the fireplace mantel. "I want to live here and work here with you, Riley 'Tell Me Your Middle Name' Thorn."

She couldn't help but grin. "You're an adorable drunk, Nick. But I'm not telling you my middle name."

"But you'll think about moving here with me, right? Because I'm an adorable drunk, and I'm super great in bed."

"And in cars and on roofs," she added. "Do you really want to live here? With me?"

"It feels right. Even though it *smells* wrong. It *feels* right."

The man had a point. Despite the fact that a body had been carted off the premises mere hours earlier, there was something right about the house.

A filmstrip rolled in her head of poker nights and client meetings and family dinners. Of Christmas trees and Thanksgiving turkeys and Burt and friends...and kids.

"Can we even afford this? And by 'we,' I mean 'you,' since you're the one who pays my salary."

He waved a dismissive hand a little too close to her face. "We've got this. I mean, who in their right mind would want to live in a murder scene?"

"Yeah, Nick. Who?"

"Us. That's who."

"I'll think about it," she said.

"Promise?" He held up his pinkie.

She hooked hers to his. "I promise."

"Cool. So about that sex?"

"Not here. And after a shower. Which we're taking at my parents' house since our bathroom and bedroom don't have ceilings anymore."

"Question. Will your parents mind if I have sex with you in their shower?"

"You've met my parents."

"Right. They're super cool. My parents would never let me have sex with my hot psychic girlfriend in their shower. They're lame."

"How about this? We shower and eat dinner at my parents'. Then we pick up dessert from your dad's restaurant and spend the night in a hotel."

"We haven't had hotel sex yet," Nick said, perking up.

"Let's go pack."

"And you'll think about the house?" he prodded.

"I'll think about the house," she promised. "You know, it's nice that you asked this time," Riley said as they trudged up the glitter-coated stairs of home.

"What do you mean?" he asked, dividing his weight between her and the railing.

"The last time we almost died, you just moved yourself in without even asking. This shows progress."

"So I probably shouldn't mention that I already put in an offer on the place, right?"

"Nick, seriously? Between getting wedged in a duct and throwing my ex-husband in a dumpster, when did you have the time?"

"When we were drinking. The real estate agent is so happy she's going to help us fumigate the place for free so it doesn't smell like corpse."

She was about to start an argument when Fred's bedroom door creaked open and a woman exited, carrying her shoes in her hand.

"Grandmother?"

Elanora's feathers were askew, and her long skirt was on backward.

"Hey! Scary Granny," Nick crowed. "What were you doing? Having a little afternoon delight?"

"You needn't look so shocked," Elanora tsked. "I am human after all. I too indulge in a treat now and again."

Riley gagged and clamped a hand to her mouth.

"You'll have to excuse Riley. She's just picturing you having sex with Fred, and it's wigging her out," Nick explained. "Ha! Get it? Wigging out? 'Cause Fred wears a rug."

"You are intoxicated," Elanora said.

"Nothing gets by you, Granny E! Can I call you Granny E?"

"No, you may not."

The doorbell rang.

"I'll get it!" Lily screeched and raced as fast as her eighty-year-old legs could carry her in what looked to be a reproduction of Queen Elizabeth's coronation gown. "Detective Weber, how lovely to see you!" Lily trilled.

"If he says one word about needing help with another case, I'm going to throw him in a dumpster," Nick growled.

"He's not here for us," Riley said, feeling her nose twitch sharply. "He's here for Grandmother."

"Detective, I've been expecting you," Elanora said, moving around Nick and Riley on the stairs.

"What's happening?" Nick stage-whispered. "Weber's not going to have sex with your granny too, is he?"

Riley clamped a hand over his mouth. "Shh. Let the grown-ups talk."

Weber appeared at the foot of the stairs. "I have something I need to ask you, Ms. Basil," he said. "Could we speak in private?"

Lily squeezed behind a large potted palm and peered out through the leaves.

"I am on my way home, Detective. Here is as good a place as any," Elanora told him.

Weber adjusted his tie. "A few years ago, my sister was taken. No clues. No contact. Nothing since. I need to know what happened."

"I need to know that it's time to give up hope."

Riley heard Weber's unspoken thought, and her heart hurt for him.

"You want me to contact her spirit," Elanora filled in.

"Oh, shit," Nick said against Riley's palm.

Weber nodded briskly. "I'm tired of questions. You give people answers. Give me this answer."

Elanora's nostrils flared. "You will join me in a room that is not coated in glitter." She turned to look at Riley and Nick. "You will also join us."

Riley removed her hand from Nick's mouth, and they trooped down the stairs into the kitchen.

"Sit," Elanora said, gesturing toward the table.

They did as they were told.

"I need silence while I contact my spirit guides."

Nick let out a giggle, then shushed himself. "Sorry. It just slipped out. Shh!"

Elanora rolled her eyes before she closed them. Riley sat holding her breath as she felt her grandmother's power rise up. The hair on her arms stood up almost as if the air was electrified. One thing was for certain, Elanora Basil was a powerful medium. And for the first time in her life, Riley wondered what it would be like to be that good at something.

Her grandmother's eyes snapped open, and Nick jumped. "Spooky," he whispered.

"I cannot communicate with your sister's spirit, Detective Weber. Because she is not deceased."

Want to know what happens next?

Read on for an excerpt from
The Blast From the Past,
book 3 in the Riley Thorn series

1

Riley was dumped unceremoniously onto the floor and immediately began fighting her way free. They'd taken her upstairs. The music and giggling were much fainter.

Someone whipped the material off her head, and she fought to get a full breath into her lungs.

It was dark, so it was the smell that hit her first, and she knew exactly where they'd taken her. The creepy, smelly closet.

She had to keep her wits about her, Riley reminded herself. Any second now, the cops would arrive and the drugs would wear off. Nick would break out of his office and find her in no time. And if she kept the bad guys occupied up here with her, everyone would be safe.

The overhead light snapped on.

"You *idiot*."

Riley blinked, trying to bring the woman into focus. She had a faint southern accent. Not the *bless-your-heart* genteel kind but the *wrestle-gators-in-the-swamp* kind.

"Here we go again," said the man who'd carried her upstairs. "You told me to bring you Dolly. I brought you Dolly. Nothing I ever do is good enough for you."

The woman gestured angrily at Riley with the gun she

held. "Does she look like the right Dolly Parton to you? I swear, I should have divorced your dumb ass years ago."

The man sneered. "Well, good news for you because my cousin Otis never got ordained, so we ain't never been married." It was Zorro. The guest who had been handing out cups of punch.

And the woman peeled off her Guy Fawkes mask and glared at Zorro.

"Lurlene and Royce, I presume?" Riley scooched up against the back wall of the closet. She could have sworn she heard a hissing noise come from the grate.

"Great." Lurlene threw up her hands. "Second Dolly knows our names. That means that tramp already opened her big mouth."

"What's the big deal?" Royce asked, dragging off his Zorro hat.

"The *big deal* is now we have to kill them all."

"Uh, can I interject here?" Riley raised a hand. "I'm sure we can work something out so no one needs to die."

Lurlene beaned her with a roll of painter's tape. "Shut her up, and then tape her hands and feet together," she ordered Royce.

"She ain't goin' nowhere," he argued.

"Well, I don't want her screaming or trying to run away when we kill her."

"Have you always been this bloodthirsty?" he wondered.

"Yes! You just haven't paid any attention to me for thirty years!"

"It sounds like you two are under a lot of stress," Riley said, frantically searching for a way to connect with her captors. That was what her favorite show, *Made It Out Alive*, always said. Well, that and don't ever let yourself be taken to a second location, which she'd already screwed up. "Running your own business isn't easy."

"Oh, for Pete's sake. Shut your damn trap, whoever the hell you are," Lurlene snarled, pointing the gun in Riley's face. "Tape her up good, Royce."

"Don't get your panties in a twist."

"If you think for *one second* I'm going back to scrubbing country club toilets or worse, you got a rock in your head where God shoulda put a brain. We have a billion dollars on the line here. I'm not walkin' away from yacht money."

"All right. All right. No need to lose your dang mind again. If you want Dolly dead, she's dead," Royce muttered. He grabbed Riley's hands roughly and wrapped the tape around her wrists several times.

"Wait," she said. But the next piece of tape covered her mouth. Which was a stupid, amateur mistake to make seeing as how she could just reach up with her bound hands and remove the tape. But she decided to keep that information to herself until she could use it to her advantage.

There was a very distinct hiss behind the grate.

Royce made quick work of taping her ankles together. "Happy now?" he demanded and tossed the tape. It bounced off the floor and hit the grate, knocking it askew.

"Not yet," Lurlene said, crossing her arms and tapping her foot.

Royce made a big show of being annoyed when he pulled a knife out of his belt and opened the blade in Riley's face. She flinched and flattened herself against the wall.

She was *not* going to die in a stinky closet during Nick's birthday party.

Author's Note

Dear Reader,

I hope you enjoyed Riley and Nick's latest adventure and that you're as excited about more from these two and their kooky cast of sidekicks as I am. Now, please hold for my authorly confessions.

Confession #1: The West Shore Farmers Market *is* a real place, but it is *not* open on Sundays. By the time I got to that part in the book/timeline, I had written myself into a corner and couldn't fix the fiction to match the reality without rewriting a lot of chapters. There you have it. But to be fair, the farmers market has really strange hours anyway, so you definitely want to make sure they're open before you plan a trip. Cool? Cool.

Confession #2: I mentioned cicadas a few times in this book as a nod to Cicada Fest 2021. After the world survived a pandemic, we were treated to a plague of the seventeen-year colony of these buzzy flying suckers. I don't know if Harrisburg always has cicadas (Google wasn't much help), and if not, I don't know what the buzzy summer insects we do have are called. But please accept this as my nod to the dozen crispy critters that attacked me while leaf-blowing the deck and not a scientific statement about the habits of insects.

Now that that's over with, if you loved *The Corpse in the Closet*, please consider leaving a review telling other readers what a diabolical genius you think I am. And don't forget to sign up for my newsletter to make sure you don't miss the next Riley Thorn installment! Thank you for reading and having great taste!

Xoxo,
Lucy

Acknowledgments

Without the following, this book either wouldn't have existed or would not have been very good.

- Kari March Designs for the original cover and fun graphics
- Amanda, Jessica, and Sabrina for their editorial eagle eyes
- Joyce and Tammy for keeping me focused on writing while they put out administrative fires
- Team Lucy, my beloved Street Team, and my ARC team for their stellar support
- Sports drinks with electrolytes for the days after I make bad decisions
- Air-conditioning and indoor plumbing, without which I would be a shell of a human being
- My author crew for never hesitating to slap me out of a funk
- Bloom Books and their entire team for putting Riley Thorn onto bookstore shelves
- Season one of *Ted Lasso*
- The 2021 cicadas
- Kenra hair spray for holding up to Pennsylvania humidity
- Mr. Lucy for being the best

About the Author

Lucy Score is a #1 *New York Times*, *USA Today*, and *Wall Street Journal* bestselling author. She grew up in a literary family who insisted that the dinner table was for reading and earned a degree in journalism. She writes full-time from the Pennsylvania home she and Mr. Lucy share with their obnoxious cat, Cleo. When not spending hours crafting heartbreaker heroes and kick-ass heroines, Lucy can be found on the couch, in the kitchen, or at the gym. She hopes to someday write from a sailboat, ocean-front condo, or tropical island with reliable Wi-Fi.

Sign up for her newsletter by scanning the QR code below and stay up on all the latest Lucy book news. You can also follow her here:

Website: lucyscore.net
Facebook: lucyscorewrites
Instagram: scorelucy
TikTok: @lucyferscore
Binge Books: bingebooks.com/author/lucy_score
Readers Group: facebook.com/groups/BingeReaders Anonymous
Newsletter signup: